CW01188198

To Sarah,
With all best wishes for 2012,
Ema x.

Child's Acre

Ema Fields

Ema Fields

authorHOUSE

AuthorHouse™ UK Ltd.
500 Avebury Boulevard
Central Milton Keynes, MK9 2BE
www.authorhouse.co.uk
Phone: 08001974150

© *2009 Ema Fields. All rights reserved.*

No part of this book may be reproduced, stored in a retrieval system, or transmitted by any means without the written permission of the author.

First published by AuthorHouse 10/28/2009

ISBN: 978-1-4490-3473-3 (sc)
ISBN: 978-1-4490-4324-7 (hc)

Cover Illustration by Glen Sullivan-Bissett

This book is printed on acid-free paper.

About The Author

BORN IN 1941, THE CHILD of an evacuee, Ema's birthplace was a Manor House in St Neot's, Huntingdonshire. Raised in London, Ema feels that she owes her love of the countryside largely to the place of her birth.

At around the age of seven years Ema began writing short poems of the Kentish countryside where her beloved grandparents took her each year to the hop gardens for the hop-picking season. These few weeks were Ema's greatest joy and further instilled in her the love of the countryside. Verse is Ema's first love and in later years she was to publish her first small book of poems, 'Land of Song and Other Poems,' to the delight and appreciation of many.

Ema was educated at convent shools in East London and feels her personality and characteristic traits were greatly influenced by the adored Mothers of the Ursuline Order. Her first employment at the age of sixteen was as secretary with London companies where, through her love of words, she soon became involved in assisting with the writing and editing of company publications.

After the birth of her four children Ema returned to work as Personal Assistant with large companies in London. Later the family relocated to Essex where she joined the Advanced Systems Division of a renowned Avionics company and, whilst seconded to the Technical Writing Departments, once again, enjoyed working on major publications.

Child's Acre is set in the early to mid nineteenth century. The period has been researched in order to provide a credible background in preparation to bring you this story encompassing life in early Victorian England.

Dedication

I WOULD LIKE TO THANK my husband for his unwavering efforts on behalf of the family and the joy he has brought each one of us. You are our inspiration.

Thank you to my wonderful and talented children of whom I am immensely proud. For their lifetime of help, care and concern, and wholehearted belief in me, I am truly blessed.

To my lovely little golden haired granddaughter and allegiant young soldier,
Lance Corporal Kayleigh Morgan. When on tours of duty thank you for always keeping in touch.

To my lovely little flaxen haired granddaughter, namesake and champion,
Ema Sullivan-Bissett BA Hons. lst. Thank you for your encouragement.

Thank you to all my precious younger grandchildren for whom success is yet to come.
To Jeannie McQuaid, my dearest friend, helpmate and confidante of 37 years, for your unfailing faith in me, I thank you Alex.

Introduction

I HAVE BEEN INVOLVED IN writing in one way or another throughout the course of my life. As a young child I wrote childish poetry until at the age eleven I produced my first serious poem. Mother Vincent at my convent school told me I had 'the gift of words', this meant nothing to me at that time. Now, I would like to think there just might have been some small truth in her assessment.

Through childhood to present day I have loved to hear and to tell stories of the Victorian Era. When telling stories to my children they were always tales of a bygone age. Strangely, I also enjoyed explaining lessons to school friends for I had a great leaning towards a career in teaching. At the age of fifteen I was sometimes permitted the joy of taking my class in the English lesson. I found I could actually help some of my classmates, at least to the best of my limited knowledge. I was also permitted to take the class in one or two Pitman Shorthand lessons and greatly enjoyed explaining the intricacies of the Pitman script.

I was to remain at the day convent until the age of eighteen when I would enter a Teachers' Training College. Unfortunately, due to circumstances beyond my father's control, I left school at sixteen. However, during my career, it seemed natural that my writing and teaching continued, as it did all through my working life.

At the age of just twelve years I promised myself I would write a book – someday. 'Child's Acre' remained a story in my heart for many years, developing its twists and turns until, eventually, I put pen to paper. I am now a grandmother of sixty eight years and this is my book. Another cherished dream was to move to the countryside.

My adored aunt Minnie Ralphs, a great storyteller, once told me that I had writer's ink in my veins and was doubtless born in the wrong century. Well, I do not know about the former but think the latter may have some merit.

Now, retired from working life, I live with my husband in a delightful old farm worker's cottage, at the edge of the wolds, in scenic rural Lincolnshire.

Ema Fields

Chapter One

THE WIND HOWLED AND MOANED, echoing the child's misery, as it tossed and tumbled the autumn leaves along the dirt track. Above her the storm clouds gathered and swirled in a menacing sky, darkening the landscape and heightening her fear. Mary, almost crushing the tiny infant to her breast, knew that she should never have attempted the journey on such a day, but winter had come early this year. If only Sarah had got better, she thought, desperately, as she struggled against the biting wind. Determined to make her way along the uneven track she wondered whether she would make it to the big house before the storm broke. There was no time to lose, which would be the quickest way? It would certainly be shorter to take to the fields that bordered the manor house, they were already in sight, but the girl knew only too well that this farmland was devoid of shelter, just open space, desolate, open space.

'Oh Sarah, what must I do?' she cried into the wind. 'We'll keep to the road,' she agonised, 'just a bit longer babe, there'll be shelter on the road, then if the storm breaks we'll be dry, come on baby, we best go quick…must be quicker. Her breathing was laboured now, her chest hurt, she was fast losing strength.

Mary knew there would be outbuildings of some kind, old barns or byres, disused milking sheds, all kinds of crude ramshackle shelters not far from the road. Yes, she thought, raising the baby a little in her leaden arms, we will take the longer, safer way.

Having made her decision and realising that a narrow track, although difficult to hurry along, would be considerably better than tramping through furrowed fields, little Mary gathered her strength and set out with stronger resolve.

The infant began to whimper, the sound barely audible above the howling wind, it was only the fact that Mary had buried her face low into the baby's wrappings that she had heard the cry at all. She attempted to gather her ragged cloak about the tiny baby boy but it was impossible. The cruel fingers of the wind tore the cloak away and whipped at her hair and head shawl. 'Dear God, let me get him there, please, please let me get him there safe' she pleaded, crying hopelessly now. About a mile and a half to go, she silently estimated, but the time she must keep moving along stretched out interminably before her. There would be no carts out on a day like this, no, folk would have more sense.

'We'll make it babe, don't you fret now, hush your crying, we'll make it.' The near exhausted girl dashed the tears from her eyes and bent her head lower against the wind. 'I promised your ma and now I promise you my love, we'll make it.' With this firm promise to her tiny nephew, the only remaining member of her family, came a determination as strong as the roaring gale, and the ten year old girl pushed onward. Burning tears again stung the child's eyes as she remembered the other promise made to her sister Sarah that very morning. She remembered crying, 'Sarah, oh Sare, don't go on that way, give over Sarah, you'll be alright, you'll be right fine, you will, you'll see, who'll tend to little Benjie if you don't get well?' Mary took up the baby from the basket lying by the empty grate. 'Look at him Sare, so beautiful, so tiny and so beautiful, you must get well, you must, you must…'

Sarah spoke very weakly but fervently. 'I will get well, course I will, in time,' her breathing shallow now as she tried to speak, 'hush your crying now, course I'll be well, but if I don't, you take 'im, you take my babe to the big 'ouse. Sarah's exertion was frightening her little sister but she went on. 'The Master there is good, I 'ear tell as 'ow 'e is kind an' I know 'e wont see no babe, 'specially no born babe, go into no workhouse or waifs' 'ome, no waifs' 'ome for me Benjie Mare, promise me, you must promise…'

Sarah held her younger sister's hand as tightly as she was able, it was really little more than a feeble touch, then, trying so hard to raise her voice, she urged, 'promise me Mare, I need to 'ave yer promise, you're all e's got darlin', an' e's all you've got now.'

Afraid lest Sarah would use up all her strength, Mary took the baby and, gripping her sister's hand whist weeping tears of rage, pity and overwhelming love, she whispered close to Sarah's ear, 'I promise Sarah, I promise.'

'He is beautiful Mary,' Sarah breathed, 'so are you, I do love you both, so much, the big 'ouse Mare, the big 'ouse ….darlin.' Sarah's eyes closed, her mouth relaxed into a half smile, 'look Mare, look' she whispered, her tired, pale and lovely face grew radiant, 'look Mare, there's Ma. Mary was confused and afraid. As she watched, the tears flowed like a great damn breaking and heartrending sobs shook her slight young body as the barely seventeen year old Sarah breathed her last.

A few spots of ice cold rain splashed Mary's cheeks jolting her out of her heartbreaking thoughts and back to the present. Her feet were cut and bleeding, her head sore from the wind tugging relentlessly at her long hair. Why, oh why did I come today, she thought, then, oh God what else could I 'ave done, I never 'ad no choice. The rain was falling faster now, Mary noticed in desperation. Breathlessly she spoke aloud. 'No, not yet, don't give way yet, another 'alf hour, that's all an' we'll be there, please God don't let the storm come yet, not yet.' There came a long, low rumble and Mary knew that soon the heavens would open. She laid the baby on the ground. 'I've got to keep you dry somehow,' she murmured frantically to the baby as she tore away her thin cloak and rolled it tightly about him. 'If you get wet you'll die for sure my lovely, and whatever else 'appens, Mary will take care of you.'

A short distance away, about two hundred yards, Mary was able to see what looked to be a shelter of some description but icy rain lashed her face blurring her vision. In a blind panic she clasped the baby close, bent her head and attempted to run against the elements. Lightning flashed its terrifying brilliance across the landscape, bare branches of the hedgerows stabbed at her as she stumbled forward, the heavens opened with a resounding clap of thunder and the rain washed over her. With racing heart that seemed to beat at the walls of her chest she drove herself on. 'We've got to make that shelter baby,' she gasped, nearly there, nearly there.' Then, looking heavenward through the driving rain, she called aloud, 'Sarah, please Sarah, if you can 'ear me…'elp us.'

Onward she struggled, every step a mammoth effort now as she frequently stumbled on the rough, uneven ground. Driving rain beat at her bare arms and face, she was growing weaker. 'Nearly there baby,' she whimpered. Tears fought with the rain as it stung her eyes, her feet did not hurt now, her hands were not cold, she could no longer feel them for her little fists were clenched so tightly into the baby's wrappings that her hands had numbed. 'Here it is little one,' the exhausted girl choked out the words as the shelter loomed in front of her, 'just a few more steps.' She was sobbing relentlessly now, 'it don't matter if I die, but dear Jesus let me live to take care of him. Sarah, Sarah, I wont fail you Sare.'

Mary almost fell into the derelict byre, it had no door and half of one wall was broken away. There was a wide gaping break in another wall, where possibly an animal had been kept at some time, but a low partition was still in tact which afforded complete shelter against the gusting wind. Stumbling forward she saw the low wall and sank down against it. 'Thank God, thank you dear Lord' she cried as her eyes fell upon the pile of very dirty but, very dry straw.

Mary swiftly pulled at the baby's wrappings then, staring wildly at the very small, very still form of her baby nephew her mind screamed, no no no. Suddenly, as baby Ben felt the raw cold strike his skin he stirred and began to complain loudly. Mary collapsed into the straw beside him, raining kisses on his smudged and moist little face, his eyes, his cheeks, thanking Lord Jesus all the while. She then threw away the baby's outer wrap, her old cloak which was sodden from the force of the rain, mercifully the cloak had kept the under blanket almost dry. As she held him to her, rocking back and forth whilst trying to gather her wits, she saw that her own clothing was seeping water into Ben's woollen blanket.

'Nothing else for it baby' Mary murmured, as she ripped off the brown dress and coarse underskirt and threw them away from the straw. Now, clothed only in a damp, thin shift, she began to work hastily and mechanically, piling high the straw and making a hollow in the centre. She was no longer cold, had not felt the piercing cold since a few moments before she entered the byre, for on reaching the shelter and seeing the dry straw her mind had fully taken over and all physical pain had ceased to penetrate the wild panic in her mind.

Crawling into the straw bed Mary drew the baby close, took off the only relatively dry wrap left to them and threw away his soiled cloth. Then, covering them both as best she could with the small blanket she pulled the dry straw around and over the top of them. The baby began to whimper again, a blessed sound except for the fact that he was now crazily hungry; his cries grew louder.

Lying half frozen in the bed of straw the ten year old girl was warm now. She felt sunshine come in through the window and pour over her. Ben's cries grew ever more demanding as she held him as tightly as she dare to her near naked little body, unable to give him the warmth and security of his mother's breast. He's safe now, she thought with overwhelming relief as exhaustion claimed her. She had brought them both to safety from the storm and, as soon as it was all over, she would take little Ben to the big house. She could still hear the driving rain as it swept through the door but didn't reach them, could hear it beating like great hammers on the makeshift roof. She could hear the screaming, howling gale as it rattled and shook the derelict shelter but she was warm. Her hands and feet were gloriously warm, the baby was warm and she could see Sarah beckoning her, it must be time for morning bread and oats. It was summer, she lie in a pleasant meadow bathed in warm sunshine, the rustling of the gently moving branches above her as soothing as a lullaby as she sank into blissful oblivion.

Chapter Two

THE GRAND COACH AND PAIR rumbled along, horses hooves sending great splashes of mud up onto the coach and into the ditches on either side of the relatively narrow main highway. The impeccably dressed gentleman inside the coach tapped his silver tipped cane on the ceiling. There was no response, the coach rumbled on for the driver could hear nothing above the noise of the storm. The passenger rolled down the shutter and, shielding his face from the biting wind, called loudly, 'Robbie, I say there, Robbie, stop the coach,' but it was no use, the driver, head down against the elements, heard nothing as the storm seemed to grow in fury. The passenger took his cane and, grasping it firmly, reached out along the side of the coach striking as hard as he could.

The horses, already making slow progress, drew to a slippery, snorting halt and Robbie MacBride climbed down from the driving seat. Sir Alexander MacKenzie opened the door for his driver, 'get in man' he yelled, and as his voice carried away on the wind they both hauled the door shut. 'Well Sir, it's been a long time since I've seen one like this, aye, a long time indeed.'

'Should it be taking this long, Robbie?' Alex Mackenzie was growing very concerned indeed.' Shelter must be found for the horses, are you certain we're on the right road?'

'I would think so, aye sir, but those fields over there, they trouble me, if they belong to Woodstock Manor then I fear I may have taken a wrong turn, but if they border Belford, as I had hoped, we should soon be at the Inn. We should nae be near Woodstock, but, in this storm, cannae see much oot there Sir. Should we wait a wee while here d'ye think? Seems wise tae me.'

Alex peered out and was thoughtful. 'Nae, Robbie,' he said, decisively, 'we cannae wait out the storm, it could take hours, even days, we must go on.'

'Thought I knew this part of England pretty well Sir, cannae believe I would tak' a wrong track, but I'm nae certain this is the main highway. Of course, the main roads here are narrow at best...

'Aye, Robbie, I was depending on ye, but nae matter now, even a countryman could get lost in such a storm.'

'There seems to be a road to the left, just up ahead sir, we could tak' a look along there, maybe there'll be a cottage where we could ask directions. At least we might find shelter for the horses, there's certainly nothing on this road for miles, if it's the main highway we're on sir.'

I suppose you're right Robbie, let's tak' a look, we must find an inn before dark.'

As Robbie opened the coach door it was torn from his hands as it slammed backwards. He forced the door shut and climbed into the driving seat. Pulling down his hat to meet his caped greatcoat he took up the reigns and yelled instructions to the two fine greys to 'trot on.' Just as the coach turned into the narrow lane, the deep muddy ruts now awash with water, Robbie saw through the oncoming darkness what appeared to be an old man staggering against the wind. He drew up alongside the man who, on closer inspection, was no more than thirty years, or thereabouts. The man was stumbling to his feet with the aid of a stout stick.

'Hello there,' the stranger shouted as he reached for Robbie's outstretched hand. 'I didn't expect to see anyone out here today, but I'm sure glad you appeared I can tell ya.'

'How is it ye are oot on foot on a day like this?' Robbie questioned, 'has ye horse gone lame?'

'No sir, cart turned over, tied Nelson to a tree, no harm done to him, thanks be, he'll be alright 'til this lot blows over.'

Robbie had some difficulty understanding the man's English country accent, hindered also by the deafening gale. Alex MacKenzie jumped down from the coach, grabbing at his cloak which was fast being tugged from his shoulders. 'Anything wrong Robbie,' he yelled, attempting to make himself heard from the shelter of the side of the coach, reluctant to step out into the open.

'Nae, not at all Sir, 'tis just that this gentleman has had his cart overturn a ways back, but the horse is nae harmed.'

'Bad luck man,' Alex commiserated, 'but nae surprising, we've seen several trees uprooted, aye, and there'll be worse before she's through. Can we tak' ye anywhere man, we're bound for the old coach house in Belford.'

'Quite a way from Belford Sir, 'bout a good 10 miles or more, yer, quite a way, but my cottage is just down the end of this lane, nowt but quarter mile away.' Speaking with a rural dialect the stranger continued, 'you'll be most welcome to warm yersels and take a bowl o' hot broth.

'Thank ye kindly, your offer is much appreciated,' said Alex, genuinely, 'but we must go on. We'll drive you to your cottage and be on our way, nae time to lose if we're to cover another ten miles before nightfall.

That such a fine gentleman would even consider asking him, in his present condition, to ride in such a fine carriage amazed Seth Wheeler and, touching his cap, he answered. 'You're a gentleman Sir, a true gentleman and I thank ya, that I do, but I wont get in the carriage, I'm not far from me cottage.'

There was no cottage in sight and Alex insisted that he would not leave the man, on foot, in such a storm. Seth Wheeler, apologising profusely for his muddy boots and dirty clothing, with great relief, climbed into the carriage.

'Nae need for apologies now, dirty work is honest work, I've yet to meet a man who can work the land and not take some wi' him,' Alex assured him.

'Thank you sir, but I've taken quite a bit of the land into your fine carriage.'

'Alex, the name is Alex MacKenzie, the coach will clean but, tell me, where is the coaching inn at Belford?'

Seth introduced himself and explained how they would best pick up the Belford Road. The carriage jolted along at a slow pace, by this time the road was truly awash and the sky grew even darker. The wind still sang its mournful lament through the leafless branches of the trees on either side of the track and, except for the amiable chatter of the occupants of the coach and the dull thud of horses hooves, all was quiet. Seth was looking out through the small window when he exclaimed sharply, 'can we stop the coach sir, something looks amiss up there.' He pointed a grubby finger towards an old, broken byre, now fallen into ruin and disuse.

'See that there old byre sir,' Seth exclaimed, declining to call Sir Alex by his first name. 'Those are rags swinging about by that doorway, don't rightly like the looks of it sir, think we'd best go see.'

'Aye, Seth, ye're quite right, we'll tak' a look, though I'm quite certain 'tis nothing but rags discarded by a passing vagrant.'

Just as Alex was about to reach for his cane to signal Robbie to stop, the coach drew to a slippery halt.

'Looks as though Robbie has also seen the barn Seth,' said Alex, thoughtfully, whilst reaching for his doctor's bag.

They stepped from the coach just as Robbie, after climbing down from the driver's seat, threw the reins over a broken tree and loosely tethered the greys. Smoothing both horses' windswept manes he spoke reassuringly, 'hold still now me lovelies, hold still for just a wee while.'

As swiftly as they could the three men made their way towards the byre, it was Seth Wheeler who stooped to pick up the sodden, muddy clothing. All three men read each other's minds as clearly as though the words had been spoken aloud. Grimly they eyed each other as they looked again at the sad little brown frock and muddy petticoat. It was Seth who broke the silence as Alex made to enter the byre.

'Could be worse than I thought, don't rightly know as I wanna go in there sir.'

Alex, breathing deeply, spoke firmly, 'come on, let's see if anyone is here.' It was an instruction.

'Aye, sir,' answered Robbie, straightening his back and steeling himself for whatever sight might meet him, but it was Seth who entered first.

Taking hold of Alex's arm, he held the taller man back. 'This is my manor Sir, I'll go, whatever's amiss maybe I'm better to deal with it.'

For the first time Seth spoke authoritatively to the two men, he was in charge now, there would very possibly be a young girl in there and Seth would do whatever was necessary, no-one else, for likely he would know her.

'I'm a doctor man,' said Alex, equally firmly, 'let's see what's to be done.' On saying this, Alex followed Seth into the Byre.

At the sight of two cut and bleeding, dirty little feet poking out from the makeshift bed, Alex moved swiftly forward. Seth gasped and paled visibly whilst Robbie, watching from the door space, held a hand across his mouth. The only other part of the child visible to them was a mass of matted, muddy hair strewn across the dirty straw.

Alex snapped into action. Opening the large black bag he issued instructions. 'D'nae touch her Seth, it may not be what we think, could be she is just sheltering from the storm, she could be still alive.'

Ema Fields

As he spoke Alex felt for a pulse with one hand whilst with the other he lifted a closed eyelid. Deftly he removed the straw from the girl's face.

'What can I do, how can I help,' pleaded Seth, as he bent to see what Alex was doing.

'Move aside now, give me room.' Alex took complete control whilst Seth watched in awe as the gentleman swiftly took off his cape, at the same time calling further instructions to his driver.

'Robbie, get away tae the carriage and fetch rugs from under the boxes.' Robbie turned towards the coach as Alex called, impatiently, ' away wi ye now.'

Alex's manner became professionally abrupt, his mind totally absorbed with the task at hand.

'It may be too late Seth, there's nae a moment to lose, we cannae do much here, but we must try.'

Alex then took in a sharp breath, 'well, well, my good heavens, what have we here then.' It was a statement of sheer amazement.

Robbie, hurriedly returning with the travelling rugs, heard the disbelief in his master's voice. 'What is it sir, how is the wee lassie? Has she a wound?'

'Nae, Robbie, not a wound, a tiny wee bairn.' Alex snapped once again into positive action. 'It's a new born, Robbie, a new born, and he's alive, at least for the moment, although,' said Alex, hopefully, 'looks quite a strong wee laddie, hasnae fared as badly as this wee gel, under the circumstances, but, och Robbie, the poor wee lassie, we must work hastily. Tak' her Robbie, wrap her quickly but carefully, carefully now man, but hurry, waste nae time. When ye get her into the carriage massage her limbs, rub her hands and feet, check her breathing all the while.'

Alex, whilst giving further orders to a bewildered Robbie, took up another thick, fleecy rug and turned to Seth.

'Seth, here, hold out this wrap now, come on man, don't go into shock on me, I have already one patient in shock.'

'Yes, yes, sir, sorry sir,' Seth stammered as he stared, open mouthed, at Ben's tiny form lying in the wrap in his arms. As quickly as he could, Seth awkwardly wrapped the rug tightly around the baby boy, murmuring, 'we've got yer now young fellah, hold still now, Seth's got yer' as baby Ben stretched and squirmed against the confines of the tightly wrapped rug. Then, 'will 'e make it governor, I mean, sir, will 'e make it?' Seth asked hopefully, looking steadily into Alex's eyes as the great black bag was snapped shut.

'Shield his head and face and get him into the carriage, they are in the Lord's hands now, but I'll say this, wee bairns can be unbelievably hardy, why, I could amaze ye with the tales I could tell about new born infants. Come away now, we're done here.'

Back in the carriage Seth handed the baby to Alex thinking, imagine him being a doctor as well, so that's why he's uncommonly helpful, a real Samaritan, and on this road, on this day.

Robbie, holding the strange little girl who lie cold and still in his arms, feeling her small body beneath his great, rough hands as he obediently massaged her arms and neck, blinked hard, swallowed hard and, diligently, with great relief, obeyed his next instruction.

'Give the lassie here, Robbie.' As Robbie handed Mary gently into his master's arms, Alex turned to Seth and asked, 'd'ye have a wife man?'

'No sir, just me, an' yer welcome to me cottage, as I said, but it's just a dirt floor, only one room with a loft, no comforts sir, but it's yours, an' I can fetch Alice from the village if the storm calms.'

Alex rubbed his furrowed brow, looking very vexed. 'Hush now a minute, I must think, where's the nearest hoose?'

'The very nearest is the big 'ouse, sir, the Squire's place, 'bout a mile along yer'll see the gatehouse, but yer can't go there sir, I mean…'

Alex cut off Seth's protestations regarding the Squire's place saying, 'hush now a moment Seth, I must tak' another look at this lassie, the wee bairn is holding his own.'

Alex pulled open the rug around Mary and rubbed her hands roughly. The girl's breathing was barely perceptible but she was breathing. He slapped her face and upper arms frantically for he had found only a weak pulse. He then took from his bag a small bottle and poured a sip of the fiery liquid over Mary's lips. She coughed, choked, and coughed again. 'Good, there's a good lassie, come on now, just a little more, that's the way,' Alex encouraged. Again he poured a little of the liquid onto Mary's lips, asking 'how's the wee one, Seth?'

'Building up to start a yellin' sir, if I'm not mistaken,' said Seth, beginning to take heart now.

'Wonderful,' replied Alex, quickly piling more rugs on and around Mary as he gently laid her on her side. Threatening tears stung the back of the big man's eyes as he tried to imagine what the child had endured to save the baby's life. 'These bairns will need careful nursing,' continued Alex, 'we must hurry. Now then, Seth, where's the Squire's house?' It was a command.

Seth didn't argue, the Doctor had made his decision, the squire's house it would be, and heaven help them all.

'If you can manage here sir, I'll show Robbie the road, it will save time.'

'Go on then man, away wi' ye.'

Seth jumped up into the seat beside Robbie. 'The Manor House it is Robbie, straight ahead to the turnpike, then yer'll see the gatehouse, I'll have you there in a trice if yer'll let me take the reins, there are one or two bad turns 'ere abouts and I know this manor like the back of me 'and.'

'Have ye handled a coach and pair,' asked Robbie, anxiously.

'Oh yer, I 'ave that, rest easy, for 'tis treacherous to be in a dire rush on a day such as this.'

'Ye may be right man, but I d'nae ken.' Robbie reluctantly handed the reins to Seth, if for no other reason than the local man would indeed know the lie of the road and if anyone could prevent an accident it would be this man. Thus, for the very first time, another man was handling the beautifully matched pair, but this was an emergency. However, it was Robbie who gave the instruction to his beloved mares to 'hup there, me lovelies,' and the horses moved in unison to bear them along carrying their precious burden.

Seth handled the mares with ease, skilfully avoiding the worst parts of the narrow lane as he drove them with care.

'What d'ye think happened, Seth?' asked Robbie, attempting to study the road ahead.

'Oh, she clearly took shelter from the storm Rob. A good thing she had the sense to get out of those wet clothes. What a little soldier, eh, that girl's got courage.'

Robbie, although unaware that this Englishman was once a master horseman, admired the way Seth handled the greys so, if his mares had confidence in their driver who was he to question their good sense?'

'Look Seth, ye seem to ken what ye're aboot, I think I'll away and help the doctor wi' the bairns.'

'Right, I'll stop here then, whilst we're moving a bit slow, 'cause when we reach the gatehouse the Manor drive is cobbled and these beauties will carry us like the wind up to the big house.'

Child's Acre

A look of alarm crossed Alex's face as Robbie climbed into the carriage. 'What's wrong now Robbie, dear God in heaven not a blocked road?'

'Nae sir, we'll be moving again directly, when we reach the gatehouse Seth says the drive to the Manor is cobbled and we'll be moving speedily, so I thought ye may need a hand wi the wee ones Sir, the Englishman knows what he's aboot.

'Well done Robbie,' Alex breathed a grateful sigh of relief. 'This wee laddie is starving, I'm not happy about the situation, ye ken.' Alex went on to explain, 'doctors meet up with many dilemmas, ye understand Robbie, and 'twas such a dilemma I had back there in the byre. I had a difficult decision to make. I knew when we found these bairns that if I had spent more time wi' the lassie, time to get the blood fully circulating then, mebbe, just mebbe, I could have brought her back with more of a chance. Cannae be certain of course, but the wee bairn was the stronger of the two for he had not undergone the struggle that the lassie had. He's hungry and in need of proper care, that meant getting him away with all speed to a woman somewhere, hopefully a nursing mother, if one can be found. I had to leave ye to do what ye could for the wee gel, and that wasnae fair to ye man.'

'Och, Sir, ye did as much as any man could, 'twas a rare coincidence indeed that it was yeself that passed along that road this day.'

All the while they spoke Alex continued to massage Mary's arms and legs, rubbing her cheek with his cheek, working on the strength of the often true saying, "where there's life, there's hope."

'She couldnae have been in the byre very long Robbie, as the wee one doesnae seem to have suffered, apart from his hunger. She clearly put his life before her own, but we have nae time to ponder that now.'

Baby Ben's complaints of hunger rose to a great crescendo and he yelled lustily. Robbie took up Ben from where he lie on the long bench beside Alex and, speaking in gentle tones, as least as gentle as his booming Scottish voice would permit, he attempted to soothe the hungry baby.

Alex, listening to Ben's wails and Robbie's efforts, said, 'ye shout now my laddie, aye, ye shout now, for 'tis a joy to hear you complain so. I have great hopes for ye, aye, that I have now, I only wish I was as certain of your young friend here.'

'Young friend sir?' Queried Robbie, 'is she nae is mather then?

'Nae, nae, Robbie, she's nae above twelve or thirteen years, in fact, if she wasnae so tall, I would put her younger than that, and she's nae his mather.

'How is she faring?'

'Still with us, aye man, but it's my judgement she may well be past her exhaustion tolerance. Also she's a little undernourished and an ordeal such as this lassie has experienced, well, everything will be done as soon as we reach the Manor. Just tak' a look at these hands, she may be in service somewhere, or mebbe she's run from the workhouse. In fact, Robbie,' said Alex, sadly, 'mebbe I shouldnae be trying so hard to revive her, poor wee wretch, but we'll soon know if she has any kin, and who they are, indeed, where they are.'

The carriage jolted to an abrupt halt, Alex almost fell to his knees clutching Mary with one hand whilst throwing out the other to support himself as Robbie's head hit the soft cushioning of the high-backed upholstered seat. The gatekeeper poked his head through the door of the gatehouse.

'What's your business, Sir?' he asked of Seth.

Alex looked out through the open shutter of the carriage and, in his very courteous but authoritative manner, replied, 'my business, man, is that I have two sick wee ones here, and I need assistance with all haste, I beg ye let us pass.'

The gatekeeper, clearly astonished at such an unheard of request, called,' I could never do that mister, yer see, I'm charged with the duty of keeping out all strangers, can't be done mister, yer'll need to…'

Alex, assessing that this situation was not going to simply be a matter of opening the huge gates, jumped down from the carriage. 'Now listen here my good man, and listen well, I have two bairns in the carriage, one near death and one very likely already past that unhappy state, let us pass, I have nae time to dally wi' ye.'

'Begging yer pardon sir, but the Master, 'e don't take kindly to…' stammered the now very nervous gate-keeper.

Out of patience Alex stepped up to the gatehouse and, speaking in a low and positively venomous voice spat out the words. 'Open these gates man, if ye d'nae want the lives of two bairns on your conscience for the rest of your wretched life, and that will be the very least of your concerns, so help me God.'

'Yes, sir, o' course sir, I didn't know sir, alright, right away,' he continued to stutter and stammer as, hastily, hands visibly shaking, he unlocked the great iron gates.

Alex jumped up into the carriage shouting, 'away wi ye, Seth'. His words trailed away on the wind and, as the huge gates were slowly drawn open, the coach seemed to sprout wings as the mares' hooves struck the cobbles. They fairly flew along the tree-lined drive up to the Manor, thankful to be out of the deep, hindering mud of the lanes.

A few moments later they came to another of Seth's incredibly abrupt halts, giving Robbie cause to wonder if he had not been a little hasty in his assessment of Seth's handling skills. Robbie made to get up.

'Stay where ye are, Robbie, keep them here until the door is open and I have explained our needs. We dare not mak' a wrong move now, after all this wee gel's suffered and may have given her life for. They depend on me now, I'll nae be a moment.'

Chapter Three

MILLIE, THE COOK AT WOODSTOCK Manor, was kneading dough for the week's supply of bread for the household. The other domestic servants were going about their late afternoon tasks complaining, as usual, about almost anything they felt worthy of complaint, but it was Mistress Hall, the housekeeper, who was the primary cause of their grievances. Millie, a short, plump woman with a florid complexion was sixty years old today. She was strong, thought to be tough, possessing a very rough tongue but a very soft heart; "a heart of pure gold and bigger'n 'erself," it was often heard said. She had borne five children, raised three, lost two in infancy and had worked at the 'big house' for the past twenty years. Hardly a day passed that Millie did not find the time to say a little prayer of thanks for her place as cook at Woodstock Manor.

The old lady sorely missed her two sons, who had left England to seek their fortunes abroad, and her Beth, her beloved daughter, now 30 years old. At eighteen Beth had married her sweetheart, Daniel Thatcher, and had gone to live with her young husband and his family, helping to farm the large acreage of fertile land that would one day be his. They were deeply in love and had remained so to this day. Millie had always had a good feeling about the match, but her true joy was in knowing that her wonderful little girl would be spared the poverty, toil and suffering that she herself had known; bitter experiences indeed.

Millie often thought of her daughter for their parting had been the most heartrending moment for both woman and girl, but Beth's happiness was her mother's reward. Millie would see her daughter at least once a year, happily a little more if Daniel had occasion to go into Chelmsford on farm business.

At such times Beth would make the journey with him and they would take the time to visit Millie before returning home.

The old cook touched her scarred cheek. Sometimes, when she was very weary, she fancied her face ached a little, then promptly told herself that this was nonsense, 'just the beginnings of a headache that's got lost,' she would say. Millie's sons and her Beth had always been totally oblivious of the mark that disfigured the left side of an otherwise lovely face. The scar began at the side of the left eye, came down across the cheek and under the cheekbone cutting away part of the flesh across the upper lip. Most people registered pity, even aversion, when first meeting Millie. Such a reaction, however, was inevitably short lived for the woman's natural warmth and constant concern for others manifested itself in the most radiant and heartfelt smile, until the offending scar simply disappeared.

Millie thumped away at the bread dough, revelling in the warmth from the range, simultaneously making a mental note that the kitchen brass and copper could do with another good clean some time this week. It was a bitingly cold day. The storm, which had been raging for most of the day, was beginning to calm. Millie sighed heavily pondering how yesterday had been such a bright and pleasant autumn day. Staring absently through the side window she marvelled that the weather was never the same from one day to the next.

The kitchen duties were, as usual, perfectly on schedule. Millie had sent the maid up to serve afternoon tea at three thirty and the next batch of bread was due out of the oven shortly. Glancing again through the misty window Millie muttered plaintively, 'terrible weather, just terrible, and the big dinner for tomorrer to be seen to, an' all those guests, hope this lot blows itself out by then or there'll be a few guests short, you see if there wont, Millie ol' gel.' Placing the dough by the hearth to prove she then took the bread from the oven, tapping the bottom of each loaf to ensure it was ready. This hard working woman greatly looked forward to the late afternoon. She would tidy up the odds and ends and then it would be her own special time. Everything was ready to start dinner at about six thirty for it was usual for the family to dine at eight thirty. At about four o-clock Millie would get Annie, the little scullery maid, to make up the fire with logs from the basket whilst she would busy herself cutting two large slices of cake or bread, or perhaps yesterday's pie, for them both. This was cook's time, when she would ease herself into the old wooden rocking chair by the big stone hearth. Then, with her tired, aching feet resting on the footstool and a steaming mug of good strong tea to cheer her, she could relax. For the next hour or two she would have her kitchen to herself with just gentle little Annie for company. It was a quiet, peaceful time of day, between meals and before the evening work began. Oh, how she enjoyed this time, the warmth; the peace; the rest. Millie was one of the world's most rare beings, happy with her lot, gratifyingly aware of simple comforts, undemanding and content.

Annie, a slightly built girl, small for her eleven years, pushed her way through the kitchen door carrying a heavy basket of logs. 'Come on girl, leave them by the fire, I've cut that wedge of cake for yer, we'll 'ave a bit of a treat today, an' it's a good un, even if I do say so mesel'. Pour yersel' a mug o' tea, an' me an' all then come an' get warm.'

Annie also loved this time of day, a time when she had Millie all to herself and Millie would tell her tales of years long gone when the old lady was a girl. They would drink tea and have a big piece of something to go with it. Millie was like a grandmother to Annie. She scolded her and praised her. She made her work hard but taught her well and always rewarded her work, always.

Annie took Millie's proffered mug and filled it with the strong dark brew, shuddering as she did so, thinking for the thousandth time that she didn't know how anyone could drink tea that was so strong. She then poured the dreadful looking liquid into her own mug until it was half full, then filled it with hot water from the huge black kettle on the range. That's better, she thought, a lovely drop o' tea.

'Can I get you another cushion for yer feet Millie?' Asked Annie, always looking for opportunities, no matter how small, to help the old lady.

'No, ta, lovey, I'm alright, but me poor ol' feet do ache a bit more'n normal t'day though.'

'Another cushion for yer back then?' Said Annie, noticing that Millie really did look more tired than usual and she liked taking care of her. Millie needed kindness, she gave so much but didn't seem to get much in return, was young Annie's mistaken assessment of Millie's life.

'Stop dithering about girl, you must be nigh done in yersel', come an' sit down and have a rest, yer've earned it t'day an' no mistake.'

'It 'as bin busy Millie, worse than usual, I thought I'd never get me work done t'day, an' the Master's been even more miserable than usual making everyone crotchety.'

'Now then, Annie, I'll 'ave none of that disrespectful talk me gel, you just mind yer tongue now, be told.' Millie scolded.

'Yer, alright, sorry Millie.' Annie quietly lowered her head and slowly sipped her tea. 'Is everything ready for t'morrer yet Millie?' She asked, tentatively.

'All but, me love, all but, an' what aint done gets left undone 'til t'morrer. I think we'll just take our rest then see to our dinners early t'day, do the dining room dinner an' have ourselves an early night.'

'Sounds lovely Millie, don't it; what 'ave yer done for our dinners?'

Annie began to yawn, Millie knew she would soon rest her back against the hearth wall and fall asleep. Then Millie would lie the girl down by the fire, place a cushion under her weary head, a shawl over her shoulders and let the youngster sleep.

As was the case with most girls in service Annie's days were long, but Millie did all in her power to ease the child's lot. Yes, Annie was, without doubt, one of the luckier ones. After Annie had fallen asleep and her childish chit chat had ceased, Millie would pour herself another mug of tea, go back to her chair by the fire and lightly doze, enjoying the silence, with no sound other than the crackle of the logs as they broke among the flames until her inner clock told her it was time to stir; but it was not to be so on this day.

The thundering of hooves on the main driveway startled Millie out of her semi-wakeful state. Before she could gather her wits there came a pounding on the doors of the main entrance to the house.

'Good Lord, 'eavens above, what on God's earth can be the matter?' Millie exclaimed aloud. 'Whatever it is I'm sure there's no cause for such a commotion,' she continued, though her outburst went unheeded by the sleeping girl. Then, on hearing the butler's hasty footsteps, muffled as they were by the distance between the main entrance hall and the butler's pantry, her heart fluttered painfully; Barkworth never hurried. She listened, standing as still as a statue, straining to hear. Placing trembling fingers to her lips she sat back again in her chair, her legs would no longer hold her. Had Master James met with an accident?' She asked the silent room. He had gone into the village that morning before the storm had broken and she had been worried about him all day as the weather worsened. 'There must have been an accident', she murmured, truly distressed now.

Through all the noise and activity Annie did not stir. Millie shook her roughly, without her usual gentleness. 'Come on gel, rouse yersel, there's something amiss out there fer sure.' By this time loud voices filled the entrance hall, Millie could hear them clearly enough now to distinguish what they were saying.

'No, Sir, the master is not available at this time.' Barkworth's coldly polite tones reached her clearly as he continued. 'I fear that certainly will not be possible Sir, Lady Woodstock is indisposed.' Barkworth indignantly informed the stranger.

'Fetch the lady of the house, man, or whoever speaks for her, I have nae patience with ye.' Called Alex, over his shoulder, as he quickly returned to the carriage.

The voices fell quiet again, merely low murmurings, but were followed by louder short, sharp instructions as Alex, carrying Mary, walked briskly passed an infuriated Barkworth. Millie could still hear the butler's voice protesting vehemently, but could no longer make out his words for the disruption in the hall as another strange voice was added to the fray. 'Dear Lord, whatever's amiss' she mumbled.

Annie, on being awakened so abruptly, was confused and alarmed at Millie's state of anxiety.

'Run across to the 'all, Annie,' Millie began, breathlessly, 'find Barkworth as soon as yer can, be quick now and find out what's wrong. Ask him if there's been an accident with young Master James, hurry now, no, not through the 'ouse, go across the yard, hurry gel, I gotta know what's 'appening.

James, the younger son of the house was twenty one years old and the apple of Millie's eye since the day he was born. Annie understood immediately the depth of cook's concern. She reached for her cloak, which always hung on a hook behind the kitchen door and, pulling it around her, turned to Millie. 'Sit down now Millie, I wont be long, nothin's 'appened to Master James, he's grown up now an' sensible an' all, too sensible to start back in a storm like that, 'e's likely still in the village.'

Millie helped Annie pull open the back door. A freezing gust of wind blew in with such force that even Millie's bulk was pushed against the wall. She leaned her shoulder into the door, slammed it shut then slotted the flat wooden bar into place. Breathlessly she stared out of the window, her face set grimly. She watched as Annie, head bent against the wind, struggled to hurry across the yard then disappear around the side of the house. She would enter through a side door, seek out Barkworth and discretely ascertain the cause of the disturbance. A few minutes later, minutes that had seemed interminable, every second passing so slowly, Annie came back into the yard. This time, to Millie's astonishment and immense relief, with young Master James' arm about her in an attempt to protect her from the wind and rain.

'Oh thank goodness,' cried the old lady, 'he's back, thank you Lord, you 'eard me prayers again Lord.' Then Millie chastised herself soundly, as was always her way in a crisis. 'Come on Millie gel, can't just stand idling about 'ere, what're you thinking of, you've got work to do.'

***

Sir John of Woodstock Manor stood over the young girl as she lie unconscious in the arms of the well dressed stranger, whilst some sort of manservant stood behind holding a small bundle. As he looked upon the ragged child's deathly face his mind went almost blank with horror. My God, no, no, it cannot be, his thoughts screamed at him. Recognising the child as "that wench's kin," Sir John's only thought was how best to get her away from his house…and the bundle? So, it was born then. He could not have his fledglings coming home to roost, not a man in his position, a pillar of society, indeed the very essence of Woodstock, perhaps even the county itself. Was it her brat? No matter, it was not unheard of, he assured himself as his mind began to race, even in the very highest circles, for a man to take a girl from his lands to pass an amusing hour occasionally. Some would even force their whims on their very own maidservants. Any false accusations resulting from such an action would result in the girl being thrown out immediately, more often than not banished from the household. Now, brought to his own door? No gentleman of note would tolerate such an outrage.

The Squire most certainly recognised Mary as the younger sister of the girl with whom he had spent the occasional hour or two awhile back. He had given not a thought to the girl, or what had become of her, since that time. His only concern at this moment was the reason for the brat being brought to his door. Why? For what? Money? Blackmail? Yes, yes, that was it, blackmail; well it would not succeed. It could be any farm boy's misdeed. I'll have you out of here this very day you young wretch, he silently vowed. Quaking inwardly he decided to take a firm stand, but tread carefully, not panic, wait.

Incredibly, only moments had passed whilst all these thoughts and questions chased across the horrified Squire's mind. Impatient at being detained and, mistaking the Master's bewilderment for compassion at the plight of the young girl, Alex spoke out. 'D'nae just stand there man, show me to a room wi' a good fire and a bed, this lassie is in dire need of help, there is nae time to lose, and I'll thank ye greatly to see that my mares are stabled and fed.'

Alex's sharp instructions brought the Squire out of his apparent stupor. 'Of course, of course,' he stammered.

With his mind still in a whirl Sir John turned to Barkworth, 'ring for Mistress Hall immediately Barkworth, she's to take care of these gentleman, whatever they need, the servants are at their disposal.' Where was he to put them? The fires were not all lit, this weather was unexpected, the only heated rooms were the drawing room, kitchens or his wife's rooms. His wife, oh God, he must think quickly. 'They may use the vacant servants' quarters,' he barked, it was a dismissal. He then strode quickly towards the wide staircase, he would spend the rest of the afternoon in front of the bright fire in the peace of the pleasant drawing room on the first floor; he needed to think.

Mistress Hall arrived, imperious and unflustered, the little tweeny maid nervously following.

'The servants' quarters at the top of the house are to be made available to you, gentlemen, will you please come this way.' Then, turning to the tweeny, instructed, 'light the fires in the rooms adjacent to the old nurseries, and be quick girl.'

'Light the fires!' Exclaimed Alex, growing steadily more angry at the lack of comprehension of these people. 'Have ye cloth ears woman? This child will nae be waiting for ye to light fires. Get me to a warm room immediately.' Alex brooked no opposition when he became Doctor MacKenzie. Thus, it was an incensed Mistress Hall who hurriedly led the way to the drawing room on the first floor, after the "contemptuous Scotsman" threatened to turn over the house until he found a room himself.

'I'm terribly sorry Sir John,' began the housekeeper, as Alex followed her into the elaborately furnished and spacious drawing room.

An enraged Squire turned to Alex but the doctor was prepared for any encounter. 'I exceedingly regret this disturbance, sir,' said Alex, curtly, and apologise for the disruption to your household but I need a warm room for this child, I thank ye for your kind tolerance, but I cannae wait for rooms to be prepared, ye understand sir?'

'Of course, of course, whatever you need. I have to say you caught me unawares, seeing the child, well, the sight was so distressing that I was not thinking straight. I was not fully aware of the urgency of the situation. Certainly you may use the drawing room, there's ample fuel and the housekeeper will attend to your needs until other quarters are suitably prepared.' Sir John made no attempt to keep the coolness from his tone and was fast taking a serious dislike to this rude Scottish individual.

Alex was not listening to Sir John's ramblings, absorbed as he was with concerns for Mary and the tasks at hand. All the while Alex worked, placing Mary on the large sofa, checking her pulse, making her comfortable, he continued speaking to the housekeeper. 'Mistress Hall, may I address you as such? I'm grateful for your assistance, will ye fetch me a woman to see to the infant, get some warm milk into him somehow. Then send to the village, he'll need a nursing mather, there'll be nursing mathers aplenty I'm sure. The storm is abating, send a cart or carriage to fetch someone, that'll nae be a problem, I'm sure.' Then, in an attempt not to further alienate the Squire, Alex turned to the man asking, 'that will be in order sir?' Without waiting for a reply, and without even a glance at the disgruntled housekeeper, Alex continued. 'I'll need blankets, warm broth, oh, and a little brandy…make up the fire and have a maid stay with the lassie.'

Alex then turned to Sir John saying, less brusquely now. 'Ye may go Sir John, I'm a highland doctor, I have no further need of ye. These wee ones are deeply in your debt and I thank ye for your charity and your good services.'

Before leaving the room Sir John turned to Alex. 'The baby, is it sick also,' he questioned. For if both these wretches were in danger the squire may just miraculously escape the unjust deserts of his folly.

'Nae, I d'nae think so, he appears well enough. It's my happy belief that we found him in time. He'll need constant care, of course, for a wee while. A nursing mother must be found in all haste. Hopefully your housekeeper will seek out a local woman, from the village perhaps. I'm depending on her knowledge of the area and the people, the wee one is not above a week old, methinks.'

Sir John was speechless, his rage almost tangible, he must regain control. There must not be a hint of suspicion that would link the girl or the brat to him. He would be a generous benefactor, for the time being. He smiled.

Instructions were being hurled fast and furiously at the maid as Alex worked. Sir John hastily left the room, his good intentions of a few moments before deserting him as, dangerously angry now, he called for the housekeeper. 'All this fuss and nonsense over a miserable peasant and a bastard offspring,' he expostulated. Breathless now, his thoughts raged on. Why, there were hundreds like her, what business was it of his? The parish or the workhouse would sort all this out, if the wretches lived.

Upstairs in the drawing room colour was returning to Mary's cheeks. She was dry and warm, her breathing no longer shallow. A little broth now and Alex could turn his full attention to the wee bairn who was hungrily sending out his wails of complaint so loudly that they reached the upper floor. Unexpectedly the squire came back into the room. As Alex pushed matted hair away from Mary's face and smoothed the covers he addressed the master of the house. 'Will ye arrange for the mares to be rubbed down and fed, sir, they'll be grateful for the attention of your groom? My man, Robbie, and the local chappie could do wi' a dram of something and a wee bite in your kitchens sir?'

Sir John met the Scotsman's gaze and replied coolly. 'Be assured that your horses and servant shall receive every courtesy sir, and no effort will be spared to help these poor, unfortunate children.'

'I thank ye man, ye are a credit to the human race and to your country. I am not unsympathetic to the upheaval we have wrought upon your household. I, er, will need a small chamber for the two of them to be made more comfortable, d'ye ken? The lassie is quite sick and in need of rest and quiet until she can be moved back to her home. But we may attend to those matters when we have completed the tasks to hand. Later we must seek out the family.'

Sir John left the room once again and headed towards the staircase that lead to the butler's pantry, a domain he did not frequent. As before his foul temper manifested itself in what was something akin to a ferocious bellowing as he yelled, 'Barkworth, Barkworth, where the devil are you man?'

Meanwhile Mistress Hall returned to the drawing room, hands flapping and without her usual composure, followed close at heel by Robbie holding the baby. Baby Ben's cries were now reaching a great crescendo as Alex laid him down upon the sofa to take a look at him.

'Here, let me help you move the sofa closer to the fire sir,' said the sombre housekeeper, nervously taking charge of the situation. 'We have a nursing mother waiting in the kitchen. One of the outside staff, Davy, has at his moment returned with her. I thought it best that you see the baby and let us know what it is you wish us to do.'

Alex smiled broadly, revealing his mature, but very handsome, good looks. 'Och, that's wonderful Mistress Hall, just wonderful, well done indeed,' he said warmly, taking both her hands in his. Now the housekeeping certainly was in a flap.

The doctor placed another sweet smelling cushion beneath Mary's head as he announced his complete satisfaction with the baby's condition, whilst Ben continued to remind them, in no uncertain terms, just how hungry he was.

Alex took up the baby, murmuring comforting highland words, words as old as the highlands themselves. Perhaps, he thought now, in his preoccupation with concern for the bairns, he may have misjudged the Master. After all, 'twas nae every day that an Englishman's castle was invaded in such a manner as this. He decided to make peace with the ill-tempered fellow.

Sir John entered the room, visibly shuddering at the sight of the wet and dirty girl lying on his drawing room sofa. Millie, having been summoned by Mistress Hall, followed a few moments later.

'You sent for me, Mistress 'all?' Millie said, mildly, as she attempted to bob a curtsey to the Master.

'Yes, Millie, we have two children here that are in need of our help. I should like you to take the baby down to the kitchen with you. The woman from the village will help you take care of him until more satisfactory arrangements can be made.'

Millie silently acknowledged the haughty housekeeper who, with the exception of the butler, was head of the household where most domestic matters were concerned.

Alex now took Millie's attention. He warmed instantly to the kindly looking woman who was doubtless weary and anxious. 'Good day, Millie, perhaps ye would like to take a seat for a moment,' said Alex quietly, indicating a chair by the sofa where the crying baby lay.

On first entering the room, Millie had recognised young Mary as one of the two girls managing alone since the loss of their parents the year previous. She had become almost transfixed at the sight of the yelling baby lying on one of the sofas, and had known at once that he would be Sarah's child. She realised also that, for Mary to have the child with her, the worst must have happened and that young Sarah would no doubt be beyond help now.

Ema Fields

Millie looked up at Alex as he lifted Ben and handed him to her. Holding the tiny baby close she rocked him to and fro. Large tears slipped down her cheeks as she thought of Sarah, and of Mary lying there so helpless; they were just children. She whispered tenderly against the baby's wrinkled little brow, 'there there now, there now me darlin', hush your fears, you're safe now me pet, don't fret, Millie's 'ere, Millie's 'ere now.' And at that moment, a bond was forged for all of time.

As Millie continued to soothe him Ben's wails slowed, his little chest heaving as his sobbing lessened. As the baby sucked on his fist Millie continued to comfort him. Calmer now, his other little fist buried deep into the old lady's damp cheek, he felt secure, for the nervous young chambermaid's attempt to nurse the baby served only to heighten his fear.

'Millie began to push herself up from the chair, 'I'll take 'im to the kitchen now Sir. Vi Carter 'ad 'er little one not but a month since, she's glad to be rid of the extra milk and 'elp this little one at the same time. She says she's got milk enough for a complete flock sir, 'tis often the way.'

With her rolling gait Millie made towards the door still murmuring comforting words. Alex, opening the door wide, smiled warmly, 'd'nae let him sleep until he has fed, Millie, but d'nae let him tak' too much at first.' Then, checking himself from issuing further instructions, Alex chastised himself laughingly, 'I forget who I'm addressing, Millie, forgive me woman, ye likely know what is to be done far better than an old man.'

'I wouldn't say that doctor, but yes, I've 'ad five of me own. 'e'll be right fine with me, don't fret on that, why, 'e'll be just like one of me own sir, getting on a bit though I may be.' Millie, at that moment, was completely unaware of how true her words would prove to be.

The doctor was alone with Mary now. The master had gone about his business, declaring that he would be available when his house was restored to some semblance of order, and that the housekeeper had complete authority with regard to bringing about that blissful state with all haste. Mistress Hall had disappeared to attend to the requisites of a sick room, instructing the maids to fetch a dozen and one things, also to kindle a good fire in the smaller bedchamber on the upper floor.

Fortunately Vi Carter lived on the outskirts of the village and it had taken but a short while to bring her to the Manor. Mistress Hall had gone with Davy to explain the situation, pressing upon him the urgency of persuading

Vi Carter, beseeching her if necessary, to help the baby boy in these dire circumstances.

Vi Carter could spare little time for she had a baby daughter as well as three young sons and her man to take care of. Despite their own circumstances they were very kind, these country folk, and both Vi and Will Carter were only too pleased to do all they could to help the motherless infant at the Manor.

As Vi pulled her cloak about her she looked into the little wooden cradle where her baby slept peacefully. Davy smiled and reached for the door latch, 'I'll fetch Vi back meself, Will, rest assured, we'll not be long, now we must get on, and thank you, thank you both.' Davy glanced around the small dwelling in which the six of them lived. It was neat and clean but quite sparse. A bright fire burned in the grate and a large pot of good smelling stew simmered gently on the hook. He looked at the three half-smiling, glowing little faces and at Will, watching the cradle, an expression of love and pride on his rugged face. They were content, these simple people, and Davy thought how little some folk needed to be happy. Assuring her family that she would not be away above an hour or two, Vi left with Davy and Mistress Hall to take her first glimpse inside the big house.

Chapter Four

FOLLOWING HER ORDEAL IN THE storm, Mary lie for a night and a day in the small room that the housekeeper had had prepared for her on the upper floor of the Manor. Today had proved to be an unusually exacting time for both housekeeper and cook at Woodstock Manor House for, as well as the additional work of caring for a new baby and sick child, it was the night of the big harvest dinner. In the normal way of things Millie and Mistress Hall worked together on these occasions, planning several weeks ahead, to provide a lavish array of harvest decorations for the large dining hall together with equally outstanding table displays. Millie's sumptuous food and succulent accompanying dishes were the talk of the county.

It was now the second night that Mary lie sleeping in the small chamber that Mistress Hall had arranged for her. The austere housekeeper had amazed the entire household with her apparent dedication to the care of Mary. She had sat with the girl the previous night, dozing by the bedside through the long, silent hours. She changed the warming pans, kept a good fire and attempted to rouse Mary in the hope that the child would take some warm broth, this she did at two hourly intervals as the doctor had requested. Also, during the still hours of the night, she crept into Millie's chamber, lifting the baby boy as he slept in order that he should not disturb the old lady. The master had declined to bear the expense of a wet nurse, thus the care of the baby, labour of love though it was, fell almost entirely upon Millie, and the late night of the harvest supper, as the huge meal was known, had left Millie unusually spent. It would be Mistress Hall who would waken Vi to see to Ben should he need a night feed. Vi was to sleep in the servants quarters with her own baby for a week or two when Ben would be fed with a bottle. But for the time being, as good as her word, Vi did everything possible to help with baby Ben.

Alex had been reluctantly invited to stay at the Manor for a day or two should he so wish. He had agreed, explaining that he would be happy to attend the child until he could determine the outcome of her condition. It appeared that she had not developed pneumonia, his main concern, but neither had she fully regained consciousness and Alex was reluctant to leave until she showed positive signs of recovery. Knowing now that, but for the baby boy, this girl was all alone in the world, Alex felt he had a responsibility of care.

In the early hours of the second night, as Mistress Hall lie fitfully dozing by a low fire, a small candle sending flickering shadows across the semi-darkened room, her patience was rewarded, Mary began to stir without the usual efforts to rouse her. The housekeeper sat up in the old rocking chair and pressed a hand to her aching neck. She shivered, the room had grown chill and, drawing her shawl more tightly around her, she wondered what had disturbed her. She reached for the poker to break up the sleeping logs, the wood crackled, sparks rose to the chimney and small flames lit the room as Mary stirred again.

Fatigued and in great need of rest the woman swiftly crossed the small space to the bed. Mary was rambling now, something about, 'soon be there babe, soon be there.' She was mostly incoherent but Mistress Hall thought she heard quite clearly, 'Mary'll get yer there.' Mary's thin arm was flailing about, searching for something, the housekeeper did not know what. She took Mary's arm and placed it beneath the patchwork quilt covered with a creamy coloured counterpane.

'You must keep warm now, keep covered up dear.' Mary was still rambling, tossing her head in anguish, she would soon be fully awake. In a fluster of excitement and joy Mistress Hall ran to the bell pull on the wall by the fire. The small clock on the mantleshelf told her it was two o-clock, she glanced quickly at Ben who was sleeping soundly in a basket then took up a taper and lighted another candle before returning silently to the bed.

There came a light tap on the door and the chambermaid came in, saying drowsily, 'did yer want me ma'am?'

"Yes, Sophie, run and fetch Barkworth, tell him to bring Doctor Alex to Mary's bedchamber with all speed. Wake up girl, be certain not to disturb the household.' As Mistress Hall sternly whispered her instructions to the sleepy-eyed maid, Mary mumbled a name, 'make haste now, Sophie,' the housekeeper urged.

'Not a sound will I make ma'am, an' I'll run like lightning,' Sophie assured her as she took up her nightgown and ran tiptoe across the room, closing the door silently behind her.

Barkworth instructed the chambermaid to arouse Doctor Alex whilst he hurriedly made his way to assist the housekeeper, their past differences now completely forgotten; at least for the moment. As Barkworth entered the small bedchamber Mistress Hall turned to him immediately saying anxiously, 'oh, Barkworth, have you summoned Doctor Alex?' Barkworth nodded in answer as he crossed the room to Mary's bedside.

'I don't know if she's delirious or not Barkworth, but I don't think so, her temperature has lessened but she's rambling all the time.' Mistress Hall's manner was humble, subdued and full of concern. A new Mistress Hall indeed, thought the bemused butler, very strange, who would have believed it?

Mary, fully awake now, was being assured that all was well as Alex entered the room still fastening the cord of his dressing gown. Appearing completely in possession of himself and equal to any situation he acknowledged Barkworth, both men calm and proficient as always. Mary looked around at her strange surroundings then to the tall woman, dressed in a nightgown and black shawl, who sat at her bedside. The frightened girl looked up at the big man in the posh silk coat, her gaze then moved to the nice looking gentleman in a long, dark woollen jacket who was holding her hand and seemed to be thoughtful as he smiled at her. She was completely disorientated as she searched for the small room in the cottage. She looked for Sarah's bed, she looked to see where the bench table should be, she looked for the door, the dirt floor, the shuttered windows, Sarah, the baby. The thought screamed at her "the baby". Mary seemed to spring to life, 'where am I' she almost cried out the words, 'please tell me where I am.' Then louder, her eyes beseeching them all as tears streamed down her hot cheeks, 'I didn't get 'im there did I? I didn't, I didn't,' she wept.

Mary had not heard Mistress Hall's words of comfort. She continued to sob as she looked pleadingly at the lady dressed in black. 'I didn't get 'im to the big 'ouse, the storm...the storm,' she sobbed brokenly, 'the storm stopped me.' Mary was most dreadfully distressed. Alex lay a cool hand against her forehead and spoke soothingly as sobs continued to choke the little girl. 'Hush now, ye must rest, we'll tell ye everything on the morrow, ye're going to be fine, just fine.' Mary raised her face to his, a look of desperation in her large eyes, and Alex continued to reassure her, 'and the wee boy is fine, truly fine, hush my little one, he's alright, aye, truly he is.' Mary's eyes opened wide and fresh sobs began to rise in her throat, she clearly did not believe Alex. He lowered his head to hers and, almost in a whisper, said, 'no, my lassie, you took wonderful care of him, look.' Alex nodded to Mistress Hall, then towards the basket, silently asking her to bring the baby to Mary. 'He's sleeping soundly lassie, we'll nae disturb him.' As Alex spoke he raised Mary up onto the pillows supporting her with his arm. Mistress Hall sat on the chair by the bed, holding the basket with the sleeping infant on her lap.

'I can't see 'im,' Mary said agitatedly, as she leaned back breathlessly into the pillows. 'I must see 'im mister,' she implored.

Alex turned to the housekeeper and lovingly took up the baby from his basket. Sitting on the bed he gently placed the infant into Mary's arms, whispering, 'see, ma gel, here he is, safe and sound, but we mustnae awaken him.' Alex smiled and winked cheekily at Mary, 'if he wakes up now he'll surely want to be fed and he has a fine pair of lungs on him, we'll need to disturb Violet, and he'll waken the whole household, be assured.'

Mary stroked the baby's hand, his fuzzy little golden head rested on her arm and she breathed deeply. Her eyes were wide and full of tears as she looked up at Alex, saying, in an awesome whisper, 'I done it mister, I done it.' I'n't 'e beau'iful mister, i'n't 'e just the most beau'iful baby you 'ave ever seen?'

A little breathless now, Mary made no protest as the baby was lifted from her arms and returned to his basket by the hearth. Her tearstained face was truly radiant as she looked again at Alex. 'Who are you? Who are these people? Are you the Squire mister?' Mary breathed the question reverently, and continued, 'Sarah said as the Squire was very kind, is this the big 'ouse?'

Alex, in answer said, 'the morrow, lassie, the morrow, will ye rest for me now?'

Mary sank into the pillows, smiling at him as she closed her eyes. Mistress Hall watched, and Barkworth, still standing at the foot of the bed, also watched as Alex pulled the counterpane up around Mary's chin, she was almost fast asleep; crying gently now, but that was alright.

Alex stood up and, straightening his back and rubbing his chin with both hands, said, 'well, Mistress Hall, Barkworth,' he gave them both a look of deep gratitude, 'we've won. We've brought the wee lassie back to us, and 'tis all thanks to the great care and the vigil ye have kept. The danger has passed, we'll say a prayer of thanks the night, aye, that we will.'

During the past two days the straight-laced housekeeper had displayed a tenderness hitherto unknown and totally out of character for this prim, curt woman. It was said below stairs that her "devotion to the sick girl had been remarkable, to say the least."

In answer to the doctor's comments Mistress Hall quietly replied, 'she is with us because of you, doctor. They are both with us because of yourself, but I am truly honoured that I have been able to serve you. Though I have no doubt that I may not have fared half so well had not Barkworth here, taken on a deal of my duties as well as his own.'

'I am indeed aware of it, Mistress, and I thank ye both.'

Barkworth spoke now, for the first time since entering Mary's chamber. 'Will you stay on a day or two sir?'

'Nae,' said Alex, thoughtfully, 'I d'nae think so, the concern has passed, there is nothing I can do for either of them now that ye cannae do better, of that I'm certain. 'tis likely I'll be away come the morrow, I've already stayed a mite too long, but circumstances required that I should. 'tis time we left, there is much to be done.'

Alex and Barkworth each bade Mistress Hall goodnight, what was left of the night, and returned to their bedchambers.

Alex did not retire immediately but sat in the big old, comfortable armchair beside the fire. He pressed fresh logs into the sleeping embers and breathed deeply as he lit the small lamp on the side table. Then, taking up his pipe, he sat back as the logs began to catch and the fire slowly crackled back to life. In the quiet comfort of the bedchamber, with its fading red carpet on which were scattered small rugs, its dark oak four-poster bed and heavy old Georgian chests, standing regally against the richly panelled walls, the man was truly troubled, what would become of them now? Low lamplight flickered, the firelight, now adding its bright flames to the semi-darkened chamber would, at any other time, have shed an ambience of perfect peace. Alex lie back in the chair and, with his feet resting on the fender and drawing gratefully on his pipe, remembered a time, eight long years ago, when a promise had been made.

***

Not too far across the Scottish border on the outskirts of a large town, the MacFarlanes had taken up residence at The Grange, a rambling old house of great proportions. Their dear friend, Doctor Alexander MacKenzie, lived about ten miles from them in a much poorer area where he determined to work as a 'true doctor' to help the less fortunate people of his beloved Scotland. It was a poor, run down area and Alex had found his work in this particular community to be immensely rewarding.

Doctor MacKenzie had attended Eleanor MacFarlane throughout her last two pregnancies which, tragically, had ended in miscarriage and was determined to be with her at the birth of her coming child. He had felt for some weeks that this birth may also prove to have its difficulties, though he prayed not, and when, two weeks before Eleanor's baby was due, he had been thrown from his horse whilst on an urgent call to one of the crofts, Eleanor was frantic. Word had reached her that she must take complete rest and that, despite the doctor's indisposition, he would be with her at the birth of her child. The message also advised Angus MacFarlane to arrange for the midwife to spend the week prior to the birth with Eleanor at The Grange. This was merely a precaution, the note stressed, Alex would be with Eleanor when her time came, they had his word.

A messenger from The Grange late one afternoon had informed Alex that Eleanor's labour had started. It was a week or two earlier than had been expected and Alex was still experiencing considerable back pain after his fall. He had quite some difficulty in walking and knew it would be impossible to sit a horse. It would take considerably less time to go to Eleanor were he able to ride, but the carriage it must be.

With all haste Alex summoned Robbie, without whose dedication to duty life would undoubtedly prove very difficult, especially at this moment in time. Robbie was the doctor's valet, secretary, butler, driver, indeed, a man of all works but, of far greater importance than all of these, he was Alex's devoted friend.

As Alex stiffly made his way to fetch his medicine bag and collect together other essentials, a crooked smile lightened his countenance. The wee mite could mebbe have waited just a day or two longer to ease my painful back, he thought, not very considerate of ye, young MacFarlane, I'll say that.

Robbie entered the room to find the doctor struggling into his outer garments, 'help me man, quickly now,' said Alex, and the anxious manservant stared in amazement. 'Och, surely not sir, ye'll nae be going anywhere wi' that back of yours.'

'Now then Robbie, who is the doctor?'

'But sir,' Robbie began to question his instruction, clearly concerned as to the wisdom of this request, for he knew the pain that Alex had endured over the past week or so.

'Robbie, please, if I've asked ye once I've asked ye a hundred times, nae more of this "Sir", all that is to be forgotten, I'm nae but a country doctor now. It's Eleanor MacFarlane,' Alex explained, 'her time has come.'

'Och, I see.' Robbie drew a deep breath, he understood the importance of Alex being with the MacFarlanes at this crucial time for he knew only too well the sad history of these good people. He argued no further. A few minutes later, the journey began.

Robbie helped Alex from the coach at the entrance steps of The Grange just as Angus MacFarlane was disappearing around the side of the house. Moments later Alex entered Eleanor's bedchamber where the midwife tearfully explained, in very hushed tones, that the child was stillborn, there was nothing to be done. The master had been told immediately as he had been waiting outside the door and, on hearing of the still birth, had fled the house. As quickly as he was able Alex removed his cloak. He glanced across to where Eleanor lay in a state of total exhaustion after her long and agonising ordeal, completely unaware that her child had been born dead. Alex turned to the midwife, 'see to the mother, I have nae time.' He looked beneath the washstand to where a small bundle of soiled linen was placed in a bowl. Gasping at the pain in his back he called to the nurse, 'the bairn, nurse, give me the bairn, how long did ye say now?'

'She was born just moments before ye arrived doctor, not above a minute or two, everything is happening so quickly, the master…'

'Hush woman,' Alex cut off the words of the distressed nurse, 'now listen, and move faster than ye've ever moved in your life.' The distraught and frightened nurse nodded, ready to assist in whatever way she could. The midwife was attending to Eleanor.

'Fetch two large bowls or basins, anything ye have. One filled with hot water, not so hot that it will scald mind, and another with almost cold water, ye ken? Away wi ye, every second is vital.

Having no time to scrub Alex worked on the infant as he spoke, massaging the little chest and trying to breathe into the tiny mouth. The baby, still warm, was soft and downy, but totally unresponsive to all of Alex's efforts. He yelled as he straightened up, entirely forgetting the pain that was caused by sudden movements. He drew a deep breath and prayed aloud, 'Dear God, if ye never give me anything again as long as I live, give me this life.'

Precious seconds ticked away, seconds that seemed like hours to Alex, until the nurse and housemaid returned with the bowls of water. 'Put them there,' he commanded brusquely, then cried aloud, 'curse this damned back.' They placed the bowls on the table where the doctor stood attending to the dead baby. Without another word Alex immersed the still little body into the deep hot water 'one, two,' he counted, then plunged the tiny mite into the cold water – no response, but there was hope, he had seen this method work at the hospital. 'One, two', then into the hot again – he looked at the baby lying in his arms beneath the water. 'One, two, three, four seconds this time,' he said, as he counted aloud then, in a flash, into the cold water, sheer determination written in those pain filled eyes. He raised the baby to the surface of the water, massaging her chest then, just as he was about to try to breath air into the still lungs the baby choked, spluttered, then choked again. Turning her upside down on his hand Alex placed his little finger deep into the rosebud mouth attempting once again to clear the choking fluid. The midwife and nurse watched in silent astonishment as tears fell freely from joyful eyes. Another cough, a choke, and the baby began to thrash about in the water, making small sounds as Alex continued to work. The little chest was rising and falling gently as the sweet black blue eyes looked up at him from a purplish little face. Tears of joy sprang unchecked to his eyes, 'well now ma bonny wee lassie,' he said softly, 'ye truly are a bonny wee gel, aren't ye now,' he said, as a deep sob caught in his throat. The baby girl lie in his arms, seemingly looking up at him, entirely oblivious to the fact that she had been snatched from a heavenly home.

'Here ye are nurse,' said Alex, also thoroughly exhausted now. 'She's all yours, pretty her up and give her to mamma when she awakens.

Alex remembered now, that time eight long years ago, when at the moment he had handed the baby girl to the nurse Eleanor had whispered 'is my baby alright Alex? Can I see my baby? Is it a wee gel or a wee son?' Then, fearfully, and in a very small voice, is there something wrong Alex?'

'Eleanor, my clever gel, nothing is wrong,' soothed the midwife, doctor Alex was wonderful, and ye have a beautiful wee lassie.'

As the midwife spoke she handed the baby to Eleanor, there were no words to describe the emotion she experienced as she placed the baby girl into the arms of her mother. She had worked all through the long day to ease the very difficult birth and, as her heart rejoiced at the survival of Eleanor's child, tears flowed silently down her tired face.

'She's real bonny,' whispered Eleanor, as the baby curled her little fist around her mother's finger. 'Och, such a wee beauty, say hello to your mamma then, my little sweetheart.'

Watching Eleanor's radiant face as she gazed, misty eyed, at her new born child, Alex knew, once again, why he had given up the easy life of the nobility to become a doctor in the country community that he loved. To take his knowledge and experience, not only to wealthy families such as the MacFarlanes, but also to the families who would, in the normal way of things, never be able to call in a doctor, not even for the very young or the very old. It would be a long time before he would forget this sight and all that it meant to him.

Still numbed with grief over this final tragedy Angus MacFarlane returned to be with his wife when she was given the news, as soon, of course, she must. On entering the house, his mind in torment, he thought he heard an infant's cry. He fought back the tears, my poor mind is going, he thought. But the cries grew a little louder and, as they gained in strength, the truth began to penetrate his despair. There had been a mistake. Dear God let there have been a mistake. The big man raced up the stairs, taking them two and three at a time and almost flew along the landing and into Eleanor's bedchamber. His swollen, tired eyes looked upon his wife, his beautiful wife, smiling wearily and tenderly up at him and, wonder of wonders, joy of all joys, cradling a tiny baby in her arms. He stood, unable to move, and breathed the words, 'thank ye dear Lord, dear God in heaven, I thank ye.'

Eleanor held out a hand to him saying softly, 'she'll be Caroline, dear, Caroline Isabelle MacFarlane, after your mother and me.' She stroked the baby's cheek as she said, 'say hello to your dadda, Caroline.'

Angus sat by Eleanor and, on a long, shuddering breath, whispered, 'Caroline.' He took the diminutive fingers and held them gently in his giant hand. As the baby gripped his little finger he said, chokingly, his eyes awash, 'hello Caroline, welcome to Scotland,' and with those words an enduring and all consuming love was born.

A while later, downstairs in the drawing room, Angus gripped his friend's hands in both his own. In a state of dazed emotion he said, 'I thank ye Alex, the midwife told me about the birth, how very difficult it had been for her and what ye did. If it were not for ye leaving your sickbed to come this night, I would nae be a father now, and when my Eleanor had learned the truth, I may not even be a husband. God Bless ye Alex, ye truly are a worthy man.'

Alex waved away the gratitude, he knew many such moments, albeit for different reasons, in his chosen work. 'Nae, nae Angus, the bairn just needed a wee shock to get her system working. She could nae clear her breathing passages wi'out a wee bit of help, nae more than that, man.'

Angus continued, 'if there is ever anything, anything in this world that I can do for ye, nae matter what, ye must come to me, Alex. Just say the word, and if it is possible to do, it shall be done, I give ye my solemn promise. One day I hope that the good Lord will give me the opportunity to thank ye in some small way for ye being here this night.'

'I have ma reward, Angus, but I thank ye, and ye may live to regret your rash promise, goodness knows I shall need help along ma way.'

'Name it,' said Angus, fervently, 'name it, and it shall be done.'

Exhausted and now in considerable pain, the doctor patted his friend on the shoulder, saying, 'I'll be away to ma bed now Angus, I leave them with a very capable midwife and an excellent nurse, they're both in good hands, and I'll just be downstairs if I should be needed.'

'Aye, your room is ready,' said Angus, as he led the way across the drawing room and along a passageway to where a spacious room had been especially made ready for the doctor to avoid the painful climb to the upper floor.

Angus left Alex at the door to his room saying, 'I cannae sleep this night, Alex, so if ye think it would be alright, I'd like to sit a wee while wi' Eleanor and ma bairn?'

Alex moved stiffly, 'my orders are, man,' he said, with mock severity, 'that ye get off to your bed, ye'll doubtless have a full day the morrow.'

'Och, Alex, ye're a hard man,' Angus smiled, 'I'll have cook mak' ye a light wee bite and a hot toddy, I'll have her fetch it to ye now.'

'No food my friend, but a hot toddy would be wonderful.'

Angus pulled the bell rope and with his hand to his chin awaited the arrival of his housekeeper who had refused to retire before the master.

* * *

Alex came out of his reverie with those words still so clear in his mind, Angus' words. "If there is ever anything I can do for ye, anything in the world, nae matter what, ye must come to me, just say the word, and if it is possible to do, it shall be done, I give ye my solemn promise."

Alex had not seen his old friends or their daughter in several years. He had become deeply involved in the research of new medicines and the lives of the people in the outlying Scottish communities that he cared for. He felt with certainty that he would be able to help the sick child, Mary, orphaned and penniless as were so many other children of her time. He prayed as he remembered Angus MacFarlane's pledge, eight long years ago.

Chapter Five

LATER THE FOLLOWING MORNING MILLIE was told the good news that, with a little rest and care, young Mary was going to be just fine. The entire household was abuzz with speculation as to whether the baby would stay at the Manor House, which was highly unlikely, or be raised on the parish, or perhaps even go to the poorhouse. But perhaps he would be one of the lucky ones and someone would take him as their own. The parish was considered to be the most likely option, for who around these parts could take on another mouth to feed without recompense for at least eight years, until the boy could be put to work, it was said. As for the girl, it was quite obvious that a child of her years, alone in the world, could not take on the responsibility of a new baby, so, what of Mary? Now there was a question indeed. She could, of course, go into service somewhere, but who would take responsibility to see her right, "'tis a sad state of affairs for her, and that's God's own truth," it was said.

Millie's heart went out to the baby boy as he lay sleeping in a washing basket at the side of the big range. She would have no idle chatter as to what was to become of him, not in her kitchen. His prospects for the future were bleak, and it distressed her to hear these thoughts put into words.

Sir John had summoned Doctor MacKenzie to join him in the library. He was vexed at the recent turn of events and was anxious to allay any suspicion of a connection between himself and those wretched peasants. He had let those girls remain on the land in the two roomed cottage after the deaths of their parents, they had been good people, right enough, and it had entirely suited his own purposes. He had thought to be hailed as a saint for his Christian charity, among other considerations, and now this, he should have known better. The Squire's thoughts were interrupted as Alex entered the library, brisk and official and wearing his travelling cape.

'Come in doctor,' said the Englishman, 'oh, I see you are ready to resume your journey.' He spoke with a forced brightness that did not go unnoticed by Alex. 'It is good news about the girl,' he continued, 'I hear she will recover. Mistress Hall informs me that the crisis is over.'

'Aye', Alex replied coolly, facing Sir John directly as he stood with his back to the high book-lined shelves which flanked the beautiful wide stone fireplace, 'she'll be fine for the moment, but someone must see to her and the wee one, where will they go? They have no kin.'

Sir John was clearly disturbed and affronted at the vague suggestions of this wretched Scotsman, surely he did not expect them to stay at the Manor, under his roof.

'Och well,' continued Alex, 'I have my own thoughts as to what might be done to help the lassie, at least. No immediate hurry, of course, she'll be needing rest for a while yet, she is still a sick gel, but 'tis as you say, Sir John, with the right care she will mend well. Strong stuff indeed, your English lassies are made of.'

'A while yet?' Sir John repeated indignantly. 'Surely you do not expect these waifs to remain here, at the Manor House with the danger past. I have a sick wife who I will not have disturbed under any circumstances, with respect, doctor MacKenzie, it is not an answer.'

Alex rounded on the Squire, 'she has barely been snatched from the grave man,' he spoke in that reprimanding, humiliating manner which had totally alienated the Lord of Woodstock from their very first meeting. 'She's mebbe just ten or twelve years old, to go back to a neglected cottage, if indeed she has even that, would mean the lung fever for certain, and all our efforts, and your good Christian charity, wasted, leaving the wee bairn with nae kin at all.'

'I see,' Sir John was thoughtful, nervous, there was much at risk, he had to think, he must think. 'I, er, did not fully understand Doctor, I was merely informed that the girl had recovered, was well.'

'Nae, Sir John, she's far from well, as yet,' said Alex, a little calmer now, then, thinking all the while that something was not quite right, he continued, 'but the battle for life is won, as long as she convalesces here, with warmth, good food and proper care.'

'Of course, I'll see that my housekeeper makes the arrangements, she may stay until she is recovered and perfectly well, why, she's a child of my village, they both are, children of my village, that is.'

Having gained the Squire's consent to allow Mary and the baby to remain at the Manor House for a while, Alex relaxed.

Sir John crossed the room and, hopelessly attempting to appear a little concerned, asked after the baby. 'Did the girl say anything, this morning I mean, have you spoken to her, about the baby's father, did she name him?' He tried to keep the anxiety out of his voice but Alex merely interpreted this unease as vexation for the way the Squire's household had been disrupted, and a natural desire to have things return to normal at the earliest possible time.

'She asked if I was the Master, I would have liked a wee chat with her but I could nae let her tax herself, then I was asked to see you in the library.' As he spoke Alex's eyes scanned the room. Rows of books and magnificent leather-bound volumes graced the dark polished wood. The sweet smell of beeswax and leather mingled with the fragrance of late blooms from the garden, arranged in tall porcelain vases. There were many old family photographs on finely carved chests. A bright fire flickered in the great hearth, adding to the beauty and comfort of this masculine room, whilst on a large old Persian rug stood an impressive red and gold leather topped writing table with a map of the estate spread out upon it. The whole was complimented by the long casement windows, with their drapes of dove grey reaching down to the deep red carpet. The English Squire's taste was impeccable and, whatever Alex's feelings with regard to the man's character, he would not have denied himself the pleasure of taking in the beauty of this room.

The Squire could ill conceal his agitation as Alex spoke. 'You have a fine library Sir John, a restful room indeed, may I compliment you on your choice of books. I see that many of the great writers are here. Were I only to have the time to peruse these shelves, I'm certain I should become utterly lost in them.'

'My library, Doctor, as indeed my entire house, is at your disposal, and should you ever wish to visit under less extreme circumstances, it would be my pleasure to accommodate you. But, with, um,' Sir John coughed and cleared his throat, trying to formulate the words, 'with regard to the boy, the baby, you see, if we knew of his father, maybe something could be done for him.'

Alex glanced at the squire with a quizzical look which made Sir John feel entirely uncomfortable, the Scotsman was getting a little too close to home and Sir John was anxious to see the back of him.

'I'll have cook pack a hamper for you and your man to see you through your journey, 'tis the least I can do after your delay.'

'Thank ye kindly Sir John, but that will nae be necessary, it will tak' but a short while to reach the Inn now. I would just like to tak' a wee look at the bairns before I leave. I may well look in on ye on ma way back, see how they are faring, I'll likely tak' advantage of your kind offer then, and a good meal before we begin the long trek hame would be welcome indeed.'

'Whatever you say, doctor. I'll come along with you to see the girl.' Sir John's face was set grimly, but even the shrewd doctor Alex was not able to ascertain the reason, something was odd, there was an underlying factor here, in this lovely old Manor House, set in the heart of the picturesque English countryside.

'Och, not at all, thank ye,' Alex replied, striding towards the door, 'I'll not keep ye from your work. Perhaps Mistress Hall would come with me, if she's free for a moment, I'll give them a wee check and be on ma way. The first gathering of the medical convention takes place this evening, I'd nae like to miss the opening speeches.'

Sir John was greatly agitated and short tempered as he summoned Barkworth to seek out Mistess Hall, and Alex, feeling a little contrite, searched for a few kindly words.

'Do not trouble yeself, Sir, ye've done more than anyone could expect of ye. Ye've put your hame at their disposal and at great inconvenience, they are fortunate youngsters indeed to belong to your village. Why, but for ye sir, they would not be here now, either of them. Ye've opened your doors and your somewhat reluctant heart, och aye, it has to be said, but ye did it nonetheless. I'll go along now, then I'll tak' ma leave of ye.'

On hearing Alex's words Sir John was somewhat mollified, though still fearful as to what that miserable wretch of a girl might reveal. 'Well, doctor, I daresay she'll likely come up with some fantastic story just to have the boy taken in by someone, some poor unfortunate personage no doubt, who knows who she will name, someone of note, I'll warrant.'

Until that moment Alex had thought little of Sir John's strange attitude during the whole of the past few days, but that last remark was undoubtedly the Squire's undoing. As if a veil had been drawn from his eyes Alex saw the inevitable. Of course, he thought, I must truly have been blinded by concern for the bairns, this Noble English Squire is the wee laddie's father. Nothing to be done, of course, none of my concern, and impossible to prove, but I'll exploit this knowledge for the benefit of the wee one. I know…and Sir John of Woodstock shall be made aware of this.

Alex turned to the man standing awkwardly behind him and, looking him squarely in the eye, said, 'well, Sir John, no doubt we'll both soon know.'

Mistress Hall was already at Mary's bedside, silently watching the girl sleeping. Mary's long hair, once dirty and straggly, had been washed and brushed and fell in long deep waves, also she had regained a little colour. She was not a beautiful girl, the woman thought, as she looked at the child, in fact a somewhat plain little thing, really. Her features were not unacceptable, they just sort of didn't come together quite right, somehow, but that abundant deep red hair is truly beautiful. Mistress Hall did not think she had seen the like before.

Still watching the sleeping girl, Doris Hall's mind drifted back to a time long ago in the north of England when, on a bleak winter's afternoon, a baby girl had been born to her. The stress of the birth had proved too much for the infant and, after a long, arduous battle into the world she had fought for life for only a short while when her strength left her. The perfectly formed, beautiful baby girl had slipped away in the arms of her bereft mother.

Doris was unmarried, she bore the baby in shame, hiding away at a home for such women to prevent them from being condemned and shunned by society but, from the very first moment she had looked upon her tiny baby daughter, the child was wholly and unreservedly beloved. The birth had been extremely difficult, a matter of touch and go for both mother and baby, Doris being 34 years old and not able to endure childbirth with any amount of ease. She had always been a demure, virtuous woman of rigid morals but had been foolish, and then, deserted by her first and only love, heartbroken and alone in her grief, she tried to pick up the pieces of her life and begin again.

Doris Hall, spinster, applied for the position as housekeeper at Woodstock Manor in the south east, leaving behind her home and the shame that she bore. However, her grief she carried with her always, each and every day. The unhappy, lonely woman had long since accepted that she would never again know happiness, but was able to provide for herself and this was all she would ask from life. Being a woman of great religious beliefs she took solace in the thought that her baby daughter was with God, it was his hand that had taken the baby from her, the Lord worked in mysterious ways and always with reason. Ours not to question why, was the only comfort she could find.

With all these sad thoughts again filling her mind she remembered how desperate she had been to find a position and somewhere to live, hopefully both under one roof. Her excellent training in service would now place her well and, down south, no-one would know her.

'You are just like I was then, Mary,' she murmured, 'with the exception that you are but a child, and there is hope for you. No home, no work and, albeit for different reasons, no kin but for the dear little baby boy.' If only… but she mustn't dwell. She let her thoughts amble on, to her adequate rooms with her own kitchen, diminutive though it was and a bedroom come sitting room, handsomely furnished with her comfort in mind. An adjoining alcove type room which housed a washstand with its bowl and jug and other toilette requisites, there was also a dressing area fitted with tall oak wardrobes, an unusual room indeed and quite delightful.

The housekeeper drew a long breath and sighed deeply. Yes, her day was full and satisfying. True enough, to say the very least, she was not the most popular person in the household but the domestic staff tolerated her and she them. She had a nimble mind where accounts were concerned and ran a tight ship. She ruled the housemaids, laundry and chambermaids and the one tweeny maid with an iron hand but they were all aware that, though hard to please, she was fair. Mistress Hall would never report any misdemeanour to the Mistress of the house and they would always know that, however they may displease her, their positions would never be jeopardised. She was not a vindictive woman, just over zealous and rather dour and, like all housekeepers, totally aware of her elevated position in the household. The Master was a tyrant and the housekeeper of Woodstock Manor would give him no cause for complaint.

Doris Hall was very comfortable in her rooms on the middle floor and wanted only to be left in peace on her off-duty periods, for peace, at least, she had found at Woodstock Manor. She valued and jealously guarded her privacy, at ease in the knowledge that her tragic and shameful past would never be known of here.

Mary was awakening, the long rest and the beef tea that she had been encouraged to take had done their work. She looked up at the darkly clad, grim looking woman and smiled, 'you was 'ere last night wasn't yer?' She said, with a degree of uncertainty as she looked around for the baby, unsure as to whether she had been dreaming of baby Ben and the kind man in the long robe.

'Yes, I was here.' Mistress Hall bestowed a very weak smile on Mary, which seemed to come from her eyes rather than her tight lips. 'Now then, I do not wish that you tire yourself, how would it be if I bathe you and brush your hair again, then I will tell you all about this little fellow here?' She said, nodding towards the sleeping baby in the basket by the fire.

'Is 'e really alright then, I did it? I got 'im 'ere? I didn't dream it?'

'If you listen in a little while you will hear for yourself exactly how alright he is, he has a fine pair of lungs.' Mistress Hall raised her eyes heavenward and threw up her hands, 'my, how he can yell for his breakfast', she said, smiling broadly now, for the first time in years.

Mary smiled up at her so sweetly that Mistress Hall's stern countenance softened and a light showed in her sad eyes. She thought what beautiful eyes this plain child had, so full of love when she talked of the baby, and was entirely unaware that the light in Mary's eyes was equally matched by that in her own.

'Come now child, Doctor Alex is to take a look at you and baby this morning before he takes his leave, which will be at any moment.' She bustled around as she spoke, fetching the jug and bowl and raising Mary up on the pillows in order to bathe her as well as she could before Alex came in to see them.

'What's your name,' Mary spluttered as a warm wet cloth was dragged across her face and around her neck and body.'

'Mistress Hall,' Doris answered in her usual stilted tone. 'I am the Housekeeper of the Manor, hush now child, do be told,' she said, a little more sternly than intended.

'You're very kind to me Mistress 'all, I wish I could really fank yer.'

Doris Hall's eyes misted over for the first time in many lonely years, then in a matter-of-fact tone she admonished, 'now then, we'll just have less of the chattering, I have much work to do and you must not tire yourself. Now sip some of this broth that cook has sent up for you, it has been especially prepared, we don't' want it to go to waste.'

'I'd really rather 'ave a nice drop o' tea, if I could, we didn't get much tea, me and Sarah,' Mary said, her voice lowering and losing its chirpiness.

The Housekeeper threw Mary a stern glance.

'But I'll 'ave the brof as well, fanks Mistress 'all, fanks very much.'

Mary sat sipping the broth, revelling in the warmth and comfort of the big bed and gazing at the low fire thinking how wonderful it would be to live and work here, at the Big House, never to be hungry again, or be cold again, and drink tea every day.

The housekeeper crossed the room to the bellrope to summon one of the maids to bring up a pot of tea.

A few minutes later a maid arrived bearing a tea tray, 'Millie sent me up with the tea Mistress Hall, tea for two,' she said, nervously.

'Tea for one Bessie'. Mistress Hall was brusque, 'now run along with you.'

The little maid needed no second bidding and the next moment the door closed quietly behind her.

Mary, now washed and changed into a somewhat large but pretty bedgown, was propped high upon the pillows in the big oak bed that seemed to almost swallow her up, looking longingly at the tea tray. She was contentedly holding a small dish of tea, savouring every sip, as Alex entered the room and sat gently on the edge of the bed.

'Well, now, ma lassie, you're looking bright eyed this fine morning and I know just the medicine to keep ye that way.' Alex winked at Mary in a conspiratorial manner as he took her tea from her, placed it on a low table and lifted the stirring baby from his basket. They both knew that Mistress Hall would object strongly, as indeed she did. The housekeeper did not seem to be as taken with the new born child as with Mary. The reason for this was quite plain to Alex for he could see that to nurse the baby with other people present was more than the woman could bear, the cause of this, however, was none of his concern. Alex handed the warm, soft bundle into Mary's arms as Mistress Hall looked on with great tenderness, an expression that did not escape the observant doctor.

'Oh, sir, I've bin waitin' for this, you just don't know, 'e is alright aint 'e, aint got no chest fever?'

Alex beamed, 'wonderful, the wee fellow is just wonderful ma gel.'

Mary gazed at the baby, Sarah's baby, through eyes streaming with tears. 'Oh, Benjie, I do love yer baby, me poor ol' arms 'ave right ached fer yer they 'ave.' Snuggling him close, her cheek pressed to his little brow, she whispered, 'I love yer so much me darlin', we'll never be parted, Mary'll take care of yer.' Both Alex and Mistress Hall watched the crooning girl, listening intently, each knowing that the day would come, and no doubt soon, when Mary and her baby nephew would be separated. Mary continued her almost silent murmuring, the room was still as Alex and Mistress Hall continued to watch and listen.

"They didn't get yer, Benjie, yer ma told me to fetch yer 'ere, an' I did, to the big 'ouse,' she went on, 'and now we're safe and no Parish aint gonna get yer now, not now.'

As the child stroked the baby's cheek and his little unfocussed eyes blinked up at her, Doris Hall could watch the scene no longer. She ran hastily from the room to compose herself in the privacy of her own apartment where she could always be alone. Alone with her heartache but, now, for the first time in eleven years, she felt the dawning of release, release from the grip of the iron band of grief that had engulfed her. Also, for the first time in all those long years she felt alive, painfully alive yes, but feeling had returned to her heart of stone.

Mistress Hall requested that she be relieved of her duties for the day, just for that day, now that the danger had passed. Of course, knowing of her vigil during the past few nights whilst the rest of the household slept, this was taken for granted and the entire staff, Barkworth, Millie the cook and the young maids assured her that all would run smoothly and that she was to rest.

Doris Hall had a day for herself, a day in which she was to weep, to pray, to rest and to weep again. After eleven years of mechanical and numb existence…the healing began.

Alex, having assured Mary that all was well and that he would call in to see her before returning home, took his leave and made his way to the library where he found Sir John in much the same mood that he had witnessed earlier, disgruntled and agitated.

'Ah, come along in Doctor, have you seen our invalid then?'

'Aye, I have that.' Answered Alex, thoughtfully.

'And how is she, and the boy, well, I trust?'

'Och Aye, well enough I think, for the present, I'm happy to say. I gave her the bairn this morning, he's her nephew, ye ken, they have only each other and she loves him quite desperately, the poor wee lassie.'

'And, ah, what of his mother, and his father, of course? She told you, I expect?' It was a baited question that Sir John attempted to disguise by lighting a cigar as he paced back and forth across the width of the fireplace. It was no use, he could not wait, as he had intended, until after the doctor had left, he had to know, and he had to know now, just how much the girl had told.

Doctor and patient had enjoyed a long easy talk. Alex wished he could make the Squire of this manor even more uncomfortable, but he had nothing to reveal, either to set Sir John's mind at rest, or to increase his agony.'

'She disnae ken the fayther', he said honestly. 'The boy's mother told the child to fetch the baby here, to the Big House. She struggled through the storm then collapsed in the old byre, that is where I found them.'

Sir John was at once immensely relieved, nonetheless he could not relax, what if…

'What do you mean man, she doesn't know? Of course she knows, she's just playing cat and mouse for her own gains,' replied the squire, impatiently. 'Not that it matters, of course, I merely wish to find a home for them both with all speed.' He attempted to cover his great unease, he must be more careful, these damned peasants.

'Well, she disnae ken the fayther,' Alex repeated, 'I tell ye, the wee gel is only ten years old Sir, no great age. The boy is the son of her sister Sarah, she was but sixteen years when she conceived, no doubt by some lustful animal of an older man, not a young lad at all. There had been no lads walking out with her, of that I'm certain, for her young life had been taken up with the care of her young sister. She had no proper care during childbirth, just a woman from the village. I have a clear picture, no regard for hygiene, no clean linen, no proper check on the bleeding. I tell ye, Sir John,' Alex's tone was implicating, he was enraged. 'If I could get ma hands on him I'd turn him over to the old women of the village, aye, that I would, and I can tell ye I can think of nae better deserts for him than just that.'

Sir John, feeling more in control now that the immediate danger was past, forced a weak smile saying, 'no doctor, 'twas surely a lad from the village, or a neighbouring village, and these wenches are often no better than they should be; perhaps we shall never know. 'Did the girl say anything at all that may lead us to him?'

'Nae, we'll nae find him, leastwhile not yet.' The doctor was playing cat and mouse now.

The squire could not leave well alone and pressed on with his questioning. 'I do not take your meaning doctor, and why should she be told to bring him here, my home is not an orphanage?'

Child's Acre

'Aye, I understand that, Sir John,' replied Alex, 'but the young Sarah told Mary that she was to bring the baby here if anything happened to her. She said that the Master of the Big House was a good man, and that he would not turn them away, especially a new born child, so she tells me. It seems your charitable works are known in your manor sir, it does you great credit.'

Alex spoke without conviction, with an edge to his voice that spoke a thousand words. 'The boy was brought here at great risk,' he continued, 'in order to be spared a life of being raised on the parish, or the workhouse.'

'Quite absurd', replied Sir John, confident now that he had not been named they could speculate all they wished, were his thoughts. 'An orphan belongs on the parish, that is why we have parish care, it is a good thing. Why, with respect doctor, if I should be guided by yourself, the next thing we'll know is that I'll have the results of all the amorous misfortunes hereabouts laid at my doorstep. Where else do orphans go but to an orphanage? Of course, the parish where possible or, for the older destitute, sometimes, the workhouse. We have no orphans in Woodstock so, if not the parish, an orphanage in the city it may well be for the baby. As for the girl, she is quite of an age to earn her keep in service.'

Alex began to collect together his medical bag and hat and to fasten the collar of his cape. 'Ye are doubtless a man wi' a heart, Sir John, that is why the bairns are here,' he said, thoughtfully. 'twould be a pity indeed if ye did not follow your heart, as ye have done thus far, and give the laddie a hame, after all, he was brought here because of the storm and a young gel's faith in the Squire. I see no reason why such faith should bring the dire consequence ye speak of, the turning of your hame into an orphanage.

Sir John was thinking that this darn Scotsman was making it very awkward for him to be rid of these peasants, but be rid of them he would and nothing would stand in his way. He said, 'I'll make no decision yet, my wife will be greatly involved in any arrangements that will affect the household, but I do assure you it will not be possible to take the baby permanently, my wife is not a well woman. In any event we'll keep a close watch on him wherever he is to be placed, and we'll try to bring him together with the girl in the future should it become possible.

'A quandry indeed' murmured the doctor then, turning to Sir John he offered his hand in farewell and took his leave, promising to call again on his way home to Scotland. Robbie was at the door with the coach, now cleaned of all the mud and grime. Pale sunlight shone on the mellowed stone of the old Manor House and a clean sweet breeze chilled the air as it blew gently across the wide expanse of lawns, still wet from the storm. The silken coats of the two grey mares glistened as they stood, tossing their silver manes, impatiently waiting to go.

The month that followed was a very happy time for Mary. She spent her days for the most part in the kitchen with Millie and Annie and it was Mary who took care of Ben, with the exception of feeding times when the woman from the village still came to see to him. The nursing was soon to become less and less as baby Ben, rarely satisfied with his feeds, was to be tried with pap food and cow's milk. Mary helped Millie all she could when Ben slept and became great friends with all the domestic staff, including the kind but formidable housekeeper and the very formal butler, Barkworth. Mary had Millie, Annie and the other maids enthralled during the long evenings after supper with stories of how her mother and father had both died of the lung sickness, after which her sister Sarah took care of her. How they had remained in the old two roomed cottage, feeding themselves mainly by helping on neighbouring farms, being paid in kind with vegetables and eggs, or picking berries from the hedgerows and fruit from the orchards when in season. She told of how they collected wood together, drank buttermilk when they were able to work in the dairies, and how they would always save a titbit from their day's labour to share in the evening in front of the fire where they slept. Her sister Sarah had told her that the Squire had allowed them to stay at the cottage until they could both find work in service but, as they wanted to stay together, it wasn't easy to find two places in the same household. "Sarah said the Squire is a right goodly gentleman," she told them on one such evening, "and we were very lucky to have such a kind Lord of the Manor," she explained, as her audience sat goggle-eyed and silent, wondering who this particular 'Lord of the Manor' actually was. If ever Mary became overly sad when telling her story, Millie would tactfully divert the conversation to Ben, now seven weeks old and the light of Mary's life.

Some weeks later the Master had received word from Alex MacKenzie that the doctor was seeking a position for Mary with reliable people of his acquaintance in Scotland. For Sir John of Woodstock this was excellent news indeed, and it was decided that, until her place was secured, Mary would be relieved of her light duties in order to spend the time that remained to her with Ben. Millie, seriously doubting the wisdom of this, was both saddened and concerned.

Instructions were given that the girl was not to be enlightened as to her forthcoming departure, just that she was to take care of the baby all the time now as the wet nurse would no longer be coming to the Manor. Mary was delighted, her happiness heartbreaking to see. She never tired of caring for her baby nephew and at night, when he needed feeding, would cradle him in her arms and talk to him of his mother. There were three other bedchambers on the top floor that the housemaids shared. Along the end of the corridor on the opposite side to Mary's little room was a kitchen of sorts. It was a room with an oven range, not the usual small fireplace. The range in this tiny room was kept burning through the night temporarily so as to allow Mary to warm Ben's feeds and tend to his needs. Her love and dedication to her tiny nephew was all consuming, she was hopelessly and helplessly devoted. So much so, that Millie truly feared for the girl when the time came for them to be parted. This little girl would be devastated, thought Millie, the ever threatening tears now falling. Her greatest fear was that should Mary remain at the Manor over long, baby Ben would also suffer the pangs of separation. For young as he was the baby boy was at his brightest and happiest when Mary would sing him a lullaby, or talk to him in her loving, crooning way, cradling him and giving him her beautiful smile. They must be separated soon, thought Millie sadly, as she watched Mary dreaming over Ben in the early hours of a cold winter morning.

Millie knew that Barkworth had explained to the Master that the peasant girl could undoubtedly prove useful below stairs, particularly now when the Manor was sparsely staffed. He made every endeavour to tactfully persuade Sir John to let Mary stay, but to no avail. Mistress Hall was not opposed to the girl working with the other maids, she explained to Sir John, and indeed agreed with Barkworth that the peasant girl might have many uses and need receive little or no monetary reward. However, like Barkworth, she had to tread warily and her efforts were entirely futile. Unbeknown to them all Sir John was determined to be rid of "that peasant and her brat" just as soon as could be managed. The girl first, and arrangements were already being finalised.

Chapter Six

I T WAS A TYPICALLY QUIET evening at 'The Grange', the town home of the MacFarlanes in Scotland. The Butler entered the drawing room and informed his master that there was a visitor, a rather distinguished looking gentleman, a Doctor Alexander MacKenzie. The Butler smiled broadly, fully anticipating his Master's surprise and delight. Angus and Eleanor MacFarlane stared at each other in disbelief as the butler announced this name from the past.

Angus was the first to move. 'Show him in Tam, show him in directly man.' It was Angus himself who had taken Alex's hat, gloves and cloak, after hurrying down the staircase to welcome his dearest friend, dismissing the maid, all the while expressing his surprise and joy at Alex's unheralded arrival.

Alex was shown into the drawing room of 'The Grange' on a bitter cold evening and was taken straight to the fireside. Amidst pats on the back and more heartfelt greetings Alex said, 'the horses…my man, Robbie…'

Alex could say no more for Angus interrupted, 'Och, di nae concern yesel'' old friend, I dare say Tam is even now taking care of them all like wee bairns,' which, indeed, he was.

Whilst Eleanor effusively greeted Alex, her husband rang the bell to summon Tam, his butler. Tam arrived promptly and equally promptly assured Angus that the doctor's man, Robbie, and the mares were receiving his best attention.

'Feed them well, Tam, have cook serve a handsome meal, which is quite within her powers even with such wee warning, oh, and Tam,' the butler turned on his way towards the door, 'aye sir?' said Tam, quizzically.

'Open a good bottle, the best in your cellar Tam, and fetch another to the drawing room for the good doctor'.

Tam needed no second bidding 'as ye wish sir.' Tam smiled at Angus and the doctor, inclined his head to Eleanor and left to attend to his task, a task he was not too often required to perform, he thought, walking briskly and smiling broadly.

Below stairs, in the huge but cosily warm kitchen, Robbie sat before the great black range and watched as cook bustled about preparing a meal for himself and the doctor. It had been a long drive but Robbie, not being overly tired, enjoyed pleasant conversation with cook until Tam arrived with a bottle of fine old Scottish Malt. Tam and Robbie settled down in front of the range, making sure that cook had ample space to move freely, for such were her proportions that ample room was wise indeed. The two men laughed and chatted whilst Robbie looked forward with relish to the meal that smelled tantalising good and would shortly be set before him. Cook, Bless her, he thought, spared no effort and certainly no expense where this particular repast was concerned.

Later, above them in the drawing room, after a long and leisurely meal, much discussion and the most excellent Malt, Alex came to the reason for his visit. Both Angus and Eleanor knew there would be a serious purpose to this much welcomed visit for, living and working as he did in country communities, it had been some very long while since Alex had been able to call on these good people, his oldest and dearest friends.

Sitting quietly Alex solemnly related the desperately sorry tale of the two orphaned children and made known his request. Reaching for his glass he sat back in the comfortable chair, a drawn and sombre expression on his face, for only now did he fully realise the enormity of his wishes, the weight he was bringing to bear upon this valued and longstanding friendship.

'So,' said Angus, after a lengthy pause and slowly exhaling a very deep breath, 'ye're asking me to take an orphaned English peasant lassie, uneducated, homeless, penniless and very likely as wild as a wee vixen, into The Grange with my wife and child?' Another pause, the doctor said nothing and Angus continued, 'to give her a hame, to permit her to live alongside of our own dear little Caroline.'

Alex was undaunted by his friend's all too accurate assessment of the situation, and said, in hushed and serious tones, 'Aye, Angus, to give her a place in service in your household, that is precisely what I ask of ye.'

Angus glanced at Eleanor, who gave no sign either of acceptance or refusal. This man, however, knew his wife well, he knew that she would remain silent until he had spoken and would then abide by his decision; Angus was master in this house. He knew Eleanor would take the child, for she had dearly hoped for the joy of another child since Caroline's birth, but had long since accepted it was not to be. Their happiness in their daughter knew no bounds, they would be thankful and be satisfied. The room was silent, Eleanor awaiting his answer, Alex still, his countenance telling all. Angus' thoughts were not for himself, had he really a choice but to take the lass? He thought not, but the decision was his. Could Eleanor cope? Och, aye, Eleanor could cope, this rare woman he had been so privileged to take as his wife. Angus looked lovingly at the portrait of his beautiful eight year old daughter, Caroline, and knew that his answer was never in doubt. Turning back to Alex he said, 'well, Alex, when can we expect her then, your little English vixen?'

Eleanor caught up her skirts and sped across the room as if borne on wings to where the two men sat and, throwing her arms around her husband in an unpardonable display of affection, giving no heed to propriety said, 'I knew ye would say yes. Angus MacFarlane, ye truly are still my bonnie wee laddie. It will be so good my dear, we'll all be just fine.' Then, turning to Alex, 'we'll give her a good home Alex, she'll be grand wi' us, we'll tak' her and be happy to, ye know we could refuse ye nothing, nor ever would we wish to.' She waved a hand at Alex as he began to speak, saying 'och, away wi' ye now Alex, it is nae too much to ask, we are both happy to help your wee Mary.'

Alex knew she meant every word, he smiled weakly, his ordeal over, and Angus read the gratitude in his eyes.

'Nae more to be said then', Angus declared, briskly, 'and that being so, let me fill our glasses and drink to,' he paused, 'wee Mary', he said, with happy conviction and smiling his bright, genuine smile.

Angus then reached out to grasp the doctor's hand in a firm handshake and, clasping hands, Alex said, 'it may not be easy my friend, but och, she's a grand wee gel. Truly a country lassie, and I know she will love it up on the estate, she'll adore the hi'lands, she has a great heart.'

'We'll make something of her,' Angus replied, 'ye'll see Alex, but whatever else, she'll have a good hame, that I promise ye.'

And so it was settled, Mary would go to Scotland, to the home of the MacFarlanes.

Chapter Seven

IN THE BUSY KITCHEN AT Woodstock Manor Millie's thoughts, as always, were of Mary's future. If only a miracle would happen, she silently prayed, and the Master would let Mary stay but, as everyone knew, he had taken against the girl, the reasons for this escaped them all but, there it was, and there was no moving him. It was no use appealing to Lady Winbourne, the Squire's wife, for that poor lady rarely saw anyone, with the exception of her sons, and had little or nothing to do with the running of the household nowadays, these duties being supervised solely by Mistress Hall.

Clara Winbourne was a sick woman whose health during the past two years had deteriorated rapidly. The doctors advised that it was the miscarriage of her third child quite late in life that had caused her ill health. She was in her thirty ninth year when she miscarried and had shown no sign of recovery, either physically or emotionally, since the loss of her child. Clara's marriage to the Master had never been happy. Since first arriving at Woodstock as a girl, and the new Mistress of the house, she had been a quiet little thing, exceptionally lovely, accepting her lot and what was expected of her without complaint. John Winbourne's ill treatment of her, his over lustful nature and the humiliation of his many escapades with women were all part, she believed, of what must be tolerated to fulfil her duty as a loyal wife. When her two sons came along she had devoted herself to them, experiencing the only true joy to come out of the marriage.

In the early days Clara had not been entirely unhappy, she had adored her two baby sons, they were her world and, if she had to endure the distasteful demands of their father, her precious boys had made it all worthwhile. Now, as John and James grew older, she often felt truly alone. The boys still visited her rooms daily and the younger, James, would stay to share a meal with her in her pretty sitting room whenever he could. The new baby was to have changed the long days and fill them with joy as before, when the boys were infants. Being with child once again Clara had been given a new lease of life, was bright, full of energy and happy. She had desperately wanted the new baby to be a girl, a little daughter to cherish, a child who would not be torn from her in the early years and sent away to boarding school before going up to Oxford. She knew that when a daughter grew from girlhood to womanhood she would not grow away from her mother as sons inevitably did.

When Clara had first realised that she was with child again she was ecstatically happy. She talked to James for hours, seriously concerned as to what his feelings would be regarding her condition, her greatest fear that he would find the new situation uncomfortable and embarrassing. Happily, Clara's concern with regard to her sons was unfounded. John had shown total indifference, saying that if his mother did not object it was nothing to him, and James had been as delighted as Clara, for it meant a great deal to him to see his mother so happy. Clara and James talked whenever possible, the subject, invariably, the new baby. James had been secretly very worried about his mother. It had been nineteen years since her last child, himself, was born and James wished with all his heart that this pregnancy had never happened. He had cursed his father a thousand times but had fussed over his mother more than ever. Clara immensely enjoyed being spoiled, her wonderful James shared her joy and her anticipation, or so he cleverly led her to believe. Lady Clara Winbourne had, at that time, believed herself to be the happiest woman in the world. Alas, when the pregnancy approached the fourth month she began to have problems. She did her best to eat the specially prepared meals that Millie would send up to her, but ate little as she worried about her child. Her other pregnancies were not like this. When Millie arrived to discuss the week's menus Clara would confide her fears. Millie would pat Clara's hand, smile and reassure her. They would discuss the menus and Clara always felt heartened after one of Millie's visits. Indeed, Millie just being there for a while would make Clara feel better. They had a close relationship, Millie and Clara Winbourne, for a deep and caring friendship had blossomed from the very beginning.

Late in the fifth month of pregnancy Clara miscarried. After lying close to death for almost a week, with the doctor and a nurse in constant attendance, she was told she had lost the baby, a baby girl. Clara was heartbroken, as was James for it had affected him deeply. He grieved for the baby sister that might have been, he grieved for his mother and prayed that she would recover, but Clara's heart had been broken and she had never fully recovered. All her plans…hopes…dreams…had come to nothing with the loss of her child.

Millie came back to the present, admonishing herself for daydreaming, remembering that dreadful time would do no one no good, she told herself. Yet still she remembered, would always remember, the shouts from Clara's rooms when the Squire was first told that Clara was with child again. Sir John had been enraged, he had told his wife that this was a disgusting state of affairs, a woman of her station, and at her age, allowing herself to get in such a condition. "Why, woman," he had bellowed, "you are old enough to be a grandmother." His contempt of his wife knew no bounds but Clara had anticipated his anger and cared nothing. This time it would be a daughter, surely. Sons must learn the business of farming and all matters relating to the running of the Woodstock Estate. Sons must grow to be independent and strong, sons did not need their mother, but not so for a daughter, for a daughter it was different.

Back in the present Millie heard the kitchen door open and snapped into action. Crossing to the range she called for Annie to 'take the scones from the oven and be quick about it gel, why, you're so slow you could be daydreaming', she scolded, hiding a small smile. She poured great jugs of strong tea but couldn't help thinking as she worked how the master had forbidden anyone to tell the Mistress of the house about Mary and little Ben. He did not want her Ladyship upset, she was not strong enough, he had sternly instructed Millie and Mistress Hall. Both women knew there would be no dissuading him, but both agreed that the Squire was making a bad judgement. Clara continued to languish by day and slept little at night. Millie felt certain in her heart that baby Ben and the Mistress would be each other's lifeline. Clara's heart would go out to both Mary and little Ben, they would help assuage her grief. The children would be given a home and, in time, Clara would not be able to part with them, they could stay together. Was there ever a man as cruel as the Master, she thought. Millie was distraught.

Two years ago, after the miscarriage, Clara had moved into the additional wing of the Manor. She had taken over a small suite of rooms on the first floor, since when her husband visited rarely, if at all. She loved her sons dearly, even though the older of the two, John, was proving to be a great worry to her.

She was very concerned at the direction his lifestyle appeared to be leading him, becoming so like his father in many disturbing ways that she truly feared for him. James, however, was devoted to her and her love for this son knew no bounds. Of late, however, James' free time was sparse as he took on his older brother's responsibilities, becoming more and more involved in Estate matters, thus Clara saw her younger son less and less. John would not demean himself with Estate concerns. Farming was not for him.

So, it appeared, for one reason or another, there was nothing to be done. Mary would be placed in service, somewhere in Scotland with friends of Dr Alex as soon as word arrived as to the date of her departure. As for Ben… what of baby Ben, the waifs' home if the Master had anything to do with it. 'Over my dead body, and only with me gone will that dear little scrap go to the waifs' 'ome', Millie vowed.

The dreaded morning arrived, the morning Mary was to be told of the plans for her future. The unhappy task of delivering the blow had fallen upon Mistress Hall. It was a bleak Monday morning, Mistress Hall had been instructed to inform the girl to prepare herself to leave on Friday at an early hour. The dour housekeeper sought Millie's wisdom, for although the two women could not, in truth, be thought of as friends, neither were they adversaries and Mistress Hall had remembered Millie's many small kindnesses to her. During the past two years, since Mistress Hall had assumed responsibility for discussions regarding the weekly menus, she had always addressed Millie as "cook" when visiting the kitchens for this purpose. Today, with such a difficult and unhappy task to perform, she decided to enlist Millie's help. The troubled housekeeper had even thought that she might delegate this trying task to Millie, for if anyone could ease Mary's pain, which she sincerely doubted, it could surely only be Millie.

Millie greeted the stern housekeeper in her usual courteous and jovial manner but, almost at once, sensed there was something seriously wrong. She did not need to guess the reason for this untimely visit.

'Can I get you a nice cup of tea, Mistress Hall? You do look a mite troubled, 'as there been a change in the menus?'

'No, Millie, thank you.'

Millie noticed the mention of her name, for it was probably the first time that the housekeeper had ever used it. Of late Mistress Hall had seemed different, somehow. Millie could not actually say when the change had begun, nor could she define this change, but Mistress Hall was certainly odd.

'Millie…' the housekeeper began again, paused, then sat down heavily, uninvited.

'It's come, aint it?' Millie whispered. 'The letter, it's come, she's to go?'

Doris Hall raised her head and looked directly at Millie, her large, expressive eyes begging the question that was on her troubled mind, 'yes, Millie,' she answered quietly, 'and she has to be told.'

Millie went over to the range and, leaning across to pick up the kettle, said simply, 'when?'

'The coach arrives on Friday, early morning, she's to be ready to go then,' Doris Hall said, sorrowfully.

'Lord love us, no, not so quick as Friday. So, it's all settled then, what you gonna tell 'er? Where's she going? Could it really be Scotland, did the Master say, or aint we to know?' Millie was clearly vexed and Doris Hall felt sorry for her too.

'She is very fortunate Millie, we have to be realistic about this, Mary is going to an excellent family, and not as a below-stairs maid either. Doctor MacKenzie has taken her under his wing, she really is a singularly fortunate child, a very lucky girl indeed…it is just that…' Doris Hall's voice faded.

'Yes, I know, girl,' said Millie, quite forgetting herself, 'I know', the familiarity went unnoticed, much to Millie's relief and she went on, 'I know what you're saying is right enough, but it aint necessary that's all I'm saying. Goodness knows we can use 'er 'ere and then those sweet souls wouldn't be parted. Who's ever going to convince Mary of her good fortune, tell me that eh, when she knows it will mean leaving that dear little baby?' Millie swallowed hard and banged about angrily making the tea both women sorely needed.

'Well, Mistress 'all, where's she to go then? Tell us the worst.' From the look in Doris Hall's eyes Millie knew they would be seeing little or nothing of Mary in the future.

Doris Hall let out a long breath, 'Scotland, Millie.'

'Scotland!' Millie shrieked out the word, 'good 'eavens above, no, I was so afeared of it being Scotland,' she cried. ''e can't do it, Mistress 'all,' Millie pleaded as her throat closed and her eyes moistened, 'she's been through too much already. And whereabouts in Scotland,' Millie raged on, 'or aint we to know?'

'The Master isn't entirely aware of the exact location, Millie, at present.' Mistress Hall explained, trying to bring a positive note into this bleak situation.

'It isn't all bad, cook, it's for the best, Mary has her whole life ahead of her, she'll be taught, trained, there will be a governess. The family has an eight year old girl and Mary is eventually to become her companion. It's the gift of a lifetime Millie, an unheard of opportunity.' Mistress Hall pressed home the advantages for Mary, 'I do see that, cook, truly, and I know you do too.'

'Yes,' agreed Millie, reluctantly, 'everything you say is right but, good as gold though she is, she aint no fit companion for a little lady, is she now?'

'Maybe not as this present moment, but she is a lovely child, we both see that, and other's will too. She will learn Millie, put your trust in the Lord and in Dr MacKenzie.'

Millie sipped her tea, glancing at the clock. 'Of course,' she nodded slowly and smiled, ' 'e would know what's best now wouldn't 'e, Dr Alex, and the Lord is giving her this chance, I see that. I know what you mean, Mistress 'all, fortunate aint the word for it, what a chance for 'er, it's hardly to be believed, but it'll make no difference to 'er, poor child, you just mark my words.'

'I fear you are right Mille, under other circumstances...perhaps.'

Millie rose from the table, taking up her empty cup, 'but it's the circumstances that's give 'er this chance, aint it, and we aint to know properly where?'

'I'm not certain at present Millie, later perhaps, we shall know.'

Millie looked heavenwards as she said, 'The Lord works in mysterious ways and that's for sure...not even to know where, it's just too bad, thass what,' she said, defeatedly.

The housekeeper looked at Millie and for the first time was not in control of the situation. She had always known what to do, brooked no opposition, was always in command...until now. Right now, her wayward heart was truly causing the woman great difficulty.

'How do I tell her Millie, when she is so very happy? What a joy it is to see them together. Ben knows her now, so well, don't you think?'

'You're right there,' Millie agreed, 'well, 'e's just off three months now, dear little soul, not much gets by him. Oh yes, you only 'ave to see 'ow those blue eyes light up at just the sight of 'er, 'e knows is little auntie alright.'

'How do I tell her Millie?' the housekeeper implored, 'perhaps I should tell her that she will be able to visit, just a little white lie. I wouldn't condone such a thought in the usual way of things, Millie, but I have to do something to help her.'

Child's Acre

'No, no,' said Millie, resolutely, 'don't go giving her no false dreams, the poor girl will just live for visits that can't never 'appen, all that way, it just aint possible. Best let 'er go an' get over it in 'er own way. Mebbe, when she's learned, who knows, mebbe she'll come back and get a place near 'ere, near 'im, Lord love 'im, mebbe take 'im 'erself, but we wont go givin' 'er no false 'opes. It's sure to be kinder in the long run.'

'Of course,' Doris replied, thoughtfully, 'whatever you say, Millie, I'm certain you know best, but we can at least promise to take care of Ben for her, we can at least do that, do you think?'

'Don't know as we can even do that. If the Master 'as 'is way that dear little baby will go to the waifs' 'ome, but you wont tell Mary that, o'course.'

'Of course not Millie, and we shall do everything possible to prevent such a thing.'

Millie, now pre-occupied with thoughts of the morning breakfasts, said wearily, 'I 'ope so, Mistress 'all, I hope and pray so.'

'Well, I'll be getting along now cook, and thank you for your time and advice, and remember, ours not to reason why.'

Doris Hall turned silently and left the kitchen, leaving Millie alone with her thoughts. Come on girl, she admonished herself, as was often her way. The boys'll be in soon and no breakfasts done. She hoped young Master James would come in with them as he sometimes did, even though Millie thoroughly disapproved and would scold him soundly, she adored the young Master's visits to her kitchen. He's a wonderful lad, her thoughts meandered on, pity 'is father wasn't more like 'im, but James takes after that dear soul upstairs. Millie busied herself.

In the small room on the top storey of the house Mary sat with baby Ben on her lap, talking and laughing with him, whilst the adoring infant reached up to pull her hair, chuckling contentedly. This was the happy scene that Mistress Hall walked in on and her sadness pained her greatly.

'Put the baby down for a moment, Mary, I want to talk to you,' said the housekeeper, pleasantly.

Mary obeyed, smiling brightly. 'Down you go me darlin', she said, lovingly, as she placed Ben in his basket. 'You 'ave a nice little rest now while I go talk to Mistress 'all, an' then I 'ave to 'elp Millie in the kitchen, but I'll take you out to the stableyard as soon as it gets a bit warmer.'

'Sit down, Mary, I have some very good news for you, very exciting news.' Mistress Hall smiled bravely and, mercifully, quite convincingly, she thought, for Mary was eager with anticipation. 'We've all been working very hard on your behalf Mary,' she continued, fervently wishing that this dreadful task was behind her, 'and Doctor MacKenzie has secured an excellent position for you, you are indeed a very fortunate girl. You understand, of course, that we could not employ you here at Woodstock, we already have Annie and Millie and the other maids.'

'Yer, thass alright Mistress 'all, I understand. I was to stay 'ere and get better so I can get work and earn our livin' '.

Doris Hall flinched at Mary's words. This was going to be even more difficult than at first anticipated. 'Yes, Mary, well…Doctor MacKenzie has found you a place,' she said, hoping Mary did not see through her contrived brightness. 'You are to be trained as lady's maid and companion to a young girl of excellent family, she is about your age, I'm told, and the family are good friends of Doctor Alex, is that not just wonderful?'

'Are you sure, Mistress 'all?' Mary replied, smiling incredulously, blue eyes wide and sparkling, 'are you really, really sure?'

Doris Hall shuddered visibly, but continued with her attempt to build an exciting, happy picture. 'Well now, you will learn to take care of the young lady, see to her clothes and personal things. You will be taught how to dress her hair, though I doubt it could possibly be half as pretty as your own,' the housekeeper told her, reaching out to gently smooth Mary's soft auburn tresses.

Mary's wide smile was innocent and trusting. Doris could no longer go on so heartlessly, she had to tell Mary, and now.

'You will go to a large house Mary, we must get you all prepared, you will need new clothes, oh, and boots, and linen, my goodness so much to be done, how exciting.' This is cruel, screamed Doris' mind once again, tell her.

Mary clasped her small, slender hands tightly, she had not understood the situation. 'Mistress 'all, I can 'ardly believe it, am I really going to earn our keep somewhere as nice as that? An' we wont depend on nobody, truly?' Mary rushed on, 'but I'll miss you all so much, and Ben is just getting to know everyone so well, when do we 'ave to go?' Mary looked over at Ben, his golden hair just beginning to thicken and gleaming in the pale sunlight which lit the small room. 'Oh, Benjie', she murmured, 'do yer know what this means, you'll never go 'ungry and cold like me an' yer ma did, an' you'll never be left alone, an' when I grow up I'll save enough to get us an 'ome of our very own.

Mistress 'all, I'm so excited I think I feel sick, I've been so scared, 'ow could all this 'ave 'appened to me?'

'Mary…Mary dear,' Doris Hall placed her hands on the ecstatic girl's shoulders, appalled at how very badly she had handled things. 'Now, slow down dear, you are going too fast, I have not explained everything yet, it is not quite as you think…you see…' Doris was quite lost for words, floundering, her eyes, despite her valiant attempts to be practical, misted over. 'Mary, I'm sorry, I…I have not made things clear to you.'

Mary looked at the housekeeper's troubled expression, she understood at once, her little face clouded and great tears sprang to those large blue eyes. ''e aint coming, is 'e, Ben aint to come wiv me?'

Doris' face did not change, she said nothing, she had failed, failed this innocent, homeless child.

Mary's words interrupted the housekeeper's thoughts. 'Well, it's a real pity, o'course, Mistress 'all, and I thank yer kindly, we both do, but me an' Ben aint gonna be parted. I'm sorry for everyone's trouble but I'll just have to find somewhere for us meself. Don't you worry none,' Mary said quietly, 'it's alright.'

Doris, now acutely distressed at her bumbling attempts to explain the situation, attempted to revert to "Mistress Hall, the housekeeper". Speaking more firmly now, she at last took control. 'I'm very sorry, Mary, but you see, it is all arranged, you are quite too young yet to take care of such a little baby as Ben. He is but three months old, no age at all.' Before Mary could protest, Doris quickly continued. 'Arrangements have been made for you to leave on Friday morning, early. The Master wishes to see that you are taken care of, and baby, of course. Doctor Alex has gone to extreme lengths to secure this excellent position, you are to prepare yourself to leave on Friday. Come now child, there is no time to lose, for there is much to be done.'

Mary's expression was determinedly set and her words came desperately, pleadingly, 'but what's 'e gonna do? I mean who will see to 'im? Where will 'e go?' Then, crying helplessly, she threw her head forward, stood up and shouted in defiance, 'well, I wont go, I wont, I wont,' she sobbed. 'We'll go somewhere else, back to the cottage, I know what to do for 'im now, Millie learned me, see.' Weeping heartbreakingly, her breath catching in her throat, she continued, for nothing could slow her words. 'Nobody's gonna take me sister's baby from me, she's DEAD,' Mary screamed. 'They're all DEAD and nobody, d'yer 'ear me, nobody's gonna take 'im away from me.'

Mary, now in danger of becoming hysterical, grabbed up Ben from his crib, she held him too tightly and, startled and alarmed his frightened cries were added to Mary's.

On hearing the commotion Millie sent Annie hurrying up to Mary's room. 'Mistress 'all, wassa matter? Millie says wassa Matter? Wass wrong?'

Doris Hall wanted to send Annie to fetch Millie but knew that cook would take far too long to climb the stairs. She took Mary firmly by the arm and, with a gentle hand under the girls chin, said, 'be still now Mary, this will serve no purpose, can you not see how you are upsetting baby. Now give him here and we shall all go down to the kitchen and talk to Millie, she will make us all one of her nice pots of tea.'

Mary's sobs abated a little, but only from sheer exhaustion. She would not release her hold on Ben. She raised him and laid him against her shoulder, patting him gently and, as her breath shuddered in her throat, continued to comfort him. 'I'm...sorry baby, Mary's sorry, sorry I scared yer.'

Ben had his little fists buried deep into Mary's hair and his crying also lessened. Mary carried him down the stairs with Mistress Hall ahead of her, Annie following closely behind. Quieter now, but with racking sobs coming intermittently, Mary sat in Millie's cushioned rocking chair by the range, she was bereft and, looking at her, Millie felt her own heart breaking.

'Give me the baby, Mary.' Millie would hear no argument and took Ben from Mary's arms. She laid him in his basket alongside the hearth and told Annie to pour some tea while Millie gave Ben a sugar rag to suck on. Ben settled down and seemed quite happy again. Mary looked up into Millie's eyes, and with just one look at that dear old face, the girl collapsed into another paroxysm of sobbing. All Millie wanted to do was cradle Mary in her arms and tell her that Millie would take care of them but, other than the Manor, Millie herself had no home to take them to. They were all dependent on the Master for their roof and their livelihood.

Millie pulled Mary up from the chair, put both her arms around the child and held her close, smoothing her hair with loving hands. The old lady knew exactly what she had to do and in her gruff, yet tender way she spoke firmly to Mary. 'It will be alright child. You see, my gel, little Benjie here will be your nephew for the rest of your life, nothing aint gonna change that now, is it?' Then, speaking a little more cheerily. 'Now then Mary, you 'ave to take this wonderful chance that's come to you, take it and learn, work 'ard and learn well, for you and Benjie there, cos e's only got you. See, Mary, when you're all growed up, even before then, you'll be schooled and you can school Ben, you can do it me gel, old Millie knows you can. Go and work and learn, for yoursel', for Benjie…and for 'is ma. Learn to read and write, learn everything you possibly can with them what can learn you. Millie wouldn't tell you wrong now, would she me lovey?'

All the while Millie spoke Mistress Hall watched and listened in complete silence, marvelling at the old lady's understanding and acknowledging, yet again, the very special human being that Millie was.

After a little while Mary collected her thoughts and understood that she must not go on opposing them. She realised also, even at her tender age, the truth and wisdom of Millie's words. Heartbreaking though it would be, Mary could see what she must do. Here, at the Manor, Ben would be wonderfully taken care of. She would leave him here for the time being, a very long time though it may well prove to be. She would learn to be the best housekeeper in the world, just like Mistress Hall, and the best cook in the world too, just like dearest Millie, and then she would come back for Ben.

* * *

The carriage drew slowly away from the Manor House. Annie stood at Millie's side holding Ben. Mistress Hall had walked with Mary to the carriage and now stood at the foot of the small flight of steps. Mary was, as they all knew she would be, devastated and bewildered. She had been inconsolable all morning and had borne her sorrow in complete silence, which greatly concerned Millie. All the clothes that Mistress Hall and Annie had altered and made for her hurriedly over the past week had made no difference. Not the new boots, the lovely linen, nor the cloak and bonnet, provided by Mistress Hall at her own expense, could lift Mary's spirits. Nothing could compensate for being taken from the precious and beloved baby boy. She leaned out of the carriage window, holding out her arms to Ben.

'Get back in the coach, Mary,' called Annie, 'wish I was coming wiv yer.' Annie tried to smile as she waved the carriage away calling loudly, 'e'll be alright Mary, I'll look after 'im for you 'til you gets back, I promise.'

The first tears of the morning streamed down Mary's face as she cried out to Ben, willing him to hear her and understand, 'I'll be back baby' she wept, 'Mary'll be back…I…I'll b-b-be back…'

The carriage rumbled along the drive and was soon away in the distance with Mary collapsed upon its richly upholstered interior sobbing pitifully, great choking sobs, and wishing with all her heart that she had died in the barn, so great was her anguish.'

Chapter Eight

BEN WAS NOW ALMOST TWO years old, there had been no news of Mary since the day she had left the Manor House and none of them, including Mistress Hall and Barkworth, dared ask the Master for news of her. Life at the big house had reverted to much the same as usual, after those first distressing weeks following Mary's departure. Baby Ben was now a strong and sturdy little boy. Millie thought it a wonder that they had been able to keep him for so long, but thanked the Lord daily for his goodness in arranging it so.

To ensure that Ben's stay with them would be as prolonged as possible he was kept, for the most part, out of sight of the household. He spent the greater part of his days in the kitchen with Millie and Annie, going for walks around the home fields in the afternoon with Annie, when weather and work permitted. As he grew older he became a little more difficult, he needed attention and demanded to be kept amused. On the whole the baby had proved to be an even tempered child and, to Millie's relief and delight, often tired himself enough to take a nap in the afternoon. Invariably, when Ben awoke, Millie would be busy with preparations for dinner and he would sit in his perambulator or play box and chat and play quite happily for a while, as long as there was a snack or tasty morsel to keep him happy, but not for long. At two years old Ben was proving to be a child of extraordinary perceptions and Millie loved him dearly.

Mistress Hall made frequent visits to the kitchen nowadays and over the past two years a close friendship had gradually grown between the housekeeper and the cook. Ben had also become great friends with Mistress Hall and, whilst the baby boy apparently looked to Millie as his mother, wanting her and only her when tired or unwell, he quite plainly loved Mistress Hall. He had begun to call her Holly, which was as much as his infant tongue could manage. Mistress Hall had happily accepted Ben's new name for her and, much to the amazement of the other staff, was now generally known as Holly. The housekeeper loved Ben every bit as much as did Millie but, as befitted her station, was very much less demonstrative where her affections were concerned

Holly often brought Ben small gifts and on Millie's fortnightly afternoon off duty, and her own monthly rest day, would take charge of him. The housekeeper, unbeknown to the other members of staff, with the exception of Millie, lived for these times when she would take Ben to her rooms and fuss over him, playing with him, cuddling and loving him to her heart's content. Ben responded to Holly's kindness joyfully for he was an affectionate baby and grew to love his Holly. It was at these times that Holly knew her first true happiness in many years.

James continued to visit Millie in the kitchens, moreso during the past year. On these occasions he would also play with Ben, laugh and talk to him and was often heard to say what a fine little fellow Ben was. Occasionally James would refer to the fact that his father was intent on placing the boy in an orphanage as soon as the time was right. Millie and Holly dreaded the day that Ben would go. Neither woman had forgotten the day Mary had left. Mary was constantly in their thoughts, for even in so short a time at the Manor her winsome ways and loving nature had left their mark. Nonetheless, both women avoided the subject of Mary and silently dreaded the day that Ben may be taken from them and put in "one of those dreadful places."

Sir John had been surreptitiously keeping a watchful eye on Ben's development. As long as the boy showed no signs of any likeness to himself, it would do no harm to leave things as they were. Nothing to be gained, he had decided, in jeopardising his "true philanthropic image". Therefore, for the time being, at least, Ben's sand gold hair and fine features guarded his secret well.

On one of James' visits to Millie's kitchen, Millie and Holly were told that the Master had decided to place Ben in an orphanage when the child reached the age of three years. Sir John felt, he had explained to James, that three years would be a right and proper age for the boy to be removed from the Manor household and put in the care of one of the many excellent orphanages in place for just such a child as Ben. Where the infant would have been placed from the very beginning had it not been for that interfering Scotsman. Ben would stay in the care of Millie until three years old as long as his care did not disrupt the peace and smooth running of the Manor household.

Millie had attempted to hide her distress at this devastating news and, understanding her fears, James endeavoured to console her with the promise that there was still over a year in which to persuade his father that Ben could grow to become extremely useful on the Woodstock Estate.

* * *

Orphaned babies and very young children in need of care were often fostered out to families living in the village or in farms or cottages owned by the Estate. Families living in such homes were allowed to remain as long as either the father of the family or, in the event of sickness or death, an adult son worked the farm or small-holding belonging to the Estate, for which a tithe was exacted by the landowner. Should there be a crop failure, or a farmer or small-holder could not pay the tithe demanded, the families concerned could be, and often were, evicted.

The villages that grew up around these Estates were almost entirely supported by, or involved in some way with, the Manor and it's lands. Villagers were either employed by the landowner in his great house, the upkeep of which would require many servants, or in the grounds of the house. The home gardens would be the source of employment for many local people. Gardeners who kept the grounds around the house in beautiful order, often following very strict instructions from the Lady of the Manor through the head gardener. Kitchen gardeners were also employed to ensure an ample supply of fresh seasonal produce for the household. The Manor would also have its dairy, laundry, stables, coach-house, gate keepers and various maintenance workers. Indeed, all manner of employment was generated from the Squire's household and Estates. Strangely enough the local people did not always live well during these times, though it is true to say that some fared better than others when the tenant farms did well.

* * *

A few months had passed since Ben's second birthday and the little boy was now almost two and half years old. Thus far Ben's infant life had been filled with warmth, love and happiness, until one winter morning when his safe little world was cruelly shattered.

It was a cold, frosty morning with a low lying mist hanging about the fields. Millie had just cleared away in the kitchen after the breakfasts. She was uncommonly tired this morning, her legs ached with the cold and she had an aching back. Because of her indisposition she had come to depend more and more upon Annie to help take care of Ben. The little boy was indeed proving to be a very lively little mite, a happy, loveable child who wanted nothing more than to run about the kitchen "helping Millie." 'He's one woman's work, Lord love 'im, a little bag of mischief let me tell yer'. Millie was often heard to say, and it was becoming increasingly more difficult to restrict Ben to the kitchen for any length of time. The day nursery had been closed up for years, but even had Ben been permitted use it, there was no nurse or nanny. Little Ben was, as most very young children are, over inquisitive. He was into everything and Millie, on occasions, simply could not cope. She was growing older, she had to admit, and Ben's boisterous energy was too much for her, but she loved him, oh, how she loved him.

On this particular morning, whilst Millie had gone to the pantry just along the kitchen passageway, Ben had disobeyed her orders to sit on the chair at the table and be still a minute until Millie returned. Annie was also in the kitchen but was totally absorbed with her task of cleaning the great copper pans and, whilst her back was turned, Ben slipped from the chair, trotted along the passageway and began to climb the stairway to the ground floor. The old stone steps were steep making it necessary for him to climb up on his knees whilst holding on to the wall for balance. The little boy looked up at the huge stairwell and the vast space above but undaunted continued to climb, thoroughly enjoying his venture into this strange world beyond the kitchen.

The Master had been preparing to take a morning ride and was hurriedly descending the upper staircase which led to a side door leading out into the stableyard. His foot struck the landing just as Ben reached up and pushed open the swing doors at the head of the kitchen steps. The Master stopped, arm outstretched to open the yard door, when he saw the golden head of "that wretched waif." Ben looked up at the Squire, giving him the benefit of a bewitching smile, but the anger in the strange man's eyes confused and frightened him, his little face crumpled and he began to cry. For the briefest of moments the Squire stood transfixed staring at the child, then brushed quickly past, yelling, "cook? Where is that damned woman?" Dashing past Ben, Sir John's great booted foot compressed the tiny fingers and the child screamed with pain and terror as he lost his balance and toppled backward down the steep steps. He landed at the bottom with his forehead cut and bleeding and his nose, also bleeding, beginning to swell. Sir John took the handle of his riding crop, pushed it under the back of the screaming boy's smock and dragged him along the hallway to the kitchens. Millie was just coming from the pantry with a bin of flour when she heard Ben's screams and the sight that met her eyes all but made her faint clean away. Ben's nose, still bleeding, had swollen and blood literally gushed from the cut in his forehead. Screaming and choking, Ben kicked out, his little arms flailing to be free. Before Millie could actually take in the scene before her, the Master addressed her in a cold rage. 'Keep this' he said, dangling the blood covered screaming Ben, 'out of my hallways, away from my house and out of my sight, Cook.' Then, gathering his wits and feigning concern, continued, 'there might have been a nasty accident, someone could have been hurt, see you keep the boy under proper control until I can make more suitable arrangements.'

Millie ran to Ben and gathered him into her arms, her mind in a whirl as she made all kinds of apologies to the Master. 'I can't think what 'e was doing Mi Lord, 'e's always bin such a good boy, 'e's never once bin on the stairs afore Sir. I'll see to it 'e don't cause you no bother no more Mi Lord, but it's me what's to blame, I'm right sorry you've bin troubled Sir, that I am'.

Sir John turned and stormed out of the kitchen making his utter displeasure with Millie known, and in no uncertain terms. Struggling with the frightened child in an attempt to stem the bleeding, her hands shaking, Millie scolded him soundly whilst the Master was still within hearing. 'Now you just stop that noise you bad, bad boy, you could've 'ad the Master over an' all you could, an' what would we do then, you just do as you're told now eh.' Little Ben, never before having heard Millie speak to him in this harsh manner, cried piteously, his head and nose were blinding him with pain, he was very frightened, and he began to sob convulsively.

Millie bit down hard on her lip and her chin shook as she cradled Ben. 'Me 'eart's fit to break me darling,' she crooned, rocking him in her great soft arms. 'That's my good boy now, stop your crying or that ol' nose wont stop bleeding and Millie's got to see to your for'ead.' Ben's sobs began to subside a little and the cold compresses had greatly slowed the bleeding. He pressed his face into Millie's breast and closed his eyes, safe and secure again. Fitfully he sobbed, 'it 'urts Millie, I fell down, my fingers 'urt me, I falled down the dairs.'

Millie turned to Annie who still stood at the sink, stricken in her own realm of terror. She had not moved a muscle since the Master had entered the kitchen. Tears streamed down her hot cheeks at the sight of Ben and the devastation she had caused. 'Go fetch Holly, Annie. No, wait a minute, fetch me another cloth first, get a clean rag, wet it well with cold water then go fetch Holly, hurry gel.'

As Annie raced around the kitchen doing Millie's bidding she glanced tearfully at Ben, her nerves were shattered, she felt responsible and could hardly think of words as she dashed up the steps, tears flowing freely. She found Mistress Hall on the middle floor instructing Meggie, one of the parlour maids, on her daily duties. 'Mistress 'all, Mistress 'all,' she called, distractedly. 'Come quick.' Forgetting all formality Annie grabbed the housekeeper by the arm and began to pull her away.

'Whatever is it girl, calm yourself, do,' Mistress Hall said, impatiently.

'Millie says to come quick, it's Benjie, 'e's...' Annie paused to catch her breath, 'e's 'urt, please 'urry Mistress 'all, please be quick.'

Mistress Hall needed no further inducement than to hear that Ben was in trouble. Wild thoughts of the fire in the range, the back kitchen door, stableyard, stone steps, her mind whirled as she followed Annie and together they all but flew along the landings and down the steps to the kitchen. Holly ran to Millie's side and gasped at the sight of Ben. 'Good God, Millie, what happened? No, never mind that now, perhaps it is not as bad as it looks, you know how heads and noses always bleed more than anything, let me see now.' Mistress Hall took control, Millie was very grateful for the housekeeper's quiet competence.

Annie was sniffing and wiping away tears with a shaking hand. 'Annie, go attend to your chores,' said the housekeeper, kindly, 'run along now, but do not stray far in case Millie should need you.'

Annie, though very upset and concerned for Benjie, was thankful to get away, she had not been scolded for her lack of diligence in watching Ben… thus far. She hurriedly escaped to her chores, the scolding would come later.

Mistress Hall took a deep breath and held a hand to her mouth in horror as she removed the cloth to examine Ben's face. Seeing the housekeeper's expression Millie spoke quietly, 'I think e'll be alright' the old lady said, looking down at her. 'I don't think it's as bad as it looks but I'm not quite sure about 'is nose, with all that swellin' it's 'ard to tell. I do 'ope it aint broke, an' I'm 'aving trouble keeping 'im awake. 'is little fingers are all blue and swelling too but I don't think they're broke, I can move 'em alright. The doctor ought to 'ave a look at 'im 'olly but we can't 'ave 'im 'ere, can we?' Millie went on to explain what had happened whilst Mistress Hall listened in silence. 'Nothing like this 'as 'appened afore, the Master was always very strict with little Master James, but never like this.' Nonetheless, the housekeeper was not entirely surprised.

'Davy will have to take him into the village, Millie, I will need to go with him, that will be best. I shall see that Doctor Wheeler examines him, just as a precaution, I'm sure he'll be fine in a day or two. Now I'm going to find Davy and arrange to take the small carriage. Fortunately Sir John will be away for the day, I have been informed that he is to dine with Lord and Lady Shelby so there's no need to wait dinner this evening, a small blessing on this day. Now, I'll send Annie to you to make a nice pot of tea whilst I attend to things.' Mistress Hall smiled reassuringly before leaving the old lady, saying, 'I'll be back directly.'

A little later, huddled inside his Holly's cloak, Ben was falling asleep between intermittent sobs. Holly spoke comfortingly to him in an attempt to keep him awake until they reached the doctor's house. She felt deeply for the little boy and murmured endearments as she pondered how best to help him.

'You must take heed my pet, truly you must, for 'tis a big harsh world outside of Millie's kitchen and you are not ready for it yet.'

In the kitchen at the Manor Millie sat in her rocking chair and closed her eyes. 'Dear Lord let 'im be alright,' she prayed, 'don't let 'is poor little nose and fingers be broke.' She wiped away more tears with her apron as Annie did her best to console her. Millie allowed the girl to fetch a footstool, place a cushion behind her head and give her some strong and sugary tea. The old cook was thankful for the girl's ministrations and accepted them only because she felt too ill to do otherwise. She gratefully sipped the hot, strong brew and with her feet resting on the footstool began to regain a little of her strength. As her practical mind returned and began working for her again Millie scolded herself soundly. No use getting in this state Millie gel, she thought, there's work to be done, chances be that baby's nose aint broke at all, an' what's a little tumble and a bashed fore'ead and bleeding nose, after all. Goodness, if I 'ad a penny piece for every bashed 'ead and bleeding nose when mine was growin' I'd be a rich woman now, that I would. Getting the morning's troubles into a better perspective Millie called to Annie. 'Bank the stove up gel and fetch the vegetables from the pantry, get going with the taters an' I'll start baking a tasty morsel for us kitchen dinners, Master's out t'night and aint that a Blessing? Come on now gel, Benjie'll be alright, can't sit 'ere all day…an' get that kettle on the stove, come on, shift yersel, lazyitits that's what you got, wouldn't do in my day,' Millie complained.

Annie gave a wavering smile. She thought that Millie was a wonder and was reassured seeing her up and about again and, above all, issuing orders. It would be alright now, Millie said so.

Later that evening young Master James looked in on the kitchen to enquire after Ben. Millie told him that 'the dear child was fast asleep, no broke nose or fingers, a mite bluish and swollen but otherwise alright.' James had promised again to speak to the vicar of the village church who would doubtless do everything possible to place Ben with a suitable family, either on one of the Manor farms or in the village. Something was puzzling him as he silently wondered at his father's mindless cruelty. His insistence on sending the loveable boy to the waifs' home caused James no undue surprise yet he sensed there was something more, something odd that evaded him, something that would continue to perplex him.

Chapter Nine

ON A CLEAR, BRIGHT, SUNNY morning Mary awoke and lie quietly listening to her favourite sound, the beautiful song of the birds, the dawn chorus; she was now sixteen years old. Looking happily around her lovely room with its pretty lace curtains and pastel drapes she reflected on the time, six years ago, that she had arrived at this house, The Grange, in far away Scotland. She recalled the day of her arrival and how, on meeting Caroline for the first time, the two girls had stared at each other in mutual dislike and enmity. The spacious grandeur of The Grange, the people with their strange sounding voices, which she had mistakenly thought to be hostile, had filled her with awe and terror and had alienated her. She did not get along with the little Scottish girl and often could not understand what was being said to her, until she had become accustomed to the strange Celtic sounds.

Lying on her bed on that lovely summer morning Mary remembered that heartbreaking time. How desperately lonely she had been, missing her friends, missing Millie, but above all she remembered the aching longing to hold Ben in her arms. How amazing, she reflected, that such all consuming heartbreak could be so short lived. This was mainly due to the firmness and understanding of Mary, her namesake, the kindly cook at The Grange. Thus, with the efforts of the Master, the Mistress and the servants, their enduring patience, tolerance and understanding of "the poor wee lassie's" unhappiness, Mary began to settle down.

As the weeks turned into months Caroline had grown to love the little English girl dearly. She greatly depended on her friend and confidante, so much so that she could barely remember a time before Mary came, and pointedly refused to contemplate a time when she would leave. Mary laughed quietly

Ema Fields

to herself as she stepped lightly out of bed and continued her reminiscences of the time before she and Caroline had become so close. After a little while Angus and Eleanor, Caroline's doting parents and Mary's newly appointed guardians, were rapidly approaching desperation. Their new young charge and their adored daughter were at "daggers drawn" almost daily. They were like oil and water, they were like fire and ice, they were an immovable object against an irresistible force - they were impossible.

Mary sat before the cheval mirror and brushed out her glossy auburn tresses, despairing of the ever present tangles in the thick mass. In a while she would join Caroline in the breakfast room. They usually breakfasted together, although Mary would have preferred to take a tray to her room. She did not join the family for dinner or luncheon, for much to Caroline's chagrin her friend had requested permission to take these meals in the kitchens with cook and the other servants. Caroline would often chat excitedly over the first meal of the day which usually consisted of porridge, sprinkled lightly with salt. Mary loved the luxury of liberally pouring sugar over her bowl of oats, as she had done often in Millie's kitchen, but that was not the way the Scots ate their national dish. The two girls would share a little tray of tea, with its separate jug of hot water, and toasted bread with cook's orange preserve. In the early days of her stay with the MacFarlanes Mary would have preferred the strawberry or blackberry preserve that Millie had used at breakfast, but soon learned not to question. There was much she would learn not to question.

As was usual at this early hour her thoughts were of baby, not such a baby now, he would be almost six years old. Mary always felt great tugs at her heart, though less painful now, when she thought of the dear baby boy she was sent away from, then only three months old. Where is he now? She would ask herself. Is he still at the Manor, or with a family in the village, or perhaps with one of the families in the farm cottages? She hoped for the latter for knew that Benjie, as she now thought of him, would love farm life as did his mother and, indeed, as did Mary herself. She had never forgotten the day she had been torn away from her beloved nephew and vowed that she would go back for him one day, a promise that was to lose none of its resolve.

In her endeavour to repay, in however small a way, the many kindnesses and respect shown her by the family to whom she had been entrusted, she had worked hard. Accepting her lessons gratefully she had learned to read and write and to speak correctly. She was schooled in protocol and social etiquette and learned how to launder and press the most delicate and the most difficult of garments. She had proved to be an ideal playmate for the slightly spoiled child to whom she was to become maid and companion and, unwittingly, had bestowed upon Caroline an education to which she would otherwise have remained blissfully ignorant, "life without riches".

The strange English peasant girl would tell of her life with her sister before her tragic death. Caroline would listen, enthralled, as Mary related her story of how she and Sarah had lived on their wits after their parents had died at the time of "the dreadful sickness." She told of her hazardous journey from their tiny cottage to the Manor House at Woodstock when forced to flee from the Parish authorities. She told what she knew of her journey in the fine coach, unconscious and close to death, with her new born nephew. The young Caroline was enthralled, she viewed Mary's stories much as other fairytales with their inevitable happy endings and would often say, "it is like a happy fairytale, and then you came to live at our beautiful house after all that unhappiness." Caroline was later to become deeply moved at Mary's life before she joined them at "The Grange" and became much in awe of her young companion.

For Mary it was, of course, a tale of opposites. She would wonder at the stories Caroline would tell, of the sheer luxury and opulence in which they lived. She marvelled wide eyed at the magnificence of the gowns, pellises and underclothing, bodices, petticoats and even bloomers, the like of which she had never before seen. She was almost afraid to touch these garments. In fact, whenever she went down to the laundry room, with its huge wooden wash tubs and great iron boilers gurgling away over low fires, she would wonder why she was laundering (not "washing" for one just did not say "washing") these perfectly clean clothes. Clothes that had been worn just three or four times and underclothing which hadn't even been worn for a week. All this work seemed to Mary at that time to be a "right and proper waste of time" but if that was what they wanted and how they lived, she would try hard and do her best, if only for the good Doctor McKenzie.

Mary felt that the household laundry maids did not really appreciate their good fortunes for Mary herself loved the laundry room, especially in winter. The laundering was much easier with the great slabs of soap that the kitchen provided, (ugh, what a smell, but very good to wash with) and she loved the warm fires. Washing in those great tubs with heated water was so much better than dousing the clothes in the stream and, of course, they actually came clean again, not that they were ever dirty to begin with. Mary found her work rewarding and at times could even help a nervous or untrained maid to finish up her task, often scolding her gently for not "getting on with it." Actually, at that time, Mary was seeking any excuse to remain in the laundry room and work with the sweet little Scottish girls with whom she could relate and who were of her own kind. She would often sit by a boiler fire on a long winter afternoon and dream of the day that she would go back to Woodstock Manor a fine and learned lady. She would smile as she thought of how she would knock on the front door of the great Manor House and say "good morning Barkworth, may I please see Mistress Hall, I'm Mary from The Grange, in Scotland." Slowly the tears would rise as she thought of her little nephew and what words she would find to say to him. "Hello Ben, I'm your auntie Mary, of course you do not remember me, I'm your mama's sister, you are going to live with me now, only if you would like to, of course. I very much hope you would like to Ben, because I've come to take you home" and the tears would flow unchecked as she sat by the fire. First there had to be a home to take him to.

Now, as time was passing, both girls knew that the time for Mary to leave would soon be upon them. It was not that her position at "The Grange" was not secure, but that she had promised her sister as she lay close to death that she would take care of her baby son. It was not her promise alone that compelled Mary, for she loved Ben so deeply that, as fond as she had become of Caroline, and heartbreaking though it would be to leave her, she had to go in search of Benjie. Mary had thought of little else for years and her heart ached to be with him, he was her kin, her only living relative, he too was alone in the world and she wanted and needed to raise him herself. Six precious years had already passed, she would let no more slip away, no more than she could possibly help.

Mary had proved an asset in the kitchen, she had shown the promise of becoming an excellent cook for since Caroline had needed her less and less she had spent much of her time in the kitchens. Caroline had always objected strongly to Mary working below stairs but the bond between them was such that Caroline would reluctantly acquiesce. On one occasion, when the request to work in the kitchens had raised its ugly head yet again, Mary had been asked to join "Ma'am", Caroline's mother, in the small sitting room. Ma'am had explained, with painstaking effort, that Mary was not required to carry out kitchen tasks. "Naturally cook and the other servants are invaluable to The Grange, but your position is as personal maid and companion to Caroline," she had stressed. "Of course you take care of Caroline's wardrobe, but that is another matter entirely and quite as it should be." Nonetheless, Eleanor MacFarlane had been obliged to grant permission for cook to instruct Mary in all that she wanted to know, since Mary had doubtless made up her mind. Exasperated, Eleanor threw up her hands and smiled, once again, her smile of defeat. At that time Mary had thanked Ma'am warmly for her kindness and explained to both Caroline and her mother that she, Mary, must make her own way in the world one day. To do this she must be fully trained in all things possible for she may be called upon to do any manner of work when raising young Benjie alone.

'I will need to be taught everything Ma'am, I want to be skilled and learned in all things, not only books and music, needlepoint and dancing. I need to be able to do everything for myself, with due respect Ma'am, there will be no servants for me, we come from different worlds Ma'am.'

It was at this time in Mary's young life that momentous events were occurring in Britain. King William IV passed away leaving his young niece, Victoria, to take his place as ruler of the United Kingdom and its colonies.

The new little Queen Victoria was just eighteen years old and Mary could not quite come to terms with the fact that England had a slip of a girl, not much older than herself, as its monarch. How must the little Queen be feeling, the little girl, princess Victoria, guarded and cherished for so many years at Kensington Palace that Mary had heard little of her until now. It was the year 1837 and England had a new Queen. The country mourned its late King but rejoiced in its new young monarch. The King is dead, long live the Queen. Long live Queen Victoria, roared the crowds. Long live the adored little princess, now Queen of England.

It was the end of an era. Old King George III, gone. George IV, Prince Regent then King, gone. His ageing brother William, King William IV just deceased, Gone. All old men but good Kings every one, if a little reckless at gambling, or oftimes thoughtless in pursuits of women.

There was no issue from George IV and his Queen, (though he would never acknowledge her as such) Caroline of Brunswick. Their only begotten child, Charlotte, died when giving birth to a son, the long awaited baby prince and, tragically, her child died with her. The country was devastated as, of course, was the King. The people were fickle where old George IV was concerned. There were times when they didn't much care for him, they disapproved of his treatment of his German wife, Caroline, their sympathies were with her, despite her own misdemeanours and rumours of adultery. She had been prevented from seeing her beloved daughter, Charlotte, on a day to day basis and, by the King's order, was banished to a private residence when Charlotte was three years old. Thus, banished by her husband, Caroline later travelled widely including the continent where she lived for some time. Caroline lived for news that her beloved daughter was delivered safely of a healthy child, be it prince or princess. Alas, this was not to be. She was notified of the deaths of her precious Charlotte and her first grandchild, a boy, a little prince, by a private letter from her son-in-law. Caroline was plunged into the depths of desperate grief. Thus, on the death of King George IV, his brother William IV was next in line of succession to the Throne.

There was no issue from William and his Queen, Amelia Adelaide Louise Therese Caroline, from the Duchy of Saxe-Meiningen. William had, however, fathered ten illegitimate children with Dorothy Jordan, the stage actress, none of whom were eligible to be heir to the throne. Hence, upon the demise of William IV, his niece Victoria was next in line of succession.

Princess Victoria had loved her uncle William and was greatly grieved at his passing. She was now Queen of England, how would she rule? She would be a good Queen, she would make reforms, she would look to the poorest of her subjects, the hungry, the orphaned children living in circumstances that greatly troubled her. She would protect her colonies. She would be a just and noble Queen.

There was to be little rest for the young Queen Victoria during the course of the next few weeks as full realisation of the enormity of her responsibilities began to dawn. Daunting though it was she knew, as she had always known, that she was destined to be a great Queen and, with the help and guidance of her advisers, God would show her the way. The country put its hopes and faith in Victoria; Victoria placed her trust in God.

* * *

Caroline sat silently studying Mary. The latter had her nose in a book, which was not in the least unusual of late. The girl sat entirely oblivious of her own special kind of vibrant beauty. Her vivid blue eyes shone like lamplights and were almost circular. Her complexion, very fair, had just a smattering of the despised freckles. Surrounding the strikingly beautiful face was a profusion of deep, yet bright, auburn hair which fell in long deep waves about her slender shoulders. Mary had grown into a true beauty, but her gradual transition from girlhood to womanhood had taken place during the time of her obsession with studying the higher aspects of life in service. Thus, she had emerged from an awkward, gangly girl and blossomed into a beautiful young woman without ever having taken the trouble to notice. But if Mary had not noticed this change, others certainly had and the inevitable invitations to dinners and balls began to flood in. "Lord and Lady whosoever, (she never could remember the countless names) request the pleasure of the Mistresses Caroline and Mary of The Grange at the occasion of their daughter what's her name's something or other celebration.

Things were becoming increasingly more difficult for Mary, she had no intention of attempting to ingratiate herself into these circles of society and had used every conceivable excuse to politely decline the kind invitations extended to her. It was time to move on. Time to make a home for Ben in her own world, in their own world. She must speak to them all…soon.

Caroline was tearful. 'You don't have to go Mary, you know you don't have to leave us. Ben could come here, we would take care of him, would we not mama?' She turned pleading eyes on her mother, 'oh do tell her mama.'

Mary sighed sorrowfully, she drew a long deep breath, this was going to be every bit as difficult as she had feared, she must not lose control, be strong, she told herself, or all was lost.

'Caro,' Mary began, using her pet name for the girl as she often did when Caroline was particularly fretful. 'I have explained many times, you'll understand one day. Your mother and father are wonderful and I do believe they would take care of Benjie, if we could but find him, but what of the boy, Caro? He is just six years old, where will this kind of life lead him? He will grow up believing he is an equal, and that he belongs with your kind, if he's raised here.'

'But he would belong,' Caroline persisted, 'you belong…'

Mary cut off Caroline's protestations and patiently continued. 'Caro, people would soon let little Ben know that he is different, unacceptable, not all folk are like your dearest mama and papa. The Mistress and the Master, well, they are very special, a true Lady and Gentleman. No, dearest, it is not so out there in the cold, harsh world. People would soon let Ben know that he is an outcast, they would be forever reminding him of his origins. You have wealth and position Caro, darling, I do not ask that you understand any other world, but one day you shall, one day.

Ema Fields

Caroline was not to be consoled and Mary knew this mood only too well. Also, she hated to see ma'am upset and Caroline's unhappiness distressed her mother deeply. Mary tried once more to help Caroline understand.

'Caro, do you remember when we were both little girls and were invited to Robert MacPherson's birthday party.'

'Aye, yes, Mary, I know what you are going to say, but we are older now and Ben will grow up one day too, it is different now.

'Caro, my love,' Mary said soothingly, 'do you remember how angry you became when you introduced me to your friends. They asked who I was, and when you told them I was your friend, Davie Sinclaire scoffed, "she's nae yere friend, she's yere maid, she does yere laundry.' Remember how you shouted at him Caro?' Mary smiled reflectively, remembering Carolines's assault upon the unfortunate boy. 'I remember Caro, I remember every word. He then said, "well, if she's really yere friend then where are her parents, which Estate does she come from, she's your maid, just a servant and servants should nae be at this party." 'Then you slapped him hard and knocked him down. We had to leave the party and you were crying. I told you at the time that it didn't matter, that he was just a silly boy, but I was hurt, Caro, so terribly hurt, I should never have been there.'

'And you didn't cry, did you Mary.' Caroline said quietly. 'I thought it truly mattered nothing to you, if only I had known.'

Recalling that dreadful day Caroline's tears broke like a tidal wave as she learned of her friend's pain, and with that knowledge came the realisation that Mary would indeed leave, had to leave.

Eleanor rang the bellcord and ordered refreshments as Mary continued softly and in a matter of fact tone. 'You see Caro, I know who I am, I know what I am. I am a Lady now, thanks to your dear mama and papa and you my sweet. I am a Lady and I do not need title or position to know this. But Caro, please look at me Caro, I am accepted now among your people, yes, but I will never be accepted into your circle on your level and, dearest Caro, I don't want to be, truly. Don't you see that never would I raise Ben anywhere but with his own kind, my own kind. Love does not overcome all Caro, that just isn't how it is. I am educated now and I will educate Ben, has it not always been my dream? Ben will be a big man in his own world, he will be respected, learned, he will know all that I can teach him and much, much more if I have my way.' Mary smiled a genuine smile as she tipped up Caroline's chin, and looking deep into her friend's sad eyes she said, 'no Caro, much as it hurts me to leave you, I must go.'

Eleanor opened her mouth to speak but Mary hushed her politely and went on. 'Because of your kindness ma'am, I have been educated, I have the best friend in the world in Caroline. It is rare in life to have such a true, dear friend and I am now equipped to teach Benjie myself. I was an ignorant child when I came here, ignorant and ungrateful, and for as long as I live I shall always remember this. For all that I shall ever have, and all that I shall ever be, will be because of you ma'am and the Master. When I had to leave Benjie I wanted to die. Millie, the cook at Woodstock, explained that I must, for I must work to take care of Benjie one day and that is why I came. Mistress Hall told me that I was a singularly fortunate girl to be coming to such a fine family. I did not understand at the time, but I understand well, now ma'am, and mere words cannot thank you.'

Eleanor listened quietly all the while Mary spoke and was deeply touched, it would have been rather difficult to speak lest her foolish tears showed through. Here was a girl with inner strength, of impeccable character and a fierce determination and with all the qualities of a fine Lady. These qualities, Eleanor acknowledged, Mary had brought with her and the Mistress of The Grange was proud to have been the one to fashion and refine the difficult little English peasant child and help make her the genuinely beautiful and gifted girl that sat before her this day. If Mary had taken some of Caroline's fine manners and delicate ways, Caroline had certainly learned humility and the wisdom to value only things of true worth in this life. Her short, sharp lessons, some of which Mary alone could have given, had done their work well; Caroline too was a fine young woman. One day Mary would understand just how indebted the Lady of the House was to the young, ignorant and proud girl who came to stay with them, purely at the request of Sir Alexander McKenzie.

Caroline had quietened, was no longer openly crying though her heart wept. She dabbed delicately at her reddened eyes and said, 'Mary, none of these people, these titled lords and ladies with their foolish ideas and their ungracious ways could ever have a shred of your goodness, I am fortunate to have had these years with my dearest friend. Go to Benjie, Mary, I wish it were not so, but I would not rob him of his Auntie Mary, and in truth I could not, I see that now.'

Caroline brightened a little and tried to look convincing when she said, 'the new railways are joining up everywhere Mary, you may be sure that we will visit each other. I hear the trains are much faster than carriages.' Caroline so wanted to believe they would see each other again.

That evening, after dinner, Eleanor and Angus MacFarlane spoke at length to Mary. Caroline had her reprieve for Angus had found the words to persuade Mary that she was not yet of an age to leave The Grange. She had a very important quest, to find her young nephew, provide a home and raise him. Another year or two, it would be better by far for both Mary and Ben, he was certain. He begged that she reconsider, 'just a wee while longer lassie,' he implored, his love for this precious child revealed in his kindly eyes, and she had neither the heart, nor the courage, to refuse him. Perhaps at sixteen years, the time was not yet right.

Chapter Ten

A WEARY, UNHAPPY LITTLE BOY hopelessly looked around his small, barely furnished room in the waifs' home; Ben was now six years old. Tom and Billy were still sleeping soundly as Ben watched them, a sorrowful expression on his young face. There were three wooden bunks, a washstand and a chamber pot in the cupboard size room. Any second now they would be called to begin the morning chores before being permitted to go to breakfast. Ben drew the grimy coverlet up around his thin shoulders, dreading the call that would inevitably come. He was hungry as always yet, despite this, did not look forward to the early morning meal. Breakfast usually consisted of two scoops of foul watery porridge and a slice of dry, and often stale, bread. Ben had been at the orphanage for almost three years, he was a very bright boy for one so young and during quiet times thought only of the day that he would leave this place forever. As he lie on his bunk he wondered for the thousandth time what it would be like to roam the fields, climb the great trees and fish in the rivers. He would remember Millie, her roughened but oh so kind hands as she splashed lovely warm water over him and pulled a clean shift over his head before Annie took him to Bed. He vaguely remembered Annie and the other kind folk at the Manor House where he had lived when he was just a little boy. He would remember his soft, warm bed, and cocoa to get him to sleep. He remembered Holly, she was the one who was always trying to tell him what he should be doing, 'baving' she called it, or be'aving, something like that. She was kind too, and smiled a lot, and she read stories to him. Ben often remembered Holly's stories and was all the saddened for remembering.

The one thought that helped keep up Ben's morale was that one day he would leave the orphanage, or the waifs' home as these places were often known; he dreamed constantly of that day. Unfortunately he would daydream all too often, for when he was sweeping the great yard or scrubbing the wide stone steps he would escape into his imaginary world and this often earned him an unexpected clout around the ear or a crack across the back with a stout switch. Ben, unlike the chubby little boy who first came to the waifs' home, was too thin, as were most of the children. In the early days of his stay at the home he was unaccustomed to the chores he was expected to learn. Also unaccustomed to the harsh ways of the people there, he would torture himself with thoughts of Holly's smiling face and Millie's loving arms. After a while Ben became a solitary child, quiet and morose and starved of love. He remembered to do as he was told no matter how hard it may seem, but his bright mind soon taught him that this was the only way to cope until he was able to leave. The sad, dejected little boy sometimes found it hard to remember all that Millie had told him, but when he did remember he would go over and over it, his mind clinging to the hope Millie had given him. She had told him of his auntie Mary, a wonderful young girl who loved him as no other little boy had ever been loved. But Mary was forced to go away to work in service so that she could come back one day and make a home for him. He tried so hard to remember everything about the story of the girl who had risked both of their lives that he should not come to a place like this. Ben would cling to Millie's words with the blind faith of a child that one day his auntie Mary would come back for him and take him far away from here. He would always feel better when he remembered the story of his auntie Mary, it didn't make him sad, it was a happy story.

As Ben sat up on his bunk and looked at his dear friends, Tom and Billy, his heart sank. There was no auntie Mary for them. If they were lucky they would go to a farm to work, if he was very lucky that might happen for him too, but his friends must go first because Mary was coming for Ben, he didn't know when, it might even be tomorrow, it could even be today.

Sunlight began to creep in through the dusty window, but there was no light in Ben's life. Had everyone forgotten him? Millie, Holly, Annie, and the man who worked outside who ran and played with him and tossed him so high into the air that he would scream until he returned safely to those big arms. He knew nothing of the letters that Davy had written him with messages from all his dear friends. He knew nothing of the food parcels that were sent to him for himself and the other children. Had everyone forgotten him? Ben continued feeling very sorry for himself as he sat in the small, cheerless room. It's so awful here, summer or winter, even at Christmas it's awful here, worse at Christmas, he silently lamented.

The little boy could not decide which was the hardest time there at the waifs' home. The freezing cold of winter when he worked in the yard or on the vegetable plots in the gardens, scrubbing steps with icy water without a woollen jerkin to protect him from the raw cold, or summertime, with its relentless heat that burned his skin and caused him great pain.

During the peak summer months the boys were not permitted to wear a cotton smock, "it makes too much needless washing" old Hawkins would say, "what are you, a boy or a girl, "can I wear me smock?" Indeed!

After a particularly bad bout of sunburn, when Ben had been forced to lie face down on his bunk for several days, he had been permitted to wear a coarse shift to protect his fair skin from the sun. His arms and neck still burned, sometimes severely, but his sore back was spared and his tender skin slowly became accustomed to the long hours outdoors and troubled him a little less.

During the bitter, raw cold winters at the home, with freezing nights and near starving days, Ben longed for the summer, he didn't care how hot it would be, just please let summer come, he would pray. But when summertime came, he would have given anything in the world to have a cold wind blow to ease the pain of his taut, burning skin, or to stand in a downpour of glorious rain and splash about in the cool water. He would dream of the rain running off his back, his face upturned to the sky. On one such hot summer day, as Ben revelled in his daydream of winter, he was abruptly brought back to the present by a hard slap about the head. Old Hawkins is a hard one alright, Ben would say to himself, flinching with pain as the rough hand came down on his reddened ears, but never a sound did he make, one day Mary would come, Millie told him so.

Ben drowsily dragged himself from the little wooden bunk, he had been daydreaming again, time to get up. He would waken the others himself, it would save them a scolding. Later that morning, after cleaning their room, sweeping the yard, cleaning out the hen houses and completing other various pleasant summertime tasks, the three went cheerfully along to breakfast. The boys sat at one great long table, the girls, at a similar table across the room. On this particular morning Ben stared in wonder at the scrubbed tabletops.

Not because of their whiteness, they were always white, for he had seen the little girls stand for hours on end scrubbing until every mark was gone from the cracked wooden boards. No, it was the food spread along the great surfaces that held Ben spellbound. He had marvelled at the dishes of gruel with milky liquid spilling over the edges. His eyes almost popped from his head in disbelief when he saw an egg placed by every dish and a thickly cut slice of bread, sweet smelling bread. He stood dumbstruck as he watched old Hawkins stirring not one, but two pots of gruel, then stoop to cut more large slices off large round loaves; the smell of the bread tantalised and tormented him, he was ravenously hungry.

That morning all the little girls wore clean cotton aprons over their frocks, patched and sewn and sometimes badly fitting, but they all looked so pretty out of their usual coarse, and often grubby, brown garments. Now Ben knew why, after morning chores, they were told to put on clean shirts and wash properly that morning. Well no, he did not at this time fully understand the reasons for these peculiar instructions, he knew only that something very strange was happening at the waifs' home. He leaned across to his friend, Tom, who was never more than a step or two away from him, the pair had become inseparable.

'What's goin' on?' Ben whispered, head bent low.

Tom also stared at the table, his mouth watering.

'It's an inspection,' he answered quietly.

'A what?' Ben asked, now even more perplexed, 'what's an insp...an inspre...'

'Ssshhh,' Tom hissed, moving closer to Ben, 'it's a check to see that we're looked after and fed proper and fings.'

'But we're not,' said Ben, in a loud whisper, trying to make himself heard over the unusual commotion of excited voices in the large hall.

'Be quiet will you', Tom spoke forcefully with alarm flashing in his dark eyes. He then muttered under his breath, 'you'll get into fearful trouble if you don't shut up. I'll tell you all about it after, just eat as much as you can, even if you go back for thirds old Hawkins will just dish it up, she'll call you a mite greedy or a cheeky lad, or some such twaddle. Ask for more bread, you wont get no more eggs but you can get more bread. Make the most of it Ben, we don't get these inspections for ages and ages.'

'Come along now me dears' said old Hawkins, showing her blackened and broken teeth. 'Finish up your eggs do and get your porridge, we don't wanna be 'ere all day now, do us?'

Ben almost tripped over his own feet in his eagerness to comply with her request. There was an elderly looking man and a stern faced younger woman, not very pretty, he thought, standing nearby. They were talking quietly and the woman was scribbling something onto a sheet of paper, but Ben's attention was swiftly taken back to the serving table. He could not remember having seen eggs at breakfast time at the waifs' home and he was anxious to take his steaming bowl of creamy looking gruel and another slice of good bread to his place at the table. Climbing into his seat he overheard the elderly man as he spoke to old Hawkins.

'Hens are laying well then, Mistress Hawkins, I'm pleased to see.'

'Right you are, Sir, right well at present' was the gap toothed smiling reply. 'In fact,' the dreadful Hawkins continued, 'we oft times have such a lot of eggs that we needs takes some to market, the money fetched is real useful.'

'Commendable, dear Mistress Hawkins, commendable,' the older man replied, ''tis a rare sense of Christian duty you have.'

The man then turned and surveyed the hall with mild satisfaction, but also with some disconcerting reservation. Things did indeed appear to be perfectly in order, nonetheless he felt a strange sense of unease, more than a few of the children did seem somewhat thin. Oh, well, he thought to himself, anxious to be away and begin his journey to town for luncheon at the Commonwealth Rooms, some children need to settle in, and not every child is naturally robust, after all. He made a mental note to call again before the usual twelve monthly inspections but, for the time being, at least, he saw no firm reason to be dissatisfied with the care at the orphanage.

Old Hawkins was anxious to distract the inspector's study of the children, 'only me Christian duty sir, as you say. I can't 'ave me own little ones but the good Lord 'as seen fit to give me thirty of 'em, oh yes sir, 'tis me who is the lucky one.'

Ben felt nausea overcome him, he heard the sickening lies and thought of all those eggs, eggs which should have been for the children, being sold at market. Anger raged within him, so much so that he was almost too sick at heart to eat.'

'Did you 'ear that Tom?' he growled.

'Yeah, I 'eard, and that's not the 'alf of it, but don't be daft Ben, eat, eat,' Tom commanded.

Ben began to eat the new bread, he had forgotten how wonderful it tasted, he ate with relish and the delicious creamy gruel, made with milk, seemed to tantalise his memory, even though he believed he had never before seen such food as this. He scooped up the gruel, as would a starving young animal, keeping his head low. Then, as Tom scraped back the bench, pushing the last spoonful of porridge into his already full mouth, he signalled to Ben to follow. Needing no encouragement Ben leaped over the bench and joined the queue behind his friend. He felt as though he might really be sick as, once again, he saw old Hawkins smile her vile smile. He took his second bowl of gruel with a somewhat thinner slice of bread and returned hastily to his seat. He sat down slowly, he was overcome with tiredness, and his tummy hurt.

Later, whilst he was digging in the half acre of ground allotted to the home for vegetable growing, Ben saw Mercy approaching. Mercy was one of the orphanage staff, there were three and, of course, the dreaded Hawkins and her mild mannered husband. Mercy was a dear soul and aptly named. The children of course were unaware of this, they knew only that Mercy was kind and tried to help them whenever she was able. She loved them all in her own way and if ever there was any small kindness she could show them to make their lives less miserable, a comforting word, a cuddle at bedtime, it would be done.

As Mercy came closer, mopping her brow in the uncomfortable heat, Ben rested from his labours to talk to her, blue eyes shone as he smiled up at her.

'Now Benjie, go on with your task, you know Mistress Hawkins will be cross with you if she thinks you are tending towards laziness, the devil makes work for idle hands,' Mercy said gently, then, smiling tenderly, she knelt down beside him, 'and how is your sunburn today?'

'It's awful sore Mercy, but if I don't move too much I can bear it, I'm six now.'

Mercy looked at the red and blistered neck and shuddered involuntarily, she said, 'well now, that's not too bad at all today, but I've brought you a cool wet cloth just the same, here, let me put it around the soreness and it will stop that ol' smock from rubbing.'

Ben flinched as the cool cloth was placed on his neck, his skin was taut and dried with fluid from the blisters, it hurt. Suddenly the pain eased away and tears filled his eyes. 'Thank you so much Mercy, that does feel good, but

Child's Acre

'I...I feel, f...feel,' Ben slumped forward and Mercy helped him sit up again, saying, 'well now, you just sit a while and you'll soon feel better. It will soon be time to go in and I'll give you a nice cool wash myself, now wont that be nice?'

Ben tried to smile and said thoughtfully, 'Mercy',

'Yes dear,'

'My belly still hurts Mercy,'

The girl replied, laughingly, 'I'm not surprised young man, methinks you ate far too much breakfast this morning, I didn't see you eating at dinner time.'

'No, because my belly hurt me.'

Mercy was close to tears but still laughing said, 'that's because your eyes were bigger than your belly, silly.'

The comment amused Ben, he smiled and said, 'you're the silly one Mercy, how can my eyes be bigger than my belly?' Then, quietly, with a serious, quizzical expression he said 'Mercy',

'Yes dear',

'I heard someone say, this morning, that we're supposed to have learning.'

Mercy looked perplexed, to give her time to think she drew a deep breath and adjusted the cloth around Ben's neck. Mistaking her hesitation for lack of understanding, Ben continued.

'You know, book learning, reading,' he explained.

'Of course I know Benjie. I know what learning is, but best you don't bother your little ol' head about such things, that's for the older children, why, you're just a babby yet.'

'But, Mercy, I'm six years old now, you know I am.'

Yes, that was silly of me Ben, I'm sorry. I'll tell you what then, my little man,' she said fondly, stroking the golden head, 'if you're still here when you are a little older you'll go to lessons for two hours a day. She smiled brightly, 'oh, but I'm sure that some lucky ma and pa will take you for their very own little boy long before then.'

'Oh, that's alright Mercy,' Ben brightened considerably, 'my auntie Mary is coming for me, I'm not really an orphan, I am an orphan but I have kin. Well, only auntie Mary really, but she truly loves me Mercy, it's just that... she can't get here 'til she's growed up...and saves some money...Millie told me all about her.'

Cruel tears stung the back of Mercy's eyes as she heard the joy in Ben's voice when he spoke of his auntie Mary and saw the light in his blue eyes. She swallowed against the lump in her throat and said, 'you truly are a lucky lad Ben, go on with your work now.'

'Mercy, I must learn to read and write,' Ben said, pleadingly, urging Mercy to understand, 'will you show me, I have to write to Millie and everyone, else they'll forget about me.'

'Ah, me pet, I fear I cannot, for I cannot read, got no use fer it, nor no time neither.' Ben looked surprised and his disappointment showed, he had so wanted to learn to read and write and had felt certain that Mercy would teach him. He looked up at her and said happily, 'that's alright Mercy, I'll learn by someone else, you'll see,' then, grinning cheekily he said, 'and then I can learn you.' They made a pretty picture sitting in the summer garden, a lovely setting with the lowering sun bathing them in crimson as it slowly made its way down through the mackerel sky. They sat quietly for a few moments more then Ben broke the silence. 'Mercy?' the solemn little boy had reappeared, he looked up hopefully and began again, 'Mercy, will you come up at bedtime and say goodnight to me and Tom and Billy, if you can?' He had wanted to say "will you tuck me in and cuddle me like Millie did?" His thoughts rambled a little, of course he would never say that, he knew that he was much too old for such baby stuff, still, it would be nice to have her come at bedtime and say goodnight in her lovely way. She would kiss him on the forehead and tuck the cover around him, careful not to touch his sunburned neck, and he would rub the kiss away saying, 'aw, Mercy, kissing is for babies.' He loved that kiss, and Mercy knew this.

'I'll do me very best Benjie, now do get on or you'll get us both into hot water. I'll try to get you in early today, but in any case it wont be long now.'

'Sorry Mercy, thank you for the cold rag, it's got warm again now though.' He handed her the warm rag.

'I'll fetch another, but you'll be in afore long.'

Ben went back to his task, much heartened by his talk with Mercy. He would need to find someone else to teach him to read and write. His young mind pondered the question, who? Then he mentally wrote his first letter, which would be to the old man he had seen that morning. He would tell him just how badly the children were treated, how hungry they sometimes were, how hard they were made to work.

Chapter Eleven

LIFE HAD CHANGED OF LATE at Woodstock Manor. Ben was still at the waifs' home, for Millie had never succeeded in her efforts to have him brought back to them. The Mistress had passed away leaving an almost tangible cloak of sorrow over the house and the staff that had loved her. Sadly she had died a relatively young woman and the fact that her death had been anticipated for some while had been of little comfort when her time came. Better in God's heaven, Millie consoled herself, than forced to live out her days tied to him who never bothered with her. Millie was convinced that her lovely Mistress had simply given up, didn't even try to get better, 'she should have tried' said Millie aloud, forcing back futile tears, 'she shouldn't have given up.'

Master John had been a deal upset at his mother's passing but had soon accepted the fact. He had loved his mother in his own careless way but they had never had a close mother and son relationship. James, on the other hand, was devastated. He had grieved excessively, if one could grieve excessively for one's mother, that is, and was, for some considerable time, totally unable to come to terms with her death. It was as though the light had gone out of his life and he had seemed to lose all sense of purpose. Holly or Barkworth would often come across him standing at his mother's long, narrow casement window, staring vacantly over the beautifully tended Manor grounds and distant farmlands. He was often seen with one of her shawls pressed against his face in a vain attempt to recapture her presence through the faintly lingering scent of lavender that she had so loved. Sometimes he would just sit silent as the grave in which she slept, other times choked by the asphyxiating sobs that were the outward sign of his breaking heart.

Below, in the kitchens, it had been James' long silences that had deeply concerned Millie, 'far better to grieve openly', she would say to Mistress Hall, 'taint natural to be so quiet, taint good fer 'im. However, the old adage was often true, time is a great healer, the only healer for some, and the only hope for young Master James.

Now, four years after his mother's death, James had seemingly recovered from his traumatic loss. His father, old Master John, suffering severely with his breathing and with gout, was even more bad tempered than before. He was miserable in the extreme and, almost totally confined to bed, left the greater part of Estate matters to his sons. He was only too aware that his days were numbered but, to be fair to the man, he had built and maintained a fine legacy for his sons to inherit. Young Master John would become Squire of Woodstock Manor and the villages and farms that it encompassed. It was a great comfort to him at this time of old age and infirmity that the elder of his sons had been the one to inherit his own strength of character, there would be no Tom foolery with John. The old man took great solace in the fact that the estate would continue to thrive, just as it had always thrived under his own rule and would still be there for his grandsons to inherit. James, however, was an entirely different kettle of fish, in the old man's opinion. James, a veritable milksop, too soft by half, the estate would surely go to the dogs with James at the helm, no idea at all, a mummy's boy that one, hadn't he proved it in no uncertain terms when the woman died. Yes, John was the lad for him.

Old Sir John found at least some peace of mind as his time drew nigh. As his chapter drew to a close he knew that the next attack of breathlessness, or perhaps the one after that, would very likely be his last. In his waking moments he would drift back to the times of his youth. He had lived a full and rich life, yes, no man could say other. Had he chosen a more temperate, less profligate, lifestyle doubtless he may have lived a deal longer, but better to have lived well and go sooner than to end his days as James doubtless would, an old man never having tasted the real fruits and pleasures of this world.

James, ah James, such a disappointment, nonetheless he had provided for him well, his mother's son, but how fortunate he had been to beget a son such as his first born. John, the very image of his father, not simply in looks but also in character. John would inherit and, unbeknown to his father, his inheritance could not come soon enough. Young Squire John, Lord and Master of the vast Woodstock Manor Estate and all that it signified. This was the thought that dominated the young man's mind almost every waking moment.

* * *

'They'll be back afore long, Annie, look sharp now and fetch the bread from the oven, the crust will be just right if I'm not mistaken. Three more trays to go up to the drawing room and we'll be about done gel.' Millie bustled about in her capable, if slightly lumbering way, ensuring that the preparations for the funeral gathering would be exactly as they should. ' 'ow many coming to the funeral, Millie,' asked Annie in amazement, 'you would fink it's 'undreds all the work it's caused, well I'm sorry about the work but I'm not sorry about 'im, and I'm sure I never saw so much food.'

'Annie,' Millie shrieked, as the girl turned from the oven bearing two more hot loaves, a startled expression on her flushed face. 'Now you just come 'ere this minute you wicked, wicked gel. What a thing to say about the Master, an' 'im who 'as put food in her mouth and give you work and a 'ome all these years, now you just 'ave a bit of respect me gel, or I'll knows the reason why.'

'S…sorry Millie, I didn't mean no 'arm, honest, I just thought…' Annie was thinking that she could not understand the reason for Millie's outburst, everyone was pleased the Master was dead, though none of them, she now realised, had ever actually said so.

'I knows that gel, I knows yer didn't mean no 'arm, 'Millie assured her, 'but it don't make no mind what we think, there's things you say and then there things you don't. Millie turned her head, a smile threatening to gainsay her anger, how could she be anything other than amazed at the girl. Lord above, she thought, the Master lying dead upstairs an' all little Annie can think about is all the work 'e 'as caused. Had Millie been alone in the kitchen she would have burst into uncontrollable laughter. Her smile showed a little, despite her efforts to remain stern faced, as she continued to reprimand Annie, albeit in a much gentler manner.

'Now get them trays I need and remember, never speak ill of the dead, let alone your elders and betters. Fetch them tray clorths from the pantry, we want everything right for Master John and especially young Master James. Mistress 'all and Barkworth 'ave got the 'ouse shining like a new pin and the outside lads have worked night and day, we don't wanna let 'em all down now. Shaking her head from side to side, still smiling, Millie began to dress the trays that would soon be laden with her most delectable fare; Millie was a Master of her craft.

The business of the funeral over, Millie, Annie, Mistress Hall, Barkworth and the other staff settled down to life under the control of the new Squire, young Master John. However, in the space of a relatively short period of time it had become evident that the young Sir John would be no less a tyrant than his father. He was cruelly without feeling, the people who farmed the Manor lands meant little or nothing to him. It was soon to be said that, at the very least, if folk had meant little to the old Master his heritage had meant everything, and for this they were grateful, it gave them a small sense of security. The Estate had been the old Squire's life, his whole purpose for being, and if the only good thing to be said of the man was his affinity with the land then it must be said. He had passionately loved his home and the vast estate entrusted to him, had been unstinting in his endeavours to ensure its continuing prosperity for those who came after him.

At present time, however, for farmers, gardeners, dairy and domestic workers alike, Woodstock no longer provided the relative security that living and working a successful estate provided. Even the lowliest farmer with the smallest acreage feared the wind of change. It was apparent to all concerned that things were going downhill due to young Squire John's mismanagement. Oh, they all knew perfectly well that Master James spent hours, no less than days at a time in the futile attempt to educate his brother on Estate matters and the laws ruling the harvests. The importance of understanding the Corn Laws currently in force under Queen Victoria and her Prime Minister, Lord Melbourne. For many years there had been a great deal of talk and groups working for the repeal of the Corn Laws but, for the present, this repeal had not fully taken place. James had a brilliant business mind but also greatly valued the knowledge and experience of his farmers. Alas, he could only advise, he did not have control and his brother was not about to be told as how best to run his own affairs; James' words fell upon deaf ears.

After one such meeting of Estate affairs John was left fuming with anger. James was getting far above himself, it was he, John, the firstborn who had inherited, who was Squire and James needed, only too often, to be reminded of this. Hence the lengthy discussions often ended in bad feeling between the brothers and inevitably word spread through the villages and farms of Woodstock.

Child's Acre

At about this time the managing stockman was experiencing much the same problems with the young Squire. Whereas old Sir John would seek the stockman's advice on all matters concerning stock before deciding upon any major transaction, his arrogant and inexperienced son went right ahead with his wild schemes. 'This is my Estate,' he would remark coldly, 'does a mere stockman, however long he's been here, dare to question how I run it?'

The wise and invaluable stockman would stand down, understanding only too well that he would seriously jeopardise his livelihood and that of his family, to say nothing of his love for his work, should he further incur the wrath of the Squire. Ill advised decisions were made and the stockman's heart would sink as he witnessed unsuitable stock being brought in. The sheer incredulity of valuable stud animals actually being sold at auction for the high price they would fetch filled him with despair. No thought whatsoever was given to future lines and strains being maintained.

Seasons came and went, despondency was all around. The Estate no longer flourished and was headed towards serious financial troubles. Indeed, if the course on which they now found themselves did not change dramatically, and soon, an entire way of life would be lost.

It was late afternoon, Millie and Annie were enjoying their usual and much needed rest hour when James entered the kitchen through the yard door. As he entered Millie stirred from dozing in her rocking chair whilst Annie slept on by the hearth.

'Why, deary me…look 'ere, it's Master James,' the old lady stammered, upset at having been found asleep in the afternoon. James was quick to note her discomfort.

'Don't disturb yourself Millie, please.' James sat down heavily on the long backed chair as Millie pushed herself up and straightened her apron.

'Nonsense Master James, you're no disturbance, whatever are you thinking, let me fetch you a nice cup of tea, an' you'll 'ave a bite to eat an' all if I knows anything.

James heaved a sigh, 'very well Millie, I concede, I'll take a cup of your delicious tea, good and strong, join me please Millie, I want to talk to you and I think you may just need a good strong cup yourself.' He smiled his bewitching smile, the smile that had enchanted her for over twenty years. She pottered about the large homely kitchen, a room James had loved all of his life. She clattered around the big black range, a sound he had loved all of his life. It pained him to see her growing a little more immobile, she had served the

Ema Fields

Manor well and was now getting old, no, she was old. Just how many years Millie had been on this earth nobody knew, but she was an old lady now and should be retired to live out her days in peace and happiness. James was fully aware that his brother John would never consider an aged servant living at the Manor house unless they worked their passage, giving James no option but to go on worrying about Millie. She had nowhere to go, the Manor was the only home she had known for many a year, oh, but to have been the firstborn, he thought wistfully.

The late afternoon sun shone through the window, the spotless old kitchen was touched here and there with crimson glints and although it was summer a fire was burning brightly, James felt a strange peace surround him and prepared to give Millie his news.

'Millie, I've some good news for you, wonderful news.' Taking the tea from her he nodded his thanks and would have continued had she not interrupted, as was her way. 'What's up then? Now you've got me all of a dither, come on with you, what are you trying to tell me?'

James leaned across the big scrubbed table holding his cup of tea in both hands, he drew a deep breath. 'You know I don't have a free hand Millie. I don't have a say in the scheme of things, cannot make the changes I would wish.' He paused to think, sipped his tea and continued, 'I have had a long talk with John and…'

'Now, now Master Jamie,' said Millie, using the term of endearment she had so often used when he was a child. 'Don't fret yoursel', I don't needs to know about these things,' Millie protested, not wanting to hear the long awaited news, so certain was she that young James had been delegated to tell her that she was too old for her work and must go. Seeing her concern James held up a hand, saying 'now do not interrupt until I have finished what I have to say. Millie, as I have just said I have had a talk with John, he really isn't so bad Millie, just a little misguided on occasions. Well, I explained to him that you simply need a little extra help outdoors. What with the kitchens and all your many responsibilities young Annie is needed more and cannot be spared to fetch wood, feed the geese, collect the eggs from the hen houses, run back and forth to the dairy and other such outdoor tasks.

At this Millie held her breath, looking frightfully anxious, young Master Jamie was going to dismiss her as gently as he could, dear soul that he was. James quickly reassured her. 'Millie, I've some good news for you, wonderful news, with a little chicanery, that is a little planning, I am quite certain I can make you a very happy lady.'

'Oh, come now Master James, I aint no lady, Lord love us, whatever next.'

'A very happy lady, Millie,' James stressed, 'the finest and the happiest lady in the land.' He laughed and Millie brightened a little. 'Now listen,' he said slowly, a determined expression in his eyes, 'I have John's permission to engage a lad to assist Annie, do the heavy fetching and carrying and all the outdoor tasks I have said. Perhaps even lighten the load for old Ned, help around the stables when you do not need him. I suggested that a boy might be more useful, but to be quite honest Millie, John wasn't at all interested, said I should have more to do than worry about the kitchens and to do what I like.

Millie relaxed, she was smiling now, she would have more help, it was sorely needed, Annie needed help, poor love, life would be much easier, Lord bless Master James, she didn't have to go...yet.

James continued, clearly excited now. 'To make the scheme more attractive, Millie, I suggested that we take a lad from one of the waifs' homes, he wasn't interested, but I could not conceal my intentions entirely, he just agreed Millie. James let out a long breath and said loudly and slowly, 'he agreed'.

Millie followed James' train of thought all the way, her eyes swam with tears, her heart quickened its beat, she was transfixed, then slowly she said 'but how Master Jamie, how can it ever be done.'

'Leave it to me old love,' James said, gently squeezing her hand, 'you just leave it to your Jamie.

In that moment of hope, hope long set aside, if not abandoned forever, Millie quite forgot her station, she caught at his arm and, holding tightly, uncaringly, truly overstepped the boundaries of a servant.

'He will still be there, Master James?' Millie asked, imploringly, her free hand rummaging in her apron pocket for a kerchief.

'Trust in the Lord, Millie. Now dry your tears and make some fresh tea, John is dining out tonight and I'll just take a tray in the study please. I will come along tomorrow afternoon, I have to address the Cattlemen's Association in the morning, then I must be off to the far pastures, but I will come as soon as I am free. Not a word now, you understand of course that this lad comes from a waifs' home, there must be no talk of young Ben coming back. I do not think John will go against father's wishes, although in truth, he has not refused, this is probably the one time that John's disinterest in the Manor is truly a blessing.'

Millie swallowed hard nodding her agreement and, pushing her wiry grey hair from her face, whispered, 'not a word Master James, I'd as soon die first.' She spoke the truth. James smiled reassuringly then hurriedly took his leave, hailing Davy as he crossed the cobbled yard, covering the ground quickly with his long stride.

Millie closed her eyes, 'and may the good Lord bless 'im for 'is goodness,' she prayed. Coughing loudly a very emotional old lady rubbed at her streaming eyes with a sopping handkerchief. Her thoughts were wildly tumbling around in her head as she murmured 'me Benjie, me darlin' boy, he must be all of nine years old now, me precious baby.' Once more anxious tears flooded her cheeks as she went about making another pot of tea, setting out a mug this time for Annie. This is one of God's good days, she told herself as she lifted the heavy black kettle from the hob calling, 'Annie, come on Annie, are yer going to lie there all day, wake up, wake up now gel.'

Annie dragged herself upright, reluctant to leave blissful slumber and her place by the hearth. She yawned drowsily, saying, 'oh Millie, not already Millie, I only just lay down.'

Millie looked tenderly at the sleepy girl whose life would change for the better soon. All their lives were about to change for the better, she had a strange conviction that this would be so, and little Benjie's life would be heaven on earth if she had anything to do with it. 'Tell you what Annie, we've still got another 'alf hour, well we aint really but Master John is dining out tonight so we'll take another 'alf hour. 'Drink yer tea, 'ere it is, and we're going to be first to taste the fresh bake today, a good slice of best gingerbread an' yer can 'ave preserve on a new cottage crust an' all, 'ow does that sound? Go and fetch it from the pantry, go on wiv yer gel.'

Annie smiled sweetly, wearily pushing strands of loosened hair into her cap as she turned towards the pantry. She loved Millie dearly and was, paradoxically, reassured that all was well when the old lady complained constantly, for Millie's true ill humour manifested itself in quite a different manner.

Millie, chastened by Annie's smile said, 'take no mind of me gel, I'm nothing but a crotchety old woman, most dead an' wont lay down.'

Annie was busy collecting things from the pantry along with an earthenware pot of preserve. 'Aw Millie,' she said, mimicking Millie's cross voice, 'you wicked, wicked woman to say such things.' Millie heard nothing, her mind was lost to all but Ben, she absently began to cut cake for them as she looked out across to the stable block to where Davy was struggling with a large bale of hay. Please, please dear Lord, she silently prayed, please let Jamie bring him home.

Chapter Twelve

BEN STOOD IN HIS ROOM staring at his little friends' wooden beds. He was excited, afraid, disbelieving, and all these conflicting emotions were causing turmoil in his young mind. He could leave the waifs' home, could it really happen after six long years, an interminable time for a young child. Years of toil, of hardship, of loneliness and fear yet, nonetheless, years of unfailing hope for Ben had never once doubted that this day would come. He would have been ecstatically happy to be leaving, if not for the fact that it was a stranger and not his auntie Mary who waited impatiently for him. Ben was greatly troubled. He cried quietly, despising himself for his tears, though his tears were not for himself. Who would take care of the younger ones now? Who would keep them a small titbit stolen from the kitchen whenever possible to give to them at bedtime? Who would tuck them in and give a word of comfort when Mercy could not? Who would cuddle them and tell them that everything would be alright for them one day? Who would teach them to pray to baby Jesus as Millie had taught him? This day, so long awaited, so long dreamed of, brought only sadness for Ben. He brushed his tearstained cheeks with the back of his hand but to no avail, a sob caught in his throat as fresh tears spilled unchecked. He would miss them all so much but he would never forget them, especially Tom, for it was Tom, with his lame leg, who had always needed him most. He smoothed the stained cover on Tom's bed and sobbed aloud, 'I'll never forget you Tom and I'll pray to baby Jesus for you every day, I will, honest I will. I wish you could come with me, I don't want to leave you here without me,' he choked. 'One day I'll find you Tom,' he vowed, 'one day.'

Ben rubbed his red eyes once more, he would not be able to say goodbye to them again. He would meet the kind gentleman and they would just leave, he had already said his goodbyes and he couldn't go through it again. He drew a sobbing breath, maybe he was not quite grown up yet…grownups don't cry.

He remembered the morning a week before when, as he was working in the shade of a large oak tree, a smartly dressed gentleman came by. The gentleman, accompanied by old Hawkins, had watched the children as they worked. Tom had been called over to speak to the man, then the stranger crossed the gardens and spoke to several other children, searching about him all the while. When he had sighted Ben he strode across to speak to him. Ben could remember thinking, as he studied the tall gentleman's beautiful long boots, one day I'm going to have a pair of boots just like those, and stockings too, when I'm really grown up my feet will always be clean and dry. Seeking Ben out among the other children the gentleman had smiled warmly at him, 'you look like a fine lad, I see they have taken good care of you here, these kind people.' The man smiled again, this time at old Hawkins. Ben looked up, 'yes sir, thank you sir,' he replied quietly, his voice barely audible.

'Benjie, isn't it?' Enquired the kindly stranger.

'Ben, sir,' he answered, a little more forthcoming now, taking note of the man's kindness.

James had remembered the chubby, loveable, mischievous three year old as he was dragged from Mistress Hall's arms sobbing hysterically. "Don't leave me Holly, please don't let them take me away, I'll be good Holly, Benjie will be good, night prayers and honest I will Holly, only please d d don't…l l leave mmmmeeeeeee."

As his mind spanned the years James' throat constricted, he coughed and swallowed. Standing before the thin, pale child with his roughened hands and grazed knees, unrecognisable now but for the sand gold hair and those unusually deep blue eyes, James put on a bright smile. 'Well now, Ben,' he said, brightly, 'I'm looking for a strong, helpful chap just like yourself to help me at home, lend a hand with the chores, you understand, help with the outside work that I no longer have time for. Do you think you would like to work on a farm? I'm certain you'll be treated fairly.'

The little boy stared up at James in silence. As Ben did not answer James continued, 'you are nine years old, Mistress Hawkins tells me, just about the age that would suit the help I need, would you like to give the work a try?' Ben remained silent. Undaunted, James knelt down, face to face now with this strange and troubled child, he continued in his gentle manner, 'I have a good and loyal staff, Ben, you would become one of them.

Ben, still silent, was bemused, it seemed to him that he had spent all his life in this place and now that he was at last to be leaving everything had gone wrong, it wasn't supposed to be this way, Mary was supposed to come for him.

James grew more concerned, what was the matter with the boy, he was sick of course, that was painfully evident, overworked, that too, but there was something else. Yes, there was something indefinable about this child that had puzzled James long ago, that would continue to evade him for many years to come; he brought his mind back to the present. 'What is it, Ben,' James coaxed, 'would you not like to come to work for me? No doubt you will be suited with another family, a fine boy like you, but why not come with me now and we'll see how we get along?'

Ben knew it had all been arranged and he must go with the stranger. Slowly, and with difficulty he broke the long and strained silence and James was dismayed as he saw alarm register clearly in those expressive young eyes. 'Sir, please sir,' Ben stammered, 'it is very good of you sir, it's wonderful sir, I do want to work for you, I do…honest I do but…you see, I can't…you see sir, it's my auntie Mary.' Ben rambled on quickly, for now that his silence had been broken the words came in torrents. 'My Auntie Mary is coming for me you see sir, she's coming to get me, Millie said so. I don't remember Millie who looked after me when I was a baby, but I remember she promised my Auntie Mary will come for me, so I must be here, you see, sir, I have to be here when she comes.' Ben hung his head and stared at the ground. James thought that never had he seen a more disconsolate soul, the child was obviously distressed as the possibility of losing his one chance to leave the home; James' heart went out to him. 'Well now young Ben,' he said, cheerily, I entirely agree with you, but I believe that your dilemma can be solved quite easily. If I were to give my word, as an honourable gentleman, that if…when your auntie Mary comes for you she will be taken to your new home, would that help you with your worries?'

Ben's large eyes widened, 'oh yes sir, it would truly sir, and you'll never have a better worker sir, I know about seasons, and planting,' he dragged a dirt smudged hand across his eyes, a light breeze rustling through the branches

Child's Acre

above him lifted his hair, and growing more animated with every second he rushed on 'and I know about wood and I can scrub floors and wash walls and peel tatties and dig and...'

'Whoa there, steady my boy,' straightening up James laughed heartily, his hopes restored as he witnessed sudden joy transform the child's sharpened features, yes, this was their Benjie. 'I do not doubt for one moment that you can do all that you say Ben, for it is plain to see you are a capable young man.'

James turned to Mistress Hawkins, who had the good grace to look a mite embarrassed, and said 'Well, then, Mistress Hawkins, I deem the matter to be settled, I will make the necessary arrangements and leave you, good lady, to attend to your own. As though to dismiss the churlish woman James turned to Ben and, speaking tenderly said, 'I'll call for you in a few days Ben, leave you time to say goodbye to your young friends.' James watched the blue eyes moisten at the mention of the other children and said comfortingly, 'a temporary farewell, you will see the boys and girls again before too long, I have no doubt.' At James' words Ben's spirits lifted visibly and his hitherto sad eyes were radiant with happiness. He drew a deep breath and said, joyously, 'yes sir, I'll be ready sir, and thank you very much indeed sir, about my auntie Mary sir.' James eyes clouded at the mention of Mary and he felt, yet again, the strangely haunting sensation that had always disturbed him.

James' thoughts were with the young girl, Mary, as he turned and walked back to where his carriage awaited him. It had been a long time since Doctor MacKenzie had visited the Manor assuring them that Mary was settled and happy with his friends, the MacFarlanes. What of her now, he wondered. He felt quite certain that Ben would never see Mary again and the thought greatly saddened him, for the boy's undaunting faith had touched him deeply.

That had been almost a week ago and now the time had come. Ben stared absently down at the tidy yard where the children were arguing, some of them were still at their chores, little Mollie was whining again and Tom limped over to her as Ben watched. He thought sadly, the kind gentleman is waiting downstairs, I mustn't keep him waiting any longer. He picked up his bundle of meagre belongings and turned to glance around the tiny room that had been his only refuge for so many years.

And so it came to be that a sad little boy stood alone in the cold and dismal upper passageway of the waifs' home. A pathetic, lonely little figure joined his hands in prayer and asked baby Jesus to take care of the children

Ema Fields

and be kind to Mercy. He tried to dry his eyes with the frayed cuff of his smock and slowly, dejectedly, made his way down the long, bare staircase for the very last time.

James had rearranged his busy schedule in order that he would be free to collect Ben from the orphanage himself, for nothing must go wrong on the boy's arrival at the Manor. He had instructed Davy to arrange his own tasks likewise and to be ready with the small carriage directly after breakfast. He had not quite decided how to approach the question of Ben's identity. How does one tell a small boy that he must pretend to be someone other than he truly is, and at the same time find justification for the deception?

James and Ben walked together in silence, out of the yard and towards the waiting carriage. They made an incongruous pair, the handsome young nobleman, the small shabby waif. Ben stopped, looked up at James and back towards the waifs' home. Shafts of golden sunlight bathed the cold, grey stone walls of that bleak house, ever grim despite its setting amid the lovely Suffolk countryside, but Ben was oblivious to all but his own silent thoughts. Could he catch a final glimpse of the children he had come to care for so much? James sensed Ben's confusion and thought that he understood the feeling of abandonment the boy was experiencing. He placed a hand on Ben's thin shoulder, gently turning him towards the carriage. 'Look ahead Ben, not back,' his new master instructed firmly, but not unkindly. Ben did not look back.

The carriage trundled along at an easy pace. James allowed Ben his private thoughts and the two had sat in silence for some little while. The horses had turned off the main highway and they were now passing through a beautiful darkened tunnel of a myriad shades of green, lit only by dappled sunlight filtering through the dense foliage of the trees entwined overhead. Somewhere a fire burned slowly and the sweet aromatic fragrance of wood smoke filled the air. Ben drew a deep breath and smiled weakly at the gentleman sitting opposite. 'Wood smoke,' he said, leaning closer to the window and looking up into the trees, 'it's my very favourite smell.' His smile widened as the gentleman closed the periodical he had been browsing through. James returned Ben's smile saying, 'methinks you are a country boy Ben. Ah, yes, I understand well for I am a country boy myself. The land is in my blood I fear, and I do agree that there is nothing in all the world more pleasing to the senses than the smell of a wood fire, snapping and crackling, smoke rising through the trees, permeating the air with its pungent sweetness.'

James spoke descriptively and with such conviction that Ben was pleased to be so well understood. He continued in his lighthearted manner, 'mayhap you and I are two of a kind Ben. Which, of course, they were.

After what had seemed a very long time to Ben the carriage drew to a halt and Davy leaped to the ground. He threw the reins over a stout branch then lifted down a hamper from behind the driving seat. He handed the large square basket to James saying, 'there you are sir, do enjoy your luncheon, I'll set awhile with the mares, you'll let me know if you require anything sir?' Leaving the carriage door open Davy grinned at Ben and nodded, 'best see that my girls behave themselves,' he said pleasantly. Ben liked the driver, he was nice too. Davy settled himself comfortably against a fallen log opening his luncheon bundle whilst the horses ate leisurely from their feed bags. The break in the journey was much needed but would also provide James with the opportunity to become better acquainted with Ben and so ensure that the child understood the nature of the problem confronting them.

'A fine luncheon cook has prepared for us, Ben, dear old Millie.' As he spoke James began placing food on the trays he had taken from the hamper. 'Hungry, Ben?' he enquired, handing Ben a hunk of newly baked bread. As Ben started to reply politely, 'no thank you sir,' James cut in, 'come along then, eat heartily, there is sufficient here to serve the whole household I'll warrant, travelling always sharpens the appetite, do you not agree?'

Ben did indeed eat heartily, encouraged as he was by the tempting fare placed before him. Munching away he listened to the birds twittering and singing in the woods that surrounded them and was lost to the world. I've never ever seen a place like this, he daydreamed, the best place to play and hide and climb trees and have dinner, better call it luncheon now though, he thought. After consuming two chunks of the delicious bread, a thickly cut wedge of home dairy cheese, a slice of game pie and an overlarge portion of plum cake he wiped his hands on the snow white linen napkin and thanked James for his dinner. 'That was the best grub I've ever 'ad sir, but I shouldn't 'ave eat so quick, forgot me manners a bit sir. I mean, the food was ever so good sir, I can speak proper sir, really I can, Mercy taught me, she said I must always speak proper when I'm with grownups and not like I talk to the children, especially if I talk to the inspector.'

'Not a word of it,' James replied with a hearty chuckle, you just be yourself Ben and, to be truthful, I was a mite hungry myself. What say we go and stretch our legs awhile before we head for home, 'tis exceedingly pleasant here and I'd rather like a word with you.'

'You want to talk to me sir?'

'Yes, I, I do Ben.' They began to stroll idly through the woods. 'Just taking a look around, Davy, back soon, he called.' Ben ambled along beside him, pausing to watch a squirrel scamper into the branches of a nearby tree. A little later James sat down on a large fallen log and motioned Ben to sit beside him. 'Ben,' he began, speaking hesitantly, 'have you any memories of the place at which you lived before you went to the orphanage?" Please Lord, give me a hand here, help me find some appropriate explanation, he thought.

'I'm not an orphan, sir, I have kin, I've got my auntie Mary, and she...'

'Ah, yes, Ben,' James cut in, 'I do realise that, of course, but do you remember where you stayed before your time at the orphanage?'

'Not really sir, I don't know where it was but... I remember a great big room, not like the one at the home, this room had a big fire all the time, it was lovely and always smelled of food, lovely food, I think. I always tried hard to remember Millie, the lady in the big room, and another lady in a long black frock, but I'll never really forget Millie sir, never, I just can't remember what she looked like.' Ben gave a small smile, 'Someone used to hold me a lot, and scold me a lot too sir, she was always scolding me.' He looked up towards the sky through a break in the canopy of the trees and said quietly, ' I remember a great big table and night prayers at bedtime, that's all I really know sir, but I was just a child then.' Ben swiftly rubbed at his eyes with the back of his hand.

James could not but be touched at Ben's reference to his adult status. 'Well, see here now young sir, methinks you would like to go back to the house where Millie lives, would you not?'

'Oh, sir, please don't think I'm not proper thanking you, I never meant to do that. I'm right glad I'm going to work for you sir, truly I am.'

James expression was grave, it was important that Ben comprehend fully, but important not to be heavy about it. 'Ben,' James began with a happy smile, 'there's something I have need to explain and I think you are grown up enough to understand. I must ask you to keep a confidence, a secret, and a lot may depend on you now.'

Ben was perplexed, 'a secret?' he murmured, his eyes wide and questioning, 'you can tell me anything sir, I would never let you down, cross me 'eart…my heart and hope to die sir.'

'Very well then,' said James animatedly, 'I have some very exciting news for you. Do you know why you were sent from the manor Ben?'

'No, sir, but I think it was because my auntie Mary had to go away so I had to go away, something like that, and she aint come back yet, hasn't, but she will.'

'Yes, Ben, you are quite correct, it was something like that, just as you say, and you were removed to the waifs home in the next county.' Drawing a long breath and edging his way carefully, James continued. 'I am the son of the old Squire of Woodstock Manor Ben. There is much I cannot explain at present, I must therefore ask that you trust me. The old Squire, my father, had you sent to the orphanage entirely in your best interest, that you may be raised with other children and have proper schooling. Well, now, I would not wish to go against my father's wishes for he was a wise man, but he passed away, sadly, and it is my brother John who is now the Squire. That is why, how, I was able to find you and bring you back to the Manor House.' Ben sat in stupified silence unable to comprehend, was sir saying that he, Ben, was going back to the Manor to work, to be with Millie again? 'Now, Ben, this is the reason for our secret, are you listening? Ben nodded but did not speak. 'My brother, the Squire, is a good man, but I fear he would not be happy to go against our father's wishes for you. Now, I, on the other hand, feel that you are much older now and able to make your own way in the world, so I believe it is a good thing for you to return to the manor. It is for this reason, the reason that we do not give the Squire any cause for concern, that it must never be spoken of that you lived at the Manor when you were a small child. Those who may know, shall know, those who should not, will not. After this conversation Ben, it will never be spoken of again.

Ben's expression was still touched with sadness as he looked into James eyes in total amazement. 'Come now, Ben,' James encouraged, 'is this not a reason for great rejoicing?

Ben remained silent, his mouth slightly agape, his eyes registering…what? James, a little discomfited, asked, 'what is it Ben, have you nothing to say?'

Ben the grown man was Ben the child again, large tears slipped down his cheeks onto his breeches. 'I'm going back to Millie, sir?' he asked, incredulously, 'is that what you just said, sir?' Still wide eyed, he began to laugh through his tears. James inclined his head slowly as Ben continued, 'oh, sir,' his breath caught in his throat and he swallowed, he smiled from ear to ear but the laughter quickly turned to sobs, great choking sobs which did not abate. He gained a little control, wiped his eyes with the kerchief James offered him, then held out his little hand. James took it and, battling with his own emotions, smiled at the boy. Ben shook James' hand in a pathetic attempt to regain his adult status, 'thank you sir', he said, earnestly, 'thank you for everything, and I'll never let you down, sir, never ever,' he said, with the deepest conviction.

James was immensely relieved that his task had been accomplished. In an attempt to restore the conversation to normal he said briskly, 'well done, Ben, that is settled then.'

'Yes sir, and I don't need to know about reasons. The little boy looked strangely thoughtful. 'Will I have to be called something different, sir, another name?' James stood up, brushed off his breeches, straightened and stretched his back and shoulders. He had considered this aspect of the deception many times during the past weeks, he smiled down at Ben. 'No Ben, there are many Benjamins in our fair country, 'tis a fine old name. Now then, what say we go home?'

* * *

Millie lie wakeful in her bed, weary and emotionally drained; it had been a wonderful day. 'Lord love us, me ol' leg 'urt something awful tonight' she murmured, 'but I don't care a mite' As she relaxed upon the warm and comfortable bed, sinking breathlessly into the downy pillows, the aching began to ease and she closed her eyes in prayer. Ben was sleeping in the kitchen on an improvised mattress at his own special request, but a temporary measure until more permanent sleeping arrangements had been decided upon. Unable to concentrate, Millie's thoughts returned to the events of the day and the happy evening they had all shared.

As the first shadows of twilight fell, after upstairs dinner had been served, the servants had all partaken of a fine meal but Ben had eaten little. On arrival at the Manor the boy had been fast asleep in the comfortable carriage and everyone knew they had not to overwhelm him after his long journey. It had been a tranquil scene beneath the great oak beams of Millie's kitchen that evening. Davy, his young wife, Rosie, old Ned, the little tweeny maid and Annie had chatted contentedly, gathered as they were around the low fire, exchanging news and enjoying a light supper whilst Millie rocked gently to and fro in her chair. A lamp burned dimly, casting soft shadows across the

Child's Acre

copper and iron pots and other kitchen implements about the room. A candle flickered and guttered in its holder on the mantleshelf above the fire as Ben sat drowsily by the great warm hearth beside Millie. Still unable to absorb it all fully, Ben listened with awe to tales of a bygone age, revelling in silence at his happiness until the old voices faded to the edge of his consciousness and he fell into a deep sleep. The old man pushed another log among the sleeping embers of the fire, 'yon lad is well done in Davy me boy,' he said, as he pushed tobacco firmly down into the bowl of his pipe. Davy lifted Ben and began settling him comfortably on the makeshift bed. 'Another pot would be nice, Annie, if you're not goin' abed yet.' Annie sought Millie's approval for the hour was growing late. 'Go on then, get us all a nightcap, not yourself, mind, it's to be buttermilk for you gel,' Millie said sternly, as Annie lifted the kettle from the hearth and placed in on the hob. Whilst Annie set about making tea the new log on the fire began to sing, the sweet smelling sap rising and bubbling upon its surface, as Millie stared contentedly into the flickering amber flames. She had her little chick back under her wing at last. She would make him a lovely good breakfast on the morrow, then give him light chores to make him feel important and needed.

Resting in her darkened room, weary and emotionally drained, her thoughts returned to the present, but despite her deep tiredness she waited impatiently for daybreak, wanting only to have the household breakfasts attended to that she may sit awhile with Annie and Ben. Once again she joined her hands in yet another attempt to pray. 'Forgive me, dear Lord,' she whispered, if I'm a mite too happy to talk to you this night, but you've give me me dearest wish an' I can't get him out of me mind…but I knows you understand.' Quietly in prayer, blissfully happy, a dreamless slumber overcame the old lady.

The following morning Ben awoke early and was saying a prayer for the children at the waifs' home as Annie crept silently into the kitchen. A few moments later Millie bustled in, the old lady was at her best in the early mornings, but on this particular morning she almost had a spring in her step. She began mixing flour and fat in a big bowl, her brilliant smile a joy to Ben's heart, whilst the tweeny maid cleaned up the hearth after lighting a bright fire in the range. 'The fire will get going quickly this morning Millie,' said the young tweeny, 'the embers were still red and hot.'

'Good gel, now you be off upstairs and see to your work.' All through this exchange Annie had been busily fetching things for Millie, her long brown skirts swishing as she dashed hither and thither. Ben, watching the busy early morning scene knew a great sense of happiness. He rose quickly and began folding his blanket and eiderdown, placing them neatly at the foot of the pallet bed when Davy lifted the latch on the back door, Ben heard his foot steps outside in the little narrow passageway which led to the kitchen from the stableyard. Hearing muffled noises from the floors above, as the servants began their preparations for the day, Ben was overcome with a sudden feeling of excitement and wonder combined with strong sense of belonging

Millie turned to her young charge, 'come now Ben, sit by the fire a minute and eat this up,' she said, pushing a thick chunk of bread spread with beef dripping fat into his hands. 'You be off with Davy now Benjie and start your chores, Davy will show you what to do. Work well now me lad,' she told him, still bustling about noisily, 'do yer work well and we'll 'ave a good breakfast ready at 'alf past eight, time'll soon go, away with you now.' Ben swallowed a last mouthful of bread with the scrumptious dripping and hurriedly followed Davy out with a none too gentle tousling of his hair from Millie's roughened hands.

'I'll work well Millie, you see if I don't,' he called, as he trotted beside Davy across the cobbled yard to the stables. It was still only six o-clock but Ben was wide awake and as bright as a button on Barkworth's uniform. He was one singularly happy little boy, he had work, food, a place to live with kind people around him, but best of all he had Millie back again. There was so much to take in, he tried hard to listen attentively to Davy but was totally mesmerised by his new environment. The stables were warm and roomy, and as the smell of hay mingled with the early morning mist drifting through the stable doors the atmosphere was intoxicating. Ben, in a world of wonder, knew he would delight in taking care of the horses and keeping the stables bright and clean.

Davy and his wife, Rosie, lived above the stables in the old footman's quarters. They comprised two large rooms plus a smaller scullery with a wide, shallow sink, a copper and a small scrubbed board table. Adjoining the scullery was a tiny washroom with washstand, jug and bowl and small wooden bench. The accommodation was adequate and housed them comfortably… for the moment.

Davy and Rosie were a devoted couple entirely happy with their lot. The only blight on their blue horizon was the fact that they were still childless after fifteen years of marriage. However, they were still young, well…not old, Davy would frequently say when his pretty wife became despondent; there was still time, lots of time. Rosie worked in the home farm dairy and was very happy taking care of the butter churning, and had become quite practised and knowledgeable in the art of cheese making in small quantities. She also attended to the milking with the help of a young dairymaid. The early morning milking in the warm cow byres was one of Rosie's favourite tasks. In fact, for domestic workers, Davy and Rosie were most fortunate. They were well educated, in a practical sense if not the academic, and well informed on matters of importance. Davy's father was Major Domo at the Manor House, an enviable position indeed and Davy took great pride in his father's status. To be engaged as Major Domo with a large establishment of the aristocracy required a vast knowledge of the multitudinous rules of the codes of behaviour, an impeccable character and a natural gentility and bearing.

As an outside worker Davy was an unusually valuable servant. Not only was he well informed with regard to the horses, the heavy breeds for farm work and the finer breeds for carriage work, but also possessed an extensive knowledge on all aspects of house management, whether practical or financial. Davy would often sit with his father for a quiet hour in the evening and, whilst they did not discuss manor house business, for that would be disloyal and could only be attributed to lack of integrity, Barkworth taught Davy all that he knew. With regard to his work as valet to the old Master and the etiquette of the day, this Davy learned as a child at his father's knee.

* * *

Ben wielded the big heavy shovel and cleared away the used straw as Davy had shown him. Mucking out the stables was to become one of his favourite tasks as he learned to take pride in the way he kept the stalls.

Davy was very pleased to have received instructions from squire John that the 'waif' should make himself useful at the stables in the early hours. He was to work with Davy, muck out and fetch the feed leaving Davy free to give his time to the young squire's latest acquisition, a fine Arabian stallion, which was to be given exclusive attention. After these early morning tasks Davy could do what the devil he wanted with the boy who, after all, was only here in the first place to appease his meddlesome brother James for a while. But, thought John, he'll earn his keep, by God he will.

On Ben's first day the young squire visited the stables to take his latest treasure on an early morning ride. It was well understood by anyone having anything at all to do with the equine world that the Arab breed could be temperamental, to say the least, and certainly require expert handling.

Kara Sheikh was indeed a proud and beautiful animal with exquisite lines and noble stance. Davy deemed it a great privilege that this fine stallion should be entrusted to his care. Of course, he loved all of the horses and had a natural connection with each one of them. Old Ned had passed on a wealth of knowledge of the animal kingdom to Davy. Alas, not all that Ned knew could be imparted to another for he was an old man and his skills largely depended upon an inbred feeling for animals that few people possessed, but Ned had long ago sensed something in Davy.

Ben was ushered into the far stall and told to keep out of the way whilst the squire was at the stables.

'That boy is to go nowhere near Arab's stall, man, do you hear?' John snapped arrogantly. 'Mucking out and feeding, perhaps he can rub down and groom the carriage horses in time but he is to go nowhere near the Stallion.'

Very well sir John, I'll attend to it, and if I might say so sir, the Arab is a fine animal, you must be a proud owner indeed sir.'

'He'll do,' replied John abruptly, 'have him ready in half an hour, bring him outside and tether him at the block.' Sir John issued his instructions in a superior and surly manner. The young Squire always spoke this way when dealing with his servants. Consequently he became disliked and ill thought of almost immediately, his superiority as the Squire of Woodstock Manor had become all consuming; he treated his people with utter disregard and his animals little better.

Davy finished tacking up Kara Sheik, soothing him all the while. A little later John expertly leapt upon the animal's back and, slipping the rein between his fingers he yanked on the bit spitefully, determined to show this proud beast who was master. The horse whinnied shrilly and reared up, throwing his head back to loosen the bit. John squeezed his knees into Kara's sides and the animal reared again in a futile attempt to unseat his rider. Laughing to hide his anger John dug in his heels and called, 'trot on, trot on, you brute, try to throw me would you, we'll see about that.' As the heels of John's boots dug into the horse's smooth flanks the Arab reared once more and took off, straight into a gallop, his hooves flying across the stableyard taking the five-bar gates in his stride. Davy watched as the beautiful, spirited stallion leaped the high hedge with ease and grace, his fluid motion a positive joy to observe. Unaware of Ben's presence he was surprised to hear a small voice enquire, 'what do we do now, Davy?'

'Quite right lad, we must get on. Come with me now, I'll show you the tack room and after we've cleared up and scrubbed the stableyard what say we go have breakfast, eh?'

Ben had known suffering, poverty and heartache to a great extent for one so young. He often thought of Tom and the others at the waifs' home. He worried about them constantly and felt very guilty about his good fortune, for he was truly a lucky boy to have been returned to Millie and the kind people he now began to remember from his early years. One might say that Ben's trials were at last at an end, for he had found a real home with work in service and would live happily ever after with the people who loved him. But this young boy was still a child with no mother, still a child who, born out of wedlock, had no name. Born on the wrong side of the blanket, some would say,

for Ben was, and always would be, illegitimate, a bastard.

James often thought about Ben, as did Millie and Mistress Hall. The boy had not a penny to his name and had no known family except a young aunt, his mother's sister who, by this time could be almost anywhere. It had been nine years since she left Woodstock and was doubtless married by now. What young woman would own to having an illegitimate nephew? An orphan at that, especially if she hoped to marry.

Davy and Ben began their task of scrubbing down the stableyard and Davy found himself in high spirits at the prospect of having young Ben around on a permanent basis. He was as fond of Ben as ever and it did his heart a power of good to see the way Rosie had cheered during the few short hours since the boy's return. Ben stopped sweeping away the water with the big yard broom and hailed Rosie as he caught site of her wheeling along an empty milk churn outside the dairy. Rosie called hello, smiling happily and returned to her task of wheeling the heavy churn. 'I like your Rosie, she's nice, all round and pretty,' said Ben, cheerily.

'I like her too Ben, very much.' Davy laughed at his own understatement. 'Come now Ben, we must get on, I'm hungry. I'll show you how we finish off the work, it must be done thoroughly, I'm very particular about my yard.'

'Aw, Davy, I can scrub and clean as good as anyone, you see if I can't.' Davy resisted the temptation to smile.'

Ema Fields

'ave I done alright though? I love the 'orses, don't you? We never 'ad 'orses at the 'ome, do you fink they like me, Davy? I fink they do.'

'Whoa there me lad, one question at a time, now let me see. Have you done well? I think you've done very well. Do I love the horses? Oh, yes, I surely do Ben…and then what? Oh yes, do I think they like you. Well, lad, the answer to that is simple, animals know who like them and who is kind to them, they understand that for themselves and, yes Ben, they like you fine, and now, young sir, I think it's time you learned to speak properly, that is, correctly.'

'But you don't always talk properly. Sorry, Davy,' Ben looked ashamed, 'I didn't mean to crit criti…'

'Criticise,' supplied Davy, with his broad smile. 'I know you didn't mean to criticise. But you see lad, I can speak perfectly well anytime I wish, sometimes, however, I do not feel it necessary. In fact Ben,' Davy continued to explain to the bemused child, 'sometimes it is better to fit in with those about you. At others, however, it is important to be able to speak correctly, be like a sort of, chameleon.'

'What's a chameleon, Davy?'

'Why, it's a creature that can adapt to a changing environment, it can change its colour to fit in with it's surroundings.'

Ben's eyes widened with incredulity. 'And can you do that, Davy?' he exclaimed in wonder.

Davy laughed raucously, 'no, no Ben, what I mean is, we must all know how to speak properly.'

'And you don't speak properly all the time because then you wouldn't fit, would you, like the cam, cam,' Ben screwed up his face searching for the word.

'Chameleon,' Davy prompted.

'Yes, like the chameleon.'

'That's right lad, now, hand me that switch, the thick one.' Ben handed Davy the stout bessom broom made up from strong thin branches. 'Who learned you to talk proper, Davy.? I think it sounds ever so nice, but I still like yer when yer's ordinary best.'

'Ha ha, you see Ben, you like ordinary Davy better because he fits in with yourself. Now you have already learned the lesson, and the answer to your question is, my father taught me all that I know about our wonderful language and how to use it to best advantage.'

'I can speak alright, Davy, because Mercy, at the home, well, she taught me a lot about talking proper...properly, she said its important, like you, but when I get excited I forget all about it, but I don't know very much, really. Will you learn me Davy?'

'Teach, Ben, the word is "teach", and yes, I most certainly will. Now then, how about breakfast, I'm fair starving.'

'I'm fair starving too, Davy.' Ben took the broom from Davy and placed it against the stable wall.

'Come then lad, let's go see what delights Millie has found for us this morning, something very special I have no doubt.' Davy gave Ben a friendly shove behind the head. Side by side they made their way to the kitchen, Davy matching his long stride to that of the small boy. Ben's first morning was almost half over.

A light breeze blew through the kitchen as Ben pushed open the door. Old Ned was already at the table, hands outstretched towards the range where the fire burned brightly alongside the ovens; a homely scene. It was customary for Mistress Hall to take breakfast in her quarters and as the housemaids breakfasted before the outside staff there was no necessity to hurry the morning meal. Millie slipped thick slices of fried ham onto the plates whilst Annie served eggs from the skillet, there was a large basket of bread in the centre of the table with a bowl of dripping alongside. Millie, having finished serving, began her usual diatribe of complaints about Rosie and her little helper being late, they were invariably last to arrive at the breakfast table. The men chatted about one thing and another, Annie asked Davy if he would want more eggs and had he noticed if Rosie was on her way. Rosie had always been a straggler, could never manage to be there when she should and after taking her to task on many occasions Millie had simply given up. She would say, 'well, my gel, if yer can't be 'ere when my good food's ready yer'll just have to see to yersel' and the little un, I can't keep up and down, up and down.' There had always been quite a turnover of the young girls who came along to help Rosie in the dairy, Millie was often heard saying "and what's this one's name, I'm sure I can't remember them from one month to the next." The current little dairymaid was Maisie, there had been one or two Maisies but Millie referred to them all as Rosie's little helpers.

As the small company sat chattering and laughing Ned dragged out a stool for Ben who was standing at the range watching Millie. 'Come on lad' the old man said, in his pleasant country way, 'sit you 'ere by old Ned.' Ben

Ema Fields

sat down and gave the old man a bewitching smile to hide his nervousness. 'That's it lad,' Ned continued, sit this end by me, you look chilled, e'en though it's a rare grand morning. Get some of this good breakfast down yer, that'll sort yer.' The old man showed a keen interest in Ben's morning and the boy happily told him all, relaxing a little as he spoke.

It was a lively kitchen, as always, and Millie did not miss the look in Ben's eyes, for they were almost popping out of his head, as he gazed at the large slices of fried ham. The aroma of the food almost sent him dizzy; he was transfixed. Looking covetously at the good smelling bread he sat in silence, desperate to remember his manners and wait until offered. Ned and Davy, still absorbed in conversation about local affairs, reached for the bread and eagerly tucked into their food. Ben watched, anxious and uncertain.

'Come on lad,' the old man spoke with his mouth half full, pointing his fork at Ben's plate, 'get your food now whilst young Annie fetches yer eggs, tuck in there's plenty more, first and best meal of the day, breakfast, and a long day ahead too, nothing more certain.

Millie drew a large dish of warmed oatcakes from the oven, placed them on the table and sat down. Adding her encouragement to Ned's, she said, 'come on me Benjie, eat 'earty now.'

Ben, without answering, smiled at Millie and plunged his fork into the ham with one hand whilst reaching for a slice of bread with the other as Annie served him two lovely fresh eggs. Millie, ostensibly enjoying her meal, watched Ben as he ate, gratified at the amount of food the boy was managing to consume, and so quickly.

As Ben finished his ham, eggs and three thick slices of bread and dripping he was handed a large tempting oatcake which he simply could not refuse, especially after the first glorious taste.

Breakfast over, Rosie went up to her quarters to attend to her own chores before returning to the dairy with little Maisie trotting along beside her. Ned and Davy lingered a while at the table, Millie sat in her rocker enjoying a restful cup of tea after her mornings work whilst Annie began to clear away.

Ben, fully engrossed with the remains of the food and afraid that the oatcakes may soon be cleared away, drew a long, deep sigh and asked in a small voice, 'can I have another oat cake please, Millie?'

'O' course yer can lovey, 'elp yersel', you's a working lad now, you don't 'ave to ask at Millie's table.'

'Ta Millie,' Ben answered proudly. Millie gave him a reproving look.

'I mean, thank you Millie, thank you,' he smiled, corrected.

'And I should think so too, ta indeed,' said the old lady with a twinkle in her eye.

As Ben reached for the dish of dripping and another tantalising oatcake he thought, Millie must know about chameleons too. Then, spreading the flapjack liberally with beef dripping all thoughts of chameleons were banished. Millie looked on in amazement murmuring, 'my word, you've seen it all now Millie gel, dripping on me oatcakes.'

Ned and Davy exchanged an amused look. They enjoyed the half hour relaxation in the kitchen after breakfast, a concession Millie had long ago permitted to evolve. Ned would fill his worn, ancient pipe as he sat by the range. Davy would stretch out his long legs and enjoy another mug of tea, Annie would potter about putting things to rights and Millie would rock in her chair, appreciating the company and the short rest, it was always the same; until this morning.

Davy stretched out his hands towards the fire, a habit he had whatever the weather, whatever the season. 'You'll get chilblains Davy, you see if you don't. I'm always telling yer aint I?'

'Yes Millie,' Davy sighed resignedly, rubbing his hands. 'You're always telling me an' I aint got 'em yet 'ave I now,' he mimicked Millie's voice, 'an you can't get chilblains in the summer.'

Millie was about to snap a haughty reply when she gasped, 'oh my Lord a mercy,' as she struggled awkwardly in an attempt to rise quickly from her chair, 'just look at me Benjie, Davy, Davy, quick.'

Davy, startled at Millie's alarm, was at her side in one swift stride. He helped her to her feet and turned to see young Ben, the reason for her distress, head down on the tabletop, grubby little hand still clutching the oatcake... and sound asleep. Davy laughed loudly and looked tenderly at the sleeping Ben slumped across the table. Millie shook Ben gently, but the sleeping child was oblivious to all. She tried again, shaking him and calling his name; Ben slept on.

'I can't wake 'im Davy, look 'ere,' she said, shakily, 'I can't wake 'im. Come on lad, come on me Benjie, wake up for ol' Millie now.' Tears streamed down her cheeks, but it was no use, Ben was long past hearing anyone.

'It's alright Millie, he's alright, sit down now, no need to fret,' Davy attempted to reassure her, but true enough, Ben could not be wakened.

Millie felt panic rising within her, her face began to contort with anguish. 'Davy, what is it, what's a matter wiv 'im.' She spoke in a whisper, imploring Davy to make things right. Davy tried hard to hide his own increasing alarm.

Ned knocked out his pipe onto the hearth and brushed the ash across the bricks then, straightening slowly, he turned to Millie, 'come now gel, you knows better than that, you knows there aint nothing gonna wake our lad 'ere 'til 'e's good an' ready.'

Millie responded to Ned's quiet confidence and unruffled manner. 'Thass not just a nap 'e's 'aving, Millie old gel, 'e's fair knocked out, seen it many a time afore, 'e's undernourished, eyes bigger'n 'is belly thass all. Half starved, tired, been working, got warm, stuffed 'imsel', now an 'earthquake wont wake 'im 'til 'e's slept it orf. Come on me lad,' Ned made to lift Ben up.

'No, Ned, give 'im 'ere, I'll take 'im,' Davy insisted. As he spoke Davy lifted Ben and smiled, of course Ned was right, Ben was sleeping soundly, and that was all, nonetheless, he sighed deeply and remained thoughtful.

Millie, feeling much better now after her shock, wiped a tear from her eye with the corner of her apron. 'Look at me poor lamb, he's been fair starved, 'e 'as.' She brushed away further offending tears and swallowed hard, turning her back to the men to hide her distress, her sadness and her anger. 'It's a wonder 'e's still 'ere,' she said, as she plumped up the cushions on her rocking chair. 'Lay 'im down 'ere in me chair, Davy, 'e can sleep whilst me and Annie get on.' Stroking Ben's head she smiled and whispered, 'sleep it off Benjie, 'cause you'll not go 'ungry again, not while Millie's got life in 'er ol' bones, you wont.' She drew a woollen shawl across Ben whilst Annie, stealing about on tiptoe, continued to clear the table.

'No need to creep around gel, aint nothing gonna wake master Benjie for a while and that's a fact.

Ned and Davy returned to their work, Millie and Annie clattered about getting on with the business of the day; Ben slept on.

* * *

The next few months passed very happily for Ben. Sir John had made no connection between the new stable boy and the young child that old Sir John had refused to have under his roof. For the greater part of the working week Ben learned to take care of the stables and horses. He found the work tiring but exceedingly rewarding. Mornings he would lift and clear the wet and soiled bedding replacing it with fresh golden straw, which he would shake about until it reached a certain depth. He would then swill out the water troughs, clean the feed buckets and fill the mangers with sweet smelling hay. Afternoons he did whatever Davy required of him. Perhaps help clean the leather and polish the brass on the great work benches in the well-ordered tack room. Apart from the stables the tack room was Ben's favourite place. He loved the redolent smell of oil upon leather, the smell of the mixture used to clean the brasses and the easy way Davy applied himself to making the huge saddles gleam before replacing them on their rack on the walls. The last Saturday of each month was his favourite day. On these Saturdays Ben would help Davy with the heavy scrubbing of the stables' floors and walls, if necessary, and together they would work companionably until their work was done. When the stables were ready Ben would proudly and happily bring in his charges to the newly scrubbed, warm and dry, sweet smelling stalls.

Ben also proved to be a Godsend in the kitchens. He took charge of most of the carrying and lifting for Millie, who found it increasingly more difficult to bend without pain. He kept the woodpile replenished, fetched and carried and generally made life much happier for Millie and Annie. As the long and beautiful summer waned and winter drew nigh Annie became susceptible to coughs and colds. She desperately hated the cold weather and as Ben took over her outdoor chores she was extremely grateful. It seemed that the entire small world of Woodstock Manor loved Ben and he, in turn, loved his home and family for indeed, over the past months, old Ned, Davy and Rose, little Maisie, Annie, Hollie, Barkworth and, most of all, his beloved Millie, had certainly become his family.

Chapter Thirteen

Ben had spent five very happy years at the manor and was now, at the age of fourteen, tall, strong and pleasantly spoken, with all the promise of becoming a very handsome and knowledgeable young man. He thought often of his dear friend, Tom, with whom he had spent his younger years at the waifs' home. Tom had been lame, not too noticeably so, except in extreme temperatures of heat or cold. At such times his wasted leg ached badly and it was only at these times that he showed a pronounced limp. On this warm, bright summer morning Ben was much quieter than usual. As he watched Millie serve breakfast he was silent. He was thinking, yet again, of Tom and how they had vowed always to be friends and never to forget each other. Had he been guilty of forgetting Tom? This question weighed heavily on his young mind. Millie was quick to sense Ben's withdrawal from the morning chatter and his apparent lack of appetite.

'Something on yer mind Benjie?' Millie asked, seemingly unconcerned.

Ben remained silent, his bottom lip pressed against the upper. He shrugged in answer.

'Whassa matter then, 'taint nothin' I can't 'elp wiv, that's for certain, said Ned, as nonchalantly as Millie.

Behind Ben's back Millie gave Ned a gentle knock on the side of his head. The old man looked up as Millie pressed her forefinger to her lips and bade him listen to her.

'What's up then lad,' she asked, again in her unperturbed way, 'spit it out then.'

Ned was watching Ben, he could understand the reason for Millie's concern, it was clear that the boy was greatly troubled.

'It's…er…oh, I um, I just,' but Ben could not formulate his thoughts, for who would understand his sadness at having left Tom and the little ones, at having so much himself whilst knowing of their plight. Ben did not regard himself as a homeless orphan working for his meals, with a temporary roof and little else. He saw himself as a very lucky young man with work, with friends and with a family he loved; Ben saw himself as rich. Who would understand him? He remained silent.

Ned pushed aside his almost finished breakfast and studied Ben, saying, 'now lad, you got troubles, well let's 'ear 'em, thass what us old uns are 'ere for, aint it Millie gel? You can't grow old without growing wise, wisdom of years is the only thing us old uns is good for, might as well 'ave the benefit lad, if I aint good for nothin' else I'm good for showing you the right road, so let's 'ave it boy. He joined his arthritic hands and placed them on the table, his weathered face was tired. Ben had never really looked at Ned until now. He was a very old man, must be in his fifties, which was very old to a young boy, but Ben loved him. Sitting across the table from Ned, Ben looked even more sorrowful as he took the mug of tea that Millie held out to him.

Ben knew he must answer them, these old people were worried about him and they loved him. He took a deep breath, eyes cast downwards. 'It's…Tom,' he faltered. 'You may think I'm soft or something, but since the time that we sent Davy with that great parcel I've not heard anything more. It's been nearly four years now, I've been here five years. Sometimes I can't believe that I've let so much time go by. But Suffolk is so far away, might as well be another country it's so far.' Ben did not look up, Millie and Ned glanced knowingly at each other but remained silent. Ned drew on his pipe and Ben reluctantly continued. 'Tom is about my age, you see, I don't suppose he's still at the waifs' home, you can't stay there forever and who will take a lame boy? He could be roaming the streets searching for shelter, or out in the fields looking for work and somewhere to sleep. The little girls would have gone into service, especially Molly, she was so pretty, and the boys usually get someone, but not Tom.' Ben looked up then, not troubling to hide from Millie the pain in those expressive blue eyes. 'Oh Millie,' he began, emotionally, 'when I think of that place I still have nightmares sometimes, I can't bear to think of it, honestly.' As was typical when anything was troubling Ben, once started, he spoke without reserve. 'Tom isn't like other boys, Ned,' he explained, turning to look at the old man, 'he's lame,' Ben repeated, longing for understanding. 'Here am I, with everything a body could hope for, while Tom…' tears began to threaten, his throat hurt and, moving his head from side to side to ease his pain he continued. 'I suppose I'm not such a man, really. He brushed away the girlish tears and went on. Tom's parents died with the lung fever when he was young. He used to tell me he missed his ma more than anything, but he missed his pa something shocking too. Sometimes, he cried so much that I cried too, and we cried together. Ben's voice lowered as his mind went back into the past. Millie turned to busy herself at the stove but Ned remained, silent and motionless, listening intently, never taking his eyes from Ben.

Ben smiled weakly at Ned, 'I used to look after him when I could, Ned. I think I was a bit younger than Tom but I looked after him, I tried to look after all of them, they didn't have an auntie Mary to come back for them. Of course, that was before I came back to you and Millie. Then I thought I only had Mary, but they didn't have anyone. Tom will never have a family like I have.' Ben looked pleadingly at the old man and, rubbing at his wet cheeks, said, 'that's why I've been worried lately, do you see, about Tom?'

Ned was acutely aware that Ben was a boy with deep feeling and concern for others. He had always been into mischief, true, always in some trouble or other, headstrong some would say, but very sensitive and his formative years in the waifs' home had taught him humility and compassion. Ben thought only of others and his empathetic nature was, at this moment, proving to be a heavy burden. 'I see your problem, Ben, 'tis not an easy one, sure it aint. You're not old enough to do anything much about it yersel', but with help... well, who knows?' Ben looked intently at the old man who had become so dear to him and his eyes begged Ned to continue. 'You see lad,' Ned shifted on his chair and re-lit his pipe, 'your friend Tom is too old now to be still at the home, he'll no doubt have found work somewhere. He may not even be in the Suffolk area, might have moved on by now. We can try to track 'im down lad, might be possible if 'e stayed around Suffolk. Don't be getting too 'opeful now, just see what the good Lord's got in mind, eh lad?.

Ben did look hopeful, 'do you really think he has left the home, Ned, really?' He urged Ned to reassure him.

Ned drew on his pipe and exhaled, 'certain of it lad,' he said, confidently.

'Then could we ask Davy to ask around if he knows anyone who knows someone from that part of the country. Perhaps Holly could talk to the shopkeepers, they might have kin in Suffolk, they all know lots of people.'

Millie had composed herself, listening to Ben she had been overcome with distress, she stopped clattering about and interrupted excitedly, 'goodness knows what gossip we'll 'ear in the village, why the things they tells me, 'taint 'ardly believable taint, why, only the other day…'

'Yes, yes old gel,' Ned cut her off, not wanting the subject of village gossip to drag on in a lengthy monologue. 'If we once puts our minds to it we can do anything,' he said with conviction.

Ben grabbed both Ned's hands in his own and said excitedly, 'you are a wonder Ned, why didn't I talk to you before? I felt so helpless, every time I tried to eat I felt ill. I must go find Davy,' he called as he opened the kitchen door, 'he's going to Mucking market this very afternoon, bless you Ned.' Ben spoke so rapidly Millie began to laugh as he continued, 'oh, Millie, can Annie go find Holly please, tell her what to do?' Ben was about to disappear when Ned halted his steps. 'Now then, young un, not so quick,' he said, 'this could take some time, lad, there's no telling where your Tom might be, even with us all pulling together it could take a long time.

Ben knew that Ned was right, of course, he was also well aware that the kind old man was concerned that he, Ben, would become despondent and anxious should the search prove fruitless.

'Don't worry Ned, I'll be doing something now, I don't feel so helpless or selfish, you understand, just to know that Tom isn't in the waifs' home makes me feel so much better, I didn't think of that. Then, speaking brightly and with conviction Ben said, 'no matter how long it takes Ned, I'll find him, I know that now and I can wait if needs be.' His bright smile had returned and his confidence was an inspiration in itself. Ned turned to Millie, 'guilt ol' gel,' he said, wistfully, misplaced guilt in a lad so young is cruel, the worst cross to carry is guilt an' it don't belong on is shoulders gel.' Ned raised himself from his seat and the quiet smile on his careworn face gave Millie great strength.

'Ned, you don't…you don't think he might be in a poor house do yer?' After all, 'e aint likely to get work is he now. I'd 'ate to think of Ben's Tom in the workhouse, them's terrible places.'

'Oh, I don't know gel,' said Ned, evenly, 'it's mainly the old, and the sick and really 'elpless that goes in them places, you knows that, you'd 'ave to be starving with no place to stay. They don't even get out, well, they can go out gel, but with them terrible uniforms people'd rather stop in for the shame of it.'

Ema Fields

'I knows all about that,' Millie agreed, 'but I've 'eard tell the food is terrible and those great big places are always overcrowded, an' anyone who can work has to work frightful 'ard. I wouldn't like to think of the boy in a workhouse. I knows they take orphans too, poor little lambs, an' Ben's Tom is an orphan.'

'Now then you daft ol' woman, you've always got to 'ave something to fret about,' Ned spoke in a practical manner. 'We wont say nothing about the workhouse to Ben, but we'll get someone to ask in the nearest one to the waif's 'ome. Still, if you asks me gel, I'd wager he's on the streets, and better for it. Now then, go find Annie.'

Millie returned Ned's smile, their eyes held in that long remembered affectionate and reassuring way, 'don't fret ol' son,' she said. As she left the kitchen in search of Annie she glanced back at her long time friend and ally, his lips were pressed together in the old familiar way when deep in thought and, slowly nodding his head, he murmured absently, ' lame boy, about fifteen years.'

And so it was that word went out and a network of farm workers, shopkeepers, travellers and contacts far and wide were asked to search for Tom, a fifteen year old boy with a lame leg.

Chapter Fourteen

As THE PASSENGER COACH ROLLED away from the Stage on the first leg of the long journey south Mary waved furiously. It was only moments later that she lost sight of Caroline and her mother through the streaming tears she could no longer hold back. The coach swept around the bend in the wide road and Mary's dearest and only friend was now out of sight and, Mary thought, almost certainly out of her life.

Leaning back in her seat Mary attempted to console herself with thoughts of Caroline's promise. Her promise, given wholeheartedly, that she would make the journey, however distant, to visit one day when Mary and Ben were settled in their new life together. But would she? Could she? Yes, yes of course, was Mary's answer to her own sad doubts but now, she thought determinedly, she must look to the future. She bathed her eyes with a fine lace handkerchief, a present from Caroline, and thought of Ben, remembering her promise to him all those years ago. Why had she allowed so much time to pass, so much precious time, a faint smile spread across her sad face and the kindly old gentleman seated opposite found the sight of a lovely young woman smiling through her tears somewhat incongruous.

'Things change,' said the perceptive gentleman, quietly addressing Mary, 'all through our lives things are constantly changing. One era ends, a new era begins.'

Mary dabbed at her cheeks with the delicate lace. 'I am certain you are quite right sir,' she answered, attempting a weak smile, 'and the new life on which I am now embarking is a time I have dreamed of for more than half of my life, but goodbyes are such very sad affairs.' She stopped speaking abruptly, raised her handkerchief once again and choked on a sob. 'Oh dear, I really must take a hold of myself,' she whispered. Then, looking at the gentleman, said touchingly, 'this is supposed to be such a happy time for me.'

The conflicting emotions of sadness at parting from Caroline and the indescribable joy of going home to find Ben had tired Mary immensely. She rested her head against the soft padding of the coach, her last words to baby Ben, screamed from the window of the carriage as she was torn away from him, echoing in her mind. "I'll be back for you baby, I'll come back to you Benjie...' Fourteen years ago, Ben was now a young man of fourteen, does he even know who I am, she wondered dolefully.

On waking Mary felt refreshed and in much happier spirits. Two other passengers were to join the coach at the next stage but, for the moment, she and the older gentleman were alone and chatted amiably. Her earlier distress having passed she began to feel alive with excitement and anticipation. Reassured by thoughts of all that she had learned and achieved during her long stay at The Grange, happiness radiated from her. She was now a young woman, educated and accomplished and quite befitted to the task of making a home for herself and her sister Sara's child. Millie will have kept him close, she thought, hopefully, or will at least know of his whereabouts. He would doubtless be earning his living somewhere, but that would all change soon, for Mary would see to his education and ensure that he secured a good apprenticeship somewhere, with a fair master. Surely fourteen was not too old to find an apprenticeship. Her thoughts ambled on, Ben would be one of the more fortunate boys, for whatever he may have endured in the past, and she dreaded to think of the blows life may have dealt him, a child alone, he would be taken care of now. Silently reminiscing about the past she remembered the tragic time of her parents' death. The two young girls left alone to fend for themselves, "go on the parish" or starve, as was the plight of so many in those days.

On reflection many things became clear to Mary now. She had been singularly fortunate because of the kind doctor Alex. How could she have been so ungrateful as to spend a whole year bemoaning her plight at being sent to those wonderful people at The Grange. Praying silently she thanked God for the way in which he had taken care of her and, in so doing, prepared her well for the task of keeping her promises to Sara and Baby Benjie. Yes, she thought, with pride and confidence, I will keep my promises now.

The coach slowed to a halt at the next stage of the journey, a small hostelry where the horses would be fed and rested before continuing to the over-night stop. Mary's food for the journey was simple fare, prepared and baked at 5.30 that morning by a dedicated cook who was most insistent upon sending "the dear wee lassie" on her way with good, nourishing food. Mary and the older gentleman shared a delicious meal of newly baked bread, creamy cheese from the dairy and a small haggis, of which Mary was not terribly fond but fully expected to find in her small hamper. There were also two small earthenware dishes, one of preserve made from seasonal berries and one of cold vanilla sauce, a ham pie and an apple pie, which were Mary's favourites. After their meal and a leisurely walk around the immediate countryside they returned to the inn to refresh themselves before going on with their journey.

Mary learned that the older gentleman was Nathan Bane, born and raised in the north of England. Nathan was travelling south to his brother's farm where he hoped to be of use in return for his brother's relentless persuasion that Nathan spend his retirement years back home. Nathan, now unable to continue working, saw no avenue open to him other than to accept his younger brother's generosity. He had not wished to do this, had always been an independent soul and had his reservations about such an arrangement. Nonetheless he was grateful to his brother, he needed somewhere to go, albeit with great reluctance and doubts as to the wisdom of his decision, a decision which had taken him many months to arrive at. So it was that Mary began to know Nathan, she felt a kind of kinship between them. Felt that her circumstances were not entirely unlike his own, with the exception that for Mary this was a joyous occasion, for she too was travelling home, to a new home and, come what may, she knew that she would be with Ben, and nothing else mattered.

The two other passengers boarded the coach but kept very much to themselves. A middle-aged couple, a doctor and his wife. The lady smiled politely, passed the time of day and settled comfortably. The rather distinguished looking doctor was very attentive to his attractive wife whose fair, slightly greying hair was worn elegantly swept up beneath a high fashion hat. Their smiles for each other told Mary that they were a very devoted couple. How nice, she thought, to have such pleasant travelling companions.

The horses hooves struck the ground once more, a comforting sound for Mary as she thought, I'll soon be with you Benjie. It was a peaceful time as, slowly turning out of the narrow lane, she settled happily to savour the remainder of the first day of her journey. Later they would approach a bridge and once across, Nathan explained, it would be no more than an hour to the

Ema Fields

English border and their overnight stop. A blustery wind began to whistle around the carriage but the storm of the previous night had passed and the sun shone brightly. The passengers were settled comfortably with shawls and wraps of varying descriptions and the coach trundled on. The doctor's wife, resting against her husband's shoulder, smiled demurely at Mary, who acknowledged the lady's unspoken words as she closed her own eyes. Entirely oblivious of the worsening weather conditions, with the sun still warm against her cheek and the wind crooning a lullaby accompanied by the rolling of the carriage wheels, Mary let drowsiness claim her and was soon fast asleep.

Only the driver was aware of the unexpected, slightly worsening weather. As the sky darkened and the wind sharpened his anxiety began to grow. It was still quite a way to the overnight stage, but they would soon be at the bridge and, once across he would make good time to the overnight stop. Having reassured himself of the widely acclaimed hospitality of the northern English folk he drew his cape tightly about him and with a gentle crack of the whip eased the team into a faster pace, taking care not to cause alarm to his passengers.

The weather continued to worsen, the road could soon become awash with mud. The driver was forced to slow the horses to a trot, progress would be hindered but safety was the all important factor. He knew he would find neither a bed for his passengers nor feed and shelter for his animals this side of the bridge for they had come too far. Once over the bridge there would be food and shelter aplenty. The anxious driver estimated their arrival at the bridge to be another half an hour or so at this pace, not long. He regretted continuing the journey, should have been more aware of the signs, should have remained at the inn but, in all fairness to himself, he had to admit the morning had been bright and mild with no sign of the storm of the previous night. 'Och, away wi' ye man,' he said loudly, 'since when has a wee bit wind and rain bothered ye, Tammy Mac?' With renewed assurance he called loudly 'come on me surefooted laddies, 'twill soon be time to tak' yon bridge.'

The storm appeared to gather momentum and as Mary grew ever more anxious, remembering another storm long years ago, fear gripped at her heart. She glanced uncertainly at Nathan, now sitting beside her, a question in her anxious eyes. 'I don't like storms, Nathan,' she said, almost tearfully.

Nathan, though concerned for quite some time had said nothing. He now smiled broadly, saying in his lovely geordie accent, 'ha way bairn, this is never a storm, why, I could tell ye tales of storms that would make your hair stand on end. This is just a squall, gel, about right for time of year, and if my judgement is anything at all, I'd say this is just the last blow of last night's storm. Aye bairn, there's not much this ol' lad don't know about contrary Scottish weather.'

Mary gave him a small smile, feeling a little better, though by no means convinced. 'You do not think it will grow any worse then?' she asked, fearfully.

'No bairn,' said Nathan, 'look ahead now, there's the bridge, we'll be back in your homeland before long now. Settle down, once into England no doubt you'll be feeling on top of the world. Wrap yesel' tightly now, it can be a bit bumpy on the bridge, nothing to worry about but get yesel' set in tightly.'

The old man glanced surreptitiously at the doctor who understood his concern. The Doctor's face was set grimly, the storm might abate, but it hadn't quietened yet, no doubt it would calm as suddenly as it had begun. He pulled the heavy wrap across his wife who was sleeping beside him. Both men knew that once across the bridge the journey would progress unhindered for the storm, though quite fierce, was nothing like the raging force of the previous night. They had seen worse, but it was growing ever more menacing out there. A short while later as they approached the bridge Mary sat up straight in her seat. She was very excited, she strained her eyes to peer through the windows but was unable to see clearly through the rain lashing against the panes.

'Look, Nathan, the bridge, I can see the bridge and I'm sure the rain is stopping, it is slowing, don't you think?' Relief overwhelmed her as she believed the rain was stopping. Her face was radiantly beautiful, eyes sparkling with excitement and her broad smile beamed with happiness registering her joy at her return to England. 'We're almost home,' she whispered to herself. 'I'm almost home.'

A few minutes later Tam MacIntyre raised his face upwards as his eyes scanned the sky. His passengers would have been heartened to see the relief that passed across his strained features as pale sunshine tried to beam through a break in the clouds now scudding across a lightening sky. Thankfully, the rain that had lashed at him not more than a few minutes earlier was now little more than a light shower. The wind, though lessening in strength now, would still be a force to be reckoned with once on the bridge, for even in mild weather the wind could always whip fiercely across the open river; but he knew his laddies were up to it. Tam called out to his horses, 'away now ma laddies, that ol' storm's given up, I'll find ye the warmest bed with the finest feed before evening's nigh, aye.'

Crooning softly to the tune of Scotland the Brave Tam's eyes were vigilant as he began to negotiate the muddy slope down to the bridge. He was an exceptional driver, experienced and able, the finest. Nursing the horses down the slope he spoke to them encouragingly, knowing all the while that his words were carried away on the wind. Tam urged the horses forward, expertly avoiding difficult patches on the uneven surface. As the wind tore at the horses' manes the murky grey water, much higher than usual, swirled and gushed beneath them. 'A wee bit slippery ma laddies, but nae real problem, he assured them.'

The crossing was uneventful, the rain had finally ceased and welcome sunlight warmed Tam's face as they approached the far side of the bridge. Mary thought she had never been so happy as she waited impatiently to hear the horses hooves trotting on to the overnight stage where she would leap from the coach and take her first steps on English soil, the first in fourteen years.

Nathan and the doctor were engaged in pleasant conversation, each greatly anticipating arrival at the hostelry, as one of the horses struck a damaged timber beneath him. The coach swerved violently as one of the lead horses went down, crashing against the weakened pylon and bringing his team-mate with down with him. Mary screamed in alarm, throwing herself across Nathan and clinging to him with all her strength. The driver fought valiantly and eventually brought the horses to their feet, but the two fine beasts were now lame and in agony as great shafts of wood struck at their forelegs. It all happened so quickly, before Nathan could gather his wits as to how to help the driver a wheel slipped beneath the edge of the bridge. Tam urged the horses forward as the coach swayed precariously on its uneven axles then, realising it was no use, he leaped from the coach in order to dislodge the wheel and enable the horses to pull the coach free. Alas, unassisted and without a seconds thought for his own safety, his shoulder barely touched the great wheel before more of the bridge opened up and crashed beneath him, hurling him into the dark surging waters below. It was instantaneous, the carriage lurched sidewards and as the bridge groaned a great gaping split cracked open the surface and part of the supports broke away causing a tremendous crashing of timber and iron. The doctor and his wife lie across the sloping floor of the coach. Nathan desperately tried to hold onto Mary as, screaming hysterically, she wrenched at the door handle. The vicious wind ripped the door from

Mary's grasp as she frantically fought to climb down from the coach. Then, with her beautiful auburn hair whipping at her face, her petticoats and cloak flailing in the wind, the last supporting structure beneath the coach gave way beneath them. That part of the bridge collapsed with such force that the carriage was torn from the shafts and Mary, seized by uncontrollable panic, slipped into unconsciousness as she was thrown from the coach just seconds before it plunged into the racing waters.

In what had seemed a lifetime, but was actually only a few mind shattering moments…driver gone, horses gone, carriage and passengers…gone.

Chapter Fifteen

EXACTLY ONE YEAR LATER, ON another of those glorious autumnal mornings when dappled sunlight shone its pale rays through the leafy branches of the trees and played on the shiny wet cobbles of the stable yard, Ben's daily routine of hard work, friendship and love of life was to be thrown into turmoil and his young world shattered. During the course of the past seven years Davy had always impressed upon Ben the importance of staying well away from the Master's horse, the beautiful Arabian stallion, Kara Shiek, known as Kara. For the most part Ben adhered to his instruction where this particular horse was concerned, visiting the stable only when it was absolutely safe. Kara was a beautiful, spirited animal who had taken to Ben at their first meeting when Ben was just a child of nine years. It had been love at first sight for both boy and stallion and Davy had been obliged to remind Ben on several occasions to stay away from Kara's stable. However, at such times when the Master was out of town Ben would go along with Davy to help groom and exercise the Arab whose affection had long been denied him. The haughty animal would always show excitement at seeing Ben. He would nudge Ben's hand whilst striking his hoof against the stable floor telling the boy that he was pleased to see him. Ben would stroke the noble head and talk to Kara in his own special way. Davy had often observed this uncanny closeness and could see no harm in letting them spend a little time together occasionally if circumstances permitted. This kindhearted concession proved to be a grave error of judgement on Davy's part. A mistake destined for dire consequences as the time to be found out, had Davy only used a little foresight, was inevitable.

Sir John had left the Manor in the large carriage earlier that morning. He was to visit a friend at Rye to spend at least a week indulging his latest whim, the purchase of a small sailing craft. There were several such vessels for sale and moored at Rye Harbour. As the carriage rolled along the great tree lined drive it seemed to Ben that the whole Manor breathed a long, deep sigh of relief. He knew that this morning was to be one of those rare and special mornings when he would go with Davy to spend an hour with his beloved Kara and he could scarcely wait. Ben knew that the stallion took as much delight in their rare and wonderful rides together as did himself. He kept the rides very short, just once around the meadow and back, though sorely tempted to go further, for these short rides were taken not only without permission, but without Davy's or Ned's knowledge. Ned had taught Ben to ride and to handle the horses. The young boy had displayed a surprising skill from the very beginning and seemed almost a kindred spirit where the horses were concerned. Requiring little schooling Ned found Ben a joy to instruct. He was a natural born rider, but neither Davy nor Ned had any suspicion that Ben had disobeyed their adamant instruction that never, under any circumstances, was Ben to ride, or even to mount, the Master's horse. After the three had enjoyed a successful and companionable morning at the stables Davy rode out to attend to business at Painters' Meadow and Ned returned to his cottage for his afternoon rest.

Ben ran directly to Kara's paddock, the horse trotted over and nuzzled him roughly. 'Steady old fellah, you'll have me over,' Ben laughed. He took hold of Kara's mane and gently patting his neck whispered, 'coming for a ride boy, yeah, coming for a ride, eh?' The stallion reared and whinnied and Ben ran him to the gate, he was almost ecstatic with joy, 'we're free today old fellah, old devil's gone to Rye.' Kara whinnied again and Ben had to restrain him in order to tack up. 'Yeah, you understand don't you boy, I really think you do.'

And so it was that returning to the Manor on that fated morning, just three hours after leaving for Rye, Sir John of Woodstock sat in his carriage suffused with rage. His anger knew no bounds as he watched horse and boy, moving as the wind with fluid grace as though each was part of the other, flying with total ease over the high hedges that Kara would often refuse at his own handling. His stallion, his magnificent, stubborn, headstrong Kara Sheik ridden by that waif, that worthless stable hand, that…that kitchen boy. The blood rushed to his head, he was crazy with anger. He reached for his cane

Ema Fields

and hammered on the wall of the coach screaming at the driver, 'the stables man, to the stables.'

As Ben expertly turned Kara towards the homeward straight and cantered him back, oblivious to everything but his own happiness, he did not see the Master's coach speed along the drive and head for the stable block. They had never been out further than the meadow before and Ben found the ride more exhilarating than ever. He saw Davy waving his arms frantically and shouting, but his voice could not be heard from this distance. Davy, Ben thought, you should be at Painters' Meadow. He saw old Ned trying to hurry to Davy's side. Ben could not understand, he only knew that something was terribly wrong. Millie was his first thought, had something happened to Millie. Instead of cantering Kara back Ben rose in the stirrups and urged him into a gallop. He felt the great surge of power beneath him when, as of one mind, the stallion responded to the urgency of Ben's command. At the final approach to the stables Ben was dumbstruck, his heart beat wildly, 'oh dear God,' he spoke the words aloud as he saw the Master's carriage and four screeching and whinnying to an abrupt halt. It was a terrifying sight. Davy's heart was racing, he was seized with fear as he ran to Ben and, dragging him from Kara's back, gasped in desperation, 'go Ben, go now, go anywhere, fly if you can but get gone. Ben would have gladly run like the wind but there was no time. No time to run, no time even to think.

Sir John leaped from the carriage as the horses snorted and shook their heads, straining against the tightened bits in their mouths. He stretched out his hand to the driver, growling slowly and menacingly, 'give it here.' The driver visibly paled, he sat speechless and afraid, he could not comprehend what his mind was trying to tell him. The sun shone, a gentle autumn breeze cooled the air, yet not a sound could be heard.

The stable yard was completely still, the world holding its breath, as Sir John, pointing to the long whip used to control the team of horses, screamed at the bewildered driver, 'give it here, I say.'

'But…my lord…' the driver stammered, as he looked in horror at the whip lying idle in his hands, 'you can't mean to…'

Sir John leaped up to the stupefied driver and dragged the whip from his hands. 'Get your belongings and get off my land' he seethed. He then turned to Ben and the terrified boy saw madness for the first time. Sheer madness in those black eyes, that purple face. The Squire breathed one heart stopping word, 'horsetheif.'

Davy's brain would not function, panic still surged through him, he could not think, he watched transfixed, struggling wildly for coherent thought. As split seconds moved slowly as though minutes he reached and grabbed Ben's arm, saying nothing, just holding fast his foolish little Benjie who stood head and shoulders above him.

'Put that animal in the paddock,' the Master almost spat the words at Davy, 'and tether him fast, I'm not done with you yet, mayhap you forget your responsibility to myself and to this house.'

Davy, thankful to have something to do but dreadfully afraid to leave Ben, reluctantly obeyed the Squire, he took Kara by the rein and led him away at a trot, anxious to return to Ben in the hope that something could be done. The coachman, Davy and old Ned knew well the penalty for horse stealing. Strictly speaking the magistrate should have been called but they were all aware that no punishment would be unacceptable for such a crime. Indeed, where a valuable animal like an Arabian stallion was concerned, the Master would be exonerated even if he thrashed Ben within an inch of his life, or worse.

Young Squire John was perfectly aware that Ben had merely taken the stallion for a morning ride and that stealing the Arab could not even have occurred to the boy. Ben had been guilty of no more than disobeying longstanding instructions, but it was all one to the young Squire who, in his present blinding rage would take the opportunity to flog the objectionable waif and, in the eyes of the county, even gain sympathy for it.

'Soooo,' the Squire drawled, his face still distorted with rage as he cracked the long whip across the yard. The very air was hushed, the sky darkened visibly, the song of the birds and the rustle of the leaves as they tumbled across the cobbles seemed to have no sound. Nothing could be heard on that beautiful morning.

Davy, flinching with shock at the crack of the whip and sickened with fear, made haste to return to the yard, his only thought being to thank God that the stable block was a little way from the house and Millie. He crossed to where Ben stood but lacked the strength to go through with this, even for Ben, especially for Ben. He glanced across at Ned, the old man stood firm, as motionless as a statue, his face unreadable.

The Squire's voice rang out into the silence, 'well, what have you to say for yourself, kitchen boy? Abuse the hand that feeds you, would you?' Another ear splitting crack of the whip.

Ben's face was ashen, his golden freckles standing out against his blanched skin. His legs were weakening, he prayed they would not fail him. He prayed with all his heart to live through this morning. Sir John drew the whip through his fingers, stroking it lovingly. 'Are you aware of the fate of horsethieves, boy? Well, are you?' he bellowed.

Ben swallowed hard, his mouth was completely dry, he fancied he could not hear so well, he licked his lips, tried to swallow again but there was no saliva. He tried to speak. 'It was his…his.' Ben's hesitantly croaked out the words, he coughed and began again. 'It was his morning exercise, Sir…my Lord,' he stammered and began to cough hard.

Ben had been troubled with a cough for the past few days and now, after the heat of the ride and with the cool breeze blowing across his face, the cough began to worsen. As Ben coughed Davy at last found his tongue. He knew nothing would stop this, he knew it was pure pleasure that drove the Master to this end but he had to try. Then, suddenly, miraculously, he had the answer and so intense was his relief that his body sagged as he exhaled a long breath. There was an alternative, an alternative he could live with, where was his mind that he did not think of it before.

Davy stepped forward without hesitation now and spoke decisively. 'Sir John, I fear you are mistaken my Lord. Quite understandable in the circumstances but, you see, I asked the boy to exercise the Arab. It was on my instructions Sir, I have an injury to my back, the boy took out the horse on my order. If you will punish anyone, if you will thrash anyone, it should be me, I disregarded your orders my Lord, not the boy.'

Standing straight and tall Ben could hardly believe his ears. His head was muzzy, he was paralysed with fear and his determination to stand strong for Ned and Davy was sapping what little strength he had left to him. He didn't hesitate for a moment.

'No, Sir,' Ben coughed and swallowed and coughed again, 'that is not true Sir, Davy did not tell me to take the exercise this morning, it was my decision Sir, for which I most humbly apologise, I was wrong to disobey Davy's instructions. It was I, my Lord, I did not ask permission for I knew that Davy would never grant it, I deeply regret that my actions have caused you such grave concern…Sir, my Lord.'

Davy shouted Ben to silence. 'Don't lie boy, don't lie for me,' he cut in sharply, clearly angry now. 'I was wrong, the responsibility lies with me, the punishment falls to me.'

Sir John glared at Davy, the latter knew that the Master had no love for him, or for anyone. He had a cruel streak and Davy thought, not for the first time, that the young Squire John was most certainly his father's son, but he'd take the old Squire any day.

'I'll deal with you later,' said the Squire, his voice full of contempt as he turned his black gaze on Davy. Then, turning to Ned he said mockingly, 'if you have no stomach for this old man I suggest you go busy yourself.' Ned remained standing on his bent old legs and, leaning on his stick, remained silent.

'As you will.' Sir John smiled his evil smile.

The coach driver, appalled at the scene he was about to witness and overwhelmed with pity for Ben, decided he must at least make an effort to prevent this flogging. Begging your pardon, my Lord,' he tentatively tried out his voice and, determined to continue, forced out the words with little conviction as to their usefulness. I do not presume to question your good judgement, my Lord…but…er, horse stealing is a very serious matter Sir.' At this moment the driver was almost as frightened as Ben, speaking as he was to a raving lunatic with a horsewhip in his hand. He continued bravely, 'do you not think 'twould be a greater justice to put him to the bench my Lord, 'tis prison for horse thieves, no less.

Davy realised that the coach driver was playing for time, Davy knew him well, but to take Ben to the constabulary would ensure a prison sentence for certain, what could be worse than that, it must be the flogging. Davy felt utter despair.

Sir John answered Ben's fervent apology as, excited by the boy's fear he caressed the whip, 'well boy, what do you say, eh?' Though still blinded with rage he was obviously relishing his task and was not about to give it up. 'Would you have me go to the law of the land and have you branded as a horsethief for the whole county to see, or will you take your punishment here and now…like a man?'

Ben was visibly shocked, the word "horsethief" hammering in his brain. What would Mary say, how could he tell her that he had been sentenced to prison for horse stealing. He had nothing to offer his mother's little sister but an unblemished character and his self-esteem; he valued these things above all else.

The master cracked the whip then raised it above his head. 'Well boy?' He bellowed.

Ema Fields

Ben flinched and gave one final plea, 'I'll be indebted to you my Lord, to take my dues now, I did wrong. He then prayed as he had never prayed before that his legs would hold him up. He tried to concentrate on the memory of the pain of the sunburn when he had been forced to work, blistered and bleeding under the relentless sun. He remembered thinking, all those summers ago, that nothing could be worse than the agonising pain of a sunburned back. He was a child then, now he is fifteen years old; a man. He began to tremble, murmuring 'dear Lord help me to bear the lash with dignity,' when the Master's voice shattered his thoughts.

'Turn around then kitchen boy, and take that rag off your back.'

Unwittingly the master had just given Ben the key to the courage and strength he needed to endure this lashing. "That rag" the Master had just referred to was the finest thing he had ever owned. Annie had sewn it for him during the evenings after a long day and Holly had beautifully embroidered his initial on the pocket. When Annie gave him the shirt he had promised to treasure it always for he so loved the people who had made it for him. Now Ben's fear turned to anger, an anger as yet unknown to him, never in his life had he hated anyone, not even ol' Hawkins, but he hated this man. Dear God how I hate him, Ben thought, and with this hatred came strength. It coursed through his veins like a power, the weakness had left him, he stood tall. Let him thrash me, let him flog me, my day will come, he told himself. Dear Lord forgive me, for I vow he will pay for calling Annie's shirt a rag. Unafraid, he slowly untied the cords of the treasured ill fitting garment and threw it to Davy giving him an almost imperceptible nod of reassurance, I'm alright, don't worry, was the message his eyes conveyed.

Davy caught the shirt and was about to vomit. He pressed the garment to his mouth and choked. The coach driver turned his horses away from the sickening scene and began to walk them slowly across the yard. Davy turned and, striding quickly towards the kitchens, dashed futile tears from his eyes. Old Ned had not stirred, immovable and silent as stone, his expression still unreadable, still devoid of emotion. Ben turned his back to the Squire, his eyes found Ned's and the last vestiges of dread vanished. He braced himself. With a deafening crack the whip tore through the air and the first lash went home. Ben felt the whip across his back and knew in that instant that no amount of sunburn could cause pain such as this. He lost his balance, struggled to straighten and vowed his spirit would not be broken. Standing squarely, fingernails almost piercing the palms of his hands, teeth clenched until his jaw was set like iron, he awaited the second lash. The Master's expression was that of utter and dangerous pleasure. 'Ride my stallion, would you,' he snarled, as the second lash curled through the air and met its target. This time Ben did not stagger but he winced and his lips pressed harder together until, as his face contorted in agony, silent tears flowed unchecked. All his being concentrated on staying upright, he did not hear Kara as he rounded in the paddock, rearing and neighing loudly as he fought against the rope that constrained him. With a resounding crack the third lash rent the air followed immediately by the fourth rendering Ben almost unconscious. With blurred vision his eyes sought Ned as he fought for control. The dim old eyes looked back and, showing no sign of surrender, the strength willed by that dear old man found Ben's heart. None of them was aware of Kara as he snorted and reared, pounding the ground with his hooves. The whip was about to strike again when Ned shifted for the first time. He leaned more heavily on his stick and, raising his eyes heavenward, prayed for intervention. 'Dear God in heaven stop this, grant an old man's wish and stop this madman.' Seconds later as the Master curled the whip in the air chaos broke out. The Arab stallion finally broke free and galloped across the paddock, leaping the high gate and turning directly towards the Master. Ned watched the enraged animal as, with ears flat to his head, he came streaking across the ground then, with hooves flying and nostrils flaring he mounted his attack on the Master just as Ben collapsed with relief, losing consciousness completely.

Sir John screamed at the animal as he raised the whip in a futile attempt at defending himself. Davy, hearing the commotion as he desperately awaited the end of the punishment, ran across to the stableyard to find Kara relentlessly continuing his assault. He made a perfunctory attempt to get near to the horse. The Master thrashed the whip but made no contact with the rearing animal and was, as yet, unharmed. He screamed at Davy, 'get that damned beast away from me or I'll flay you alive.' Davy continued to make a show of bringing the horse under control when, as the Master's attention was diverted, Kara's hooves struck him to the ground. Davy rushed at the stallion for the angry animal was within seconds of taking the life of the Master. In that split second Davy wanted to do nothing, just let Sir John be pounded to death, yes, that was what he wanted, but sanity prevailed. Davy had both arms held high before the furious animal and danced about in front of him shouting, 'back, back,' then louder and with purpose 'back now Sheik, back I say, back. The horse began to respond to the command and with great relief Davy gently

Ema Fields

reassured him as he tentatively reached for the headcollar. 'Whished now, there's a boy, there's a boy, there's my lad.' Davy made every attempt to calm the horse that for so long he had lovingly called The Sheik. He needed Ned but knew that the old man was stooped over Ben so, with all his strength and love and powers of persuasion, he coaxed the rearing horse to stand. Kara continued to shake his head and whinny but as Davy stroked his flank and whispered close to his ear the animal began to clam. Davy did not so much as look at the still form of Sir John, but turned instead to Ned who nodded affirmatively and, in answer to the question in the younger man's eyes, said, 'go on lad, be about your work, our boy's gonna do well enough, I'll see to 'im, you see to the Arab.' Old Ned's eyes spoke a thousand words as he looked at Davy and said 'tend him well.'

By this time Barkworth had appeared on the scene and was helping his Master. He knew well what had been happening and instructed Annie that on no account was Millie to go outside. Sir John had taken powerful kicks from Kara's front hooves and was being helped to his feet when his eyes focussed on Ned and the housekeeper as they attended to the boy who lie motionless on the ground.

Dazed and confused the Master yelled, 'leave him be, leave him I say,' as he staggered upright throwing off Barkworth's hand. Holly looked directly at the Squire, 'if you will forgive me, my Lord, we had best not leave him, he may well die here, it may not be wise for the boy to die whilst on the Manor property.'

Still enraged and in a great deal of pain Sir John spoke incoherently, 'just get him off my land, do you hear, my word is law here, he'll have no attention from this house, throw him off.' His words were slurred and came in short bursts, he was holding his head, the world swam about him. Ned remained silent but Holly assured the Master that she would take responsibility for having his instructions carried out. Her words went unheard.

Barkworth caught his Master as he turned and stumbled and with an arm around the injured man assisted him into the house. Ned watched until the two had almost reached the door to the main house then said, 'now Holly, go fetch Davy, he had to see to the Sheik but he'll be settled alright now. Tell Davy to bring the small cart, we've got to get the lad over to the hay barn.'

'But Ned, the hay barn, he'll take cold, we can't, he'll need nursing, look at the weals on his back' said Holly, agitatedly.

'Do as I say, Mistress, he cannot go into the house, too dangerous, get Davy, fetch the cart, don't dally now, be gone.'

Holly ran off to meet Davy as he was closing Kara's stable door. She relayed the recent happenings and Ned's instructions. Within five minutes Davy and Mistress Hall were helping a dazed Ben to his feet and pressing him onto the cart. He could not walk, such was his weakness and his pain, and they certainly could not carry him. Eternally thankful that his ordeal was over Ben was allowed to rest for a short while before he must find a vestige of strength to climb the ladder to the loft in the barn. Now, shivering violently, his body in shock, it was difficult to know how to keep him warm without exacerbating the injury to his back. He began to cough and asked why he was to go up to the hayloft. Ned told him that all would be explained on the morrow but, just for now, he must trust old Ned. Ben looked at the resolute old man, 'thanks Ned, thanks for waiting by me, it was easier with you there.' Then, almost with a whisper the weakened youngster said 'I'll go up to the loft, Ned, but not if I'll bring trouble upon you, any of you.'

'No trouble lad, it will be easier to tend your back without Millie getting over fretful, I'll explain everything in time, now you must climb up lad, Davy'll help you.

Four days later a watery, early sunlight spread through the mist and filtered through the cracks in the shutters of the dusty loft. Ned moved stiffly, his old bones creaking with the cold. He looked at Ben who was lying much too still, his breathing shallow and, placing a hand on his forehead, tidied the covers around him. 'No fever now, but no improvement yet,' Ned murmured beneath his breath.

For the past four days Ben had refused the food that had been especially prepared for him and yesterday it had been impossible to get him to take even a few spoonsful of broth; he was growing weaker. Ned sat on an old milking stool by Ben's bed. He was bitter and perplexed as his thoughts recounted events of the past few days. Men had been thrashed before and as thrashings go it could have been a lot worse. The Arab is getting older now, the young Master has had no real interest in him for years, he's kept only for stud, why then the flogging, and why was the boy not getting over it. The wounds, though still a way to go and angry looking, were healing well enough, the pain was certainly less now. He's sleeping too much, that's the wrong of it, Ned told himself. Sleep and rest are the medicine lad, anybody knows that, leastwise at first, to help nature with her healing, you see. Ned's thoughts continued as he wished he could get through to Ben. You should be getting a mite hungry now lad, and you must drink. You've got to get up, walk about. Speaking aloud now as he searched his pockets for his pipe, 'somethin' aint right boy, there's more to this than those weals on yer back. What you need boy is a reason to fight.' Ned made up his mind at that moment that he would somehow make contact with Master James. It was high time now and young James will know what to do. Nodding his head wistfully he pressed tobacco into the bowl of his pipe. 'That Mary gel,' he went on absently, 'that's who we need, aye, the young gel; a miracle.

There came a short gust of wind as Holly opened the door below, she had brought warm beef tea, fresh water and cloths to bathe Ben's back and more warming pans. Ned rose to take the basket from Holly as she climbed the ladder. 'I'm goin' t' try an' get 'im goin' this morning, 'olly gel. Too deep into that sleeping, I don't like it woman, I tell yer, I don't like it, we'll 'ave 'im up the morn.

During the past week with Millie sick, Davy away on Estate business, Barkworth and young Annie helping Holly with Millie's work and Emily, the latest little dairy maid, being fully occupied, it had fallen to Ned, with Holly's help whenever possible, to take care of Ben. Until Davy returned, Ben was well again and Millie back in her kitchen, the Manor House was struggling greatly with the absence of servants. Incredibly, in the short space of the four days since Ben's punishment, the old man and the housekeeper had reached a new understanding, which came about through their mutual concern and affection for Ben. The old retainer, come stablehand/veterinarian, no longer addressed the remote and snooty housekeeper with her formal title, Mistress Hall, she had become "Holly", a kind and caring woman as concerned for Ben as Ned was himself and a great comfort to the old man at this dreadful time. To Holly Ned was no longer the stableman, she now knew him for the wise and knowledgeable kindly old man that he was. A somewhat frail old gentleman now, who had demonstrated the wisdom of Soloman and the patience of Job when so very desperately needed, an old man whose heart, so it seemed, was bigger than the man himself. Ned had shown the stilted, self important housekeeper friendship, patience and kindness and had become a father figure to the misguided, lonely woman. Holly silently bemoaned all the wasted years that this dear old man had dwelt just a half acre from the house and she never even taking the trouble to speak, or to grant him greeting of any description on their rare meetings. Holly was ashamed of her behaviour, there had been no excuse, but it was her own loss, not Ned's. She felt an unfamiliar humility when in his presence and as they sat alongside Ben, quietly chatting over times gone by or in companionable silence, they reached a new understanding, and with that understanding came a new and abiding friendship.

Holly stepped onto the floor of the loft as Ned took from her the things she had brought. 'You have done all you can Ned,' she said, looking towards Ben as Ned placed the basket on the floor, 'here, let me bathe him this morning.'

At first, immediately after the flogging, Ned would permit none but himself to attend to the dressings. He was not envied his task and it was silently acknowledged that only Ned would have what it would take to dress the wounds. Now, as the welts began to heal, Holly would be able to take on more of the nursing. Ned thanked her and poured himself a mug of broth then, sipping the broth appreciatively, watched Holly as she began her work. Heartened to see that the wounds were healing and now looking much less angry she said. 'He should be able to get dressed before long Ned, if he would only try…oh Ben…Benjie.' The old man looked at Holly and nodded in agreement whilst she spoke to Ben telling him how things were needing his attention around the place and that Davy, Millie and Annie were lost without him. Ben slept on.

'Can you help me lift him Ned, we'll raise him and get him to drink something.'

'Aye gel, 'tis time to take the hard line, don't fret now.'

They raised him to a semi-upright position and pushed a bolster behind the pillows. Ben opened his eyes.'

Holly, determined not to show her relief and delight, said firmly, 'morning Ben, my, but you are a sleepy head, I've bathed your back and you are doing just fine. Time for you to freshen up for the day, then we'll see about some breakfast, just broth I think for now and we'll bring over a good meal later.' All Holly's attempts at normality came to nothing, Ben sighed and sank heavily down into the pillows. Turning his head away from the spoon that Holly held out to him he moved his lips stiffly but no sound came. With difficulty he tried again and whispered, 'not hungry, thank you Holly, so tired…too tired,' and almost before Ben had spoken these few barely audible words he had slipped back into sleep.

Ema Fields

***

Later that day, at about noon, Davy stared into his jug of ale at a tavern in the town. He had accompanied Matt, the stockman, and they were to spend the day at market hoping to conclude livestock transactions. It was restful in the small tavern with its low oak beamed ceiling and small mullioned windows that helped dull the noise and bustle of the market place. Outside the weather had turned sharply which was not uncommon for that time of year and, gratified by the comforting warmth of the fire as it sparked and flamed in the huge old grate, Davy began to relax. Peering through the haze of the smoky room, amidst the low hum of cheerful voices, he smiled to himself as his gaze fell upon three old men engrossed in conversation, chuckling at tales of the old days as they puffed lazily on their pipes. Matt returned to the table and took up his jug. Looking across at Davy he said, 'we'll get this bite to eat and best be about our business, it's getting busy again out there.' As Davy didn't answer Matt drew a long draft of ale before continuing. 'No sense worrying man, I knows you got the boy on your mind but yer can't do nothing this far away and that's a fact, come on, look alive, there's a right buxom beauty a coming with our food, and 'ere's the lad who can do them both justice, aye, I'll say.' Davy was quite aware that Matt was merely making a futile attempt at bringing him out of his misery. He felt a little ashamed, they were to be at market all day, he could at least make an effort to be cheerful, even if he could not enjoy the day as they always had on their many previous visits. He smiled at Matt and said, seriously, 'it's a real worry Matt, Ben was not doing well when we left, in just these few days you can see he's losing weight, and he's hardly awake. It'll take something to take my mind off him, that much is certain, and the old lady has taken it real bad…real bad. But you're right, we've business to see to, and Ben will be fine with Ned and Holly, I couldn't do anything, useless, I'm better here doing what I do best.'

'That's the spirit,' Matt replied brightly, 'you'll notice the difference when we get back, you see if you don't.' Smiling at the pretty young server he laughed aloud now as he forcibly attacked the steaming pie that was set before him.

Davy thanked the girl politely and disinterestedly began to break his bread. 'You know, Matt,' he said thoughtfully, if we could only find that little girl, well, she must be in her twenties now, but that would be the medicine, the only medicine that I can think of. You know, Ben's young aunt, Mary's

Child's Acre

her name, lovely child she was, just lovely, never should have been separated you know. Seriously Matt, I'm worried half witless.

Matt then reached for his ale and was just about to reassure his troubled friend once again when, thrusting his stool backwards Davy leaped up from the table knocking over his ale and calling out as he fought his way to the door, 'wait here for me Matt.'

Matt grabbed the little table as it almost toppled over and as his ale spilled onto his food he shouted, 'what the, Davy, have you gone mad, come back here for pity's sake, Davy! Matt was wiping his wet hands with his kerchief when the server came over to him, 'is anything amiss, sir, is the mister alright?'

Whilst Davy had been idly breaking the crusty new bread he saw a dirty, ragged boy stagger past the open doorway. A young boy, very thin, with matted dark hair hanging loosely about his shoulders. Davy sat there thinking, poor lad, there must be hundreds like him, poor little beggar, and with that limp as well. Suddenly the word "limp" screamed into his brain. A dirty ragged boy, with a limp. He thrust back his stool, made or the door and dashed after the boy. As he turned from the tavern the boy was still in sight, he didn't appear to be hurrying but on market days the streets were very crowded. Davy dodged along as fast as he could, there were many side alleys, the boy could turn down any one of them and disappear, for this was the main monthly market taking up many streets, little squares and pavements, where tradesmen plied their wares over every spare inch. He shouted, 'hey boy, hey you boy, stop, wait.' The boy turned, perplexed, was that stranger shouting at him? Davy waved and shouted again, 'wait boy, you, yes, you with the limp, please, please wait.' Davy's heart was racing, the boy heard him, the man was waving at him and shouting, he was really angry, what if he had recognised the boy as someone who had stolen from him. The boy was scared, he had to get away but his leg hurt, it always did in cold weather. He had been scouring the market hoping to get something to eat, people sometimes took pity on him, he didn't always have to steal. He knew he would not be able to outrun the man so, accustomed as he had become to thinking quickly, he decided to run for the church and take shelter there. But the man was close behind him, what if he didn't reach the church, he may well get another beating. He dodged in and out of the crowd, losing his balance and being cursed along the way, gasping as he fell, pulling himself up and leaning against the railings around the churchyard. Exhausted and breathless he dragged himself up the few steps to the church door. He turned his head and there was the man, just

Ema Fields

a few feet from the church, well, he couldn't run any further, he just couldn't, he would stay on the church steps, maybe a vicar would come and save him. His leg pained him severely, tears slipped down his dirt smudged face, he brushed them away.

Davy approached the church steps, 'I mean you no harm,' he panted, holding his chest. He studied the boy's appearance. Rather small, he thought, perhaps too small to be about seventeen, but there was no doubt about it, with his long, thin face and those dark eyes that now looked back at Davy, if the age was right, this dirty little ragamuffin fitted the description of the boy, Tom, perfectly. Davy's heart pounded, he must choose his words with care. Reason told him that any lame beggar boy would be thin, with sharpened features and sad eyes, but this was Tom, Davy knew from somewhere deep within himself that he had found Tom. Must ask the right questions, mustn't give anything away. The boy continued to stare with those dark frightened eyes.

'Wha'd'ya want, whatya starin' at me for mister, I aint done nuffink.' A London accent, thought Davy, I don't remember Ben telling me that Tom was from London. Oh, no, no, no, I haven't got it wrong, dear God tell me I haven't got it wrong. 'I'm sorry lad,' he spoke quietly, attempting to put the boy at ease. 'You've done nothing wrong, I...er, I thought I recognised you as someone I once knew, that's all.' Davy breathed deeply telling himself, think man think, what did Master James say, what did he say, oh yes, relief flooded through him as he knew what he must do. He gained a little time whilst formulating his next words, the boy remained silent and Davy continued. 'Seems I don't know you, but I'm sorry if my shouting alarmed you. Listen now, I've been looking for a young man you see, for quite some time, a lad about your age, he's a sort of distant relative, I thought if I could find him, well, he could come and work for me, on my farm. How old are you lad?'

'I'm sixteen mister, nearly seventeen though, well, nearly, honest I am, I know I don't look it 'cause I'm not very big.'

Davy sat down on the steps below the boy and smiled broadly now as he said, 'really, nearly seventeen eh, already a man. Well now lad, it seems to me that you wouldn't say no to regular work, eh? I don't have much, not a rich man, but I dare swear that doesn't matter to you now, does it?' The boy's eyes looked suspicious whilst at the same time revealing sheer disbelief. Havoc and chaos were all about them as Davy went on. 'How does, er, board and found sound to you, with a day off every month and a half day once a fortnight, you

Child's Acre

wont find me hard but you will have to work, and we'll talk about your wage later. Now, what's your name lad?'

The boy's eyes opened wide, now it was his turn to stare at the stranger.

'But you don't know me, mister, I could be a fief, or shiftless, or worse.'

Yes, lad, you could be any or all of those things, but if you're shiftless I'll send you packing with no wage and no supper and, as for stealing, well… you'll only steal from me once. So, what do you say?'

Total incredulity lit up the dark eyes, he must surely be dreaming. For years he had tried to find honest work with a roof to sleep under at night, even a barn or stable would have been real fine, just to have the right to be there. This fellah didn't understand, he was lame, his bad leg tired him and slowed him down, he couldn't work proper, but cor blimey Lord I'll try, he silently vowed.

Davy's eyes questioned the boy as he sat, transfixed, saying nothing. His thoughts ran away with him as he waited the boy to answer. He must know the truth, how can he be certain, he would not be able to fool Ben, not even in his sickness, neither would he wish to, but how could he be certain. Oh Lord have I got it wrong, what if I've got it wrong, please Lord don't tell me I've got it wrong, please, he prayed. Sensing the boy's distrust and noticing tears beginning to well up in his eyes Davy said, 'just a business proposition lad, what's your name, eh?'

The boy still didn't answer, he sniffed loudly, dragged his dirty cuff across his face and swallowed. 'You must have a name, eh?' encouraged Davy. Reason tormented him again, Tom, he must say Tom, he will say Tom, we are a long way from Woodstock and Suffolk, this boy probably has never heard of the search for the orphan Tom, if he says Tom, it is him. Davy could barely breath so great was his anxiety and his chest still pained him

'Sorry mister, it's just that…you reminded me of me bruvver for a minute, he was real kind an' all, see.'

Davy heard no more. The noises of the marketplace, the bleating of the lambs, the shrill squealing of the piglets as they were hoisted from the carts, the loud voices of the auctioneers, the raucous laughter of the farmers, the shouts of the piemen. All the noise and hubbub left his mind, he heard nothing but those shattering words "you reminded me of me bruvver; bruvver; bruvver." He felt cheated, devastated, this boy was not Tom, oh, but he had been so sure. It took all of Davy's will not to break down right there and then. He pressed his hand to his forehead, then dragged his fingers roughly through his hair, his expression was that of utter defeat. He had promised the boy work, given him hope, he would not take that hope away. The silence that ensued between them seemed endless. Thoroughly confused the boy spoke again, his words hushed and full of sadness, bringing Davy's full attention back to the present.

'O' course, he aint me real bruvver, just an orphan like me, but we said we'd always be bruvvers, as long as we lived, we said that, we made a promise.' The boy spoke so softly, so obvious was his sorrow that Davy barely heard him as he murmured 'me little bruvver.'

So overcome with emotion was Davy that he did not know whether he was laughing or crying. Tears swam in his eyes as he spoke one word, 'Tom.'

The boy dragged the heel of his hand across his nose, sniffed, then said, 'you know me name. 'ere mister, 'owd'ya know me name, 'oo are ya?'

Davy caught Tom's hands in both his own, his mind blinded by the words, be certain, be certain, be sure. Urgently, with excitement coursing through his trembling body, he gushed, 'where was the waifs' home, Tom?'

Staring at the stranger as though he had gone quite mad Tom made to back up onto a higher step as he answered, 'Suffolk, it was in Suffolk, 'ere mister, you sure you aint drunk or somink?'

Davy charged on 'and your brother, Tom, what is his name, please lad, his name, I'll explain everything, but this is so important,' Davy stressed.

'Benjie, mister, it was Ben.'

Carried away by his certainty Davy urged Tom to answer further questions, no longer afraid of the answers. 'Ben had a relative Tom, do you know the name, did Ben ever tell you?'

Tom began to laugh now, as the stranger's intention began to dawn he thought, this nutcase might know Ben, might know his whereabouts. Catching Davy's excitement he said eagerly, 'you must mean Mary, his auntie Mary, Mary and Millie, yeah, that's them, he only talked about those two, all the time 'e did.'

Davy was ecstatic, as he drew Tom up from the church steps the excited, bewildered boy seemed desperate, he trembled as he said, 'd'ya know where 'e is mister, me bruvver? If ya know where 'e is please tell us, I gotta get there.

Davy held Tom by the shoulders and, pressing firmly against the jutting bones he reassured the quaking, pitiful little figure. 'I've a great deal to tell you Tom, but it's a long story, first…we eat. We've been searching for you far

Child's Acre

and wide for the best part of two years, come now lad, take my arm.' Davy held out his arm as Tom hopped down the steps and leaned against him. 'Heaven has smiled on us all this day, Tom, but food first.

Borne along by excitement and wonder as they made their way hurriedly through the crowded market Tom's mind was whirling. ' 'oo is this stranger in farm workers getup? Will 'e truly give me work, and food and a bed?' I dunno, I don't care, 'e knows Ben, I can get to Ben, an' even if I don't get work I can show Ben 'ow to live on the streets, I can fieve for 'im, I can fieve for us alright.

Back at the tavern they ate heartily, Davy and Matt drinking a little more ale than was usual, as Davy told his story. Over a veritable feast of mutton stew followed by cheese and bread, Tom listened intently. Then, relaxing, his story told, Davy sat quietly watching Tom devour with relish his first good meal in a long time. Feeling as though his heart was close to bursting Davy raised his tankard to his lips and murmured 'I've found him, Ben, I've found your Tom.

The next morning a blanket of early mist covered the fields as Holly hastily crossed the yard to the barn. She had just greeted Ned and was about to speak to Ben when the sound of a cart rumbling along by the dairy reached her ears. Ned, also hearing the noise, looked enquiringly at Holly and simultaneously they crossed to the shutters of the loft. Holly leaned out through the opening wondering what could possibly bring such an early caller to the Manor. The driver of the small cart looked up, raising his hand.

'Just been sent here from round the back there,' he called, pointing backwards towards the kitchens. 'I've a message for a Mistress 'all, ma'am, is it here I will find her?'

Holly pushed the shutters open wider and leaned out further to see more clearly. 'I'm the one you seek sir, I'm Mistress Hall, I'll come along directly.'

Lowering herself onto the loft ladder she raised her face to Ned and said, anxiously, 'I'll be just a moment Ned, whatever can be amiss?' She hurried across the yard to the man on the cart, it was obvious to the stranger that the woman was distressed.

'Steady there mistress, no cause for alarm,' the man spoke sympathetically with a deep, rough but kind slow drawl. 'I've a message from a Davy Barkworth.'

'Yes, yes, go on, what is it?' said Holly, distractedly.

Ema Fields

'Well, ma'am, I come across him on the road aways back, 'bout ten miles or so, I reckon, Chelmsford way.'

'The message,' Holly cut in, urging him on impatiently.

'Well, ma'am, seems they 'ad a bit of 'ard luck, wheel came off, cart overturned on a bend.' Noting Holly's horrified look of alarm the man endeavoured to speak more quickly. 'Oh, they's alright ma'am, as I said, no cause for alarm, but they'll be late back, says to tell you as they's sent for wheelwright and don't expect them 'til the morrow.'

Holly, having no particular time at which to expect Davy and Matt to return, thought this message rather strange, and to send a man out of his way, well, that was indeed a needless thing to do. She attempted a weak smile as she answered, 'oh, dear, dear, that is indeed most unfortunate, thank you so much for taking the trouble to advise me, it is appreciated. Look, I'm afraid I'm not being very hospitable, but we are experiencing a difficult time at present, sickness, you understand, come to the kitchen and take some refreshment, 'tis a sharp morning.'

Holly was shivering quite violently as the messenger flicked the reins, saying, 'I thank ye ma'am but I should be getting on, hoping to get to Tilbury the day, good day to you

ma'am.

Holly drew her shawl more tightly about her and made to hurry back to the barn when the messenger called out, 'a moment ma'am, I almost forgot.' She turned and looked back, shielding her face against the chill wind.

'Your Davy, 'e says to be sure an' tell ye that 'e found Tom, good day again, ma'am.

'Tom?' Holly mouthed the word in sheer stupefaction then shouted, 'Tom, he found Tom, did you say? Oh, can it be?' She hurried to the cart as the horse began to clip clop out of the yard. 'Sir, a moment please. I understand your haste to be on your way but you must permit me to insist that you take a meal. Allow me to repay you in some small way for being the bearer of such wonderful news. Come now, I'll not take no for an answer, come and warm yourself by the kitchen fire.' Holly, hardly pausing for breath continued her verbal assault on the driver. 'There's a stable over there, a half an hour will matter not one way or another.' Still she went on, and still with the smile which transformed a plain, middle-aged woman to a beautiful warm creature. 'See that your horse is fed, there'll be feed and water, then come back here and wait for me.'

Not requiring an answer Holly turned, lifting her skirts high as she ran across to the barn.

'Ned, Ned,' she called, as she mounted the ladder.

'Lord a mercy, woman,' said Ned, quoting Millie's well used phrase as he helped Holly step up, 'what's amiss?'

Holly's face was alight, she drew in a deep breath, then gasped, almost laughing, 'they found him Ned, they found Tom, isn't it wonderful, 'tis just what we have needed, just what Ben needs, he has wanted to find that boy for so long, too long.

'Nay lass, don't ye be getting so hopeful now, could be a mistake.'

'No, Ned,' she exclaimed, 'Davy would take care to be certain. He sent the man especially out of his way to inform us. Ned, I must go, I must take the man to the kitchen, Davy is waiting for the wheelwright, a broken wheel, I'll explain later, they'll be delayed until the morrow.' Then, searching Ned's eyes for reassurance she said, 'it will be alright now Ned, he will get better now, surely, yes?'

Ned's expression was frank, his ever honest eyes told Holly what was truly on his mind. He realised that she was not as familiar with death and grief as he was, she had not lived his years, he felt such compassion for this woman, the woman that all had disliked for such a long time. He took her hand, saying, 'Holly, me gel, 'e's gonna be just fine, now get away and take Millie the good news, then get me a bite to stay mesel', I'll wait by the lad, go put them all out of their misery. Hollie hurried away.

Since Millie had first learned of Ben's foolhardiness and subsequent barbaric punishment she had taken sick. The old lady could not cope with shock, she was a tough woman who had known much hardship and worry but Ben's young life had also been fraught with suffering in his early years, and now this. Millie had feared for Ben for years, wasn't he always bringing trouble on himself somehow. Even as a tiny boy, although he had been scolded many times, he would always go against what was best for him. She remembered the time when he tried to climb the high stairs to the upper hall and was cruelly kicked down them by the old Master. The times Ben had told her that he had been caught stealing food at the waifs' home for the little ones when they were so hungry through the night that he could not bear their cries. Oh, Benjie, you've got a heart of gold, but why do you bring such grief to yourself. Millie, quite literally, could not bear it.

Ema Fields

Holly, Barkworth, Annie and Rosie had tried so hard to keep their manner bright, reassuring Millie that Ben would be fetching in the wood for the stove and getting under her feet again before she knew it. But Millie was not to be fooled, she knew how bad things were. Meals had not been up to standard in the kitchen, although nobody had really noticed. Millie spent many hours asleep in her chair as she grew steadily weaker and, for the first time in memory, left the running of the kitchens to Annie. It was Ned alone who had realised that as Ben grew weaker, incredibly, Millie also grew weaker. Millie had now taken to her bed and as Ben's young life was beginning to fade right before his eyes, the old woman also seemed to be letting go. It was almost as if there was an uncanny bond between the old lady and the young boy.

On this particular morning Annie was so desperately worried that she had urged Millie out of bed on some pretext of sitting by the fire and advising Annie.

Holly hurried into the kitchen bidding the messenger to be seated at the table, then smiling at Millie, watching her struggle to rouse herself from dozing by the fire, she said 'you should not be out of your bed Millie but, as you are, we have some wonderful news.' She spoke gently, quietly, as Millie straightened in her chair, 'Davy has found Tom, he is bringing the boy back, it is most certainly Tom, our troubles are surely over Millie, thank the Lord for his goodness.' Leaving Millie slightly bewildered with a question on her lips, Holly turned to Annie. 'Annie,' she said brightly, 'see that this gentleman received the finest hospitality this house can offer, your most excellent breakfast, Annie, then perhaps you will see that Millie takes something light, stand no nonsense now.' Indescribable relief washed over Holly as she took her leave. She turned hurriedly, her skirts swishing about her, 'oh, and Annie, I had almost forgotten,' she said, laughing now, 'a tray for Ned, I'll be back in a few minutes and I'll take it to him myself.'

'Yes, Mistress Hall,' called Annie through the closing door, and she turned to her work with wings on her feet.

'Found Tom?' said Millie, the question in her sad eyes speaking much clearer than her words.

Annie, dashing hither and thither, threw thick slices of ham into the pan on the range then, crossing the room she clasped Millie's hands excitedly in a desperate attempt to cheer her. 'Yer, Millie, an' when our Benjie sees his old mate from all those years ago, goodness, 'e'll be so 'appy that 'e'll be over 'ere to see us afore you can say Tom Fumb, now I gotta get the man 'is breakfast, there's so much to do.'

Annie was so happy, Ben would surely get well now, he just had to, this place would die without him. She sang as she worked, speedily and competently, and a brilliant smile lit up her face as she heard Millie call gruffly. 'You mind now gel, don't forget, never puts the eggs on afore yous done the black puddon, come on gel, my, if I didn't move a mite quicker 'an that we'd all starve, we would indeed.'

'So great was her joy at hearing Millie scold her that Annie all but flew across the kitchen and as she hugged Millie, tears of relief and happiness beginning to overwhelm her, that grand old lady whispered, 'fetch us a dish o' tea, gel, an' make it a good brew.'

Chapter Sixteen

NED SAT THOUGHTFULLY BY BEN'S side hoping that Davy and Matt would return soon with the boy, Tom. All the firmness and kindness Ned had mustered when caring for Ben had been to no avail. There Ben lay, consumed by shame and anguish, making no effort at all.

A cloud of anxiety and inactivity seemed to engulf the Manor House. In the kitchen only the scraping of Annie's knife as she cleaned and prepared vegetables disturbed the almost tangible silence. Impatiently Millie and Annie waited for the distant sound of horses hooves or the rumble of the wheels of the cart, as yet entirely oblivious to the quite astonishing day that lie ahead of them.

'That's them,' Annie exclaimed, throwing down her knife and hurrying to the door. 'It's them, Millie, they're here.'

Millie wrung her hands and closed her eyes, her heart skipping a beat at Annie's words. 'I knows you didn't bring the boy Tom 'ere for nothing Lord, make 'im well, Lord, make me little Benjie well, pray make him well.'

Annie dragged herself away from the doorway and returned to her task, chatting as she worked. In her now weakened state Millie breathlessly hauled herself out of her chair. She crossed to the big white sink and began to pump water into a large kettle, but swayed alarming as suddenly the room swam about her. Almost before she had time to grip the edge of the sink Annie was at her side. Allowing herself to be helped back to her chair she warned, 'steady old gel, steady, there's work to be done.'

Outside in the yard Holly hastened to meet Davy, Matt and the young boy just moments after their arrival. Ned left Ben and followed Holly with his usual unhurried gait. Leaping swiftly to the ground Davy acknowledged Holly with a smile and addressing Ned asked, 'how's our boy then, Ned?'

Ned felt he could not speak freely in the presence of Holly but his eyes gave Davy the answer to his question. What Ned actually said was, 'well, lad, he has a way to go yet, but he'll be very happy to see his old friend.' Then turning to Tom he said cheerily, 'let's get on up lad, a word with young Ben and then off to the kitchen for a good meal, eh, I expect you're all in need of it. Do ye think ye can manage the ladder up to the loft?'

Tom had been very subdued since the cart drove around the perimeter of the Manor and through the farm gate into the yard. These strange surroundings, the great house set in grand expansive grounds, the acres and acres of land stretching far into the distance, the obviously poor old man and plainly dressed woman. All the incongruities of the scene bewildered him. He felt sadly and wholeheartedly disappointed, for Tom truly did not believe that his Ben could be here, in such a place as this, he felt certain there had been a mistake, his spirit was crushed. However, in answer to the old man's question he said, 'course I can mister.' Tom was about to follow Ned into the barn when he turned and looked at Davy for permission.

'Go on up lad,' said Davy, with forced brightness. 'See what you can do for our Ben. I'll put this old girl in her stable and assure Millie that I'm still in one piece.' He climbed back onto the cart and Tom heard the gentle clip clopping of the mare's hooves echoing around the yard as she happily trotted towards the stable block.

Ned led the way to the loft and motioned Tom to sit beside Ben. Tom remained standing, he now knew that this man was not his Ben, this great lengthy youth. It had not occurred to him that Ben could have grown to be such a tall fellow, for in Tom's mind he hadn't changed, he knew Ben was about a year younger than himself and he couldn't be as big as that man lying there. He looked at Ned, uncertain, afraid. 'Blimey mister,' he said, shaking his head, 'that aint my Ben, is it? I fink it must be someone else, mind you, the 'air's the right colour.'

'Aye lad, this is yer Ben, you'll see when he turns 'round, wake him quiet like.' Tom's mouth was dry. Ned eased Ben into a position where he lay partly on his side, no longer face down on the ticking. Tom attempted to speak but his voice croaked. Overcome with emotion he looked at his dearest friend in amazement, he coughed, swallowed hard and again tried to speak.

Ema Fields

'Benjie, 'allo mate, it's me, Tom. Ben, you gonna say 'allo then?' No answer came from the still form, Ben did not stir. Tom looked to Ned for direction.

'Go on lad,' Ned encouraged, 'keep talking to 'im, just like that, give 'im a bit of a shake, easy now, quiet like, just keep talking.'

Tom went on, 'Ben, blimey, fancy seeing you 'ere, been a long time since the waifs' 'ome aint it mate? You remember ol' 'awkins, crikey I do. Ben, Benjie.' Tom fell silent as Ben began to stir. On hearing Tom's voice in the distance Ben's mind was back at the orphanage, his back was badly sunburned, he could feel the pain, but it wasn't as bad now. He called for Mercy, the helper at the orphanage.

'Mercy, is that you Mercy? Came the feeble reply.

'It's not Mercy, Ben, it's me, Tom.' As Tom sat awkwardly by Ben he knew that this great big chap was indeed his Benjie, his friend and brother, Ben. So great was the surge of love, pity, anger, Tom was rendered speechless.

'Tom? T...Tom?' Ben's words, spoken in a whisper, were confused, questioning.

Tom exhaled a long breath, 'yer mate, I'm 'ere.'

Ned motioned to Tom to assist him and together they raised Ben to a semi-upright position. Realisation began to dawn for Ben, he was not dreaming, or was he? He tried to think, am I asleep, was it all a dream, did I hear Tom, is Tom really here? Am I at the Manor, was I really flogged, disgraced, banished, branded a horsethief? Did I really just want to die? Is that Tom, did they find him? Ben's mind fought through the haze of tiredness and confusion as he slowly became fully awake. His mind began to clear, there was old Ned. He moved his head, took in a deep breath, then as his eyes met Tom's he stared in wonderment for, to Ben, his old friend looked almost exactly the same. Perhaps a little taller but the skinny, dirty, ragged waif, with the most beautiful face in the whole world, smiled down at him. Tom remained silent as, smiling, he grasped Ben's hand, the hand of the only person he could ever remember having loved, he didn't know much about love, he had loved little Emily, the kitchen maid at a house where he had worked for a short while. Yes, he had loved her, he thought he'd die when she became betrothed to the blacksmith's son, but this was a different kind of love, the love for his brother, his acknowledged brother, Ben. Tears filled his eyes once more as, joyfully, he began to laugh, tentative and uncertain though the laughter was. Then, blinking away the threatening tears, he whispered incredulously, 'Ben.'

Ben feebly attempted to raise a hand, he swallowed hard, never taking his eyes from Tom's face, gulping again he said, hoarsely, 'Tom, Tom, how did you get here, how did they find you?' His hand found the thin face and pressed Tom's cheek for just a moment, as if to dispel the fear that he could still be dreaming. Then, ruffling the dark, straggly hair he said weakly, in Tom's manner of speaking and with such a depth of feeling, 'good Gord Tom, it's real good to see yer, bruvver.'

The scene witnessed by Ned on that cold autumn morning was a scene rare indeed, he saw the love of one human being for another, and both of them young men, brothers could not have been closer.

Tom chatted on for a few moments longer. 'We'll 'ave a long talk later mate, I'll come back the night, we've got so much to talk abaht, cor, could I tell you a tale or two, fair make yer 'air curl it would, I can tell yer. But 'ave a bit of a doze now mate, yer look as if yer could do wiv it, yer look done in.'

Ben eyes sought Ned's as the old man sat by the shutters drawing on his pipe. 'He can stay 'til the morrow Ned?' His weary eyes were beseeching the old man to say yes. Ned could see that this reunion was taking its toll on the lad, he was too weak, just a few minutes had tired him considerably, but his spirit had been nourished, his spirit was alive and well, now, very soon, so too would be the body.

Ned answered, 'aye lad, your Tom don't be goin' nowhere, we've seen to things. Now, mind you just get some sleep,' real sleep, thought Ned, healing, restful sleep, 'and leave those to be doing as can be doing.'

'Thanks Ned. You know, I'm so tired, you'd never believe how tired I feel, but before you go back to work, do you think I could have a jug of tea from the kitchen?'

'A dish of beef tea'll do yer far better, lad, but Millie's tea it is then, for now.'

As Ned turned to warily tread the shaky ladder to the floor of the barn, Ben was already sleeping soundly.

''e looks pretty sick, don't 'e mister,' said Tom, anxiously, 'd'ya fink e'll be alright, what really 'appened to him mister?'

Ned, watching the rise and fall of Ben's chest and hearing his regular breathing, answered Tom in a thoughtful tone. 'I reckon, Tom lad, I reckon

Ema Fields

that from now on our lad is gonna do just fine. Still a prayer or two wouldn't go amiss just the same.'

Aint got no time for all that praying stuff, thought Tom, but did not think it kind to say so.

'Come on lad,' Ned motioned with his head for Tom to follow, 'let's get to the kitchen, our task will soon be over now, thank the Lord.'

They descended the ladder carefully, the lame young boy, the frail old man.

Tom's introduction to Woodstock Manor was certainly a most enlightening experience. Nothing of the like had ever happened to him before. The servants, it would appear, were a rare assortment of folk of all ages. The family type banter, the concern for each other, this is all a bit odd if yer ask me, Tom thought as he listened intently.

In the kitchen they discussed Ben most of the time. Millie, the old lady who appeared to have assumed the role of matriarch, fussed like an old mother hen with a brood of chicks. Calling out orders from an old rocking chair by the range, she readily, and unquestioningly, took Tom under her protective wing. Tom watched as Millie fussed over Ned, but the young man could understand that, for the old man looked exhausted, if Tom was any judge. Tom had walked into an entire sequence of events of which he knew nothing. It was like watching a stage play unfold before his eyes, but better than that, for the stage was real, and the players were real.

Before Tom could even begin to marvel at his new circumstances the kitchen door opened, everyone looked stunned, except Tom, for he had never seen the tall, immaculately dressed man standing in the doorway. Not a word was spoken. Tom wondered why everyone had gone so quiet. A stillness had fallen across the busy kitchen. Who's 'e? Thought Tom, Is 'e good? Is 'e bad? Why didn't someone say somefink.

It was the old woman who broke the silence. She rose from her chair, turned directly to the stranger, held open her arms and cried, 'oh Jamie, Jamie me boy, Master James, is it really you?' She wept openly and no force on earth could have stemmed the tide of tears that flowed down the drawn face at seeing young Master James. Master James, younger brother of the Squire of Woodstock Manor, placed an arm around the old woman's shoulders whilst Tom sat, wide-eyed and silent.

'Hush now Millie,' James soothed, 'hush now, I know all about it, everything will be alright. I'm home now, James is home.' He held her as she wept on, tears falling freely as she attempted in vain to apologise for her total lack of control. James' anger

knew no bounds as he watched this grand old lady weeping like a child, a thing unheard of in all of his years. He looked across the top of Millie's head as he gently guided her back to her chair. 'Summon Barkworth for me please, Annie, ask him to fetch brandy, then get some tea for Millie.' James' masterly tones startled Annie into movement.

'Yes sir, Master James,' said Annie, nervously, as she hurriedly ran out through the door.

Ned stood by Millie, his hand resting lightly on her shoulder as he attempted to comfort her. 'There, there old gel, hush now, 'twill be right now, don't fret so gel,' he took a seat by the fire.

James felt murderous towards his brother John who had wreaked such pain, such mental and physical anguish on these beloved old retainers of his mother's. Yes, at this moment, murderous was the only way to describe the feelings of the gentle, mild mannered, kind hearted James.

After seeing Millie supping her tea, Ned took the dish of strong black liquid that Annie handed him and stooped over the range to knock out the dottle of his pipe. He always took tea at the greatest strength Annie or Millie could produce. James smiled affectionately at the old man, thinking, there will be no more work for you, old man, you are one old workhorse who from this day will be put out to pasture. The remainder of your days will be spent in peace and security, rest and contentment, you'll want for nothing, this I swear. Then James spoke to Ned, 'get you off to your bed old man, I'll take over now.'

'With yer due respect Master Jamie, an' it's right good to see yer back, if I may say so lad, but there are…'

James spoke more firmly now, it was difficult to be firm but he must take control. 'Never you mind Ned, get off to your cottage, your fireside and your bed. Or am I no longer Master James of my father's house? Annie will fetch you a meal later, your task is done, and a rare grand job you did too, by all accounts our young Ben owes his life to you. Be off with you old man, and leave everything to those as can be doing,' he said, remembering old Ned's words from the past, the oh so distant past.

Millie, her weeping ceased, brushed away the small glass of brandy that Annie held before her and encouraged Ned to do as Master James directed, 'we're all in good hands now lad, off you go then, Benjie'll be well and Master James is home, away with you now.'

Ned's old bones creaked as he raised himself from the settle by the fire. He was suddenly overcome with an incredible weariness, his very soul cried out for rest, for peace and silence, for a mind free from worry, from the great responsibility he had carried this past week, was it truly only a week since all this sorry business began.

'I'll be off then Jamie, lad.' The term of familiarity did not pass unnoticed by anyone in the kitchen that morning. But to Ned, the man who stood before him with a look of deep concern in his eyes was his Jamie. The little lad whom he had scolded a thousand times for hanging around the stables. The little lad who had been admonished a thousand times for asking a million questions. Yes, Jamie, the Mistress' special little lad.

'There'll be no need to bother Annie with me dinner the day, I'll just put me ol' bones to bed with a bowl of Annie's broth that's waiting by me fire.'

Ned turned and slowly, gratefully, left the kitchen, once more squeezing Millie's shoulder as he passed her. 'Be right now ol' gel, yer little lad's getting better an' yer big lad's back home.'

An old man, now mentally and physically exhausted, knew a lightness of heart that morning such as he could not recall having known before. He reached his cottage, it would be a bright new day the morrow, he looked forward to seeing Ben, for the boy would certainly gain strength now, his job was done, Jamie was home. Millie would get right now, she would have her chick back. The boy Tom would work out well, Ned had taken to him. The bent old man threw a log into the glowing embers of the fire that he had lighted at dawn that morning. He hung a kettle of water on the rail above as the log flickered into life. He would make a good pot of strong tea after he had rested. A small covered pot of broth sat on the hearth waiting to be warmed. He drew in a deep breath, his work was done, Jamie was home, his load had been lifted, he must give thanks. The old man was weary, bone weary.

So it was that, stretched out on his wooden bed beside the crackling fire waiting for the comforting sound of the kettle singing, a tired, beloved old man, on whom so much had depended, drifted into a joyful, peaceful sleep; a sleep from which he was never to awaken.

Back in the kitchen, James turned to Tom who was still mesmerised by this entirely new world. 'Well, now, you must be Tom, in the absence of any introduction I will assume to be correct. The household is in something of disarray this morning, I fear, but I have heard much about you from young Ben. Welcome to Woodstock, Tom, it has been no mean task finding you, I believe.'

Tom stood up somewhat cumbersomely, he had hardly understood a word this Lord was saying and was in a highly nervous state. Receiving no answer, James attempted to put Tom at ease.

'Well, Tom, are you a strong chap?'

'Oh, yer, Lord…I mean, yes sir, Lord.'

Although still very saddened and mutinously angry James had to summon all of his control not to collapse with laughter, he was, in fact, very close to losing the battle but Tom's discomfiture prevented him.

' "Master James" will do fine Tom. I'm Master James, my brother, Sir John, is the Squire, you will address him, should you have occasion to, as Sir John. Now then, that's settled I think, yes?'

'Yes, Lord, er, Master James, an' I'm strong an' all,' Tom lied, but oh, so convincingly.

'Well, Tom, that is indeed splendid, young Ben will be up and about again before very long, I do not doubt, but for the present you will assume his duties. I will speak to Davy, you will receive your instructions from him. I doubt we shall meet frequently, Tom, I am an exceedingly busy man and soon I expect there'll be not a moment to call my own. It is a pleasure to meet you, young sir, glad to have you with us.'

Tom remained silent, his mouth slightly agape, still overwhelmed by this tall, authoritative Lord for whom, incredibly, these people showed no fear. This is a strange place right enough, they all seemed to like each other, he thought for the umpteenth time since his arrival early that morning, and was to think at least umpteen times more during the weeks that followed.

James gave Millie a stern look, but the twinkle in his eyes belied his frown as he scolded her. 'Well now old woman, I'll have no nonsense from you, lest I put you out to grass, now away to your bed and take a rest.'

'Old woman, indeed,' retorted Millie in a shaky, somewhat uneven voice. 'I'll 'ave you know young Master James that I'm not ready yet to lay about and let others earn me bread. Oh no, you'll wait a long time afore that day dawns,' she parried, in mock haughty tones with the utmost indignation, 'but I will take a rest this day, yes, this day is one of God's good days.'

'That's my girl,' said James, smiling as he spoke. 'I'm away to see Ben, then to arrange for his removal to the house. Annie, a tray of tea and a light breakfast in the library in a short while, if you will.'

James arrived at the barn and swiftly mounted the rickety ladder. Holly was tidying the bare, dreary loft. She had swept and cleared as best she could with Ned's help, and had brought a bright patchwork quilt from her own rooms in a futile attempt to bring a little comfort to the place. There was a pot of tea on the big old box containing various old pieces of tack from the tackroom, alongside the tea was a basin of broth. Holly had hoped that if Ben had been wakeful he might take a little more sustenance. She turned her head as James appeared at the top of the ladder.

'Well, Holly,' he said cheerfully, 'how soon can this bright young lad be removed to more comfortable quarters, soon, I trust?'

Holly was greatly surprised to see Master James, she had known he had been contacted and informed of the troubles at the Manor, but did not know he had arrived back this morning. He surely had returned with all haste, she thought, as she struggled to regain her composure. She smiled hesitantly and drew back the quilt and white sheet that he may see the dreadful marks left by the whip. James was horrified, he crossed to Ben and, replacing the covers, sat alongside him. He took Ben's hand in his own and made to entwine his fingers through Ben's in an attempt at waking him gently. James was dumbstruck, he could not believe what he saw and groaned in shocked astonishment as he turned to look up at Holly. The woman's expression was serious as she said, meaningfully, 'you see Master James, the wounds are healing nicely, Ned has nursed him well.'

At length, noting Holly's direct gaze of understanding, James whispered hoarsely, 'who else knows?'

Fully comprehending his meaning Holly replied in hushed tones, 'Millie, naturally, who nursed him from an infant, myself…and of course Ned, who has been taking care of him, took charge from the beginning, but no other.

'You understand what a great shock this is, Holly?'

'Of course Master James,' was all she said.

'I need to think, Holly.' James spoke in bewilderment, he felt his legs would barely support him. Weak with pity and a combination of so many emotions and regrets nausea almost overcame him. He had been shaken to the core, as Holly knew he would be.

James pressed a hand to his forehead, saying, 'I, er...my brother, John, does he know?'

'No, Master James. Sir John is not aware that Ben was brought up here to be tended, it was a sad and regrettable deception. Ned would not hear of taking Ben to the house, he felt he must adhere to Sir John's orders, at least as far as was possible. He would not do other.'

'We must give thanks that these wounds are not even greater.' James shook his head slowly from side to side and, letting out a long breath, murmured with hardly a sound, 'what devil had possessed him.'

James then pushed himself upright and, appearing to assume command of this new situation said, 'Ben is to be moved to the house, Holly, he's to be put in the upstairs sun room, overlooking the meadow.'

Holly looked at James with ill concealed alarm in her eyes, 'the yellow room, Holly,' said James, with authority.

Holly nodded her assent as seemingly blindly James clambered down the ladder and crossed the yard to the house. A few minutes later he was in the library pouring himself a very unaccustomed, very large glass of brandy. Sitting by the great log fire, his long legs stretched out before him, James sipped the much appreciated spirit which somehow helped restore his ability to think and afforded him a modicum of calm.

A light knock on the door and Annie silently entered the room bearing a tray laden, on Millie's last minute instructions, with a not so light breakfast. Placing the tray on a side table she bobbed a curtsey and, closing the door behind her, just as silently left the room.

James eyed the delicious meal, albeit entirely disinterested now, and thought what an agreeable soul Annie was to have around. He pressed his palms against his forehead and sighed, as one tormented, 'what to do? Dear God, what do I do now?' In the tranquillity of the darkly panelled library his mind began to clear a little and he considered his options regarding Ben. He could remain silent, say absolutely nothing, for surely the loyalty of his mother's servants was entirely without question. The secret would remain a secret, for even Ben was ignorant of the fact. On the other hand, however, he could admit to the world that the waif, brought to the Manor soon after his birth, was in fact his very own brother. Born out of wedlock, true, the wrong side of the blanket some would say, but James' very own brother by blood, there is no room for doubt.

'It's all becoming clear to me now, Ben.' James said aloud, 'I always knew there was something about you. Something indefinable, yet so endearing, well...now I know, yes, now I know...all these years, and now I know.' James sat staring into the fire, inhaling deeply as he swirled the remainder of the brandy in the bottom of the glass. His thoughts roamed to his brother, John, and to his excesses. Excessive drinking and gambling and constant revelling. His idleness where Estate matters were concerned. It pained James to think of the Estate, his very own heritage, and now, perhaps Ben's also. He thought of John's tendency often to show cruelty and now cruelty in the extreme. He pondered on John's avaricious nature and other failings that James would rather not give thought to. In fact, James' brother John was a scoundrel of the highest order. John was so like their father that James no longer thought of him as a brother, but rather as an evil part of the family to be tolerated and dealt with as best as one could. But Ben, the boy Ben, how had he escaped such traits. Ben had such compassion, such unusual values in one so young, his love of animals and all nature's wild things. His love of the land, his honesty, except perhaps whilst at the orphanage. James smiled slowly as again he expressed his thoughts aloud. 'His folly, oh yes, for 'twas folly indeed to ride the Squire's horse. Oh Ben, Benjamin...what a dilemma you have set me this day.'

James continued staring into the fire, growing sleepy as his thoughts strayed to the past. To have such admirable qualities you will have come from honest folk Ben, good folk. Your young mother would have been a lovely girl, just like my own dear mother, but dead, dead because of my father and his lusting ways. It was with that thought James' decision was made. John would contest, of course, but he would be no match for James, not now. James thought again of his younger brother lying across the yard in the cold, dusty barn, beaten in mind, body and spirit. A half brother, true, which mattered nothing, for Ben was worth a thousand brothers such as John. Ben was also the indisputable son of an English nobleman. James reflected on his thoughts, scrambled as they were, when he first saw that the middle fingers on Ben's hand were joined together. Not necessarily a hereditary trait, he knew, but the mark of the family for centuries past and doubtless for centuries to come. James did not have the webbed fingers, not every family member did. But his father had, and his brother John's middle fingers on one hand and middle toes were joined. James did not know if this family peculiarity had a medical name, it had always been referred to as webbed fingers or toes. This trait was totally unnoticeable, fingers and toes were perfectly formed and the joining was totally imperceptible, thus had Ben's paternity gone unnoticed except to those very close to him.

A knock on the door interrupted James' thoughts. He bade the caller enter. Mistress Hall crossed the room and stood before him, making a brave attempt to control her acute distress as she made her apologies for the intrusion.

James rose immediately. 'Come Holly, be seated, do, and tell me what is the cause of such distress.'

Holly straightened her back and fought for composure. 'I have come directly to you, Master James, as I believe it to be the wisest thing,' she coughed, dabbed at her eyes and tried to continue, 'in the circumstances,' her breath then caught in her throat. James had never seen the competent, resolute housekeeper in distress, but these were trying times of late. He guided her to a chair beside the fire and, pressing her into it, bade her continue. 'Go on,' he coaxed.

'It is Ned, Master James.' Turning her head she dabbed again at her eyes and almost wept as she tried to continue. 'I called at his cottage on leaving the barn, I thought he might like a fresh pot of tea, he is, was…always so partial to,' Holly had said too much, she should have been brief and to the point as befitted her station. The tears flowed unchecked.

'And,' James encouraged gently.

'Well, Master James, he was still abed, you see, I thought he was sleeping at first.' Holly drew a sobbing breath but was gaining composure. 'He was a wonderful old gentleman Sir, a rare old soldier indeed, as soft as whey where his animals were concerned but as tough and as strong and as dependable as any rock when it was required of him.' James let her continue, 'I learned that, oh yes, I learned that during this past week, Master James. Please forgive my lack of restraint, but,' the tears flowed freely again, 'this is so ill timed.'

James pressed Holly's shoulder reassuringly but said nothing. He crossed the room to the heavy Georgian desk and brought down his fist with such force that the quills flew into the air and rolled onto the rug. Holly rose from the chair, smoothing her skirts. 'Have you any instructions Sir?'

'Holly', James turned to face her, a "little boy lost" look in his saddened eyes as he remembered days of his childhood with Ned, 'have you spoken to the others?'

'No, Sir, as I have said, I came to you directly.'

James stared vacantly. 'I had not even the time to tell him of the new cottage I was to build for him on Little Acre, did not even tell him.'

Holly understood the irony of James' words for Ned had always loved Little Acre more than any other part of the Manor lands. Little acre was where he tended all of his sick animals, a little plot of land, actually about three acres in size, which ran along beside a brook overhung with willows. A heavily planted area was Little Acre, full of old oaks, hawthorns, rambling roses and deteriorating dry stone walls, always rejected for farming because each generation in turn was loathe to take the plough to such a picturesque spot. James had intended to build two small cottages in this favourite place of his mother's, a cottage for Ned and another for Millie. Well, it was too late for Ned now, but not so for Millie.

Holly was beginning to cope a little better with the shock now. It had helped her enormously to be with young Master James at this time and she thought perhaps that it would not be too presumptuous of her to offer a few words of comfort. Hesitantly she said, 'if I may say, Master James, I came to know Ned very well during this past week or so, and do you know what I believe the old gentleman would be saying now, were we only able to hear him?'

James smiled a kindly smile, ready to accept any words of comfort the older woman had to offer. Holly continued 'he would say, "come on now lad, I've had a good life, an' a bit too long already, now there's things to be seeing to, the Estate to be run and work aplenty. Folk don't live forever lad, and I surely don't want to be the first."' James listened to Holly's words with great affection for old Ned, his eyes were smiling lovingly as she went on. 'He would say, "Be about your business and your tenants lad, the Manor, the Estate, it all depends on you now, they all depend on you, so don't be fretting about an ol' man who should 'ave met 'is maker long since, aye, and been thankful."' To James, hearing Holly speaking, or trying to, in Ned's rustic manner it was as though Ned himself were sending the words to him, yes, fanciful, he knew. '"See to Millie and the boy, they needs you, I done my work, 'tis you they needs now, you be the one Jamie."'

James' eyes filled with tears at Holly's last words. This was so difficult. 'Oh Holly,' he said, 'you are such a wise lady, don't think I haven't seen through you but, I do believe you are right. You know Holly, Ned was the grandfather I never had. We will finish his work, you and I.'

Chapter Seventeen

THE EVENTS OF BEN'S TROUBLES and Ned's death had added considerably to James' burden of responsibilities. Ben had loved old Ned, as did all who knew him. He would accept Ned's passing, albeit with deep sorrow, owing to the great age of the old man, but the recent news, learned at an hostelry in the north where James had stayed overnight on his journey home, was the news that troubled him greatly. How could he tell Ben now, he simply could not; not yet.

James reflected on how he came by the tragic news. He had been seated at the fireside in the main room of the inn, idly reading notes as he enjoyed the local chit-chat. He had found it a little difficult to understand all that was said owing to the strong northern accents and had been concentrating more on his notes than the conversations. The entire room was abuzz with talk of the accident that had occurred when the bridge was damaged in a recent storm. It appeared that the entire party, carriage, passengers, driver and team were lost as the bridge, weakened at the English side, gave way. The coach, due at the hostelry early evening, had not arrived. There had been a severe storm on the previous night, but the following day the weather had improved enough to allow scheduled journeys to be undertaken. Local people were bringing in varying reports of what had actually happened. Vaguely listening to the conversations going on around him James had felt truly sorry for the people involved in the accident and for their kinfolk. As descriptions of the passengers were told and retold he began to pay closer attention. Disjointed conversations came to his ears from all sides. Some said there had been a doctor travelling with his wife, a middle-aged couple, well respected who would be greatly missed. The driver had been in his forties, "best driver in these parts, so it be said, left young bairns too."

Several scraps of conversation came to James' ears but it was the somewhat muffled conversation of two older men at the bar that made every nerve in his body come alive as he strained to hear. 'Geordie heard it, aye, shocking, but the greatest tragedy was the young lass,' 'aye', agreed his friend. 'Coming back to England she be, so some do say, be goin' to some village or other down south.'

James made his way to the counter as quickly as he could, ordered a jug of ale and leaned against a great oak support beam. He listened intently to the lovely old northern voices as the conversation continued… 'Down south, aye, so old Geordie tells me, they found the driver, aye, still had the passenger list and timetable in his belt carry. How true it is well, who can say, aye, pretty little thing, by all accounts. 'bout in 'er twenties Geordie said, deep red hair she had, wasn't with the coach…found the 'orses, why aye, the coach floated and the 'orses did swim to the bank, in a bad way though, poor beasts, but no bodies yet, 'cepting the driver's. Terrible, terrible…aye…terrible bad.'

James had been in shock as he listened to the incredible story unfold. He had only just learned the news of the troubles at the Manor and was on his way home; now this. Dear God, he thought, it was simply not to be borne. He introduced himself to the men, ordered their tankards refilled and begged their patience as he questioned them carefully. He then left the inn and made extensive enquiries at the local constabulary. He was left in no doubt that Mary had been travelling in the carriage on that fateful day, the driver's book had substantiated his worst fears.

James felt devastated as he thought of young Ben back at the Manor. The boy's faith that Mary would come back to him had never once faltered, and he had been right to believe where others, including James himself, had not, how wonderful to have been proven wrong. Ben's faith had been rewarded, Mary had been coming home. Now Ben would wait no longer.

James thoughts returned to the present, yes indeed, how to tell Ben. Not yet, not when he is so sick and hurt, that much at least was certain. So much is happening, how can I keep abreast of things. What shall I do, it simply is not to be endured. Take hold of yourself man, Ben must first gain strength, must accept Ned's death, that is enough for the present little brother. I knew there was something special about you, Ben, I knew it years ago. I knew.

Child's Acre

With each day that passed Ben greatly improved. He now had Tom with him, what a miracle. Had it not been for the flogging Tom would not be with him now. Millie's words must be true, "the Lord works in mysterious ways his wonders to perform," Ben had heard those words so many times.

Ned had been laid to rest. It had been a sad time for all of the Estate workers and most of the villagers too, but it was the household that had felt his passing so acutely and it had fallen to Tom to comfort Ben and get him through those early days. Ned had left a note for Millie, the paper on which it had been written was smudged and creased. What Ned had written would remain for Millie only to see, it would be a farewell, it had been written long ago, that much Millie had told them. The old lady had accepted Ned's death surprisingly well. James had sat her down by the fire and had told her the news as gently as he could. Millie had known by the sadness in his eyes as soon as he had walked through the kitchen door. She had remained silent for a few moments before her ashen face smiled up at him then, looking past him, said, 'she got it right me lad, Mother Nature's had her way an' she got it right. I knows 'tis how you would have chose it. Don't fret about us ol' lad.' Then to James she had said, 'He saw you come home Jamie, he left us in peace, it was his time to go. Do you know, when Ned left my kitchen just this morning he said, "I'm off to me bed gel, a strong tea by me fire an' a great weight gone. I could sleep 'til the morrow but keep me dinner for me, no more fretting." Then 'e said, "this is one of God's good days". He said my words Jamie, he was happy, so don't fret my love, old lad has only gone 'ome.' James knelt by Millie's side and held her hand as she smoothed his hair and, paradoxically, it had been Millie who had comforted James.

Six months had passed since the black day of the flogging. Ben worked harder than ever since Ned had died and he revelled in the absence of the Squire, as did everyone, not least of all James. Tom had gained weight and was now a fine looking young man. Davy had cut Tom's hair and it curled slightly around his neck, giving him the look of a child, a handsome child. His leg still troubled him at times but was growing stronger and with his new life, good food, proper rest, the pride he took in his work, the comradeship of Ben and Davy, Tom had blossomed out of all recognition. Both boys were happier than they had been in their lives.

Holly was transformed from a 'sour old maid' type of woman to a pleasant, happy soul whom Ben adored and of whom Tom had become very fond. Millie and Holly had shared their grief over Ned's passing, though each had their own reasons for their sadness, and had been a great comfort to each other. Davy's Rosie was now with child and, so great was their joy that, as they told Millie and Holly their news they had both laughed and cried simultaneously. Since Tom had proved to be such a help and Ben had taken on more and more responsibility Davy worked more closely with Master James and Matt, the stockman. Each day was a joy to Millie and Annie as they provided for the ever increasing needs of the household, Annie becoming ever more skilled and Millie, outwardly, ever more quarrelsome; Annie had never known such contentment. Whilst Davy and Rosie awaited their firstborn Barkworth's days were filled with eager anticipation of his much longed for grandchild.

Shortly after Ned's death Ben had left the Manor house and had moved to Ned's small cottage where he had spent a few weeks convalescing under the watchful eye of Holly. Master James had proposed that Ben make his home at the house. Ben thought this the most amazing suggestion and could not possibly imagine why Master James should even think such a thing. He had assured James that he was recovering very well and would like permission to move into Ned's cottage. A more suitable dwelling was to be found for Davy and Rosie now that baby was expected, and it was agreed that Tom would use their rooms over the stables when the time came. It had been observed that, from the way young Tom had been shyly eyeing the little dairymaid, perhaps he would be in need of those rooms before too long! On being informed of his new quarters Tom was to think, yet again…this is surely no ordinary Big House; but, then, had it ever been?

Of course, on any large Estate such as Woodstock there are constant changes and at about four weeks before Rosie's child was due the Manor was to face another great sadness. Another tragedy which struck at the heart, the very substance of the great house, when Barkworth, it's revered and much loved major domo took sick and was lost to them within just a few short days. Hollie was distraught, Davy was inconsolable and only the thought of the imminent birth of his child gave him any comfort. Only the thought that he must help Rosie through this bereavement, a loss so great that it could easily portend even greater tragedy. He must protect Rosie and the baby and it was for them alone that Davy found the strength to face each day without his beloved father. He would sit in the cool of the evening in the lovely old dowager cottage that James had allocated to them. The cottage had been meant for James' mother in the event of the death of his father and John's marriage. James thought it fitting that a new generation be born there, his mother would approve. Davy would sit, resting his hand upon Rosie's belly where his son or daughter slept, he would sigh and say, 'Rosie, my darling girl, the Lord giveth and he taketh away, Dad will see his grandchild, have no fear.' Rosie would answer, 'he knew about the child, Davy, it brought him so much joy, we have that much at least to comfort us. He didn't know how sick he was, that was truly a Blessing, he left us a happy man love, 'twill be alright, you'll see.'

Events moved quickly at about this time. The manor was thrown into deep mourning for Barkworth. It was a sad time indeed for he was so greatly missed by all. A quiet, diligent man, a gentleman of the highest order, loyal to the family for the greater part of his life, having first come to the Manor when a boy, at the time of James' grandfather. Squire John did not return to the Manor for Barkworth's funeral but did return a week later when, assuming his rightful position as Squire, he carried out interviews for Barkworth's replacement. Within a month a new major domo was installed and the Manor attempted to function with this daily reminder of its great loss. Ben had been instructed by Davy to continue his work as usual but was told that, temporarily, the greater part of his time would be assisting Matt with the home farm herd of cattle. Ben had been very happy and greatly relieved. He had never learned that on Master James return, after the flogging, there had been the most dreadful quarrel between the two brothers. Had never learned that, even in John's shocked and injured state, James gave no quarter. John had been so shaken by his weakling brother's verbal onslaughts and single-minded authority that the young Squire had left the Manor, ostensibly to take convalescence, but shamed beyond all tolerance.

All was not doom and gloom by any means, for there was always light on the horizon…Rosie's child was born. The baby, a girl, was the cause of great rejoicing. There had been no organised celebrations, and Barkworth's loss had been brought to the fore once again, but with the birth of the baby girl the joy that enveloped the Manor had been almost tangible; they named her Hope.

For the folk of Woodstock Manor yet more glad tidings were to come. They were given the astonishing news that young Squire John was to depart for America in order to establish business interests in that great land of opportunity. James has already assumed full responsibility for the management of the Estate and, during past months under his direction, Estate business had begun to improve. The tenant farmers had such faith in James' sense of fairness and love of the land that they had supported him, to a man, had given their all for him and with him. The tenant farmers and Estate workers were not slow in realising the inevitable rewards for their toil and, likewise, the Estate benefitted greatly from their sacrifices and endeavours. Woodstock Manor was beginning to flourish once again. Yes, those were good days indeed.

James had never before known such a year as this. Life was moving fast, events would overtake him then, just as he felt he had the reigns firmly within in his grasp, some other problem or trouble would beset him. When happiness came, it seemed to James, it came in abundance, for whilst these had been times of great sorrow, they had undoubtedly been times of unprecedented joy, not least of which was the joy he found in his work and the promising prosperity of the home and lands he so loved. The rewards in James' daily life were considerable, he took great pride and satisfaction in all he did but, inevitably, there was a dark cloud on his horizon. This particular cloud would not go away until he faced it, he knew he could put it aside no longer.

Chapter Eighteen

BEN'S SIXTEENTH BIRTHDAY WAS JUST three months away and James had not yet summoned the courage to tell him about Mary. Now, as he rode out to Painter's Meadow shortly after dawn one perfectly beautiful summer morning, he again contemplated the problem that had caused him such anguish. He had not been able to sleep, life was so good right now but there would be no peace for James until he had performed this painful duty. The question that plagued him was whether to wait until after Ben's birthday before he destroyed his dream of Mary coming back to him. A dream Ben had cherished and believed in since he had been a very small boy, the same dream that had given him a thread of hope during his time at the waifs' home, or whether it be kindest to tell him now.

James brushed aside a dew soaked branch as he rode beneath the trees of Painter's Meadow. A green and gold patchwork of fields, framed with a lacework of hedges rolled away in the distance bathed in the crimson of the sunrise. The smells of wet grass and foliage filled his senses with a sense of peace and belonging, it was little wonder that, save for the clamour of birdsong, the silence of this glorious morning gave James time to think clearly and time to reach a decision. It had to be done, and soon, for each time Ben spoke of Mary, and how he would take care of her, James' stomach lurched and he felt physically ill.

Having made his decision James hoped that by the time Ben's birthday came around he would have accepted the truth and be able to look forward with new hope for the future. Pulling gently on the rein James turned his mount and, feeling much relieved, changed gait to a canter and enjoyed his ride back. He had been so busy of late with pressing Estate matters and

Ema Fields

working closely with the stockman to restore the blood lines of the cattle, that there had never seemed an opportune moment to speak to Ben, either of Mary's tragic accident or of his true parentage. So many decisions, for how could he present the boy with a brother at one moment, and in the next destroy the dream of his young lifetime. Ben's true identity must be shelved for a little while. This morning seems to be a morning for decisions, thought James, I did right to ride out, unclutters the mind. Yes, there would be no more running away, he would speak to Ben about Mary this very morning.

Ben thought it most odd that Master James should summon him to the library. The tack room or the Estate Office, yes, there would be nothing unusual in that, for James and Ben often discussed stable management and other aspects of the Manor farms in those places. Sometimes the library was used to discuss business, but only with the Squire or the stockman, sometimes Davy.

Ben washed and dressed carefully and made his way across the yard to enter the house the back way through the kitchen. Unbeknown to him James watched in dread from the drawing room window, hoping desperately that he would find the right words to ease the crushing burden of pain he was about to deliver. He hurried downstairs to meet Ben.

Ben entered the room where James stood looking out over the grounds and across to the farmlands. He did not feel uneasy but was most certainly in awe of the beautiful room that he had not seen until now. Never had he seen such wonderful furniture, such elegance yet combined with a strong masculine ambience in so much space.

It was a beautiful morning, the sounds of people at work drifted through the open doors onto the gardens, the Manor was a veritable hive of industry. Across the fields two great shire horses were plodding along in their desultory way, James could just hear the sound of their hooves as they clip clopped down the lane, they were being moved to temporary stables for their was no work for them at this time. He attempted a smile which died on his lips and said, 'do come in Ben, take a seat, please.'

Something was obviously very wrong, the bright smile faded from Ben's flushed face and his expression became solemn as he sensed the enormity of whatever had caused Master James to summon him. Could it be to do with the flogging, had the Squire branded him a horsethief after all, it could only be that, or was Tom to lose his place. Ben's thoughts reeled around in his head, but he did not speak. James motioned him to a seat by the open Georgian doors. Close by a vase of fragrant summer blooms adorned a highly polished side table.

'Ben,' James began, tentatively, 'I have asked you to come here this morning because,' he halted, thinking that in a few moments this would be over and this happy youngster's world would be shattered. Ben, I will…will not try to soften the blow of what I am about to tell you, for it is most dreadful indeed, and I am pained that it rests with me to bring you this news.'

Ben's thoughts raced, I'm to be imprisoned, or worse, hanged. His face, already pale, drained of all colour and his eyes registered complete panic, he couldn't have spoken had he tried.

James went on, 'it is about Mary, Ben, your Auntie Mary.'

Not a horsethief, Auntie Mary, Ben's confusion was total and James now realised more than ever how very young he still was, for although soon to be sixteen years Ben sat before him like a frightened child.

'Auntie Mary?' Ben looked questioningly. 'Bad news? 'You mean she is not coming back for me.' His face clouded, that must be it he thought, Mary is not coming back, she couldn't be bothered, she had her own life, probably in a fine mansion, why bother with him, and he just a farm hand. Might as well go to prison, or hang for a horsethief, it didn't matter now; nothing mattered anymore.

Utter defeat was written on Ben's face. His eyes spoke a thousand words and James could hardly bear to go on with what must surely be the most heartbreaking task of his life. 'Ben, lad, it's worse than that, far worse I fear. You really are a man now and are going to be required to behave as a man. For Millie, Ben, you understand, she loves you very much and your pain is her pain. You must be very strong.'

Ben was truly afraid now. James knew he was making a hash of this and fervently wished he could turn back the clock just fifteen minutes and begin again.

'You said worse, Sir,' Ben prompted, 'please tell me what could be worse than my Auntie Mary not wanting to see me?' He looked hurt and desolate.

No more hedging, James determined, the boy was going through enough. 'Mary died in an accident, Ben. She's gone.'

James turned away for try as he might he could not muster another syllable, either of comfort or of wisdom, and neither could he look at Ben's face.

Ben slumped in his chair. His blue eyes seemed to darken, his skin turned blotchy and his gulping for air could be heard across the room. James turned to him. 'What can I say lad, I feel for you, that I do, but I can offer no words to ease your pain this day.'

Ben took out a large red handkerchief and held it to his eyes. 'How, when?' he asked, his throat constricting with the immense struggle required to prove he was a man.

'It may help you to know Ben, or it may not, but Mary was on her way back to Woodstock to make a home for you both. I made certain the young woman travelling in the coach was truly Mary before telling you. I have already exhausted every possibility of a mistake, you may be certain.'

Ben wiped furiously at his face with the sodden kerchief, he looked up, tears gushed as his eyes pleaded with James, 'not dead, Sir, not dead.'

James poured a small brandy and silently offered it to Ben. 'She was coming home for me, Sir. My mother's little sister was really coming home for me.'

James saw the agony of disbelief in the face of his younger brother and was powerless to help him. Ben dashed the brandy glass from James hand and fled, stifling loud asphyxiating sobs as blindly he stumbled through the open doors and ran across the grounds to the fields beyond.

James poured another brandy and swallowed it in one gulp. He remained sitting by the open doors. He understood Ben's grief, who better than he to understand such pain. His mind travelled back across the years as he said aloud. 'I lost my mother lad, I was alone, but you are not alone, you have an older brother, and he will not fail you.'

Chapter Nineteen

A MONTH AFTER BEN'S SIXTEENTH birthday Sir John sailed for America. The atmosphere at the Manor could only be described as euphoric. The reason for the Squire's departure was widely speculated upon. He had become even more unpopular among the tenant farmers and villagers since his barbarous act of lashing the fifteen year old orphan lad in his employ and his notorious reputation as a less than honest speculator had become widespread. Millers and other local traders were becoming ever more reluctant to deal with him which, in time, would have placed the growing prosperity of the Estate in jeopardy.

Sir John, a scoundrel through and through was, as one would expect, no man's fool. He was only too aware of his boring brother James' respect and popularity in the county, of his dedication to the Estate and his integrity as a businessman. New farming techniques and agricultural progress had always left John quite unimpressed and nothing could ever persuade him to dredge up an interest in the boredom of fiscal matters. The attendance at farming conventions and, worse yet, the ever dreaded discussions on the improvement of bloodlines, left him quite cold. Surely if he was to continue to enjoy his liberty in the manner to which he had become accustomed in his father's day, America was the place. America, where a true English nobleman was a high ranking personage indeed, from all he'd heard tell.

The legalities of the change in management of the Estate had been concluded, an allowance from the Estate to be paid to John annually through the bankers had been settled and James went to work with renewed fervour. Of course John's allowance would place an added strain on Estate finances but James would cope, oh yes, James would most happily cope; somehow.

Ben had resigned himself to Mary's death and though it was now a new, somewhat older young man who faced them each day, the most difficult time had passed. He and Tom had shared an even closer bond and it was becoming clear that Ben's young mind was, as James had hoped, turning to thoughts of the future.

Once again all was well at Woodstock Manor. Rosie's baby, little Hope, was "getting on" as Millie often said, "beautifully". She had the prettiest little heart-shaped face and her fair hair, entirely without encouragement, had begun to fall into golden ringlets about her neck; Hope was a beautiful baby.

Rosie had taken to calling in at the kitchen each morning before her day at the dairy began for it made Millie so happy to see little Hope. Before baby came, Rosie didn't see Millie until breakfast.

It had been decided that Rosie would continue with her work at the dairy as the baby could go with her. Hope would lie awake in her basket, cooing and chuckling, whilst her mother worked, and in the afternoons she would sleep soundly, often until Rosie's work was done. Hope was an undemanding baby, a joy in every way. Rosie and Millie had agreed that now the mornings had grown chill it would not be possible for baby to be in the dairy, thus, to enable Rosie to continue her work, little Hope would stay with Millie and Annie in the cosy warmth of the kitchen. And so it was that, on a clear, bright, autumnal morning, as Millie sat at the great table in the immaculate kitchen with baby on her knee, she drew a deep breath and, smiling up at Annie, said, 'Annie gel, this is one of God's good days.'

Yes, these were jubilant times. Woodstock Manor had indeed experienced its share, more than its share some would say, of trial and tragedy. However, as is almost always the way, the dark days pass and, with hard work and perseverance in the face of adversity, happiness inevitably returns, and returns tenfold.

The new butler, Stebbings, was working out very well. A gentleman whose professional pride could not be denied and, yes, it must be said, one who, without exception, was the very soul of graciousness. In view of all the good fortune bestowed upon the manor of late, James decided this could well be an opportune time, if there were such a time, to tell Ben of his true parentage. It had occurred to him, of course, that this incredible fact would come as a great shock to the boy, perhaps even an unwelcome shock, and James was not at all certain how to approach this delicate subject. Remembering their last formal meeting in the library brought a shudder and James would prefer never to remember that day again. He had therefore determined that, on this occasion, he would speak to Ben in the tack room, on the boy's own territory, for surely never again would Ben wish to be called to the house, there to be reminded of the darkest day of his young life.

It was mid morning, James strolled across the yard to the stables where he knew Ben and Tom would be working at this hour. He greeted the pair cheerfully and asked Ben to join him in the tack room in half an hour. Having been assured that there were no ill tidings Ben happily went to his cottage to clean up for his meeting with James. On entering the tack room Ben found James examining one of the old harnesses, he seemed relaxed as he looked up and smiled at Ben.

'That's a beautiful harness Sir, real workmanship, I oil it myself, you would never believe its age.'

'You have certainly done a fine job Ben, I remember this harness from years ago when Ned would sit and oil the leather and polish the brasses, it was old then. I thought it had been cast aside and was somewhere in the loft of one of the barns.'

It was Sir, I brought it down, I've a bit of work to do on it yet though. It's still a little brittle in places, but one day that old harness will be as good as new again, you have my word on it, but I'm not here to talk about harnesses, am I Sir?'

'No Ben, indeed not. As you have guessed I have something of great importance to discuss with you, maybe the tack room is not the place I should have chosen.'

'I'm very happy here Sir, it's one of the places I come to when I just want to be quiet. I take up an old harness or saddle and work on them. Sometimes I completely forget what time it is, it's a good place to work, Sir.'

'It is that, Ben, I came here often as a boy, I'd sit for hours with Ned, helping him, or being scolded by him as was too often the case. Father would not have permitted it, of course, but mama didn't mind, I remember how I would tell her of my afternoons in the tack room with Ned. It was a sort of conspiracy.' James laughed aloud as he remembered. 'I did not ask you here to bring you bad news Ben, but you will need to be sitting when you hear what I have to say.'

'Does it concern Mary Sir?' Ben asked quietly, his smile fading.

'No Ben, but you remember our talk when I told you of Mary's accident, how you said that you were completely alone in the world, that Mary was your only family.'

'Yes Sir, I remember, that's true now.'

'Well, Ben, we shall not dwell on painful memories, I had every intention of telling you this news that day in the library but so great was your burden, it was simply not the right time.'

'My burden has not lightened, Sir, but I'm learning to accept, so whatever you have to tell me it may as well be now, I'll never forget, and nothing could be worse.'

'Never is a long time Ben, and time itself is the greatest healer of all. But as to being alone in the world, it is my happy task to inform you that you are not alone, for you have a brother. A brother by birth, a fact which was made known to me but a short while ago.'

Ben stared at James in wide eyed astonishment. He knew that James would never lie to him, for any reason and, unless James had truly been misinformed, his word would be God's own truth. 'It cannot be, Sir, for surely if I have a brother, Mary would have told someone, Millie…or Holly, all those years ago. We would know Sir, truly, it cannot be.'

James was feeling anxious, was he going to make a hash of this as well, just as before. He went on 'it was not such a simple matter Ben, you see, Mary did not know of your father, or his family, it will become a little clearer when I explain. There is much you will not understand at this time, but which will become clearer as you grow older. For the time being, Ben, I must ask you to trust me, and believe that I have your best interest at heart.'

'Ben's insides began to churn, his eyes were begging James to convince him that the information was true, that he really did have a brother, of course he would always love Tom, nothing could ever change that. He would never forget Mary, the younger sister of his mother, both of whom he had never known, but a brother, a true, real, living brother. 'Who? How? Where, Sir, where is this man who says he is my brother?'

First things first Ben. Does it not occur to you that you may well be disappointed in your brother, once you have been made aware of his identity?'

'Never Sir, never. If it is true my brother could be the devil himself and I would not complain. Forgive me, Sir, you understand me, of course.

James saw the complete irony of Ben's words, he hadn't actually dwelt upon the fact that John also was a brother. Ben's eyes shone, his face was alight for the first time since he had been told of Mary's death. He hurled questions at James, 'who is he Sir? Do I know him? Does he know me? Am I truly awake, or is this a dream just like I prayed every night that I was dreaming when you told me about Mary?'

'It is not a dream Ben, you are, in fact, one of three sons, alas, one of your brothers has proved to be a great disappointment to the family and has gone away to seek his fortune abroad. You will hear nothing of him, for he thinks only of himself and will no doubt come to a bad end.'

Ben looked solemn, how could anyone leave their family, leave a brother when Ben would give the whole world away this very day to have a brother, kin of his very own.

'The um, my, er' Ben stammered, he was unable to take in all this information, so many questions to ask.

'Your other brother, Ben, the brother who wishes to see you, is that what you were about to ask?'

'Who, Sir?' Ben beseeched him. He was standing and had let the harness fall to the floor. Feeling positively ill, he continued with his questions. 'Is he a little brother, or an older brother?'

'He is thirty seven years old lad, or thereabouts, an older brother.'

'Thirty seven!' Ben exclaimed, 'as old as that', he emphasised the last word.

'Yes, Ben, I'm afraid so,' James could not help but laugh aloud as he said, 'as old as that.'

Perceiving that Ben's emotions were about to overcome him James said, 'Ben, I still do not know how to tell you this but,' James pushed his fingers through his hair and, smiling broadly, said 'your brother sits before you. I have known only a short while.'

Ben sat down, or it may be more accurate to say that he stumbled to a large wooden chest and fell onto it. He stared at James, who looked back in silence, for what could he say. Ben was the first to speak. 'You, Sir...you are...my brother?' He spoke slowly, incredulously.

'Just James, Ben, just James, should you wish.'

'My brother? We...are brothers?' Ben continued to repeat himself like a demented parrot. James could only nod and smile.

Ben found his wits, 'Master James, why did you not forget this? I am just a farmhand, an illegitimate stable boy, never in this world or the next will I be your equal, never good enough to be your brother, especially since, since,' his voice died away.

'I'm afraid, Ben, that it is out of your hands, or mine, for we have the same father. None of our making, of course but, speaking for myself, having known you all these years, since you were born, I am proud to call you brother.'

'But,' Ben struggled for words, 'if your father was also my father, who then is, was my mother, how…?' His mind was scrambled as he tried to think.

Speaking quietly James said, 'there is much to understand Ben, remember, I too knew nothing of this until quite recently but, rest assured, we are brothers. In time all will be explained but, for now, enough…agreed?' James reached out to shake hands on the agreement but, to his amazement and chagrin, Ben rose and stepped away from him saying vehemently, 'no, sir, I'll pull you down, your name will be disgraced. I wont do it Master James, you cannot own me as a brother, after all you have done for me and Tom, everything that is good in our lives is because of you. I'll never let you do this, I don't know exactly how it happened, but I'm not so young that I don't understand…some things, and besides you mean…' Ben hung his head, then looking James straight in the eyes said, 'you mean too much to me. But I will know you as my brother, and God could not have given me more if he had given me the earth.'

James was very moved by Ben's words, he said, 'we'll go into everything later Ben, but as for not disclosing the fact, it is already done. The Estate solicitors have been advised, but there is much to do. It is enough at this moment to take in the fact that you are no longer an orphan, the proof of which is indisputable, I am only distressed that I did not learn the facts sooner and could therefore have spared you all of your earlier trials. You see, Ben, you are, potentially, a wealthy young man.'

Ben took up the harness and held it close to his chest. It was all too much to take in, his thoughts were racing as to how he would have been able to take care of Mary had she lived. Of how his home and Tom's would be safe forever, for if James had wanted them to leave, he would never have made public this momentous truth. 'I am a rich man,' he said, then turning to James, 'I'm the richest man on earth.' He was positively overcome with emotion, his expression at that moment could not be described; such joy James had never witnessed.

James forced a smile and said, somewhat sadly, 'well, Ben, perhaps not quite the richest man on earth.'

'Oh, but you are wrong, Master James,' Ben said fervently, 'I am truly the richest boy on earth, for today I have been given a brother, and that brother is you. Never in my most impossible dreams could I hope that this could happen to me. Never will I ask another thing as long as I live.' Tears did fill his eyes now. 'I'm not bred enough, really Sir.' Ben's usually correct way of speaking had deserted him, he said whatever came into his head, but of one thing you may be certain, he did not believe himself good enough to be the brother of James and son of Woodstock Manor. 'You will always be Master James to me sir, could I want more than you have given me this day, the right to call you brother.'

James was very deeply touched. His decision had been a sound one and a very great wrong had been righted.

'May I take Melody out, Sir? She is in need of exercise and I would sorely love to ride awhile.'

James opened the tack room door, motioning with his hand that Ben was free to take out the big bay mare. Ben pressed both his hands across his eyes and rubbed hard. 'I can't think Sir,' he said, slowly shaking his head from side to side.

'Go take your ride, lad, Tom will finish your work, ride for as long as you wish.'

As James left the tack room a little later he caught site of Ben riding as never before with one hand on the rein, the other held high in the air. He watched as Melody, with her lumbering gait, carried the boy across the lower pastures, rising, and amazingly clearing, the hawthorn hedge and on towards Little Acre. James grinned from ear to ear, he was inordinately pleased with himself and the way he had managed his talk with Ben. Relieved and happy he silently congratulated himself and, strolling back towards the stables, made yet another courageous decision. Firstly, he told himself, he must speak to Tom, for doubtless the lad would be concerned, to say the least, at seeing Ben ride off without so much as a backward glance. After a brief word with Tom he would take a leisurely lunch in the library then, after lunch, he would set right another matter that had been outstanding for some time.

Chapter Twenty

FOUR WEEKS LATER JAMES AROSE at dawn, he had instructed Stebbings to ensure an early call. James wrapped his dressing gown closely about him whilst Stebbings poured tea. When the butler silently closed the door behind him James took up his cup and, gratefully sipping his tea, his thoughts strayed to the day he had told Ben of his parentage. He had much to do at this time of year as did all the landlords and tenant farmers. If James had believed that by this time Ben would have taken up residence at the house he was to have been greatly mistaken. There had most certainly been a change in the boy since the knowledge that he and James were brothers. Were it possible Ben had become even more industrious. He whistled and hummed as he worked and enjoyed his long talks with James about the Estate and how well it had fared of late.

Ben worked overlong hours most days, it was mid autumn and he felt that there could be nothing more worthy of his labours than to work for the good of his brothers' Estate. Though his labours were for James alone for never did he spare a thought for John. Tom was also becoming an asset around the place, for him no task was too great or too small and in this happy state both boys progressed towards full manhood.

James and Ben had had frequent discussions with regard to their true patrimonial ties. It had taken Ben a long time to accept the fact that James had made his true parentage known to him. He had asked James if they might restrict the knowledge of the new situation to just those of the Manor servants who had always known and the solicitors, as it was too late to withhold the facts from them. Ben was adamant that he would not have Tom told, not yet, for Tom would surely feel that Ben now belonged on a higher plane than himself and, though he would inevitably rejoice for Ben, would feel hurt and saddened in the belief that their closeness must change. James had readily agreed to Ben's wishes…for the time being. He understood that Ben's first thoughts were always for those he loved. Ben and James were not unalike in many ways and James had a notion that their similarity was inherited from their paternal grandparents, both of whom had been loved by all who knew them; a very possible theory.

James had made many changes since he had formally taken over the management of the Estate. His was no ordinary household, he was no ordinary landlord. Owing to his commitment to ensure the upkeep of his brother John's allowance from the Estate, good profit margins were even more essential, nonetheless, the young Squire James never failed to acknowledge the needs of his tenants and servants. In return each of his workers continued to give their all and, despite John's allowance, or perhaps because of it, Woodstock Estate continued to thrive.

Ben was still a youth, not yet seventeen, and had not fully grasped the extent of his heritage. Still foremost in his mind was the fact that James was his brother. He had no desire whatever to change his way of living or to discuss finances. James was a great deal older than Ben, twenty one years senior to be precise. It was for James to be concerned with finances and Ben to be concerned with the running of day-to-day business whenever and wherever he could for he had much to learn.

The household was running smoothly and efficiently but somehow things had never been the same since Barkworth's passing. Davy had become more involved with instructing Tom and Ben of late but, despite his joy in his family, had seemed very disillusioned with life. James was completely aware of Davy's potential, he had all of his father's qualities and great knowledge had been passed down to him over many years. James was mindful of the fact that Davy had hoped himself destined for greater things and was concerned that, after his initial relief and subsequent celebration at the birth of his baby girl, Davy had become frustrated and unfulfilled.

James, still thinking of the day he had spoken to Ben in the tack room, remembered, once again, that he had also intended to put another matter to rights. He deeply regretted his failure to do so and upbraided himself for permitting business concerns to consume so much of his time. He was certainly putting his house in order and determined that, as soon as his morning's tasks were completed, the matter he had so long neglected would be attended to.

* * *

Davy was very agitated, he straightened his collar, took a last look in the mirror above the washstand, turned, took up his cap and went out of the scullery door. It was a good day for Woodstock Manor when Master James took over. Yes, thought Davy, as he turned the corner of the dower cottage and walked around the little arched porch, a good day for us all. What could Master James, he mentally corrected himself, Sir James, yes, Sir James, it had a good sound, what could Sir James possibly want with him. The new butler was working out very well, not a particularly cheerful fellow, well, I suppose he shouldn't be, really, but an excellent butler and very mindful of his duties, according to household chatter. Davy continued with his thoughts as he entered the house and made his way to drawing room. Why, oh why was I so blind and stupid as to go for my father's position when Sir John was hiring; what on earth possessed me that day. Remembering with painful clarity the humiliation suffered at the hands of Sir John at that never to be forgotten interview, Davy was filled with shame. How could he have thought that he might carry on his father's work when that terrible day eventually came. Oh, dear Lord, he thought, whatever James wants me for, please let it not be bad news. Davy was a little short of breath, due in the main to his nervousness, but the climbing of the stairs had not helped. I must take a hold of myself, he chided, catch my breath. James wouldn't let me go, would he, not now I have little Hope to provide for…no. Assuring himself that everything would be alright he mopped his brow with a kerchief and continued agonising over the reason for being summoned to the drawing room, of all places. 'The drawing room,' he murmured, 'I wish James hadn't chosen the drawing room,' he mopped his brow once more, 'on the other hand,' he whispered, who would call someone to the drawing room just to let them go?' Feeling positively nauseous he tentatively knocked on one of the huge oak doors.

'Yes, come in.' Answered James.

Davy felt he needed every second to calm himself before entering the room, ignoring James answer, he knocked again.

'Come in.'

Davy pushed open the heavy door. James was seated in an armchair by a bright fire with a mess of papers spread out on a small table in front of him. It was a relaxed smile that welcomed Davy, but he remained stiff and on edge.

'Ah, yes, Davy,' said James, in a formal tone but with a glint in his eye. 'Be seated, do, I'd like to have a word with you, shouldn't take up much of your time, I imagine there are other more urgent matters requiring your presence. Rather be attending to them than wasting your time here, I don't doubt.'

'I'm very happy to see you Master…Sir James.' Davy stammered, embarrassed by his slip.

'Yes, Sir James will do fine Davy, can't be doing with all that 'my lord' nonsense, but 'twill take some little while to become accustomed, I assure you.'

'Yes Sir, I'm afraid it will Sir, but a happy change indeed, oh, er…if it is not to impertinent to…'

James roared with laugher, 'no Davy, I quite agree, for 'tis a happy change indeed, though I could have wished the circumstances to be other.'

Davy nodded his head respectfully and exhaled deeply, for James' laughter had gone a long way towards putting him at his ease.

'Well now, Davy,' said James brightly, 'for the purpose of this discussion let's revert to Master James, or just James, within these walls.' James noted Davy's anxiety, nonetheless, gave in to an overwhelming urge to play cat and mouse, probably the first cruel act he had performed in all of his life. 'Sit down Davy,' James pressed, indicating the chair opposite him whilst slowly lighting a cigar. He leaned forward in the large leather winged chair, drew deeply on the cigar, then stood up and, raising an elbow, rested against the mantlepiece.

Looking a little more serious now, James began. 'A great deal has happened over the past few months, a year perhaps, you will agree? It is no secret that I am now Squire of Woodstock, a great responsibility indeed and, of course, it will become necessary to make changes if we are to continue to prosper.' Davy's heart beat faster and his mouth went dry. 'I realise, of course,' James went on 'that, in the short term changes are not always welcome but, in the fullness of time I am hopeful that these new arrangements will benefit the Manor.'

Davy inclined his head, indicating his understanding thus far. His expression showed concentration and concern as he silently waited for James to continue.

Ema Fields

'One of the changes I am about to make is that I intend to take on a new footman. You will agree, no doubt, that it will be far more practical to employ a footman come groom who will have some knowledge of veterinary work, than for the Estate to consult a professional vet in every small matter.'

Davy, ever more anxious and growing closer to panic thought, what is all this to do with me, unless I've lost my place, but listened intently to what James had to say. Assuming Davy's silence indicated agreement, James continued.

'We'll never find another Ned, of course, he was simply magic with the animals, but with young Tom proving himself far more useful than I had ever anticipated and Ben becoming such an asset, well, I feel that our circumstances are not what they were, say, a year since. The Estate is faring well, Davy, but it is plain that changes here and there are essential.

Whilst Davy understood that James was not exactly discussing Estate finances, he realised that he was being treated as an equal. He straightened in his chair and, despite the headache and nausea, was clearly absorbed in all James' proposals, even to the extent of shelving his own precarious position. James continued 'I need to consider all aspects Davy and, with the best will in the world, your present work here is being carried out perfectly well by young Tom and Ben, thanks to your diligent tuition.'

Davy nodded again, he was about to speak in his own defence but, what would be the use, instead he said, 'I understand.'

Noting Davy's expression James felt thoroughly ashamed. He should first have offered Davy his new position and then continued with the discussion about the new arrangements. He greatly regretted his approach and the way he had handled things, thus, without further preamble, he came to the point.

'Well now, Davy, I have thought the work schedules through very carefully but it all depends on your own decision.'

'My decision, Sir?' Davy spoke with ill concealed hope in his voice.

'Yes, Davy, you see, I hope very much that you will take up the new position I have in mind for you.'

Davy's grim countenance vanished and James thought, I can read you like a book old friend. He said, 'yes Sir, I will be very happy with whatever position you have in mind, very grateful, and I will serve you well, Sir.'

'I'm certain of that, Davy. Well, as you know, nothing ever remains the same. It was a very sad day for this house when your father left us so suddenly, yes, a bitter pill that. He had been with this family since he was twelve years old. Started as assistant to the first gardener, I believe, always had his head in books, the story has it. Still, you are quite aware of the old tales.'

'Yes, Sir,' Davy was visibly relieved and had sat back in his chair, 'my father was very happy here, always.' He would often tell me how singularly fortunate he had been.'

'I'm happy to hear that,' answered James, thoughtfully, 'I would like to believe it, yes, he was a good man, none better, possessed of every quality, diligence, honesty, integrity, unquestionable loyalty, and all of these attributes he passed on to you Davy.'

'I thank you for that, Sir, it is the greatest compliment a man can be given. Father loved his work. As you know, our fathers grew up in the same household, albeit on different sides Sir, my father greatly loved and respected your grandfather, the old Squire, Sir.'

'Yes Davy, and it was mutual I do assure you, and I'm glad that my own father had a childhood friend, I'm sure there would have been many times when he would have been in need of one.'

'We all have our time, Sir, I hear the new butler has worked out very well.'

'Indeed he has Davy, Stebbings is a grand fellow.'

Davy swallowed hard, he wished he could hide his acute embarrassment. Had James been told of that dreadful interview with his brother John? Well, Davy simply had to know, he could stand the suspense no longer, he would ask James what his new position was to be. Of course it could only be lower in the political scheme of things, but he would still have a position, still be able to provide for his family and he would be the best darned, whatever it was, that any Squire had ever known.

Davy plunged in, 'my new position Sir?'

'Yes, of course, your new position Davy, forgive me, I get carried away when talking of old times. Well, now, I hope you will do me the good service as to consider taking care of the Squire and his household, follow in your father's footsteps, as was always intended. It can only make sense to keep to the old way of things in this regard and, who knows,' James eyes twinkled as he said, purposefully, 'perhaps even, in the fullness of time, establish a tradition.'

Davy had no feeling, his senses were numbed, he could not even respond to James' amusing remark. Still smiling, James came to his assistance and said, 'my house needs the attributes of a Barkworth, Davy, and I can think of non better equipped to fill your father's shoes. I know he prepared you well for this day.'

James had spoken seriously, reverting to his position as Squire. He looked at Davy whose heart was racing for he could not believe what he had just heard, tears threatened, he coughed and swallowed hard. James turned towards the fire and looked deep into the coals in order to give Davy time to compose himself and, hopefully, not realise that his reaction had been noticed. Taking up a poker he prodded the coals and continued casually. 'Of course, there are things to attend to before you take up your new position Davy, assuming your answer is yes. Stebbings is a champion fellow as I have already mentioned but, you know, I feel certain he will be much better suited to a London household. He is of the town, I fear, is Stebbings.' James thought it kinder to continue and to put Davy's mind at rest with regard to Stebbings' future. 'Have no fear Davy, Stebbings will have great opportunities, will go to one of London's fine old families, but you understand that I could not speak to him of my decision without first discussing the matter with yourself.' James now turned to face Davy who by this time had quite regained his equilibrium. 'May I take it that your answer is yes? Or would you like a little time to consider?'

Davy stood up, still holding his work cap in his hands he made an incongruous figure as he said, positively and very formally, 'yes Sir, of course Sir, I am deeply indebted to you Sir.'

'Nonsense, you're my man, Davy, always were.' Realising he had touched another emotional nerve James quickly went on. 'You will need the tailor, of course, new uniforms and what have you. We'll talk again later and discuss the new way of things then. Well now, dare not stand here idling much longer, eh?'

Davy's smile was enigmatic, alight with happiness, yet tinged with sadness, 'no, Sir James,' he replied. He turned to leave the room but as he opened the double doors he heard James call out, 'oh, and Barkworth.'

Davy turned, clearly non-plussed, 'yes Sir?'

'Nothing,' said James innocently, and with a crooked smile and happy gleam in his eye, 'just wanted to try the sound for size, it fits you well.'

Davy did not return the smile as he said, 'Yes Sir, thank you Sir' before silently closing the door.

It was all too much, he must get down to Millie, but first he must go to Rosie. His heart raced fit to burst and he thought he would never breath normally again. The words, "Personal Aide", Major Domo, Valet, Butler, rang in his ears. He would take up his father's work, Major Domo to the Squire of Woodstock Manor. He stopped at the wide curved staircase, placed his fingertips to his trembling lips and murmured, 'father, oh pa, I will not let you down.'

Davy almost fell through the kitchen door so great was his hurry to speak to Millie. Millie, Millie, come on now, leave that, sit for a moment, you must listen.' Still breathless Davy could contain himself no longer and pulled Millie away from the range.

'Lord a mercy, what's a matter now Davy, nothing can be so important as to take me away from me oven with the bread almost done. Annie, see to the bread, another minute or so.' Continuing to scold him she reached for the kettle. 'Comin' in 'ere, disrupting my kitchin, wheres you got no business at this time o' day, all this commotion, what is it Davy?' she demanded.

Davy gently pushed Millie into her chair, saying, 'this is where you sit until I've told you, then I'll leave you in peace until supper.'

'Yer, you will an' all, I'll see to it mesel. What is it now, your jaws wont shut and that silly grin might take root, Lord I do 'ope not, for your sake, I do.'

'Hush, woman, for mercy's sake, I've just been speaking to Master James and he has told me his plans for the butler of the Manor.'

'Hmmm, an' 'ow can that possibly put you in such a dither, unless Master James is giving ol' Stebbings his pack and pennies.'

'No Millie, nothing like that, Master James is very happy with Stebbings. But, not a word now,' he turned to Annie, 'you cannot hear this conversation Annie.'

'What conversation, Davy?' Annie replied as she noisily drew a loaf tray from the oven.

'Good girl. Davy turned back to Millie, drew himself up to his full height of five feet nine inches and said, imperiously, 'I'll thank you to treat me with a mite more respect in future, Millie, yes indeed. I will also thank you to address me by the name best befitting a gentleman of my elevated station. Henceforth you will address me as "Barkworth", if you please.' He turned to Annie, 'you too young maid.'

'Sorry, Davy, I can't hear this conversation,' she replied, cheekily.

Ema Fields

Millie stared in disbelief, she put a hand to her cheek and her eyes spoke volumes. Again Davy thought how soft hearted this outwardly caustic old lady really was; a dear, dear soul.

'Oh, Davy, Davy me lad, it should always 'ave been you, Lord what wonderful news.'

She pushed herself out of her chair, caught him by the waist with her rough, plump hands and they pretended to dance around the great table. 'We got a Barkworth back agin,' she said, and her eyes brimmed with tears of happiness. 'How will I work now, you've upset me day right an' proper you 'ave, 'tis all too much. Do you think the new Squire would object mightily if his new butler takes a drop o' tea an' a slice of new bread wiv an ol' woman, eh Barkworth?'

'The new Squire will not mind at all, always providing he may join you, that is.' The voice came from the other side of the kitchen door and, as James entered, Millie was flustered, 'Master...Sir James, I...' she stammered out the words.'

'We will all share a nice pot of tea and take a slice of your wonderful warm bread, Millie.'

'Sir James, shame on you,' she pursed her lips and shook her head in mild disapproval. 'Just you go on up to the drawing room and Annie'll fetch up a tray. 'taint fittin for you to take tea in the kitchen Sir, not no more Sir, just aint fittin'.'

Oh, we'll not lose our standards Millie, have no fear. Woodstock has always been the finest Estate and Barkworth will see that it remains so. But for now Millie, may your Jamie have one last cup of tea and slice of bread with his dear friends in your fine kitchen.'

They sat around the big table and chatted like old friends whilst Annie served them tea and Millie cut into the big round crusty loaf. As the tantalising smell of new bread filled the kitchen Ben's tall frame appeared in the doorway and, grinning widely, he dumped himself unceremoniously into a chair. It was well known by all that whenever and wherever food appeared, Ben also appeared, uncannily it had always been so.

'Well I never, wouldn't you just believe it,' shrieked Millie, 'e's gorn and done it agin. Can't get a minute wivout 'im where there's food about.'

James literally roared with laughter and the little company joined in heartily, for they all knew the tales of Ben's fortuitous appearances when cake was being taken from the oven or Millie had been sampling her beef puddings.

It was a happy scene and one not to be witnessed too often in the years that followed, after all, " 'taint fitting'."

Some time later on that happy day James smiled satisfactorily when, returning from his last task of the day, he glimpsed Rosie as she lifted Hope from her perambulator which stood in the shade of the old oak outside their home. He watched, obscured by the surrounding hedge, as Davy hurried to her side, placed his arms about his wife and child and held them closely. They stood in front of the cottage with the late autumn roses tumbling over the porch, adding their lovely yellow, sweet scented blooms to the deep greens of the Ivy as it reached its tendrils to the eaves, framing the windows in its path.

Perfect…James was getting it right.

Chapter Twenty One

ANOTHER HAPPY, SUCCESSFUL YEAR LATER as Ben's seventeenth birthday dawned, a young woman sat quietly alone in an Ursuline convent in the far north of England, looking out of her window in her cell like room. Enjoying the stillness of the hour she awaited the impending knock on her door which would tell her it was time to join the nuns in the chapel for morning prayers. The deep glow of the sunrise grew lighter, creating a halo of burnished copper as it caught her hair, heightening the paleness of her skin. As she sat looking over the small courtyard to the dew covered fields beyond she made the sign of the cross and prayed to the Holy mother, as she had prayed each morning since her arrival at the convent, that one day soon her memory would return. She loved her work here in the big old run down house that served the nuns as their small orphanage. She loved the children for whom the sadly equipped building provided a temporary, but loving, home. She now understood the industrious, sometimes harsh and frugal way of life. Loved her peace with God and the wonderful Ursuline nuns who had devoted themselves to her recovery.

As the somewhat sad young woman continued to drink in the beauty of the morning the same questions tormented her. Did she have a family? Had she married? Did she have parents, brothers, sisters? Could she ever find true peace until her memory was restored; questions, still so many questions. She crossed to the small table that, with the exception of the low wooden bunk, was the only furniture in the room. Now known as Sister Paul, Mary poured water from the jug into the basin. She must hurry a little now for she had wasted time with her daydreaming again. However, it was difficult for her at this solitary hour, a time of thought and prayer, not to let her mind drift back to the story of her arrival at the convent that fateful morning almost two years ago.

Sister Paul had been found caught in the boughs of a partially uprooted tree that had been treacherously overhanging the river after a particularly bad storm two days previous. The bridge had been damaged close to the bank on the English side of the river her coach had been crossing. It was truly a miracle that her fall had been broken by the overhanging tree and she had survived. Father John had discovered her whilst on his way to the convent on one of his infrequent visits. Trundling along on the lopsided old cart he urged his donkey onward. He had hoped to reach the convent in time for the Angelus, midday prayers, and was thinking that he had made excellent time when he saw the damage to the bridge. He steered Barnabus, his ancient donkey, over to the verge and climbed down to take a closer look. There appeared to be no sign of travellers, the scene was peaceful but the bridge looked as though it had been badly damaged by the storm. Turning back to the cart something bright caught his attention. He stooped at the edge of the downward slope in order to see more clearly, then gasped and, almost choking on an intake of breath, made the sign of the cross, exclaiming, "Holy Mother of God, the poor woman." The priest could see quite clearly now, as he tentatively lowered himself another foot or two down the bank. There was a woman clad in green, but were it not for the white petticoat he may not have seen her. Her body seemed to be twisted among the branches of a partially uprooted tree. Father John could not think how to reach her but knew that, should he leave her whilst he sought help, the tree could easily give up its fragile grasp on the bank and take her crashing into the river below. Of course, Father John realised she may well be long gone from this world but he had to be sure. He must be certain for, as he had told Sister Paul on many occasions since, had she already gone to her heavenly home, why then was he there, on that particular day, on an unscheduled visit to the convent.

Father John had taken off his cloak and tied Barnabus to a stout bush. He then swiftly rummaged around in the back of the cart, found a rope and, securing it to a tree a little way from the edge of the slope, began to pray. 'I sincerely trust you do not want me just yet Father, for as you well know I still have much to achieve.' He then made the sign of the cross, asked God to be with him and slowly descended the hazardous slope. On reaching Sister Paul he was saddened to see that she was a very young woman. He began to free her from the branches, praying as he worked that his movements would not loosen the tree's roots still further and that he would be given the strength to somehow bring her safely up the bank. As he made his first terrifying attempt to lift the unconscious girl a voice shouted down to him.

'Ha wey there Fairther, wait now boy, be still, I'll give ye bit help, I'll coom doon.'

Father John looked up and saw two men in labourers' clothing. As one man tied a length of some kind of lashing around himself the other secured it to a tree. The smaller of the two began a slow descent. 'Thank you Father,' the priest said aloud, 'I knew you would not fail me.' Some thirty or so heart-stopping minutes later, back on safe ground, he expressed his profound thanks and bestowed God's blessings upon those two brave and wonderful geordie lads. Father John then made all haste to St Angela's convent whilst Sister Paul, unconscious but blessedly still alive, lie wrapped in his cloak in the back of the cart. He prayed he had made the right decision to take the injured girl directly to the nuns. The two young men had assured him there was no infirmary hereabouts, thus, although the convent left him some little way to travel, he prayed to the Holy Mother to grant him speed.

So it was that Mary arrived at St Angela's convent, unconscious, badly cut and bleeding and with horrific bruising but, incredibly, without serious physical injury; she had remembered nothing from that day.

The nuns had tried to seek out information regarding the damaged bridge and how it had come about, but the convent orphanage was quite some distance from the town and neither nuns nor priest frequented the ale houses or market places where the tragedy was discussed. Inevitably, town gossip was very soon forgotten and in their rural environment no news had ever reached them. In the weeks and months that followed Sister Paul was to be examined by several medical people interested in the field of the subconscious. Reverend Mother had not stinted in her endeavours to find help for the woman in her charge, but all that had been learned about her was her incredible fear of storms, the true reason for which remained locked away in her mind. It had been agreed that, so great must have been the trauma on the day she could, most certainly, have lost her life, the mind had simply refused to remember.

A light knock upon her door brought Sister Paul back to the present, she picked up her missal and left for chapel. After morning prayers the day began much as usual. The nuns, novices and Sister Paul busied themselves with the early chores that were attended to before breakfast. The Ursuline Order is not a silent Order but meals were taken in silence. Sister Paul always looked forward to mealtimes, especially breakfast, when all the Mothers and novices shared the first meal of the day in grateful and companionable tranquillity; before the children were up. After the early meal the nuns parted company. The novices left to continue with their instruction in the ways of the Order, with its disciplines and devotions, after which they would often study their specialised subjects. They may also be required to help with practical tasks as well as join the nuns at times set aside for prayer; there were two novices at St Angela's at that time.

Sister Paul left with Mother Agnes to cross the yard to the makeshift orphanage where she spent her days scrubbing, cleaning, teaching and, above all, loving the little ones in her care. The Ursuline Mothers diligently went about their work. They had timetables for the kitchen, laundry, vegetable gardens, children's home, schoolroom and chapel, not forgetting any whitewashing of walls and other minor restorative tasks. They had their religious devotions each day and also special subject studies including teaching and nursing.

Sister Paul was neither nun nor novice but wore the habit of the novice at her own request. During her time at the convent it had become her dearest wish to join the Novitiate and study with the novices to take her final vows and enter the Ursuline Order. This request had been denied her many times. Mother Vincent, the Reverend Mother, would not consider Sister Paul's wishes until her memory was restored which, she had been assured by the doctors, could be at any time. The old nun had decided that it would be too cruel a fate should a young woman find herself torn between her commitment to a life in God's service and the bonds of love for a family she may have left behind. Sister Paul must be free to make the right choice when the time came.

* * *

On the evening of that day, at the other end of the country, James sat relaxing in the drawing room of Woodstock Manor. He ached from head to toe despite the fact he had just bathed away the rigours of the day. However, it was a pleasant exhaustion for the Manor was enjoying a very successful harvest time, thus many concerns were reaching a long awaited conclusion. James looked forward with anticipation to the quiet restful evening but, as he happily sat enjoying this tranquil time, a knock upon the door disturbed him. He sighed deeply and bade the thwarter of his peace enter, entirely oblivious to the fact that on that very evening the entire course of his orderly life would be turned upside down and changed…forever.

A very upright and elegant Barkworth opened the high double doors saying, 'I do apologise for disturbing you Sir, but a travelling man of the cloth called at the house whilst you were taking your bath. I showed him to the kitchen and Annie is attending to a meal Sir. Naturally I offered the priest the hospitality of the house Sir, but he would not hear of it, instead asked that he may wait in the kitchen. I thought you would not wish him to leave without your knowledge Sir.'

'A priest, Barkworth? Yes, of course you did right.' James rubbed a weary hand across his chin. 'I should have a word with him before he leaves, I suppose. Has he specific business with the Manor.' James asked, puzzled.

'It seems not Sir, I did enquire, naturally. A little rest and refreshment was his only request. He is somewhat travel-stained and appears exceedingly weary. I have asked Tom to take the priest to his rooms in order that he may refresh himself.' James rose and, arching his shoulders and stretching his neck, said decisively, 'take a message to, did you get his name?'

'Yes, Sir, it is Father O'Donnell Sir.'

'Take a message to him Barkworth, have him join me in the drawing room after his meal. Don't take no for an answer, I'll come along and see him myself if he is still of a mind to refuse.'

'Of course, Sir,' Barkworth replied and left to speak to the reluctant Father O'Donnell.

Some thirty minutes later Barkworth showed the Irish priest into the drawing room. James rose from his chair by the window and crossed, with hand outstretched, to welcome his visitor.

'Ah, good evening Father, do come in, James Winbourne.' James introduced himself as they shook hands, 'very happy to welcome you to my home, it is Father O'Donnell, I believe.'

'Yes, son, it is, and a good evening to ye too, and thank ye for the foine hospitality, Oi'm sorely weary, so Oi am, to be sure.'

Father O'Donnell spoke in the wonderful lilting way of the Irish. He did indeed look extremely tired and James showed no hesitation in guiding him to the most comfortable chair. 'There is no need to thank me, Father,' said James, smiling his charming smile, 'I am very pleased to have your company for a while. The evenings are usually very quiet here, for which I am entirely grateful most of the time but, this evening, well, a little good conversation is heaven sent.'

Father O'Donnell waved a hand, dismissing James' need for conversation as an excuse in order that the priest should not deem his presence an intrusion. 'Oh, nonsense Sir, Oi'll have none of it, ye are very gracious son.'

'Well now, Father,' James began, as his unexpected visitor leaned back gratefully in the big worn old chair, 'what brings you to Woodstock? The nearest Catholic church is in Swanbridge.' James crossed the room and pulled the bell cord that would summon Barkworth.

'Aye son, that it is, and aren't Oi the foolish auld fellow that be finding the wrong road. Well James, it'll not be the first toime of that ye may be sure. May Oi call ye James, Sir.'

'James it is Father, I insist.' Said James, thinking how quickly he had taken to this good humoured old gentleman, yes, he liked Father O'Donnell, he liked him very much.

Father O'Donnell continued. 'Oi'm making for Rochester, Oi'll be crossing the river the morrow, it is to be hoped, but Oi thought that whilst Oi was in these parts Oi'd visit an auld, auld friend of moine, Father Kelly, he's at the parish of St Andrews in Swanbridge. Sure an' Oi couldn't be passing so close and not take the trouble to call on him.'

'Ah yes, St Andrews, of course. Well Father, you are some little way off your track, Swanbridge is at least four miles from here, you were surely not intending to walk?'

'Aye, indeed son, we do not carry much with us, as no doubt ye will appreciate. Oi'd been walking an hour or two but, would ye believe, Oi did go an get mesel' lost, so Oi did, would ye be thinking Oi could be so careless. Oi was taking mesel' into the village but me ol' legs had decided other, so Oi sees the house from the track and, Lord be praised, didn't the little gairly in the kitchen make me a foine meal, so she did.'

Barkworth entered the room smiling briefly at Father O'Donnell before looking to James for instruction.

'Bring us a bottle of your good malt, Barkworth. I think this is an occasion to indulge ourselves, just a little.'

'Certainly Sir, will there be anything else, Sir?'

'Not at the moment Barkworth, thankyou.'

James turned to the priest who said promptly. 'Now don't ye be troubling yesel' on moi behalf, son. Ye've already been more than kind, so ye have, indeed, more than kind, to be sure.'

'Nonsense Father, after a day such as this a nightcap or two will be just the thing, and I must own to be enjoying an unexpectedly pleasant evening.'

'Father O'Donnell shifted in the deep, comfortable chair, 'a drop of the medicinal would indeed be "just the thing",' he agreed. It had been a long time since the old priest had had an opportunity to share a glass of anything and he smiled in anticipation, truly enjoying the friendship of this young English Squire. What a thing to happen to him, he would indeed have a story to tell Father Kelly and the folk in Rochester, that he would.

James and his guest shared a most unexpectedly stimulating evening. The conversation was good and the tales of the old priest were most amusing. James had invited Father O'Donnell to stay the night as a guest of the Manor and after a few moments of firm persuasion the priest gratefully accepted. The evening continued merrily until James, feeling uncommonly hungry rang the bell pull once again and suggested that Barkworth find them a light supper. Whilst they awaited the food James noticed the old gentleman draw the folds of his sleeves about him. How pale he looks, thought the younger man, and how remiss of me not to realise that he might be feeling the chill. 'Well now Father, is there a chill in the air, or is it too warm to put a spill to the fire?' Not requiring an answer James rubbed his hands, removed the tapestry fire screen from the hearth and lit the fire, which was always laid in readiness. In a few minutes the kindling was burning brightly, sap crackled as sparks flew up the chimney and Father O'Donnell sighed with pleasure.

Barkworth had decided that an appetising meal of good farmhouse fare would be most suited to the occasion. A little later, after arranging an immaculate tray cloth, a simple but delicious supper was served and the pair, continuing with their raucous laughter, thoroughly enjoyed their supper; they were having a rare old time.

After a while, inevitably, the conversation became slightly more serious. The priest had many experiences to impart and the younger man listened attentively. Father O'Donnell, enjoying his audience, proceeded to relate stories of his day to day life in the priesthood. Then, suddenly, the conversation took an unexpected turn. James was savouring his drink, revelling in his mellow mood, the cosiness of the fireside and Father O'Donnell's scintillating company. The resonance of the old priest's undulating tones continued…'Oh,

Child's Acre

yes, moi son, ye would not believe the work we are called upon to do. Whoi now, only last month Oi be having a bit of a chat with me ol' friend Father John, he was at a parish up north 'til about, oh, let me see now, must be three months ago, at least. Well, he be after telling me as how he was on his way to the good Mothers at the convent orphanage when he was called upon to rescue a young woman.'

James continued listening, not overly attentive now but still enjoying another fine tale, and as the priest continued the fug began to clear from his mind.

'Be all accounts,' Father O'Donnell warmed to this remarkable tale, 'she was trapped at the side of a river bank. Well now James, Father John says it was a turrible sight. So, he starts down the bank when the good Lord sends him help and two men came to his aid. Well now, between them they gets the woman, a young thing too she was, up the treacherous bank, whoi, ye should hear the way Father John tells it, he being there, of course. So, he takes the little lady to the Mothers at St Angela's, that's the convent ye see, and she's been there ever since…Oi tell ye the Lord's own truth now, James, moi son, she has remembered not a thing from that day to this, so she hasn't.'

His mind began to clear very quickly now and with every word James dared to hope, he sat forward abruptly. 'Father, would you repeat that story please?' James said urgently, dragging his fingers through his hair as if to clear his head, he was unaccustomed to taking more than one small drink, if any. In fact, it was usual for him to have a hot drink before retiring. 'I think what you say may be of the greatest importance Father.'

Then, absently, he murmured, 'no…it surely cannot be.'

'How do ye mean, son?'

'Father John, as I have said…' James cut in and, leaning further forward, 'Father, where was this place, this place that your friend found the young woman? Was it in Scotland?'

'Well, it was up north o' the co'ntry, cannot be certain mind, but up by the borderland, the bridge had been damaged, you see, and the little woman has not remem…'

'Yes, Father, do you know anything about the young woman?' James spoke in earnest, 'try to think Father, it is of the most dire importance.'

'Ye don't say now, really, well now…let me see. They do call her Sister Paul, I knows 'cause moi ol' friend is most proud of his work that day.' Noting the impatience on James' face Father O'Donnell said, 'aye son, Oim trying,

Ema Fields

heavens above, the impatience of the young. Well now, she had red hair, yes. She had been wearing a travelling frock but had no belongings. She was just a gairlie on her own, that's about it son, she having no memory ye see, there's really nott'n' else to tell, except she was young.'

'When did this happen Father, if you could only remember when?'

'Whoi, that's easy, James,' the priest took another sip from his glass. James was on edge, he had never known such torment. 'Sure 'twas only last month Father John did tell me. 'Two years ago, aye, two years to the month last month. I know because my birthday follows a month after and 'twas moi birthday last week. Two years, James, no doubt at all.'

'This is most incredible Father. You know, I do believe you may have brought the most momentous news. It would seem Father that I may well have a story to tell you.'

Just then Barkworth knocked lightly and discreetly lighted the small lamps on the chiffonniere. Then, crossing to a low table he lit the large lamp. James lowered the wicks and let the oil lamps bathe the darkening room in a gentle golden glow. He then offered the priest a cigar and, as flickering shadows danced about the room, the two relaxed by the fireside and smoked companionably whilst James told the story of Mary and Ben, beginning at the beginning, recalling all that he knew.

Father O'Donnell listened, enthralled, until James had finished his story then the old priest said. 'Well, son, I agree wid ye, given that your Mary had been living in Scotland just across the border, and had always intended to come back, it does indeed sound loike the yo'ng woman could be her. Ah, James, I fear I must advise true caution but, even so, I have a greater reason for believing the yo'ng lady is possibly your gairlie.'

'You do, Father? Said James, intensely.

'Aye moi son, for wasn't Oi after wondering whoi on earth I be here in a Manor House I have never heard of, looking for moi auld friend, Father Kelly, and him as far as four moiles away now. Oi was meant to come here, son.'

The next morning James bade his new friend farewell. He had instructed his footman to take Father O'Donnell to Swanbridge to visit his friend and then drive him on to the river crossing where he would continue his journey. They had promised to keep in touch and Father O'Donnell repeated his thanks, assuring James he would be in the old priests thoughts and in his prayers.

After that dramatic evening James wasted no time in visiting the convent. He would not speak to Ben. He felt in his heart that the girl had to be Mary, but first he must be certain. There was only one Convent in that area, Father O'Donnell had assured him. He anticipated no problems with locating it; and encountered none.

During the long journey north James tried to recapture the image of the ten year old Mary. Hopefully her features would not have changed too much. She had been very thin at that time and the scraggy little vixen had a temper like a shrew. He smiled, remembering.

On his arrival Mother Agnes, who sent for Mother Vincent, the Reverend Mother, received James at the convent. Mother Vincent welcomed him graciously and after thanking her for seeing him without prior arrangement he told her of his hopes. Mother Vincent was very happy for James to see Sister Paul but was adamant that he must not reveal his true identity should she prove to be the Mary he was looking for. The nun told James that she had every reason to believe Siser Paul was the girl he sought. James readily agreed to Mother Vincent's condition and assured her that he would be guided at every step. Should Sister Paul prove to be Mary, he would not wish to jeopardise her recovery in any way. Reverend Mother decided that the Holy Father would forgive a small deception, thus James would be introduced as a medical man; he met Sister Paul that very day.

Hoping against hope James waited with Mother Vincent until a slender young woman entered the small, pleasant room as quietly as if she had glided through the doorway. Everything about her was quiet and gentle. She exuded an air of the sweetest serenity and with one look at that lovely face, and those tranquil eyes, James, quite unwittingly, fell utterly and hopelessly in love.

Mother Vincent introduced the young man as Doctor James Winbourne. Sister Paul inclined her head, murmured softly, 'good afternoon doctor', gathered the folds of her skirts and sat down. James was shocked and deeply affected that the gentle face, shyly returning his gaze, was the very image of Ben. The same fair complexion, the same large, wide set eyes with the most exceedingly long lashes, the fair eyebrows and the full lips. They were so alike they could easily have been brother and sister. Mother Vincent, aware of James' stunned recognition, took up the conversation in a pleasant, matter-of-fact tone. James gathered his wits and smiled at Sister Paul. He had been instructed as to the few questions he would ask but, as he looked into those deep blue eyes, he was lost. She was quite, quite lovely.

Following that first brief meeting James had been assured by the Reverend Mother that, as Sister Paul did not belong to the Order, there would be no visiting restrictions, always assuming she suffered no distress. James immediately determined that he would visit Sister Paul whenever business permitted; which he did.

Chapter Twenty Two

THE WEEKS PASSED BUSILY AND happily for Sister Paul as her very special day drew closer. She had been baptised into the Roman Catholic faith the year previous and soon, after long months of preparation, she was to make her First Holy Communion. Her dearest friends, Sister Bernadette and Sister Luke, the two novice nuns, had helped her with her studies and, under the guidance and tuition of Father John, Sister Paul's understanding of her chosen faith grew, as did her love. She had worked so hard with the two young novices who were ever at her side during free hours. Together they helped her study the catechism. They listened as she laboured over the prayers of the Catholic faith. "The Apostles Creed", the "Hail Holy Queen", the sixth prayer of the rosary, the "Glory be to the Father", the "Act of Contrition" and many others. The novices were endlessly patient as Sister Paul struggled with the alien sounds of the Latin Mass. They guided her through such Latin prayers as "The Pater Nosta", The Lord's Prayer, the "Ave Maria", the Hail Mary. They studied the Saints with her. They smiled and encouraged, laughing at her and with her. They helped her remember the order of the Commandments, the Stations of the Cross and the Blessed Sacraments. They praised her successes and made light of her failures. Her triumphs were their triumphs, they had the very patience of Job. It was no surprise therefore, that when Sister Paul's First Holy Communion date was set, the three hugged and laughed in the most unseemly manner.

With her First Holy Communion day now a reality and drawing ever closer Sister Paul became uncharacteristically lighthearted and was, to Mother Vincent's relief, becoming less anxious by the day with regard to her loss of memory. One morning after breakfast she skipped across to the kitchen

Ema Fields

garden where Mother Jude was stabbing with a hoe at a particularly solid patch of earth. Doctor James Winbourne, or James as she now knew him, had visited her the previous day and his visit, coupled with her forthcoming First Holy Communion, had lifted her spirits enormously.

'Hello Mother Jude,' Sister Paul greeted the young nun, 'what is the problem, I would certainly not like to be that piece of earth, you must use a fork, Mother, not a hoe.'

'I have already used the fork, Sister, that is, I jumped upon the…the… fork, and after I finally got it into the ground, I couldn't get it out again.' Mother Jude pointed to a garden fork standing up with its tines stuck fast in the ground. 'See?' said the nun. Her voice rose with sheer frustration and Sister Paul could not help but laugh merrily, her very genuine amusement infuriating Mother Jude.

'Well, Mother,' said Sister Paul, 'you are truly not the most robust person I have ever known.' Sister Paul was still laughing and Mother Jude began to mellow a little. She smiled briefly as Sister Paul continued to tease her. 'In fact, Mother, you are quite feeble, look at the size of you, as if you jumping on that old fork would have any impression on it.' They both looked at the fork stuck in the earth and, as Mother Jude gave the offending implement a hefty kick, the two fell into peals of laughter. It was Mother Jude who spoke first.

'Well now, Sister, you are certainly in fine fettle this morning, did I notice the young doctor again yesterday?'

'Yes Mother, Doctor Winbourne.'

'He's a nice young fellow isn't he. Is he able to help you at all? He has been to the convent several times, I hoped, perhaps, that you were making a little progress.'

'Oh, I don't think so Mother, it will just take time. He is nice though, have you ever spoken to him?'

'No, no, I haven't, just nodded hello,' Mother Jude replied, rocking the fork back and forth in the ground in a futile attempt to loosen it.

'He's, well, different to the other doctors.'

'Different, child, surely a doctor is a doctor, how can one be different from another?'

'Well, Mother, he doesn't seem to ask the same questions. In fact, most of the time we just chat about our likes and dislikes. Yesterday he asked Reverend

Mother if we may take a stroll in the garden to conduct our interview, he seems very interested in my problem.'

'Yes,' said Mother Jude, thoughtfully, 'it would appear so. Is it three or four times he has questioned you now, Sister?'

'I have only seen him three times, twice before and then yesterday. I think he has quite some way to travel.' Sister Paul was smiling and her blue eyes sparkled. Sister Paul was unaware of this; Mother Jude was not.

'So,' ventured the nun, 'what do you think of him Sister?'

'Well, he's a gentleman, of course, Mother.'

'But of course, Sister,' said Mother Jude, with mock solemnity.

'And I suppose,' went on Sister Paul, thoughtfully, 'really quite dashing.' As these last words left her lips Sister Paul turned and fled, amused and surprised at her boldness. Oh, to shock Mother Jude in such a way.

Mother Jude, smiling fondly at the retreating back, shook her head from side to side exclaiming, 'dashing! Dashing indeed! With her thinking to become a nun. Saints preserve us, and when I think about obedience, well, I darest not think about obedience. Paul, Paul, whatever shall we do with you?'

Sister Paul was so very happy and no longer troubled herself as to why. A few weeks previous she had reached the momentous decision that she would fret no longer. She would put herself in God's hands and accept whichever road he chose for her, life was good, she was happy; and Doctor Winbourne would visit again soon.

During the course of the past few weeks Mother Vincent had watched closely the continuing change in Sister Paul and was not in the least surprised when, early one morning, on a day that had begun as any other, the world of her young charge was thrown into utter turmoil.

A week after James' last visit, as Sister Paul was crossing to the children's home, she saw a young girl carrying a basket of laundry, the girl was about fourteen years old, she had long fair hair and hummed as she walked. Something flashed in Sister Paul's mind as she watched the girl, but so fleeting was the sensation that before she could grasp it…it had gone. As the girl turned the wind caught her hair and a different pretty young face flashed before her again. An older face this time but, so quick, so elusive. 'Who is she?' Sister Paul murmured. 'Who is the girl that I am seeing, remembering?' She pressed her hands to her cheeks as she realised the significance of the word "remembering". The sight of the girl had triggered something in her mind.

Tearful and afraid she almost ran to the convent hurrying through the big broken gate and across to the annex where she knew Mother Agnes would be at this time. Sister Bernadette, seeing her haste, watched with concern as her friend disappeared through the annex doorway. It was most unusual to see Sister Paul in such a hurry. Entering the annex her ears were assailed by the cries of one of the very young infants. The baby was screaming lustily, for no other reason that she wanted her feed. Sister Paul stopped abruptly and, as the cries continued, the memory of another tiny baby, wrapped in a tattered shawl, clouded her mind. The cries grew louder and as Mother Agnes turned into the corridor the sight that met her eyes was most distressing. Sister Paul was holding her head against the wall and sobbing aloud, 'no, no, I wont, I wont leave him, I wont,' she cried heartbreakingly, distress muffling her words.

Mother Agnes ran to the sobbing girl, Sister Luke poked her head through a doorway, a baby in her arms, 'fetch Reverend Mother, Luke, it's an emergency,' whispered the older nun, hurry Sister, do.' Sister Luke disappeared, fear clouding her eyes.

Mother Agnes gathered Sister Paul into her arms. 'Come now Paul,' she soothed, 'we'll go along to your room, you must rest awhile.'

Sister Paul raised her eyes to Mother Agnes' sweet face and pleaded, 'what's happening to me, Mother, I will not leave him, please, what's happening to me?'

'There now child, there now, let it all come.' Slowly Mother Agnes began to guide Sister Paul out of the annex and through to the convent. 'You must rest now Sister, rest now my pet, you are remembering something distressful, that is all, it cannot harm you now.'

Mother Vincent met them in the corridor, she exuded an air of competent serenity as she took Sister Paul's arm. 'What is it Mother Agnes?' she enquired, calmly, 'is she remembering something, I have been expecting this.'

'I believe so, Mother Vincent.'

Reverend Mother spoke to Sister Paul as though she were just a frightened child. 'Come now, Sister Paul, has that old memory of yours finally decided to wake up, well it is certainly not before time. Now then, go along with Mother Agnes, I'll be back directly. Compose yourself Sister, it is no more than we have wished, there is nothing to fear.'

Mother Vincent went hurriedly to her office, took a sheet of notepaper and wrote, simply, "Doctor Lind, please come with all haste, Sister Paul has need of you. Reverend Mother, St Angela's Ursuline Convent." One of the novices was told to ride the donkey over to the next farm. The farmer would then send someone to ride over to Doctor Lind and deliver the message.

Sister Paul was still crying softly as they reached her room. Mother Agnes settled her to bed and comforted and reassured her that all would be well. Mother Vincent returned with a glass of hot milk and a sedative. She knew the girl must sleep, must let her mind rest to do its work. She sat by Sister Paul's bed and spoke of pleasant things. She took up Sister Paul's favourite book and promised to read to her until she fell asleep. Sister Paul became drowsy as the sedative began taking effect. It would act as a restorative and Sister Paul would feel the stronger for it after a night's rest.

The next morning Mother Vincent instructed Mother Agnes to go to Sister Paul and stay with her in her room until she joined them.

Mother Agnes found Sister Paul awake, refreshed and composed. She placed the tray of tea on the side table and they sat calmly and quietly discussing the events of the previous day.

'I remember a baby, Mother Agnes, a tiny baby, do you think it was my baby?'

'No, Sister, 'twas not your own child. Now remember all that Doctor Lind has told you and do not fret. You must be obedient Sister.' Mother Agnes smiled, thinking how difficult it had sometimes been for Sister Paul to follow the rule of obedience. She did not hold to any great hopes.

Mother Vincent arrived, followed by Sister Bernadette bearing a breakfast tray. Sister Paul raised troubled eyes to the Reverend Mother. 'I think I remember a baby, Mother, whose baby I do not know but…I will remember, and then, perhaps, the nightmares will go away.'

'Sit quietly now Sister, have your breakfast, it has been specially prepared this morning, I'll return a little later and we can have a long talk.' Mother Vincent's calm authority always dispelled any fears Sister Paul may have. She thanked the older nun and began to eat.

Later that afternoon, as Sister Paul sat up on her bed resting against the pillows with Mother Vincent at her side, she tried to answer Doctor Lind's questions. It was explained to her that she was beginning to remember things in stages. It had been a slow process, the reason for which lie mainly in Sister Paul's anxiety over her condition. The nightmares she had experienced were possibly the manifestation of her memory trying to return. Now that her mind was peaceful and her body fully recovered, there should be no reason, at least none that Doctor Lind could envisage, why she should not be restored to perfect health. 'It is my considered opinion young lady,' Doctor Lind assured her, smiling warmly and patting her hand, 'that within a few days, a week perhaps, you may well have full recollection. Now then, it is most important that you do not over exert yourself. Don't try to work anything out, do not tire your mind with the effort of remembering and, above all, do not allow yourself to become vexed or anxious.' The doctor spoke firmly but continued in a friendly way saying, in hushed tones, after all Sister, it is a very exciting time, but you must guard against it, nonetheless. Nurture thoughts as they come to you, do not dwell upon anything that may cause distress, it all belongs in the past and cannot harm you now. You will have happy memories also, think about these.'

The doctor smiled at Mother Vincent. 'Well, Mother, I'm delighted with our young lady. Keep her quiet for a while, there is no cause for concern.'

Sister Paul smiled weakly at the doctor. 'Thank you doctor, I cannot believe I am going to be well and after all this time, to know who I really am.' She drew a shuddering breath and relaxed against the pillows. 'Doctor... Mother,' she began, haltingly, 'the baby I remembered yesterday and this morning is my nephew, my sister Sarah's baby, Sarah died a little while after he was born, she was only seventeen. I took him to the Manor House to save him from the Waifs' Home, for I was just a child, only ten years old, I couldn't take care of him.' Silently the tears welled again, but they were healing tears now, she was perfectly calm. The doctor motioned to Mother Vincent to let her continue.

'Sarah told me to take him to the Manor, "the big house", she said, and I did as she told me, but I was sent away. I promised baby Ben that I would come back for him. He did not know, of course, he was only three months old, so beautiful,' she said, absently, then, smiling through her tears, 'I think I love him more than anyone in the world. I have lived all of my life since that time, just to learn everything I could, to go back and make a home for us both. My mother and father died of a fever, before them my two little brothers, then Sarah. There is only Ben left, and I'm all he has, just me.'

Mother Vincent looked anxiously at Doctor Lind, his expression reassured her and they allowed Sister Paul to continue. She told them of her years at the Grange, of Caroline and her parents, wonderful people who loved her. When, a few minutes later, she said,

'Mother, I'm so tired, I'm not afraid, everything will be alright now but, it's still so muddled.'

Doctor Lind laid a comforting hand upon Sister Paul's arm saying, 'all is well Sister Paul, everything is going to be just perfect, I promise, do you understand now? I promise.'

Sister Paul smiled at the doctor and said, wearily, 'I want Ben, Doctor Lind, I just want to find Ben.' She would have wept again but for the doctor pressing her hand and saying, 'now young lady, did I not tell you that everything will be perfect, I have never broken my promise to a pretty lady yet.'

This caused Sister Paul to smile genuinely and the doctor spoke with mock severity as he said 'you do exactly as Reverend Mother says…to the letter mind.'

'Yes doctor, thank you, I will.' She closed her eyes, truly exhausted now and, before drifting into a restorative sleep, said, 'Mother Vincent'.

'Yes dear,' the nun answered gently.

'My name is Mary, Mother, Mary Pargeter…but I did so love Sister Paul.'

'I too child, I too.'

Mother Vincent's eyes were brimming over and she spoke lovingly saying, 'sleep now my little one, sleep now…Mary.'

The next morning the sun shone brightly through the small window in Mary's room. She had awakened refreshed and was experiencing a joy such as she had never known. Smilingly radiantly she bathed at the scrubbed wooden washstand, then hurriedly dressed with trembling hands. She had missed morning prayers, of this she was certain as the familiar sounds of morning hustle and bustle reached her ears. On leaving her room she tripped lightly along the corridor to the dining room where the tables would need to be set in readiness for the breakfast hour. Mother Gertrude was on duty with Sister Luke and she greeted them both warmly. Despite the apparent radiant wellbeing of her would be helper, Mother Gertrude was uncertain. 'Sister Paul, I'm sure you should be still abed. I do not think I should encourage you to be working when you need to be resting, what will Reverend Mother say?'

'Oh Mother Gertrude,' Mary threw her arms wide in a display of rapture, 'how can I possibly sleep, I have slept for two days, I am so happy I simply have to be with someone. I want to shout and jump and climb to the top of the spire and tell the world, shout as far as Woodstock and tell them all, "I'm coming home".' Suddenly the lovely smile faded and with trembling lips she struggled with her next words, 'oh, but Mother Gertrude, how shall I leave you, and the children, how shall I leave you all?'

Seeing her distress Mother Gertrude decided to take Sister Paul's mind away from the inevitable sadness that parting would bring. 'Come now child, if God has decided that your work is to be elsewhere, then so be it, be happy in your good fortune, you will always be with us in our hearts, and you will most certainly visit.' Then with mock exhasperation, for Mother Gertrude was practiced at exhasperation, she said, 'heavens above child, you talk as though we were on the other side of the world.'

'Mother Gertrude you are a wonder.' Mary was beaming again. 'I don't know about wonder,' the nun answered, cheerfully, 'but 'twill be a wonder if I ever get these tables laid with your good help, Sister Paul.' They set to work. As they worked Mary told Mother Gertrude and Sister Luke that she would now be known by her given name, for she would need to become accustomed to being called Mary again. Her happiness restored, she looked forward to breakfast.

Later, during the midday meal, Mary recounted the events of the past forty eight hours. Could it really be just two days since she had found herself again? Sitting quietly she thought about the kindly old man who did odd jobs around the orphanage and the gardens. They had become staunch friends and it was not until now that she realised, with happy certainty, that the dear old gentleman had been her travelling companion on the journey south, Nathan, who for almost two years had said nothing. Nathan, how can it be, her thoughts roamed on, how did you survive that day. I cannot believe you are here, I cannot wait to tell you that I am well, I cannot wait to see you. Mary no longer needed to think of Father John's story, she remembered it all, up until she had tried to climb down from the coach but, as Doctor Lind had instructed, she did not dwell upon the past, for truly it could not harm her now.

After the midday meal Mary went out to the garden where Sister Bernadette was on duty. Mary's dear friend welcomed her warmly saying, 'now you are not to be doing any work, Sister Paul, we have all had strict orders and heaven help the one of us that Reverend Mother catches allowing you to help. Oh, Sister Paul, it is just the most wonderful news,' she exclaimed, with great feeling and not a little sadness.

'I suppose you will call me Mary now, Sister Bernadette, my name is Mary; I remember everything.'

Sister Bernadette asked no questions but said, 'I am so happy for you Mary, so very happy.'

They embraced and Mary said, 'it's alright Sister, I am neither nun nor novice, I may embrace my dear, dear friend.'

Mary knew that today was usually one of the days that Nathan called to give a helping hand. She awaited him anxiously, keeping watch down the lane, until at around two thirty, the old man ambled around the bend on which two huge oaks partly obscured the view of the lane leading to the convent. Through the foliage he saw Sister Paul waving frantically and calling, 'Nathan, Nathan, do hurry.'

The old man jogged along a little more quickly, waving his hand-hewn stick in acknowledgement as Mary opened the gate and ran towards him. He was a little concerned that something was amiss but, as Mary reached him and took both his hands in hers, he realised that a miracle must have happened since his visit the previous week.

'What is it, Sister Paul, ye remember something, d'ye not?' It was perfectly obvious that this wasn't the quiet, troubled little Sister Paul he had come to know and love.

'I remember, Nathan, I remember, my name is Mary, I remember everything. Oh, Nathan, how is it that you are here, you were travelling to your brother's, I remember now, you told me.' She was brushing away the happy tears that came unbidden to her eyes.

'Well, this is indeed wonderful, Sister Paul.'

'Call me Mary, Nathan,' she interrupted, 'everyone is to call me Mary now, after all, Sister Paul was just a borrowed name until I found myself.'

Nathan placed a woollen clad arm about Mary's shoulders saying, 'it's a canny story Mary, how I came to be living here and helping the Mothers. Come, if ye have no chores we'll sit in the garden and I'll tell ye how it all began. They ambled across to the old hut in the vegetable garden and sat outside, enjoying the sunshine, whilst Nathan told his story. Mary listened, intrigued, as Nathan related the succession of events that led him to settle close to the convent.

'Well, 'twas like this, lassie ye know how I told ye that, like yeself, I am more or less alone in the world now. If ye recall I told ye that I was going to my brother's home in the north, but that I wasn't truly happy about it.'

Nathan paused, clearly concerned, he did not know quite how much of the story he should reveal. There may well be aspects of that dreadful time that Mary still had not remembered and he did not want to upset her.'

'Do not worry, Nathan,' Mary said gently, 'I remember it all now, please go on.' She was relaxed and smiling. Nathan continued.

'At the time of the er, accident,' Mary nodded and patted his hand reassuringly. 'I don't know how but I found meself in the water. Well, I was a very strong swimmer in me young day and somehow I found I hadn't forgot. I was carried along with the current mostly and didn't know how I was to help meself. Well, the river bends a bit further on from that bridge and I found meself being swept across to the other side. At some stage the bank seemed to be growing out of the water and mercifully I was thrown against it. I dragged meself onto the land and must have collapsed, likely with relief and shock. It was night when I woke up and I was freezing cold, how I didn't die of the cold,' he paused, Mary listened earnestly and with no signs of distress encouraged Nathan to continue. Intending to be as brief as possible, he went on with his story.

'Well, as I shivered along the road I thought I saw a light. It were at a distance but I was so cheered that I walked quickly to keep meself warm and before long I was rapping on the door of a small farm. An old man lived there alone and when he opened the door he pulled me inside and made me sit by the fire. He didn't ask any questions, well, I must have looked a fearsome sight. He fetched some clothes and built up the fire and it wasn't long before,' Nathan took a deep breath, 'I was sitting by a blazing fire with a bowl of hot broth, the finest broth I had ever tasted in all of me years.' He smiled, remembering.

'Yes, Nathan, yes, what then?' Mary urged.

'Oh, now then, I told the old man, Tavish he is called, MacTavish really but he's always been known as Tavish. So, I told him what had happened and he just couldn't do enough to help me. As you can imagine I had taken a very bad chill and was poorly for some while. Tavish was very good and it was only his kindness that brought me well again. He went to see about the accident for me, to ease my mind, you know, but was told that all the passengers were lost, and you being so young and so pretty, I was sorely grieved, but later, it seemed true enough. Tavish had been told there had been a search but, of course, by that time Father John had found you, and the rest you know.'

Child's Acre

'How did you come to live near here, Nathan, when Tavish's farm is nearer to the bridge?'

'Yes, Mary, I'm getting a wee bit muddled aren't I,' he laughed. 'So, on the first morning that I got up from me bed, Tavish gave me breakfast outdoors, he said he has his food with the birds whenever he can, they expect it and wait for him. I tell ye, Mary, when I went out of that little farmhouse for the first time I didn't expect to see such a place. Tavish had collected fallen branches and made an arch over the doorway, an old wild rose had spread all over it and I could imagine it in the summertime smothered in the little pink blooms. The farmhouse itself was pretty as a picture with ivy climbing the walls and a little cobbled path led to the well. Tavish had planted trees around the well to keep it shaded. There was heather all over the place, for Tavish and his wife had moved here from Scotland, they loved the heather and the blues and purples were everywhere. Oh, Mary, Tavish's place is a little heaven on earth. He keeps six hens and a goat and has a wonderful old mongrel called Dog. Around the side of the house there's a stall for his pony and shelter for the cart. As I ate my food there was such peace. Tavish was sowing seeds in a box, Dog was lazing at his feet and the birds twittered and hopped around me demanding to be fed. You, know, Mary, 'twas then that I knew I wanted to stay around here, somewhere. Mind you, Tavish's bread wasn't much to speak of but, truly,' Nathan laughed genuinely, then said with conviction, 'his oatcakes, well now, they're wonderful. So I had fresh eggs, Tavish collected them that very morning, and oatcakes warmed in the oven. When I was getting better Tavish gave me me girdle, all the sovereigns were there. I'm not much for churches, Mary, but that day I thanked the Lord for helping me and I thanked him especially for my sovereigns, which were all I had in the world.

A little while later Tavish helped me look for a place of me own. There wasn't anything very near there so we looked in this area. After a few weeks Tavish took me to a little place that was just right. I needed to be busy and, my goodness,' he laughed merrily, 'there is enough to do in me little house to last me the rest of me days. You see, it was because of it being so bad that I could get it, and that is how I am here today. I planted and weeded and made the garden. I dug the earth and planted out the vegetables. Tavish took me to market and I bought five hens. I mended the fences and painted the house. I made a little hut, just like this one,' he looked behind them at the hut and smiled, 'and I have never known such peace and contentment in all of me years as I do this day. Tavish is a dear friend, he brings his pony and cart over to see me from time to time and I'll go over to see him. We have so much to do and oft times we even work on me ground together. He knows all there is to know about growing, does Tavish. He's not much on mending though, I do bits of mending for him. I think Tavish is glad of a friend too, he lost his wife five years ago, ye see.'

Mary was still mesmerised, she begged Nathan to go on.

'Well, girl, that's about it, ye know. As ye would expect, over the past two years I've got me wee bit of ground sorted out, it's about three-quarter acre I reckon. I grows vegetables for the convent and the little ones. I've got a dozen hens now and they're fine layers. I fetch most of the eggs up here and sometimes Tavish takes some to market for me. I've got me little house grand, two rooms down and two up and a washhouse as well. Done the holes in the roof, mended the walls where the birds was nesting, laid a few flags in the washhouse and cleared the chimneys.'

Mary could understand the pride and happiness with which Nathan told his story. The old man had made it sound like a fairytale; which, to him, it was. She was eager to know more and listened contentedly as Nathan continued.

'The immediate garden was so overgrown, there was even a broken old hut that I didn't even know was there until I started clearing the ground, but 'twas too old and damaged so I made me new one. The weeds had run riot and the wild rose grew everywhere strangling everything in its path. Mind you, I do love the wild rose, one of me favourites is that but you have to control it. I tell you Mary, I didn't know where to look first, and as for making a start, well,' he laughed again, rubbing his chin, 'I had to take it a little bit at a time and I loved every minute. Now you are wondering how I came to be at the convent.'

'Oh yes, Nathan, do tell me, I had better go in soon, Mother Vincent insists that I rest in the afternoon as though I were sick, she says I must remain rested.'

'You must indeed Mary, if that's what Reverend Mother says. You know, canny lass, it was helping the nuns that gave true meaning to me life. I'm not a religious man, never have been,' he said solemnly, 'but I have me own faith Mary, oh aye, I do. I don't know who he is, but he's there, the Lord is there, that's all I know and that's all I needs to know. I still don't have any time for this religion thing, but I sorely needed that sad little old house with its clogged up well and its overgrown garden. Oh, aye, I'm truly thankful. You know Mary, when I first saw me little place it looked as if it had been just waiting for me, and d'ye know what, I think it was. Still, as I have said, 'twas the nuns who gave me true purpose. They needed someone on the gardens and I love the land. They needed fixing doing that they couldn't do and it was heartbreaking to see them struggle. I often passed the convent when I went walking. There's lovely countryside hereabouts and one day I walked so far that I saw the convent. On one of those days as I was about to walk back I took me courage and just went through the gate and spoke to the nun who was working there. The nun went and fetched the Reverend Mother and I told her I would be happy to lend a hand. So, I don't go into the convent, naturally, but I help in the bairns house and I help with the planting and weeding. I didn't see you at first Mary, what with the cloth,' Nathan nodded at Mary's novice habit,' but one day ye were playing with the bairns outside, ye had on an ordinary pinafore and ye're hair was blowing free. I tell you, it was like I had been struck by lightning, I almost jumped for joy, would have too but me ol' legs wouldn't let me. When I spoke to you...'

Mary interrupted, she had loved Nathan's story, 'I told you that I had been brought here by Father John, and everything had become clear to you.'

'Aye, canny lass, it did. I could do nothing for ye, ye were well and being cared for, it was simply a matter of waiting. I told Mother Vincent what I knew of course, but I had no address of the village down south, had no family name, just Mary, just Ben, there was nothing to be done, I wouldn't leave ye. Ye will go back to your Ben now? Aye, of course ye will. Ye know, ye were meant to come here Mary, doubtless in the Lord's good time we'll all know why.'

Mary hugged the old man, 'I do love you, Nathan, these past two years you have been the father I did not have.' Then, sadly, remembering Mother Gertrude's words, she said, 'but I will not miss you, for you will be with me, always.'

Kneeling in the chapel later that evening Mary made the sign of the cross and prayed for guidance. Almost soundlessly she heard a footfall and, looking up, saw Mother Vincent walking towards her. They sat in silence for a few minutes then Mother Vincent said, 'I saw you come into the chapel Mary, are you troubled child?'

'Yes Mother,' Mary answered, a little vaguely, 'troubled, uncertain, confused.'

Ema Fields

'Of course Mary, you are wise to pray for guidance to work through these feelings. Come, now, we'll go to the kitchen in the children's home and you must tell me your fears.'

In the kitchen Mother Vincent placed more fuel in the stove saying 'I think we may be forgiven a little extravagance this evening.' She went to fill the small kettle when Mary said, hurriedly, 'oh no, Mother, please sit down, I will do that.'

With her usual quiet dignity the nun turned to Mary, 'do not be so shocked child, it is not unknown for me to make a drink. Sit by the stove now, and tell me what troubles you.'

A few minutes later Mary was sitting by the open door of the big round stove revelling in its warmth and sipping hot milk. She felt much better now, she always felt better when Mother Vincent was around.

'It is so difficult for me, Mother. You see, I wanted to join the convent so much. I wanted to become a novice, the life here Mother, I love it so, but… oh but Mother, I must go to Ben, and not out of duty, I want to go home, I want to be with Sara's child. I want to do it for Sara, for Ben and for myself, I loved that baby so, Mother, and I promised them both.' Mary spoke a little too quickly but the nun understood her perfectly, who better?

'You say you will not be returning to Ben out of a sense of duty, do you really feel this to be so, Mary.'

'Oh, yes, Mother, but such a decision, to leave my life here, to abandon my hopes of becoming a novice,' then, looking directly at Mother Vincent and speaking decisively, Mary said, 'I must go back Mother, I want to take care of Ben, I need to be with him. You knew, didn't you Mother, you have always known.'

Mother Vincent smiled serenely, 'you know child, not all who seek to become nuns may do so. Sometimes, for many different reasons, a woman may not be suited to convent life, no matter how great her love. Those that are, of course, have several years to make the decision to take the final vows. Where you are concerned, child, you must follow your heart. Go where your heart will lead you. There are many ways of serving God and, one day, your way will become clear.' Mary smiled, she felt so much better. The Reverend Mother continued, 'return to your sister's son, Mary, be happy, the reason for your stay here will be made clear to you when the time is right. If you are to become a nun, that also will be made known to you, when the time is right. Perhaps you are meant to have fifteen children,' Mother Vincent quipped, as she was sometimes known to do, 'therefore God has sent you here to learn how to raise them.' She was smiling reassuringly and Mary laughed aloud so great was her amusement.

Mary felt as though a great dark cloud had been banished from her mind, a leaden weight lifted from her heart. 'Mother, you have made everything so clear to me. Why did I fret so, thank you Mother, thank you so much for helping me to understand. I will go back to Ben and I will visit all my dear Mothers, if they will permit me.'

'Of course, child, and always remember, it is not only nuns and priests who serve.'

'I know Mother, I see that now. Mother…?' Mary became suddenly anxious, 'I will make my first Communion, Mother, I could not bear to lose my faith.'

'Of course, Mary, of course you will, such a thing to say, you will never lose your faith child come what may. You will make your first Holy Communion here, in the chapel, and we shall all be there, the nuns, the novices and the children. You are aware, of course, that Sister Bernadette is being recalled to the Mother House for her final year and that Sister Luke is to go to a hospital in East London for her third year.'

'Yes, Mother, I know.'

'Have no fear, we shall make certain they are both here for your Holy Communion Day.'

'Oh, please, Mother, if you could.'

'Come now, the hour grows late, you must retire, be happy child, remember…The Lord's timing is perfect, and a new and wonderful adventure awaits you.'

Chapter Twenty Three

A SLIGHT BREEZE ENCIRCLED THE house at Woodstock Manor as James arrived back from London. He had attended a very satisfactory meeting with the Estate's bankers and was not a little pleased to be home but now, the day's business concluded, thoughts of Mary returned to taunt him. Since the evening with Father O'Donnell, James had travelled to the convent on three separate occasions. His first journey, ostensibly a business concern, had caused minor difficulties with the running of the Estate, as it was not an ideal time to be away. He had, however, arranged his subsequent visits more conveniently. Now, his thoughts turned, as they invariably did of late, to Mary for, despite all his efforts, images of her lovely smile pervaded his mind almost every waking moment. When James first sought to ensure that the young woman at the convent was Mary, he had assumed that it would simply be a matter of course that she would return to Ben when her recovery was complete. The only uncertainty at that time was, could the young woman be Ben's Mary? After meeting her, however, he had not been so sure that her identity would be his only concern, for the startling realisation that Mary hoped to become a nun was beyond his wildest imaginings. He was upset at the affect Mary had had upon his settled existence. He had so wanted to bring about the reunion, knowing what it had always meant to them both, but his meeting with Mary had greatly disturbed him. Despite the long journey ahead of him he was inexplicably happy after having made his arrangements to visit then, after he had seen her, he was restless and unhappy, seeking answers always to the same questions. When Mary's illness had passed and her memory was restored, would she still wish to join the convent? Indeed, and he banished these thoughts almost before they were formed, when Mary learned that Ben was no longer alone, that he had a brother, that he had an inheritance in his own right, would she feel released from any responsibility she may have felt with regard to his future. Would she then, happily, fulfil her own dream? It simply did not bear thought. Feeling wearisome, unable to concentrate, his troubled mind turned to Ben. His dilemma at this moment was, when should he tell his young brother that Mary was alive and well, but without memory? If the decision had rested with James, Ben would have been told immediately on James' return from his first visit to the convent, but he had been obliged to assure the Reverend Mother that he would wait. Both the doctor and Reverend Mother felt that Sister Paul had recently made small steps towards a full recovery. They believed that should her nephew make contact of any kind at this crucial time, a natural and very delicate balance may be placed in jeopardy. Thus, it was in this disconsolate frame of mind that James attempted to deal with the mail Barkworth had left for him. It was two weeks since his last visit to the convent and he stared absently at the handwriting on the envelope he held carelessly before him. 'Latin script,' he muttered, 'news from the convent perhaps.' His fingers were ripping open the envelope almost before his thoughts had grasped the significance. He did not read the letter from the beginning, so great was his haste to find the news he sought. The meticulous Chancery script flowed on as his eyes scanned the page to where, in the last two paragraphs, he read

> "it is my happy duty, therefore, to advise you that, after an emotional and traumatic interlude, Mary is now preparing herself, both physically and spiritually, to begin her life anew. Her joy at this time can only be described as a gift from the Holy Mother herself, who has been with Mary every step of the long road to recovery, I am sure. As it is Mary's wish that she return to Woodstock, Doctor Lind has advised that, in view of her close associations with the convent, unnecessary delay will serve no good purpose. I understand you may prefer to stay her hand with regard to an early departure in the event that you may wish to aid her journey.
> Be assured that it has been my great pleasure to become acquainted with you. Goodbye Sir James, may God's Blessings be with you.
> Love and prayers,
> Mother Vincent
> (Lady Harper-Smythe)"

The letter was signed "Lady Harper-Smythe." So Mother Vincent was a Lady in her own right, mused James, incredible.

James, though ecstatic, was hesitant, for now he must face Ben, not only with these wonderful tidings but also with the fact that all had been kept from him. Leaving the letter for the most part unread he leaped to his feet, summoned Barkworth and, pacing furiously back and forth attempted to assemble his thoughts. 'Mother Vincent I love you,' he laughed aloud then, arms outstretched he cried joyfully, 'she's coming home Ben, your beautiful auntie is coming home to you.' The door opened, 'yes, Barkworth thank goodness you are here.' James showered a thousand and one instructions upon Barkworh who remained professionally calm whilst attempting to absorb James' many requests. On hearing the momentous news Barkworth also was overcome. Nonetheless he appeared to take everything in his stride as he left the room to attend to the business at hand.

Without further thought James hurried along the upper corridors, down the staircases and across the yard in search of Ben. He found him about to drive off to the upper pastures in the big cart. Ben pulled gently on the rein to turn the horse in the direction of the gate when he caught site of James hurrying across to him. 'Whoa there fellah, stand boy.' he called to the huge Suffolk Punch who obediently stopped walking and began to strike his hoof against the ground, his way of asking for a titbit.

James approached somewhat breathlessly. Ben smiled, saying, 'I'm off to the top pasture to take a look at the ground, thought I'd call in on the Wheeler's whilst I'm up there, see how old man Wheeler is, he was ailing a bit last time I saw him.'

'It will keep, Ben. I must have a word.' In his uncertainty James spoke seriously in a tone that Ben had come to dread for when James spoke thus, he knew that his older brother had something on his mind. Ben always expected ill tidings, and this time was no exception.

'Can it not wait, James,' he hedged, 'until later?'

'No Ben, come over to the...' James had not thought where he would take Ben to impart such monumental news, or even how he would tell him. Would anything ever come easy, he thought. He took the reins and guided the horse to the edge of the orchard where he tethered him on the lush grass. Where better to give Ben the miraculous news than in the orchard by the fields he so loved. James remained serious for, once again, he was not at all certain as how best to handle the situation. Would Ben be furious and upset? Ben was first to speak.

'There is bad news for me James, well, I would like to have done with.' Ben was so full of respect for his elder brother that his nervousness was plain to see.

James took a deep breath and smiled genuinely as he said, 'not this time Ben, not this time little brother. Nonetheless I am very much afraid that what I have to tell you will come as a great shock.'

'No greater shock than when I learned that you and I are brothers, James.'

'Possibly not, but equally so I assure you and most certainly every bit as happy, even more so, much more so.'

Ben's expression was uneasy as he said, 'James, what could be happier news than to learn you are my brother? I live in dread of news of any kind, I do believe if I had my way I should go through life with my head in a sack, and happily so. What is it James? Please be done with.'

James drew a deep breath and sat at the foot of the tree, Ben sat alongside him. 'Ben, I have no way to tell you, I have not taken time to think, but...'

'James, for pity's sake,' Ben urged.

'tis Mary, Ben, Mary has been found, she is alive and well. She did not die in the coaching accident. I just did not know how best to break the news to you, after all you have suffered.'

Ben was silent, his expression unreadable, it was as though he had been struck deaf, dumb and blind. James, sensing the shock, spoke very quietly. 'I do not wish to discuss the accident at this time Ben, we already know of that. However, it appears that Mary was thrown from the coach and rescued by a priest very early the morning after.'

Ben now looked at James, he made to speak but no sound came, he swallowed, cleared his throat and began again. 'Truly, James, truly, not dead?' His young face registered disbelief, anger, pain, but most of all, the emotion James saw in Ben's eyes was that of fear. James attempted to stem the avalanche of questions that were about to be hurled at him, but to no avail.

'James, how long have you known? Are you absolutely certain? How could you have such news and not tell me? Why...'

'Wait now Ben,' James put up a hand to quieten the boy whose mind had been thrown into turmoil, and not for the first time. 'Now, Ben, first things first. I have known for just three months.'

'Three months,' Ben cut in, almost shouting.

James continued, unheedful of the protest. 'Do you remember the priest who came to see me, some three months ago, or thereabouts?'

Ben acknowledged his recollection of the stranger and James went on. 'You see, Ben, the priest brought news, entirely without realising, that there had been a coaching accident way up north. He had learned the story from a colleague of his, another priest, it seems. He told me that a young woman was found the morning after the accident. The young woman had been taken to a convent where it had been established that she had no memory whatsoever of what had happened to her, either at that time, or any other. I asked Father O'Donnell when this had happened and he confirmed my hopes that it was two years ago. I knew the young woman must surely be your auntie Mary for I had already established that she had been travelling on that coach, do you remember?' Ben nodded again and James continued, 'well, I had to be certain, Ben, do you not see, I had to be certain, after all you had been through, to give you false hopes, I simply could not.'

'James,' cried Ben angrily, 'you have treated me like a child, protecting me. You should have told me, I should have known if there was even a possibility that Mary was alive, I should have been told,' he shouted. 'I am seventeen, James, seventeen.' Ben emphasised the very great age he had attained and, with all the rage of a seventeen year old believing himself as aged as Old Father Time, said, 'I am not still a child.' James looked at his brother, I have handled this very badly, he thought. There were tears forming in Ben's eyes and James was saddened as Ben blinked them back saying, vehemently, 'I'm a man now, James.'

James was at a loss as how best to ease the situation and the strain between them. This should have been such a happy time. James was miserable and so terribly disappointed that it showed in his demeanour. 'I'm sorry Ben, I truly thought I was acting in your best interest, mayhap I assumed too much, I can only apologise wholeheartedly, but it was such a difficult decision, such a burden of responsibility. I do not always get things right.'

Ben was still confused, but feeling most terribly remorseful now. He had still not absorbed the full impact of what he had just learned, but to see James so unhappy, after bringing such wonderful news, was beyond endurance.

Ben put a hand on James arm, 'no, James, 'tis I who should apologise, for even with all your other concerns, you made the journey north, such a journey, and for me. Forgive me James, I am an ingrate, but I am afraid to believe it. I am afraid, James, truly.'

James smiled his brilliant smile, a smile that would melt any maiden's heart, thought Ben, as he looked at this dear brother.

'It is certain,' said James, convincingly. 'You will have many questions and there is much to tell. Shall we dine together this evening? I promise I will explain everything as I know it.'

Ben did not answer for his thoughts were elsewhere. He and James had not dined together as yet, Ben had always shown great reluctance to share a quiet dinner and James had not pressured him. The two were standing now and as Ben began to accept the enormity of the situation his fears came to the fore. 'But will she want to see me?' his voice pleaded, 'James, I am so afraid.'

'Calm yourself lad, I received a letter from the convent only a few minutes ago, from Mother Vincent, the Reverend Mother, I came directly to find you, Mary is coming back Ben, Mary is coming home.'

Ben held James by the shoulders. 'She's alive James,' he said, his voice shaking as excitement mounted, 'how can it be, she was once coming home to me, my mother's little sister, and now she is really coming home. James, don't you see?' he cried. Of course, James did.

'Dinner this evening, Ben, in the small dining room, we will celebrate, yes?'

Shock, relief, indescribable joy caused Ben to disregard anything further that James might say and, without taking leave of his brother, he began to run, he ran like the wind, far across the fields. James watched as Ben ran and ran, ran as never before.

Soon, out of sight of the house, Ben's whoops of joy were borne away on the wind. Tears rained unchecked as, gasping for breath, he slowed a little. He did not stop to rest but ran until his chest hurt, hurt so badly he could not go on then, holding a clenched fist to his throat and still gasping for air he fell to the ground. Laughing and crying he panted for breath and with all energy spent he lie there until the spasm subsided and mighty asphyxiating sobs released him from all the pain and suffering he had ever known.

Later that evening the brothers were seated at a side table in the small dining room, a grand, spacious room where, placed in the hearth of a high, decorative fireplace, stood an arrangement of gold, white and rust coloured chrysanthemums, the last of the season. To Ben's eyes the room was another delightful mixture of comfort and opulence and, although in no way could it compare with the spacious dining hall where larger functions and dinners were held, the "small" dining room was not at all what Ben had expected. He looked across to the large highly polished table, with its heavily carved legs, its great ball and claw feet, admired the high backed, ornately carved chairs and was very pleased that James had ordered dinner to be served at the smaller side table. At James' request Barkworth had moved the small table to the open window at the far end of the room.

Ben sat quietly with his thoughts. On the one hand he knew that he belonged here, how frequently had James said so. On the other hand he felt that he may never be at home in these surroundings and, perhaps, neither would Mary. He had Mary to consider now, where would she like her home to be.

James, surprised and delighted that Ben was to join him for dinner, had determined that this would be a memorable, happy evening. He dressed casually, almost carelessly but, to his chagrin, was only too aware that Ben was pre-occupied and ill at ease. James interpreted his younger brother's thoughts and attempted to banish them. 'Well, Ben, we have a great deal to discuss,' he said, cheerily, 'but first I have a letter that I want you to read, it is the letter I received this morning from the Reverend Mother. The letter will answer most of your questions and I will fill in the gaps wherever I am able. As James spoke Barkworth bustled about serving the meal unceremoniously, smiling at Ben and entering into the casual dinner time conversation, generally making no distinctions between the two, his behaviour reassuringly informal. The smell of the delicious meal, which looked good and, Ben was relieved to see, satisfyingly substantial, made him realise how hungry he was, ravenous would not be too strong a word, not for Ben.

A cool, almost chill breeze reached them through the open window and, together with the heady scent of blooms, complimented with a glass of ale, created an ambience so very pleasant that Ben could not help but relax.

After the meal, over which the pair discussed the incredible events of the past two years, they began to make their plans to bring Mary home. Totally relaxed now, albeit with anticipation and trepidation still lurking around the edges of his mind, Ben began to put his thoughts in order with regard to where he and Mary should live. The subject of Ben's right to reside at the family home was naturally discussed, and just as naturally rejected.

James was painfully aware that he must not demonstrate any untoward authority or influence where Mary was concerned. Wisely, he employed the ruse of including Ben at every turn. Mary was Ben's family and James would be seen to respect this for, despite his wayward heart, Mary and James were comparative strangers. He would defer to Ben, and rightly so...for the time being.

Ben was a proud, independent young man and this misplaced pride, at times, had been known to cause difficulties for James; this was one such time. James conjured with words to deal with the situation. He could not possibly offer Mary a home, that was Ben's responsibility, or so Ben firmly believed and the lad was very sensitive where the question of Mary's welfare was concerned.

'For the time being, Ben, the very least I can do is offer Mary the unreserved hospitality of our home. Your reunion will be a profoundly emotional occasion for her. What do you think, Ben? I believe it may benefit her to adjust to the immediate days ahead were she to be among friends. I'm sure she will wish to reaquaint herself with Millie and Holly, do you not agree?'

'James, none of this would ever had happened without you and were I to thank you a million times it could never be enough. What I would do without you, James, I darest not even imagine.'

So it was settled. At last, thought James with some relief, I have managed to get something right.

The evening was greatly enjoyed by both Ben and James; Ben was exceedingly happy. I have no words to describe James' feelings. As they talked it was decided that Ben would accompany James and that they would travel on the Monday of the following week, leaving ample time for a letter to reach the convent advising Revered mother of their plans. They agreed that Mary should accept James' hospitality to stay at the house for an indeterminate period, but whatever he had in mind, James acknowledged, a young woman of Ben's forebears would doubtless have quite a mind of her own. Naturally Ben was to stay in his own place, Ned's cottage, that he loved so much, and all arrangements for the future would be made in the fulness of time.

Ben had a thousand questions but his jumbled thoughts could not formulate them. In nine days he and James were to travel to the convent to bring Mary home. That fact alone was as much as he could contend with. They laughed and chatted for a while, recalling events of past years both happy and sad. They jested and hurled insults at each other with positive gusto, neither giving quarter. James had told Ben how emotional Millie had been on hearing the news of Mary's safety and recovery and the fact that she was soon to return to Woodstock had made the old lady happy beyond words.

'She's such a happy old soul, Ben.' Said James, reflectively, for he did indeed have much love for Millie.

'Happy!' Shrieked Ben. 'Which Millie, our Millie? Happy! Dear brother, where have you been for the past thirty eight years?'

They cried with laughter and, with a kerchief to his eyes, James said, 'come now Ben, I demand a little respect or I shall have no alternative but to thrash you within an inch of your life.'

At this Ben threw back his head and howled with laughter. Then, falling to the floor feigning helplessness, he patted James on the head saying, 'were you ever to be big enough, old man, you will not be young enough.' He thumped James on the back and they left the room, stifling their laughter like two young children.

They had found common ground. James was no longer lonesome. It was a wonderful night outside despite the chill in the air and, enjoying the stillness of the hour and having no desire to sleep, they walked, talked and made plans. Ben thought it very unlikely that he could ever be this happy again. He told James, 'to have a brother, to have you as my brother, you can never know what that means to me. To be able to help you on the land, to work with Tom, there really is no other quite like you, James…and now Mary. Mary is coming home, and not because she needs to but because it is what she wants. How can any one person be so fortunate and so happy?'

They continued to walk until they reached Ben's cottage, he hadn't even noticed the direction James had taken. When Ben said goodnight to his brother he grasped James' hands in both his own and said, quietly and with great depth of feeling, 'thank you James, for a wonderful evening…and a wonderful life.'

Chapter Twenty Four

MARY AROSE AT FOUR THIRTY, she had been wakeful for what seemed an age and, unable to bear the sleeplessness any longer, slipped silently from her bed and tiptoed along the corridors to the kitchen. She stooped to poke the sleeping embers of the fire and hung a small pot of milk to warm. Coaxing the fire she watched as small flames began to lick at the new tinder then her eyes roamed affectionately around the room, as if to take it all in one last time, the room where she so loved to be. She poured the heated milk into a small bowl and happiness swept over her. Her reluctance to leave the convent had now been overcome. The reassurance of the nuns and her belief that her destiny was to lie in a different direction had restored her faith in the future. Mary felt at peace, confident that her stay at the convent was part of a greater plan. Endeavouring to contain her excitement she sipped the milk gratefully and murmured, 'today, today I'm going home.' Her thoughts struggled with the fact that this was the morning she had dreamed of for so long, almost as long as she could remember.

James and Ben had made the journey north together, in a few hours they would leave the inn to come for her, in just a few hours they would be here. Mary attempted to analyse her fears. 'Am I truly terrified,' she whispered, hugging herself tightly, 'or is it excitement that makes me tremble so?' Reverend Mother had told her that Ben had sand gold hair, that he stood over six feet tall, that he was a fine lad, honest, industrious and very caring. James Winbourne had told Mother Vincent much about Mary's young nephew. How Ben had always known about his auntie Mary, had always believed that one day she would return to him, for Millie, the cook at

Woodstock Manor, had told Ben all that she knew of his family and of the little auntie who had loved him so.

Mary sighed deeply, her mood changing by the second she now felt despondent, defeated. 'I can be nothing but a stranger,' she said, tremulously. 'Little Ben, dear little Benjie, please do not be a stranger.' She stood now, put down the empty bowl, joined her hands across her lips and closed her eyes in wonder as excitement, once again, rose within her. In a few hours she would see him, speak to him, go home with him…Sarah's son.

James and Ben fell silent as the carriage sped them towards their destination. They had departed from the overnight stop, an inn not too far from the convent, at eleven. It was now noon and they were scheduled to arrive within the next thirty minutes.

James reflected on their conversation since they had left Woodstock. Yesterday Ben had been in such high spirits it had been a joy to travel with him, but now he was greatly agitated, his courage, if indeed it was courage that he needed, had deserted him. To James' consternation Ben seemed troubled, not at all the eager, happy young man of the previous day. James looked again at Ben, he was at a difficult period in his life, that time between boyhood and manhood, and as he stared out of the window James could not begin to imagine the conflict that existed in his young brother's heart.

The countryside was glorious, the greens, russets and golds of autumn reaching out to meet above them along the narrow winding lane. They passed a cottage garden here and there, this final stage of the journey was so special, but only James enjoyed the beauty.

Ben turned his head and saw James watching him with concern. 'Soon be there, James,' he said, his expression unchanging.

James smiled his special smile and Ben almost felt a little better. 'Another twenty minutes or so, Ben, I am certain Mary will be waiting, it has been a long time for her too. You are both the last of quite a large family, I know Millie has told you, and soon you shall learn of them all.' James tried to laugh, 'someone certainly must have been a very tall fellow, you stand over six feet and are not done yet, I have no doubt. Come now Ben, do you want your Mary to see you with such a dour countenance.'

'I'm so nervous, James, do you think she will like me? She will be disappointed, I think, do I look suitably well?'

'Hmmm' James made the sound slowly, 'you are a big lout, I'll grant you that, with not the finest of features and, of course, you will never make a dandy…but, you will do well enough.' He smiled affectionately.

Ben laughed aloud for the first time that morning. 'A dandy! James, may heaven forefend.'

'You look fine Ben, quite presentable.'

James had chosen plain wear for Ben, beige breeches, cream linen under a well cut olive green jerkin and plain brown boots, from a selection of clothing he had commissioned for him a while back. He looked appraisingly at Ben, he truly was a strikingly handsome boy, so like his auntie Mary; she was beautiful.

'Tell me again, James, what does Mary look like? I swear I cannot remember. Ben was smiling now for James, as always, had reassured him.

'Well, as I have said at least a hundred times,' he laughed and Ben laughed with him. 'Mary is tall for a girl, almost as tall as myself, I do not recall too much of her features.' James permitted himself this small untruth then, speaking quite casually, 'I could not see her hair, of course, but I expect it will be much the same as yours.' Ben relaxed as James told the story…again.

They drew closer, a signpost told them they were not far away at all. James pressed a firm hand on Ben's shoulder. 'Come now lad,' he encouraged, 'a few minutes and we shall arive.'

Moistening his lips Ben turned to his brother, full of trepidation, his heart drumming wildly he said, 'almost there James, thank God you are with me, if I do not die from fear I shall…' The carriage trundled through a high gateway.

Mary sat in solemn silence whilst Mother Vincent smiled down at her. 'Come now child, is this not the day you have so long prepared for. Could you not manage a smile?'

Mary raised anxious eyes to the Reverend Mother, her face even more pale than usual. 'He does not know me, Mother, I love him so but…I am a stranger. Am I doing the right thing, Mother? Or do I merely force an unknown aunt upon a young boy? Perhaps I shall be an intrusion into his life, perhaps it is all too late.'

Mother Vincent smiled sympathetically. 'Now Mary, you know well that is not so. James wrote that your nephew has long awaited your return. Where do you find such notions? 'tis the red hair,' she said, teasingly, 'I always thought that redheads were a little crazy.'

Mary smiled up at her. 'He shall be here at any moment, Mother.' She began to pace the floor of the small room, growing increasingly ill at ease with every passing moment. She had prayed so fervently for Ben to accept her that now the time had finally arrived her fear had reached its height. She jumped, thrusting a hand to her throat, as the door opened and Mother Agnes entered.

'All is prepared for luncheon, Mother Vincent,' she said, smiling radiantly at Mary.

'Thank you Mother Agnes, our guests have not yet arrived but tell Mother Jude we shall be along presently.' Then, turning to Mary, 'now child, you must compose yourself, this is a happy time.'

Feeling faint, Mary sat by the open door. 'Mother, I think I should like to meet Ben in the garden, not within doors. May I take a slow walk around, I feel so faint, it is such a lovely day and I do believe I shall go crazy waiting, I should love to walk in the garden, it is always so lovely after the rain.

'Of course, my dear, come.' Mother Vincent extended her hand, 'I'm a foolish old woman not to have thought of the garden myself.'

Mary was standing beneath a willow tree as the carriage approached the convent. She stood with her hands clasped at her waist and her breath caught in her throat as she glimpsed the carriage through the sweeping folliage.

The sight that greeted Ben and James as the coach jogged to a final halt was that of a young girl, standing partially concealed beneath a willow, her bright auburn hair falling in deep waves and blowing in the breeze. She was tall and uncommonly slender, and wore a plain grey frock with a white collar and white at the cuffs.

James sat watching her, transfixed, thinking he had never seen a more perfect picture. Ben was simply too afraid to move. Mary walked to the edge of the low green curtain of willow then stepped out into the sunshine where she could see more clearly. It was as Mother Vincent welcomed her guests, as they climbed down from the carriage, that Mary first saw Ben. He was so tall, so beautiful, could it really be little Benjie. Where was her baby, where had his childhood gone, she wanted to cry. Hesitantly she walked a little way along the path, her senses numbed, her heart pounding.

Mother Vincent took James' arm and turned towards the house. Ben, seeing this, said, 'please James, don't go.' James turned to the carriage on some pretext whilst Mother Vincent left to oversee luncheon.

Ben looked across the garden to where Mary was standing. He could not see her too well from this distance but managed a tentative smile.

Mary thought, he is so young, he looks so…lost, I must go to him. She slowly approached the pathway, desperately seeking appropriate words of welcome. As she drew closer all thought of words abandoned her. She stood, motionless, as she saw Sarah's child, with his mother's face, his mother's eyes and his mother's smile. She spoke but one word…'Sarah.' Quickening her step she raised a hand and called, 'Ben.'

Ben could not move but smiled brilliantly and, as Mary sped towards her nephew he opened his arms wide and she flew into them, encircling his waist and hugging him to her. Tears flowed as she wept openly and unashamedly. 'Benjie, it is you, oh, it is really you my boy, you are the living image of your mother. She stepped back and looked up at him saying, 'oh Ben, such a long time, such a very long time.'

At the mention of his mother he looked at Mary, he was overwhelmed, standing before him was his auntie Mary, his mother's little sister. At first, unable to speak, he just looked at her, then said, 'Mary…I…Mary,' he fought the hateful, girlish tears but to no avail and, weeping together, they hugged again.

James had watched the scene with disbelief. He had not seen Mary other than in her novice's habit. He would not have known her, she was so vibrant, so absolutely lovely.

Mary threw back her head, laughing now, her magnificent hair blowing across her tear stained face. She caught Ben's hand, 'how did you get to be so tall?' Then, still laughing, 'it is because of your grandmother, she was all of five feet ten in stockinged feet. Oh, Ben, I have a thousand things to tell you, so many things.'

'And I have a thousand things to tell you and ten thousand questions to ask. You do not look as old as twenty seven, Mary, not nearly so old, you certainly do not look like an aunt.' At this childlike ungallant observation Mary laughed helplessly, all fears of their reunion banished forever. 'You must tell me everything about yourself and my mother.' Ben said happily.

Mary smiled at his boyish impatience then, speaking softly, said, 'I shall tell you everything Ben, we have the rest of our lives now. I still cannot believe you are here, it has truly happened, I have finally found you.'

So absorbed were they in their own private world they did not see Mother Vincent approach with James. It was Mary who turned and saw them.

Whatever am I thinking Ben?' Mary fluttered a delicate hand 'we must go to lunch.'

'Come along now you good people, 'Mother Vincent called, laughing merrily, 'I have asked Mother Jude to serve luncheon in the garden, we have one of Nathan's fresh vegetable platters and Mother Gertrude's wonderful new bread. Now then, gentleman, if you would like to refresh yourself after your journey, I know that Mary will be delighted to join you for luncheon…' her voice trailed away on the breeze as James and Ben followed her into the children's home.

A few minutes later James and Ben joined Mary under the great gnarled old oak where a table had been set for three and James smiled his special smile for the beautiful young woman who had eyes only for Ben; until that moment.

'James,' said Ben, with immense pride, 'it is with the very greatest of pleasure that I introduce my mother's younger sister, Mary.'

James raised the extended exquisite hand then, bowing, brushed it lightly with his lips in the most gracious manner, saying, 'it is my greatest pleasure, Mary.'

Mary could have fainted clean away but, happily remaining standing, replied, 'hello Sir James, I remember you now, from the Manor, of course I do.'

Seated at the table Mary began to serve from the vegetable platter as Ben said, 'Mary, was my mother beautiful, like you?'

Owing to the close proximity of James, Ben's words caused Mary to colour deeply. Lowering her head she continued to serve then, replacing the fork, looked into Ben's eyes and, smiling serenly, said, 'no, Ben, she was beautiful like you.'

During the course of the journey home the three enjoyed each other's company immensely. Mary and Ben spoke of their lives during the years of separation and James explained all that had happened with regard to the good people at the Manor and the current state of affairs within the household.

Inevitably, there were periods of tedium for the happy threesome as the journey progressed but their jubilant spirits remained unaffected. Mary had demonstrated extreme patience and fortitude but as the long journey south neared the overnight stage it was plain to both James and Ben that she was growing weary and needed rest. The following morning, bright as the buttons on Barkworth's uniform, they climbed into the carriage and, after settling themselves comfortably, James said, 'well, folks, let us go home.'

The journey was over. Mary looked up in awe at the great house for the first time in seventeen years. She remembered with agonising clarity the day she had been forced to climb into the carriage that would take her away from her beloved baby Benjie and the wonderful people at the Manor. Showing reluctance to approach the steps a light touch on her arm interrupted her thoughts. It all happened at once, she looked up at James, his face smiling encouragement, Ben took her light portmanteau, the great oak doors opened wide and Mistress Hall appeared at the top of the steps. James propelled her forward gently and Mistress Hall smiled radiantly.

In her mind's eye Holly still saw a ten years old girl with matted red hair and was not at all prepared for the tall, elegant young woman who now climbed the steps towards her. Amazingly, to Mary, the housekeeper looked almost as she did all those years ago, a little softer, somehow, perhaps just a little older. Remembering a hundred kindnesses Mary stepped forward and took Mistress Hall's outstretched hand, saying, 'Misrtess Hall, oh Mistress Hall, you are a Blessing to my eyes.'

Holly clasped Mary's hand, 'Mary, Mary my dearest girl, you are quite astonishing. 'Come now, all of you' she said, as she took Ben's arm and her misty eyes smiled up at James.' ' 'tis wonderful to have you all back safe and sound. Annie is waiting an early dinner, everything is ready, you must take some light refreshment and retire to your rooms until dinner for you will all be sorely weary after such a journey.' Then, looking up at Ben, she said, 'Ben, have a word with Millie, do, she has been over anxious these past days.'

Mary looked back at Ben, 'tell me I shall not awaken, Ben. Tell me I am not dreaming.'

As Mary entered the house she found that, although everything appeared as she had remembered, there was something different, something she just could not fathom, a lightness, somehow. There were little maids hurrying hither and thither, Davy appeared in his butler's uniform and welcomed her warmly before going up to James' rooms to prepare a bath.

'Go along with Holly, Mary,' said James, as he caught up with her, 'I'm certain she has prepared your rooms admirably with your every comfort in mind, but do ring if there is anything at all you require. We shall take a little refreshment in the drawing room in a short while then, I feel certain you will agree, a long rest before dinner is the order of the day.'

Mary did not answer, merely smiled her agreement for she was more than a little bewildered. James followed Barkworth around the bend of the staircase and disappeared, leaving Mary in Holly's care. Ben touched Mary's arm saying, 'I'm off to the kitchen, Mary, to see Millie, are you quite alright?' he asked, concerned to see how she had paled visibly before him.

'Yes, of course, Ben,' she replied, then, looking from Ben to Holly, said 'would it be possible to come along with you Ben, I would like to see Millie before I go for my rest, if I may?'

'Of course you may, Mary,' answered Holly, 'but do not stay over long, you really must rest and you will have all the time in the world…tomorrow.

Yes, Hollie, thank you, I shall not stay long.' Mary put a hand to her head and clutched at Ben's arm to steady herself. Ben was so alarmed he almost forbade her to go anywhere other than directly to her rooms.

'I'm really quite alright, Ben,' she assured him, with gentle laughter. 'Things are so different, this is such a happy household.'

'It certainly is Mary, a truly happy household, and James says you must regard it as your home, remember? But Mary, please go to your rooms now.'

'Just a moment, to say hello to Millie, I could not retire without seeing her, Ben, I truly could not.'

'Just one minute then, you promise, auntie,' he stressed the word "auntie."

'Only if you promise, young man, never to refer to me as "auntie" again,' she said, gently mocking him.

They reached the kitchen chuckling like old friends and Ben smiled at the familiar and welcoming sight of Millie crossly instructing the highly efficient and very talented Annie who, you will not be surprised to hear, had just taken a cake from the oven. Mary did not recognise Annie, now a young woman of about her own age, but as her eyes rested on Millie her heart went out to the old lady struggling to rise from her chair. Millie stood awkwardly and, looking at the young woman she saw only a lovely little girl, with her giant of a nephew standing protectively at her side.

'Mary…Mary me gel,' she said, overwhelmed at the sight of them both, together, and choking back the tears that welled in her eyes, 'me little love.'

'Mary sidestepped the big white table, ran across the huge kitchen and, throwing her arms about the old lady she cried, 'nanna, nanna Millie, oh how I've missed you. Thank you, thank you for keeping him safe, for taking care of him, I owe you so much. Oh, nanna Millie, I do love you, I have thought of you every day, other than during my illness, I swear I have thought of you both every day, I've missed you so.'

Ben stood in the doorway, for him it was like watching a stage drama being acted out before him.

'Hush child, hush now, 'tis alright, Millie's here.' Millie reached out a hand to Ben and he crossed the room to join them. 'Yous are together now,' she said, reaching up to place a loving hand to Ben's face. Ben stooped to embrace them both and Millie's voice cracked as she said, huskily, 'a new life now, my children, this is one of God's good days.'

A month had elapsed since Mary had returned to Woodstock. She and Ben had begun to know each other very well. They found similarities in their characters almost daily and had learned much from each other. Mary had spent many hours in the kitchens, which was not altogether frowned upon but neither was it approved of by the old woman who had insisted that "kitchins is no place fer a Lady". Mary had delighted in baby Hope and had befriended Annie and Rosie.

On this particular day Mary was enjoying her usual early morning ride, though these early jaunts caused her to miss Carolines's company for they had loved riding out together. She felt exhilarated when on horseback, for nothing compared with the thrill of the ride, and in the beautiful Essex countryside, the place of her birth, she felt confident she would find her true place. Mary was entirely content, so much so that her life would be perfect but for the one question that hovered about her like a dark cloud, and this ever present question weighed heavily upon now. She must do something, of this alone she was certain, for it would be very wrong of her to accept the fact that James would happily provide for her. Such a prospect simply could not be countenanced. She loved Woodstock. Loved the people. Loved Ben, oh how she loved Ben. Of course, life seldom follows one's plans to the letter, Mary's experiences had taught her that, and she understood she could not ask Ben to leave the place he so loved, the people he loved and the home that he loved. Truly she would never contemplate such a thing. Ben did not need her now in the sense that he needed her to provide for him but, he needed her nonetheless, and she needed him. It was crazy but Ben was more than a nephew to Mary, he was everything. She had come home to Woodstock, but what now?

Shortly after her return Mary had written to the Mothers at the convent enclosing a missive to Father John. She had also written to Caroline and her parents and her final letter, to Nathan, she would take down to the village today. Caroline's father, Angus MacFarlane, by taking care of her financial obligations, or at least those she misguidedly felt her responsibility, had made Mary a young woman of independent means. She must now assert herself in this respect and do something about the question of a home of her own.

As Mary cantered Melody around the outskirts of Painters' Meadow she prayed that a solution to her dilemma would present itself. She slowed to a trot, the morning was one of nature's most glorious. The peace was spellbinding, the countryside picturesque. Suddenly a blinding thought struck her, impetuously she wheeled Melody around and galloped for home.

Chapter Twenty Five

A FEW DAYS BEFORE MARY had taken her inspirational ride out to Painters' Meadow, her possessions being so few, Holly had taken her on a shopping trip to London. James had previously offered to accompany her in order that she may make some purchases but, feeling flustered and gauche in his presence, she had politely declined. This foolish young woman liked James, she liked him immensely and was greatly indebted to him, why then this reluctance to be with him. Why did she tremble so at the very mention of his name? Why, when in the same room with him, did she just want to flee?

After her morning ride Mary had lunched with Ben and Tom. In the afternoon she had slept, bathed and slept again, luxuriating in the tranquility of the lovely rooms chosen for her. Evening came and she dressed carefully in the simple but elegant emerald green that Holly had helped her choose and had paid special attention to her hair. Dinner that evening began even more lighthearted than usual. In the lovely emerald gown with the high, ivory lace bodice that tapered to her tiny waist, her abundant hair shining in the lamplight, Mary looked exquisite and blushed frequently at the admiring glances of the attentive and disturbingly charming James.

James was seated across from Mary, adding to her discomfort, whilst Ben sat on her left. They had talked for hours over dinner and, once again, seemed to have touched on every subject imaginable including plans for the future, the waifs' home carefully avoided as mention of it had always upset Mary.

Ben found Mary's stories fascinating whilst James, for the most part, sat quietly absorbing the beauty and grace of his house guest, with her lovely eyes sparkling, her smile bewitching and who, though not by birth, was a natural

Lady. It would no doubt be quite some time, James thought, though not unkindly, before Ben and Mary will have exhausted conversation, months maybe, perhaps even years, but he could wait. His brother had suffered much, as had his young aunt and James had known only joy at their reunion; but would Mary ever notice him? Mary had always attempted to avoid conversation with James for, to her chagrin, she was inclined to become very ill at ease. James had misinterpreted Mary's manner as that of indifference for should he touch her hand in greeting, or when taking his leave, she would avoid his steady gaze, his intensely dark eyes, his wonderful smile but, to all of this, James was completely oblivious.

A little later, relaxing around the fireside, Mary decided to enlighten them as to the momentous decision she had come to earlier that morning during her ride. She looked at her nephew who gave no indication of weariness and, despite her disqiuetude at James' nearness, wished this time with them both never to end. She hoped James would not suggest they retire, despite the lateness of the hour, but unbeknown to her James was of the same mind and Ben, well, Ben was simply indefatigable at any time. Mary leapt to her feet, she must tell them, and now. Standing with her back to the fire, the golden lamplight above playing on her hair, she faced them.

'Ben, James,' she began, seriously, breathless with excitement. 'I have decided I must see Mother Vincent.' There, she thought, much relieved, I have said it. The expressions on the faces of her two companions cannot be described as they watched her, waiting in stunned silence. James was rendered incapable of coherent speech, the words, no, no, I cannot lose her, whirling around in his mind whilst his heart thundered with panic. As for Ben, his alarm was plain to see. Mary inhaled deeply, her eyes shone with such brilliance they may well have lit up a darkened room. She is magnificent, thought James.

'I am going to open an orphanage,' she gushed, excitedly. The silence was deafening. She held out her hands, palms upwards, 'say something, both of you, either of you, please…say something.'

Ben was first to break the silence. 'Mary, I, well, that is, that is truly incredible. I thought that you were home…where?' Ben was clearly confused, but not so Mary. She spoke animatedly now for as the idea took firm hold she knew it to be right.

James was alone with his thoughts. I should have declared myself sooner, now it is too late, she shall move away for certain, there is nothing to hold her, I must do something, but what, how, you fool James Winbourne, you fool.

Mary continued, 'I understand this has come as a shock, it is a surprise to me also, but most amazing is the fact that I did not realise it sooner. 'Ben, do you not see, the waifs' home, though 'twas none of my doing, I see clearly the reason now. We both know how such children suffer. Ben, it does not bear thought but, I want to do more than just think, I want to do something about it. In my small way I will help, I will give at least some orphans a loving home.'

So great was Mary's excitement, her certainty, she was abound with energy. Ben stared in love and wonder at this young aunt of his whilst James was overcome with admiration. James' plans, though not fully formulated in his mind, had certainly not taken into account any such notion but, watching her now, he could not deny there would be no stopping her.

'An orphanage?' Ben asked, 'are you certain it is what you truly wish?'

It was as though James had not been present. Mary had not intended to exclude him but had been borne along on a wave of destiny. She took Ben's hands in hers and James wished himself in his brother's shoes, to be so loved by her. 'My little Benjie,' she continued, 'being sent to The Grange, oh, I learned so much, there is little I cannot do. I can cook, sew...I can teach the little ones. As the boys grow older I will engage a tutor. I shall teach them languages, Ben. The girls I shall teach needlepoint...and music. Suddenly Mary became aware of Ben's acute sadness and was thoroughly ashamed for not explaining her intentions clearly. Ben's expression was a picture of despondency and rejection. 'I will need you to help me Ben. When you can be spared, of course, for I shall need your strength and your support. Will you help me, Ben?'

Ben's eyes lit up and he smiled for the first time, so happy to be included in Mary's impossible plans. If anyone could do this, she could, he said, 'Mary, do you really feel you need to ask?'

Mary hugged him, 'oh, thank you Ben, it means so much that you understand.'

Mary continued to explain her reasons for her passion about an orphanage whilst James watched on, his spirits crushed, could it really be possible that he should lose them both. 'The accident, Ben, when I was travelling back to make a home for us. My time at the convent orphanage,' she laughed, 'I am a veritable wizard with accounts. I believe it was all to teach me, to prepare me. When you and I were left alone in the world there was no such place for us. Think Ben, think, if there had been we should not have been separated. I shall never separate families,' she vowed.

Mary then turned to James who was smiling his captivating smile, much relieved and thinking…she is not to return to the convent. You fool, she would never take Ben away from Woodstock, Mary may have her orphanage; I can wait. James could do little else…for now. Mistaking the warmth of James' smile as enthusiasm for her orphanage Mary crossed the room to sit beside him. 'You agree, James, I see it in your face. James,' she went on, with slightly pleading eyes, 'does it sound to you to be such a crazy dream.'

'No, Mary,' he answered truthfully, 'I feel it may well be an ambitious dream, but crazy, no. Have you given thought to your own life, this really is so sudden, what of a husband, children?'

'Oh, James, I shall have many children, they shall all be mine. You are quite right though and, one day, should God decide, I shall have babies of my very own, and a husband.'

'But…not in that order, I trust.' James smiled mischievously. Mary's heart thudded and, catching her breath and blushing furiously, she said, 'James, do not tease me, this is a serious matter.' Oh how she loved him. Work, hard work to fulfil her plans, that is what she needed; she told herself.

James had little time to ponder the new situation. He was ecstatically happy for Mary's reaction was not lost upon him, dare he hope that she might care…given time. She hastily left his side and crossed the room to safer territory. Smiling at Ben, she said sadly, 'if only I had come back sooner Ben, I may have spared you at least some of the years at the waifs' home. If only I were older when you were born, if only.' Her eyes conveyed a thousand words. Words of torment, of regret, of love.

James came quickly to her aid. 'All things have their reason, Mary. Because of the waifs' home both Ben and I understand the sad places these institutions are, though, it is only fair to say, Ben was placed in the best that could be found. Now, to positive intentions, the time for these painful memories is long past. This will take quite some thought, Mary. Where your orphanage would be best situated, how it will be funded. We have much to tell you but surely you tire yourself, we shall speak again on the morrow.'

'Forgive me, James, I am forgetful of the hour.'

'Oh, what matter,' James laughed, 'for look, 'tis Sunday, and Sunday is rest day.'

They talked on into the early hours. Mary had made her decision. She had learned so much that night, they spoke at length of the incredible fact that James and Ben were brothers. Mary said, 'it seems I am not needed after all,' then, immediatley, 'but far better to be wanted for oneself, 'tis truly a happy day.'

When Barkworth looked in to say goodnight and to enquire as to whether they wished further refreshments James said, 'goodness, Barkworth, we have kept you late from your bed, but a tray of tea would be gratefully appreciated.'

James placed another log on the fire and turned to Mary. 'We shall decide where your children's home is to be, a small house perhaps, at first.'

'Yes James,' Mary replied, 'we shall find a suitable dwelling, or raise one ourselves. Now that my decision is made and my way is clear to me, I do not have the greatest impatience. Though it shall take much thought for every consideration must be given to all aspects of my orphanage. I have no cause to think further at this time for I know well that, once the building is found and children have need of me, the rest will come. The authorities may well prove difficult, but Mother Vincent will deal with them.' She laughed gaily saying, 'and you, James, do not think you will escape, you must vouch for my character. What say you, Ben, shall James speak well of me?'

Before Ben could answer James said, 'I have not as yet been obliged to vouch for an addled-brained redhead, 'twill require some serious consideration.'

Mary made to cross to him then hastily withdrew. Instead she leaned forward from where she stood saying, with mock infuriation and eyebrows raised, 'well, my good Sir, there is always a first.' At this, the imperturbable James became abashed.

Later that night, as James lie quietly in his semi darkened room with moonbeams making silver patterns on the huge four-poster bed, he thought how quickly fortunes changed. Mary would open her small orphanage, of this he had no doubt, and that confounded pride would prevent him becoming involved. Not that he wished to become involved with a children's home for in truth, he did not, but now that he had found his enchantress he would not let her go. He smiled as the thought came to him, there was something he could do. He placed a hand beneath his head and told the silent room 'Mary is not the only one who may have flashes of inspiration, I know exactly how

I can keep her close, keep them both close but, for now, James Winbourne, to sleep.

Morning came too quickly as Mary drowsily rubbed a hand across her brow in a reluctant attempt to clear the dreamlike haze that dulled her mind. She looked across at the large window overlooking the farmlands then, for a moment, was entirely disorientated as she stared up at the satin and lace canopy that draped the huge oak bed. As her eyes roamed around the bedchamber she recalled how the dainty white and gold furniture and gilt framed pictures of cottages and countryside had delighted her when she first saw these rooms. Was it just a few weeks ago, had she truly known James for only four months? First as Doctor James Winbourne, then as James, her friend of seventeen long years ago. Just four short months and now Mary could not imagine a day without James in her life. Foolish heart, she told herself, we are of different worlds, our worlds could never be one, Sir James of Woodstock Manor, and Mary Pargeter…a peasant girl. Despondently she glanced across at the clock on the mantleshelf and was vexed to see that it was already eight thirty; how had she slept so late. Listening for the sounds that would tell her the household was busy she realised how she longed for a morning drink. The sleepy girl was also ravenously hungry but had missed breakfast with Ben, Tom and the others. Stepping out of bed onto the soft Turkish rug she tiptoed across to the bell pull that would summon a maid and almost immediately the little tweeny appeared.

'Good mornin' ma'am,' she said sweetly, dipping a curtsey.

'Good morning Alice, I trust I have not taken you from your duties?'

'Oh, no ma'am.'

'Do you think I could possibly have a pot of tea, Alice? I have missed breakfast but shall get something from the kitchen a little later.'

'Yer can 'ave breakfast 'ere ma'am, if yer wants, that is. Mistress 'all says 'ow I was not to disturb yer if yer slept late, and I'm to look after yer. Will I fetch up water for a tub, ma'am?'

'No, thank you Alice, I shall attend to my own needs, if you would just bring the tea, please.'

'Yes, ma'am.'

'Alice,' Mary called, as the maid reached the door.'

'Yes, ma'am.'

'I should like some help with this,' she said, pushing both hands into her long unruly mane and holding it upwards, a helpless expression on her face.'

The tweeny smiled, 'yes ma'am, I'll brush it real nice for you, I will, an' I wont be long wiv yer tea ma'am.'

'Thank you Alice.'

A few minutes later Mary sat sipping her tea and relished the muffin, topped with orange preserve, that accompanied the wonderful brew. Alice had brought up hot water and had left it in the adjoining room where a marble topped washstand, with rose patterned jug and bowl, held all her toilette requisites.

Fussed over by Annie, Millie and Mary shared a delicious late breakfast. Millie came down a little later these days for there was no call on her time and it was rather special having Mary around. Millie still lived at the house for the cottage that James had had built for her on Little Acre was much too far away now, she wanted no changes at her time of life. It would have been different, of course, had Ned not passed away so sadly, for his new cottage had also been built, even though he would never see it.

After breakfast Mary received a message inviting her to accompany James and Ben on an afternoon ride around part of the Estate, always providing she had no other commitments. They were to take a picnic hamper and lunch in a particularly lovely spot that James felt certain she would enjoy.

Mary was thrilled for she dearly loved to ride and was never happier than when galloping across the fields or cantering along the hedgerows. She could scarsely wait for the time to pass. At around noon she changed into her dark brown riding habit, a welcome home gift from Ben when she had arrived. She pushed and pulled her hair into the riding snood, securing it as best she could, and left for the stables where James and Ben were waiting. Ben rode the seventeen hands gelding, the biggest horse Mary had ever seen. James was mounted on his own horse, Monarch, sixteen hands high, broad and muscular, his black coat gleaming like ebony who, with his rider in black jacket, cream stock and beige riding breeches made a magnificent picture. Mary's heart missed several beats.

Almost as soon as the ride had begun and James headed out toward the far pastures Ben knew their destination. How clever of James, he thought, Mary would love Little Acre. Mary, as always, found the ride exhilarating. Until that afternoon she had always taken Melody, a dear, "safe" good-tempered mare, but James now had confidence enough in Mary's horsemanship to allow her a better ride; her mare today was called Chassie and they soon became friends. On recognising her rider was a competent and sympathetic handler

Chassie went easily into the gallop and the three headed into the distance towards the woodland. Holly and Millie watched from the kitchen until all they could see was Mary's riding dress billowing in the wind beneath a banner of flame as her hair was whipped free from its constraining net.

As they approached Little Acre sunlight filtered through the foliage of the tall trees, shedding a glow of autumn colour upon the leafy ground as they slowed the horses to a trot. They reached the narrow stream, winding its way towards two newly built cottages. Mary dismounted and, stooping beneath a tree overhanging the stream began to drag a handkerchief through the clear, ice cold water. She made a matchless picture with her skirts spread about her, a curtain of hair falling across her shoulders and shimmering red and gold in the dappled sunlight. She breathed in the fragrant air as she bathed her cheeks and smiled up at Ben and James who were watching her, the latter somewhat intently.

'This is the most perfect place on earth,' she said, addressing neither in particular but seeming to speak rather more to the trees and the stream.

James smiled, 'this has always been my favourite spot, Ben's too.' He looked across to Ben.

'Ned loved this place,' Ben said absently, as though he were distanced from them. 'When he was a younger man he built boxes here and treated the hurt and ailing animals, sometimes he would ride out daily. I always enjoyed his stories. Yes, Mary, I agree, this is the most perfect place on earth.'

'Those sweet little cottages…and the stream,' Mary said in wonder, drinking in the beauty of her surroundings.

'Come,' said James, excitedly, as he loosely tied the long rein to the branch of a tree, 'tether the horses, we will leave them to graze and I shall take you into the cottages. One was to be Ned's,' he went on, 'sadly he was never to know of it, but I had it built just the same. The other is for Millie, but the stubborn old lady will not leave the house, too far from everyone perhaps, or just too sad without old Ned.'

On entering the little stone cottage through the low wooden doorway Mary was captivated, for whilst the cottage was new, James had kept its tenant in mind and had planned it in the older style, entirely without modern embellishments. The floors in the front room and the two upper rooms were laid with wooden boards whilst the floor of the living room and scullery at the back were laid with flagstones. The little front room had a small, simple black iron fireplace over which was a high wooden mantelshelf with other shelves on either side. This room looked out to the stream where several trees had been planted by James' grandfather. In the living room a small iron oven with dampers was fitted into a high open fireplace in front of which was a wide stone hearth. On either side of this large firespace were shelves set in open brick arches, where alongside the lefthand arch a door opened onto narrow winding stairs. In one of the upper rooms a little dormer window opened out under the eaves from where Mary could see the stream. The other room had two small windows giving panoramic views across Little Acre and the Woodstock farmlands. It was from this window that Mary looked across the fields to where she saw the church spire and thought she could just make out a narrow track. 'James, come, look across there,' she pointed towards the church as Ben came into the room, 'Ben, oh, there you are, I thought you were in the other room.' Then, speaking incredulously, hardly believing the question she was about to ask, 'James, is that a little lane I see, look, over there past the first field?'

'Yes, Mary, it is the track the carrier cart takes, it encircles the Manor lands and joins the main highway.

'James, I do believe that is the track I carried Ben along when I was trying to reach the Manor House. It is,' she said in amazement, 'Ben, look, look at that little lane, there, see? You were only a few days old the last time I walked that track. It is too incredible.' Mary took hold of Ben's arm, saying wistfully, 'is it not wonderful, Ben, to be home?'

As they made their way downstairs Ben cracked his head and complained woefully whilst Mary stood by, laughing unsympathetically, and James said, 'I cannot imagine why you came up the stairs, Ben, when you could just as easily have looked through the upper windows from the outside.'

'A slight exaggeration, brother,' said Ben, rubbing his head.

They left the cottage, Ben stooping almost in half in an exaggerated attempt to pass through the doorway unscathed.

'It's enchanting, James, simply enchanting, and spacious too, for a cottage, Ned's world,' said Mary, in a small voice, remembering the old man from long ago and thinking he was so like Nathan.

They strolled to where the horses were idly grazing and James led them to a small clearing where, to the left farmland stretched into the distance whilst to the right the narrow stream meandered into the sunlight, reflecting a hundred shades of autumn as the trees swayed gently above. The three stood in silence, as silent as the two little white cottages behind them. It was James who broke the spell. 'This is in truth a beautiful spot, Mary, a tiny patch of land, barely three acres in size.'

'Little Acre,' Ben told her, ' James favourite place, isn't it James.'

'It is indeed Ben, and it is my wish that it should never change.' James became serious, hesitant. He said, 'Mary…Ben,' then faltered.

Ben became exceedingly anxious. Not again, he thought, not now, is James about to throw another of his thunderous shocks, please Lord, no.

Mary looked up, 'Yes, James,' she said happily.

'It is about your orphanage, Mary.'

Ben's face blanched as certainty brought the inevitable alarm and he thought…she is going away, he is going away. James took a very deep breath and Ben recognised the pattern of his brother's manner. James had brought them here to tell them something dreadful, he just knew it, but could not stay to hear it. He said, 'James, Mary, do you mind if I take a walk along the stream, I shall not be overlong, I shall be back before you lunch, you may be certain. Without waiting for an answer Ben ran along by the stream beneath the trees and waited, praying that he may have wrongly assessed the situation, but with little hope.

James turned to Mary, 'you are still of a mind to try to run a children's home?' he asked.

'James, I am still of a mind to run a "small" children's home,' she assured him without the slightest hesitation.

'Mary,' James was as nervous as a new born kitten, I have to do this, he told himself, get on with it man or you shall lose her. 'Mary, he began again, I would deem it the greatest of honours if you would consider having your "small" orphanage here, on Little Acre, using the two cottages.'

Mary looked at him in astonishment and, with her lips agape, breathed deeply.

'Now, before you protest,' James waved a hand to still her refusal for she simply must agree, 'the land is quite adequate, but a little extra would not pose a problem. Please do not reject my suggestion out of hand, Mary.'

'Ben watched the two, thoroughly ashamed of himself but praying he would observe a happy situation, this was not to be so. He saw Mary's shocked expression, I knew it, he thought, and was close to tears.

Mary, still looking at James, was rendered speechless and James took her silence as an indication that she would prefer not to accept his offer. Endeavouring to keep desperation from his voice he went on. 'This land,

Mary, is part of Ben's inheritance by right of birth. I know his feelings on the matter and it does him great credit…but changes nothing. You need a place to open your orphanage, Little Acre is acceptably close to the village, why not here?' James, receiving no answer and entirely unable to read Mary's expression, decided to suggest more acceptable terms. 'Naturally, he began, in a matter of fact tone, 'if it would suit you better you may use the cottages and land temporarily on loan, if you insist, then, when you need larger accommodation you may seek another situation at some future time.' At last a reaction, Mary pushed her hands through her hair, 'James, I, this has come as a great shock…I must think.'

'I understand, Mary, but, do not concern yourself with objections, the cottages are ready, in truth they should be put to good use, and what better use for them than to begin your orphanage.

Mary shivered from head to toe with emotion, thinking that people just did not give help of this magnitude, but James is family, at least, he is Ben's family, and 'twould only be until other accommodation could be found… 'twould mean no prolonged delay.

Overcome with gratitude and disbelief Mary knew with absolute certainty that this was meant to be, that it was her destiny to build an orphanage, her whole life and Ben's had led them to this day. She looked again at James and said, falteringly, 'but this is all so sudden James, I am greatly confused, so much has happened.' She held a hand to her chin, anxiously pushing at her bottom lip.

'Life is often that way, Mary,' James explained. People's lives remain on an even course, so it would appear, for many years then, it has been my experience that, almost overnight, worlds are turned upside down, as in your case, and Ben's. Fortunes are made and lost overnight, families once lost are found again, it is not so very uncommon.'

Whilst Mary thoughtfully turned things over in her mind, Ben watched anxiously, her expression told him all he needed to know. He ran along the stream until he was breathless, then rested awhile before slowly walking back to join them for lunch; but knew he would not be able to eat a morsel.

James knew it was now or never, but how to speak, what to say. 'Mary,' he began, taking her hands in his. Mary almost swooned then, at the look in James' eyes her heart pounded. James' heart reciprocated as he stumbled on, 'Mary, my dearest girl, forgive me, for I had not intended to speak to you out in the fields, I imagined wine and roses, an orchestra, a ball perhaps.' Mary's head was spinning, what could James possibly mean, not…no, surely not, don't be foolish Mary, she admonished, how desperately unhappy you will become when you learn how sadly you have been mistaken. James continued, 'you see, Mary, please forgive my schoolboy bumbling, but, my dearest…' Mary's eyes were as blue as the sky as she inwardly pleaded with James to go on but dare not speak lest she be mistaken and be shamed forever.

'Mary, do you think you could ever…care for me, in a small way, given time, for you see,' James raised a hand to Mary's cheek as he said, 'Mary, I love you so desperately. Maybe, with time, is there a chance for me, some little hope that…perhaps?'

Mary's heart beat wildly and with such joy she thought that it would surely burst and, placing her hand over James' at her cheek said, 'no, my love, I cannot love you with time…'

James skin paled, 'do not answer yet, Mary…'

She placed her fingers to his lips preventing him from speaking and, smiling her most radiant smile said, 'for I think I have you loved all along.'

'You have? Y…you do?' Stammered James, 'you love me, Mary? 'His eyes opened and closed and opened again and with indescribable joy he caught her by the waist and swung her around, 'she loves me,' he shouted, 'Mary loves me, do you hear Little Acre? Do you hear world? Then, letting her feet slip to the ground but still holding her close James looked deeply into Mary's eyes and said, 'I love you Mary Pargeter.'

Ben approached the small copse by the cottages with leaden heart and, brushing his wet cheeks, the sight that met his eyes defied belief. In utter stupefaction he said aloud to the trees, 'James is kissing Mary, James is kissing Mary,' then, with eyes popping almost out of his head, 'James is st..i..ll kissing Mary.' Ben ran back away from them, ran for all he was worth then, out of hearing distance, threw his arms into the air and whooped with happiness.

A few minutes later Ben approached them calling, 'have you not put out lunch yet, what on earth have you been talking of all this while?'

James and Mary laughed aloud and exchanged glances conspiritorially, each silently acknowledging that they would tell Ben their news later. 'Come, Ben,' said James, we have much to tell about your orphanage.'

All three laid out lunch from the hamper. They were the happiest people on earth. Ben thought, at last James, I feared you would never speak, any blind, witless fool could see that Mary loves you, and as for you, well, you were so obvious dear brother, we all know how you feel about Mary.

Settled comfortably and enjoying their lunch they explained all that had been discussed regarding the plans for the orphanage. 'But the funding, James, for the orphanage,' Mary said, then the solution hit her with remarkable clarity.

'Do you accept Mary? What do you say, Ben? We will discuss funding later for it would be just a few children?' He questioned, hopefully.

'Oh yes, James, just a few, certainly not above a thousand or so.' She was laughing merrily, tears of mirth falling freely.

James roared with laughter as he expostulated, 'two thousand?'

Mary, though still trembling with the shock and joy of this day, was smiling now. 'About twelve children, James, the cottages will house between twelve and twenty children if we use the front rooms for accommodation. We'll think about a larger dwelling if needs be, later, much later.'

'Then it is settled?' He said, his voice questioning, still uncertain, 'you accept?'

Mary looked up at Ben who, through all this discourse, had remained silent delighting in his secret knowledge. 'Do we accept James' most wonderful offer, Ben?'

Ben took his brother's hand and, shaking it firmly, said, 'we do indeed, we accept, James, we accept, oh yes, we accept.' Ben hugged James, and for the first time in all of their years together the young man and the younger boy felt that special love that is known only to brothers.'

Mary then became very serious. 'I will accept not a penny to run the orphanage, James, on that point I shall not be moved. The orphanage will provide for itself, I promise you. Help will come, we shall be provided for, I am certain it is already arranged,' she said, mysteriously, 'and, James, you are to be the founder.'

James waved a hand in firm protest, 'Mary,' he began, but Mary stood firm.

'Those are my terms, James, or we cannot accept, which would be a great pity for Little Acre is where I wish our orphanage to be.'

James conceded and with eyes full of love and wonderment said, 'it shall be as you wish, Mary, entirely as you wish.'

'Little Acre, a beautiful name, I cannot believe this day, James.' Mary linked an arm through Ben's. 'We will work hard Ben, there is much to do. You will continue your work with James, of course, and live in Ned's cottage, do you agree?' She did not wait for an answer but continued joyously. 'I shall be here, Ben, at Woodstock, we shall all be together, oh how simply unbelievably wonderful.'

Ben was taken up with the magic of the moment, Mary's orphanage was to be on Manor land, he also felt this too wonderful to be happening. But the most wonderful news he will be told later, he knew. 'I shall work hard for the Manor, Mary, none harder, and I shall move into the orphanage with you when it is ready, just until you are established, I will help you every step of the way. Mary, James, I do believe I am the happiest man on earth.'

Not quite the happiest little brother, thought James, but kept his own counsel.

Mary shaded her eyes and looked across to the cottages where they were to open their orphanage. She looked up at Ben, her arm still linked through his, and said, determinedly, ' "Child's Acre", we shall call our children's home "Child's Acre"…for every child shall be special. I lost your childhood, Ben, and had little of my own, but together we shall have many childhoods.

James was awestruck at the incredible strength of character of these people, his family.

And so it was that, after seventeen long years, on a lovely autumn day, with his arm linked through Mary's and his brother also at his side, Ben looked across to the cottages where their orphanage stood, where "Child's Acre" stood…waiting.

After all the years of separation, of hardship, of trial, of hopelessness and intolerable grief, Mary and Ben had come home, home to Woodstock and to "Child's Acre."

They stood in silence. For Mary and Ben this was an overwhelmingly emotional moment. Mary was lost in a communion of her own. Ben reached out a hand and James grasped it firmly in unspoken recognition of a journey completed, a chapter of their lives reaching its conclusion, a new chapter soon to begin. Then, as of one mind, which is often the way with brothers, a thought struck them simultaneously and they said in unison, and with great emotion –

"This is one of God's good days.'

Chapter Twenty Six

A YEAR LATER MARY'S ORPHANAGE was ready. Just as she had predicted the funds began to come, slowly at first, then more frequently until the donations had veritably flowed in. So respected were James and Mary that, on hearing of Woodstock Manor's intention to open a small orphanage the local traders gave what they could financially but also gave materials of every description. The county landowners gave generously and, surprisingly, when approached by James, even the County Town administrative offices supported the scheme and granted a donation. Local people even sent seeds and plants to begin the gardens. Angus MacFarlane provided the furniture and furnishings and would not hear of Mary's refusal, assuring her that his part in the venture was to "help the wee ones". Thus, "Child's Acre" came into being.

Events had moved incredibly quickly at that time. Firstly, news had arrived that about three months earlier, James' elder brother, John, had died of a gunshot wound after a gambling dispute. James did not grieve for his brother, but grieved sorely for the loss of a young man's life, a young man who should have had everything to live for. However, I shall not dwell upon this.

Not only did Woodstock have the excitement and achievement of converting the cottages and opening Child's Acre for, another year on and James and Mary had married. They were wed in the tiny village church which, too small to accommodate all of their guests, had its doors opened wide so that villagers and tenants outside could be part of the ceremony. James and Mary had insisted that each and every member of the little Woodstock community followed on to the Manor where a grand reception was held.

They were a devoted young couple, so very much in love, and their shared interest in the Estate, the orphanage and the tenant farmers provided many an occasion for them to work closely together. They had been greatly blessed when, at Christmastime, Mary realised she was to become a mother and both prospective parents were astonished, overjoyed and impatient in their anticipation of their first child, expected in the autumn. The house was a happy place indeed these days with never a cross word to be heard…unless Millie was in the kitchen. The manor had begun to entertain again, in a small way, and Mary had proved to be a beautiful, gracious and accomplished hostess. They would entertain a little more after the baby had arrived and invitations to the Manor were to be jealously coveted.

Ben had worked hard combining and converting the little cottages to serve as the orphanage, and both he and Mary had been moved beyond words to see 'Child's Acre' completed in its picturesque setting.

A while after James and Mary's wedding, Ben had spent some months at The Academy for Young Farmers studying new farming techniques and the development of new farm machinery. He was to take a more active part in the finances of the Estate since James had become involved in local politics in his quest to improve the lot of local people. Ben's homecoming was to be a celebration for he had been sorely missed by all and did not as yet know that he was to become an uncle, a fact that was to make him, as was his way, whoop with happiness.

Having adamantly refused to move from the house, Millie was delighted to see the new cottages used for Mary's orphanage. When, eventually, Ben had agreed to live at the Manor, Millie had wasted no time in informing James that she would spend her retirement years in Ned's old cottage closeby. James, having no sway in the matter, had two large rooms built onto the side of the little place and Tom was to take care of Millie's small but pretty garden. Surprisingly, Millie was enjoying her enforced retirement in comfort and ease, surrounded by the family she so loved.

Annie had taken over Millie's kitchen and was running her own little world with all the pride, competence and devotion that Millie had instilled in her. Samuel, the footman, come groom, come stableman spent time in the kitchen when work permitted. Both Annie and the young man enjoyed many a quiet hour in the late afternoons in companionable contentment; was this history repeating itself!

Barkworth had proved to be following in his father's footsteps with all the diligence and success anticipated. His evenings were, for the most part, his own. At around seven he would finish up his tasks and go across to his family. James would take care of his own needs after that time but Barkworth was always on hand if called upon. At home in the Dower cottage he would sit at the kitchen table reading his father's big book in which guidance notes on special requirements and advice regarding the running of the household had accumulated over the years. Rosie would sit by the window knitting or crocheting for, in the spring of next year, little Hope was to have a playmate; Rosie also was with child.

Holly, industrious as ever, excitedly awaited the birth of the new baby. It had been decided that Mary would not engage a nanny, perhaps a nursemaid, for Holly was to help with the baby in any small way that she could, her household duties permitting. Holly was now a happy and contented woman much loved by all.

Tom, well now, Tom was indeed a fortunate young man always mindful that he owed everything in his life to Ben and James. He loved his work, especially loved mealtimes in the kitchen, loved the people he worked for and had recently become betrothed to the little dairymaid who had been with the Manor for two years; by the way, this one's name was Polly. Polly was head over heels in love with her handsome Tom and in a year or two they would plan their wedding.

Matt, the indispensable stockman, lived in the village with his family and was relieved and delighted to see the Manor Estate flourish, his position at the Manor no longer in jeopardy, the wellbeing of his family assured.

James had increased the number of villagers employed on the Estate and Manor gardens and this had worked out well. "Child's Acre" had four little ones, from two to eight years, and Mary had engaged kindly women from the village to work days, with a woman and young girl to work through the nights. She would engage more help as it became necessary; which it certainly did.

Christmastime once again and the Manor House and lands created a scene of breathtaking beauty. Smoke curled from the chimneys of the many snowclad rooves of the "big house" and the countryside was a winter wonderland straight from a poet's dream. The trees, stark and bare, were clothed in gowns of glistening white reaching their branches in filigree patterns towards the sky whilst, as far as the eye could see, the land rose and fell beneath a coverlet of deep velvet, dazzlingly bright.

Young Master James was now three months old and the beautiful golden haired baby boy melted the hearts of all around him. It was the most wonderful Christmas any of them had ever known. The Manor was alive again, a thriving, happy household and in the not too distant future its halls would ring with the gleeful sound of children's laughter.

My friend, this is one of God's good days.

B/72/P